BEAU GESTE REVISITED

Beau Geste Revisited

The Pentland Press
Edinburgh – Cambridge – Durham – USA

John Quentin, 1996

First published in 1996 by
The Pentland Press Ltd
1 Hutton Close
South Church
Bishop Auckland
Durham

All rights reserved
Unauthorised duplication
contravenes existing laws

ISBN 1-85821-380-0

Typeset by Carnegie Publishing, 18 Maynard St, Preston
Printed and bound by Antony Rowe Ltd, Chippenham

*To Joan Coaker and Heather Morgan
for their help and encouragement*

*A Golden Thread runs throughout
the Trilogy – the Spirit of Beau Geste*

ABOUT THIS BOOK

Beau Geste Revisited

P. C. Wren's famous trilogy telling of the adventures of
Beau Geste, Beau Sabreur and *Beau Ideal,* edited and rearranged
(with supplementary notes and comments)
by
John Quentin

There is no such thing as 'coincidence'. A powerful, higher
force sees to it that 'events' take place, when and so
ordered – what takes place is meant to take place.
(Anon)

This book deals with:
LOVE : WAR : HATE

A man's love for a woman

A man's love for a man

A woman's love for 'her' man

The French Foreign Legion retains an abiding interest for many people in the world today. Perhaps it is the most famous and widely known of all the regiments that have ever existed!

Contents

	About this book	ix
	This book deals with	x
	Introduction	1
	The First Book: *Beau Geste*	5
1	The Disappearance of the 'Blue Water'	9
2	Joining the Foreign Legion	12
3	North Africa	24
4	Sidi-bel-Abbès	28
5	The Desert	39
6	Of the Strange Events at Zinderneuf	44
7	How George Lawrence takes de Beaujolais' Story to Lady Brandon	64
8	The Fall of the Fort at Zinderneuf	66
9	The Journey Home	91
10	John's Return Home	98

The Second Book: *Beau Sabreur*

    Foreword   103

Part I – Failure   105

1. Out of the Depths I Rise   107
2. The Blue Hussar   111
3. Africa   119
4. Zaguig   123
5. Raoul d'Auray de Redon and Others   129
6. Abandoned   134
7. The Great Oasis   138
8. Fears Confirmed   143
9. For My Lady   152

Part II – Success   155

    Introduction to Part II   157
    The Making of a Monarch   159

1. El Hamel   159
2. El Habibka   164
3. The Confederation   167
4. Voices from the Past   169
5. The Emir and the Vizier   174
6. Maudie   179
7. Buddy and the Blues   181
8. Maudie and Buddy   184
9. A Mixed Bag   186
10. The Parting of the Ways   190

The Third Book: *Beau Ideal*   197

	Introduction	199
	The Story of Otis Vanbrugh	207
1	Isobel	209
2	The Angel of Death	215
3	Encore Zaguig	220
4	The Mystery of the 'Blue Water' Solved	226
5	John and Otis	233
6	The Legion	236
7	The Zephyrs (or Joyeux)	244
8	Zaza	248
9	Brothers	255
10	Exit Selim	265
11	The Departure	267
12	Return to the West	269
	An Ending	275

Appendix 1	277
Appendix 2	278
Appendix 3	281

Introduction

PERCIVAL CHRISTOPHER WREN (1885–1941), born in Devon and educated at Oxford, had a varied and much travelled life. He joined the French Foreign Legion and wrote a series of successful books dealing with adventure and life in the Legion.

The books for which he is principally remembered are *Beau Geste* (1924), *Beau Sabreur* (1926), and *Beau Ideal* (1928). *Beau Geste* is described in the *Oxford Companion to English Literature* as 'the first of his Foreign Legion novels, a romantic adventure story which became a best seller'.

One hates to cross swords with the *Oxford Companion* but the fact is that *Beau Geste* was not Wren's first Foreign Legion novel! In 1916 Wren wrote *The Wages of Virtue* and in 1917 *Stepsons of France*. The principal character in *The Wages of Virtue* is a delightful character, John Bull (Jean Boule), and the novel gives an excellent account of day-to-day Legion life in the garrison town of Sidi bel Abbès. A secondary character in the book, Reginald Rupert, could be a forerunner of Michael Geste. Characters from *Stepsons of France* reappear in *Beau Geste*. Sergeant-Major 'Suicide-Maker' could be a pattern for Adjutant Lejaune.

No mention is made of these books in the *Companion*, nor of several other Foreign Legion books which Wren wrote later. *Good Gestes* (1929) is a series of short stories concerning the Geste brothers; *Soldiers of Misfortune* and *Valiant Dust* (1932) form a set and, as far as can be ascertained, were the last of Wren's French Foreign Legion novels.

In writing about these books, and in effect reviewing them, with accent on the trilogy, it becomes evident that Wren outlined the trilogy at the time of writing *Beau Geste*. The novels came out at intervals of two years and yet they hang together in remarkable fashion and in only a few instances can chronological error be spotted.

Life is no doubt based on or made up of a series of coincidences. That coincidences happen there can be no denying. And they happen, frequently, throughout the stories. They do not detract from the stories as Wren has a knack of running events smoothly into one another, without jarring the reader's susceptibilities. But it is worthwhile and even just to note the coincidences.

Although we know when the three books comprising the trilogy were written, in the reading of them it is almost impossible to pin-point the period Wren is writing about. For example the only motor cars mentioned are those that take people from the railway station to their stately homes, and vice-versa; all other transport is either by railway or by horse-drawn vehicles.

'Beau Geste' (part of the trilogy) and other works by Wren were re-popularised by the making, by Paramount, of the film, 'Beau Geste'. The black and white film was released in 1939 and featured Gary Cooper as Beau; Preston Foster as Digby; and Ray Milland as John. The villain, in the shape of Sergeant Markov (Lejaune in the book), was played by Brian Donlevy. Teenagers whose parents had read *Beau Geste* in their youth, now in turn, thanks to the Paramount film, discovered the P.C. Wren books.

Does anyone read P. C. Wren books today? So far as can be ascertained none of the books of the trilogy, *Beau Geste*, *Beau Sabreur* and *Beau Ideal*, nor any of his other books, *Stepsons of France*, *The Wages of Virtue*, *Soldiers of Misfortune* and *Valiant Dust*, is in print.

Recently, an abridged version of *Beau Geste* was published in paper-back form. The original Wren books were published by John Murray in hard-back, paper-back being unknown in those far off days.

The abridged version of *Beau Geste* is published by Penguin Books in its Puffin Classic series. Acknowledgement is accorded John Murray in the colophon (in very small print).

Whilst the author is indebted to Penguin Books for a description of the physical appearance of P. C. Wren, 'tall with blue-grey eyes and a military moustache', he cannot agree with some of the conclusions drawn by the editor of the abridged version. Robin Waterfield, the editor, states that Wren, 'followed it [Beau Geste] up with several more books about the Geste brothers.' He did *not*. One other book, *Good Gestes* (of which mention is made in this book) is a collection of short stories and as its title implies is about the Geste brothers.

The second and third books of the trilogy, *Beau Sabreur* and *Beau Ideal*, hardly make mention of the Geste boys. In *Beau Sabreur*, Henri de Beaujolais mentions them *en passant*. In *Beau Ideal*, John, the youngest of the Geste brothers, plays an off-centre part of some importance. Digby is given a cursory mention and Michael (Beau) is mentioned only in that his final testimony clears up, conclusively, the facts concerning the disappearance of the 'Blue Water', the mystery concerning this priceless gem being central to the trilogy.

Robin Waterfield and I agree that the Paramount production of 'Beau Geste' was by far the best and most famous of the Hollywood film productions.

Waterfield labels the books 'escapist'. To some readers they may well be; but others discover that they throw a direct light on the attitudes to life and living in the early days of the twentieth century.

Waterfield notes: 'Wren, along with many of his contemporaries, included elements in his writing, which could, in one way or another, be jarringly out of date today. These elements have been excluded . . .' Shakespeare could be 'jarringly out of date' to some in our modern world.

This author, however, feels that the complete absence of foul four-letter words, the absence of explicit sex and the sheer basic decency of the main characters, excuses Wren his small lapses in calling a man a 'Jew' or a 'dago' or a 'nig'. Today, we of Anglo-Saxon descent are called 'Brits', 'Poms' and 'Limeys', and we have to accept this, even if we don't like it.

What could be annoying to some and refreshing to others is the superiority Wren accords to Britishers and Americans; then come the French (*Beau Sabreur*). But his characters, from whatever nationality, even those 'lesser breeds' (Kipling), are always judged by their honesty and their bravery:

> When two strong men stand face to face,
> though they come from the ends of the earth.
>
> Kipling.

The First Book
Beau Geste

A man's love for a woman
Waxes and wanes as the moon
A man's love for his brother
Is as constant as the stars

CHAPTER I

The Disappearance of the 'Blue Water'

P. C. WREN'S TRILOGY revolves around the disappearance of a fabulous gem known as the 'Blue Water'. When Wren wrote of this gem he valued it at thirty thousand pounds sterling, which at the turn of the century was a fortune. The stone belonged to Sir Hector Brandon of Brandon Abbas, and was kept, for safe-keeping, in what was called 'the Priests Hole'. This was a secret vault secluded behind oak panelling, and had been at the time of Cromwell exactly what its name implied.

As Sir Hector was virtually an absentee landlord, habitually away on safari, the ordering of the Brandon Abbas estate was in the hands of his wife, Lady Brandon. Before her marriage Lady Brandon had been Patricia Rivers, and she was known to those others living at Brandon Abbas as Aunt Patricia.

Some of the main characters of the trilogy live at Brandon Abbas. They are three brothers, Michael (Beau), Digby (his twin) and John Geste. The boys are orphans – no mention is made by Wren of their parents.

Living also at Brandon Abbas are:

Claudia, 'an extraordinarily beautiful girl, whose origin was mysterious, but was vaguely referred to as a cousin.'

Isobel Rivers, Aunt Patricia's niece. The Geste brothers bestow on her the title of 'Faithful Hound'. She is regarded by all as a 'pretty young girl'.

Augustus Brandon, a nephew of Sir Hector Brandon and known as 'Ghastly Gustus'.

The Chaplain, the Rev. Maurice Ffolliot, a minor character, but one who shares a dark secret with Patricia Rivers.

What better place could these children wish for in which to grow up in than a country estate in Devon with its ponds, streams, lawns and rolling hills? Amongst the many and varied games and pastimes indulged in by the Geste brothers and their admirers, Isobel and Claudia, was a particular favourite called by them, 'Naval Engagements'. The game was played out on the giant lilypond at Brandon Abbas and involved two model warships – one British and one French. These models were authentic replicas of ships of the line and their small cannon fired live ammunition. The vessel losing the engagement was burnt in a form of ritual known as a 'Viking's Funeral'.

Wren gives a description of a 'Viking's Funeral' and even though this is anachronistic in the context of British and French naval battles, it suited the style of the Gestes.

> Now a 'Viking's Funeral' cannot be solemnised every day in the week, for it involves, among other things, the destruction of a long-ship. The dead Viking is laid upon a funeral pyre in the centre of his ship, his spear and shield beside him, his horse and hound are slaughtered and their bodies placed in attendance, the pyre is lighted, and the ship sent out to sea with all sail set.

After one such engagement culminating in a 'Viking's Funeral' words are exchanged which are to manifest themselves many years later and in a place far from the green fields of England. As a losing vessel ends its 'life' in the pall of smoke and fire of a 'Viking's Funeral' Michael is heard to say:

> 'That's what I call a funeral . . . I'd give something to have one like that when my turn comes . . .'
>
> 'Righto Beau,' said Digby, 'I'll give you one . . .'

An occasional visitor to Brandon Abbas is a certain Major Henri de Beaujolais of Spahis – a North African cavalry regiment. Although French, his mother had been a Devonshire Carey and a neighbour of the Brandons. He is able to talk, too, to Lady Brandon of her friend George Lawrence. This officer imprints an indelible picture on the minds of the young Gestes.

Some years after a de Beaujolais visit, the Geste brothers are down from Oxford on half-term vacation when Claudia suggests that it would be a good opportunity for them all to see the 'Blue Water' and admire the priceless gem. The Chaplain brings it from its secret hiding place and places it on the table, cradled on its velvet cushion and covered by a glass dome. After they have all exclaimed over the beauty of the stone, and fondly handled it, the Chaplain replaces it on its cushion.

At that moment the lights fail and the room is plunged into darkness. Situated in the country as they are this is not an unusual occurrence and no one is particularly distressed, that is until the lights come on and the 'Blue Water' is no longer lying on its cushion.

Aunt Patricia at first treats the matter as a practical joke and asks the 'joker' to replace the gem. The joker does not do so. Isobel suggests that the lights be turned off for a brief period and during that time the joker should replace the stone. Her suggestion is acted on; when the lights come on again the cushion is still bare.

Aunt Patricia then questions each of her nieces and nephews in turn and each denies having taken the stone. Seething with suppressed anger Lady Brandon leaves the room stating that if the 'Blue Water' is not on its cushion by morning she will summon the police as she can only conclude that there is a thief in their midst.

Morning comes and the gem is not there; neither is Michael Geste. Beau Geste is aware of two things – he knows something of the true value of the 'Blue Water' and he is practically certain of who the thief is. He absconds ostensibly to draw suspicion to himself. Digby is left a note in which his twin confesses to the theft and states only that he will take care of himself; he leaves no forwarding address.

Shortly thereafter Digby follows his twin and several days later the third brother, John, disappears. In John's case desertion is not so easy to come to terms with as he and Isobel are in love with one another and he has declared that love.

John is about to tell us his story. The trilogy novels are all told in the first person, except for a portion of Beau Sabreur, in which the third person is used.

Before John begins his story it would be as well if we look at how John, this twenty-year-old soldier of fortune, views his brothers:

> Michael, generally known as 'Beau' by reason of his remarkable physical beauty, mental brilliance and general distinction.
>
> I have met few men to equal Michael and Digby in beauty, physical strength, courage, and intelligence; but I was 'longer headed' than they, and even more muscular and powerful.

Digby, 'loved fun and laughter, jokes and jollity'. He was also 'Michael's devoted and worshipping shadow'.

It is strange that the character in Wren's trilogy around whom the novels are built, Michael (Beau) Geste, plays, physically, a relatively minor part in the plot; it is his character which runs like a golden thread through the novels.

CHAPTER 2

Joining the Foreign Legion

IT IS WELL that we look at the relationship between John and Isobel before we look at John's flight to the Legion.

John and Isobel had grown up together and were what in those days was called 'childhood sweethearts'. The disappearance of the 'Blue Water' precipitates their engagement. John knows that he will follow, as if drawn by an irresistible force, his brothers to the Legion. Before he goes, though, he must make his feelings towards Isobel quite clear to her.

She helps him. In the quiet of the drawing-room she approaches him and asks him,

'Did you take the "Blue Water", John?'

On receiving the answer 'No', she puts her arms around his neck and kisses him on the lips and John can do no more than to declare his undying love for her. This must have been extremely difficult for him to do knowing that he would shortly be departing for the ranks of the Legion.

In order to soften the blow of his departure John writes Isobel a long letter in which he explains that he cannot remain at home whilst his brothers are away and drawing the guilt of the theft of the 'Blue Water' to themselves. He must share in this 'guilt', even though he is not guilty and is positive that Michael and Digby are not guilty.

> Now you'll be the first to agree that I can't sit at home and let them do this, believing them to be innocent. And if either of them were guilty, I'd want, all the more, to do anything I could to help . . . You'd despise me, really, in your heart, if I stayed at home . . .

And so John makes his plans which he trusts will reunite him with his brothers.

> From the moment I had learned of Michael's flight, I had somewhere, just below the level of consciousness, a vague remembrance of the existence of a romantic-sounding adventurous corps of soldiers of fortune, called the French Foreign Legion.
>
> When thinking of Michael and seeing mental pictures of him in the setting of Brandon Abbas, our 'Prep' school, Eton and Oxford, one of the clearest

Joining the Foreign Legion

of these dissolving views had been a group of us in the Bower, at the feet of a smart and debonair young French officer, who had thrilled us with dramatic tales of Algeria, Morocco, and the Sahara; tales of Spahis, Turcos, Zouaves, Chasseurs d'Afrique, and the French Foreign Legion of mercenaries; tales of hot life and brave death, of battle and of bivouac. At the end, Michael had said:

'I shall join the French Foreign Legion when I leave Eton . . . Get a commission and go into his regiment,' and Digby had applauded the plan.

[The 'smart, and debonair young French officer' was none other than Major Henri de Beaujolais.]

We are immediately confronted with a problem. Michael avers that he will 'join his regiment'; but de Beaujolais was of the Spahis and not of the Foreign Legion.

Michael had not joined the Legion after leaving Eton, but had gone up to Oxford, and is in fact an undergraduate at Oxford at the time of the mysterious disappearance of the 'Blue Water'.

John, nevertheless, feels certain that his brothers have enlisted in the Foreign Legion and he determines to follow them. From Wren's point of view there could be no argument about the brothers' desire to join the Legion – the disappearance of the 'Blue Water' provides the *raison d'être*.

John's progression into the Legion makes interesting reading by today's lights. Brandon Abbas, we are told, was near Exeter in Devon. John states that the journey from Exeter to Waterloo was 'horrible'. This word describes his feelings – not the state of English trains pre-Great War. They were, if anything, cleaner and more punctual in those far-off days than they are now.

He resists the temptation 'to go to the quiet and exclusive hotel that the Brandons had patronised for many years . . .' His reasons are twofold – he might be recognised and more important, having come away with only five pounds in his pocket, he is short of cash. So short in fact that he is forced to visit a pawnbroker so as to convert his disposable possessions into cash. The visit to the pawnbroker throws some light on the mores and attitudes of the time. The shop lies across the Westminster bridge – that is, to the south. There is no record of Wren being anti-Semitic; in fact, one of his bravest and most stoical characters is Jacob the Jew. One can only wonder whether the following account of John's encounter with the pawnbroker would be received tolerantly today!

I entered and found a young gentleman, of markedly Hebraic appearance, behind the counter . . . His bold brown eyes regarded me, his curved nostril curved a little more and his large ripe lips, beneath the pendulous nose, ripened while I watched. He said no word, and this fact somewhat disconcerted me, for I had hitherto regarded the Children of Israel as a decidedly chatty race . . .

I want to sell my watch and one or two things, said I to this silent son of Abraham's seed . . .

' 'Ow much?' asked the child of the Children of Israel . . .

The watch was of gold and had cost twenty-five pounds.

For the watch, John's gold cigarette-case, gold pencil, dress studs, cuff links, plus a dispatch-case containing a pair of silver-backed hairbrushes, a comb, a silver-handled shaving-brush, razor, an ivory nail-brush, a tooth-brush, and a silver box containing soap, the 'spoiler of the Egyptians' parts with five pounds.

The exercise is interesting in that it shows that a young gentleman of John's standing was no match for the pawnbroker when it came to bargaining. It shows us, too, that in the early years of the century a young man's accoutrements were of gold and silver and his dispatch-case of genuine leather. Not many young men aged twenty would be thus kitted out in this day and age.

The pawnbroker does not like John. He feels sure that he is dealing in stolen goods and is not prepared to pay too high for these quality items. John does not dislike the pawnbroker he pokes fun at his origins but acknowledges his bargaining skills. If anything John regrets not being able to drive a harder bargain.

John now has ten pounds in his pocket.

Not being prepared to risk lodging at the family hotel John considers the following hotels: the Ritz, the Savoy, the Carlton, Claridges, the Grosvenor and the Langham! Would he have received change from ten pounds in 1905? Remember he has still to pay for his fare to Paris. Cost, however, does exercise his mind; and the risk of meeting someone who knows him finally persuades him to try for something more modest.

So what does he do? He 'approached one of those mines of information, or towers of strength or refuge, a London policeman.' This worthy advises him to go to Bloomsbury, and so he does. One wonders how a London 'Bobby' would react these days if approached with a similar request for information!

Is John's encounter with the pawnbroker offensive? Is it amusing? Try selling a Kruger Rand to a Cockney coin dealer! Treatment received from him will not be much different than that meted out to John by his pawnbroker!

Wren does not tell us of Michael's and Digby's journeys to France and the Foreign Legion. One cannot help feeling that they would have handled matters in far better fashion than did John.

Of the 'modest' hotel in Bloomsbury John has this to say:

> I had an edible dinner, a clean and comfortable bed, and a satisfying breakfast, for a surprisingly small sum . . . The 'young lady' at the bureau of this chaste hostelry did something to enhance the diminished self-respect that my Israelite had left to me, by making no comment upon the fact that I was devoid of luggage, and by refraining from asking me to produce money in advance . . .

There are not many hotels around these days which admit guests without either cash 'up-front' or a pull of the guest's credit card.

John is quite frank in admitting: 'I was glad to get away in the morning and to seek the shop of a hairdresser, after sleeping for the first time in my life, without pyjamas, and bathing without a sponge . . .'

Then comes the journey from London to Paris. In order to spare his funds and enable himself to eat and have something over for an hotel in Paris, John wisely decides to travel third class – a bit of a comedown, one must conclude. We are informed that he turned his pounds sterling into francs at Charing Cross station, and 'felt much richer'.

John is familiar with Paris hotels; the Maurice, the Crillon, the Bristol and the Ambassador's; but again, he fears meeting someone who might know him. Once again he approaches the law, this time in the shape of a gendarme. This worthy directs him to the Normandie in the Rue de l'Échelle.

It is difficult in our day and age to believe that people behaved in the fashion that John behaved in, whilst waiting to check in at the Normandie:

> . . . trying to look like an eccentric foreigner who habitually went about without walking stick or gloves in order that he might keep his hands in his pockets . . .

Then to overcome his acute embarrassment at lack of luggage he pretends to be an American by talking to the receptionist in what he fondly believes to be American slang!

How did one go about joining the Legion? John does not know but soon finds out from a loquacious barber, who considers the members of that famous regiment to be a bunch of rascally scoundrels, mostly from Germany. Despite his dislike of the Legion he is able to tell John that the recruiting-office is in the Rue St Dominique. Taking a fiacre to this address John finds the *Bureau de Recrutement – Engagements Volontaires*.

At last a ray of hope lightens John's life – he learns from the Colonel in command of the recruiting station that he, John, is the third Englishman within the last few days to have signed on for the Foreign Legion. John enlists as 'John Smith', but makes a foolish mistake by signing the form 'J. Geste'. The kindly Colonel tears up the offending form and prepares a new one which John duly signs as 'J. Smith', his chosen *nom-de-guerre*.

Wren is hardly original in the names he gives to his heroes; Michael chooses 'Brown' and John 'Smith'. Digby's *nom-de-guerre* is unknown; in the Paramount film he is simply known as 'Digs'. As the brothers had not ever discussed *noms-de-guerre* it is amazing that they do not duplicate names by mistake!

A rail-warrant for Marseilles sees John on his way to Fort St Jean, the military depôt in that town. John is met by a Sergeant whose duty it is to meet the Paris train and escort recruits to the depôt. John reports:

> I rather liked the look of the Sergeant. He was a dapper alert person, and his bronzed face, though hard as iron, was not brutal nor vicious. He wore the usual uniform of the French infantry, but with a broad blue woollen sash around his waist, green epaulettes, instead of red, and Zouavre trousers –

The Sergeant: 'Another Englishman – well it might have been worse.'
John is naturally thrilled to hear these words.
Having had nothing to eat on the train, John is by now, ravenous.

> I waxed diplomatic. 'A sergeant would not share a bottle of wine with a recruit, I suppose, Monsieur?'
>
> 'He would not *bleu* [rookie]. Not from a natural sense of superiority, but also because it would be against the regulations. Some sergeants, properly approached might refresh themselves, perhaps, while a deserving *bleu* did the same . . .'

John hands him a five franc piece and the sergeant goes off to a wine shop and John goes to a café where:

> I hungrily devoured my last civilian meal – and rose, feeling what Digby would call, 'a better and a wider man'.

On re-meeting the sergeant that worthy asks: 'Have you any more money, *bleu*?'

> *John*, feeling somewhat disappointed in him: 'Yes, sergeant.'
> *Sergeant*: 'Because if you have not, I shall return you three francs.'
> I assured him that this was wholly unnecessary, though a very kindly thought, and regretted my suspicions.
> *Sergeant*: 'Then I will give you some good advice instead. Beware the Algerian wine – the blessing and the curse of the army in Africa. I have just drunk two bottles of it. Excellent . . . Beware of women, the blessing and the curse of all men. I have married three of them. Terrible . . .'

He goes on to warn about absinthe:

> 'Absinthe is the uncle and aunt of the grand-parents of cafard [desert madness]. It is the vilest poison. Avoid it. I was brought up on it . . . Terrible . . . I had some just now, after my wine . . . Now you have talked more than is seemly. Silence, *bleu*.'

And so John concentrates his attention on the Marseilles water-front:

> People from all over the world . . . Arabs, Negroes, Levantines, Chinese, Moors, Annamese, Indians and Lascars and seamen of the ships of all nations . . .

and, to John's delight: 'much evidence of the "English flag".'

On entering the barrack-room at Fort St Jean, John is disappointed at not finding Beau and Digby there. However he meets two characters who are destined to play an important rôle in the trilogy. But before we meet Hank and Buddy officially, we find John wrestling with a window in an attempt to open it and gain some fresh air.

> I am not in a position categorically to affirm that this was positively the first time that a window had ever been opened in Fort St Jean, but it might have been to judge by the interest, not to say consternation, evoked by my simple action.

This 'simple action' is challenged by one of the recruits.

> *Vogué:*   'You want that window open?'
> *John:*   'Monsieur is intelligent.'
> *Vogué:*   'Suppose I want it shut?'
> *John:*   'Come and shut it.'
> *Vogué:*   'Suppose we all want it shut?'

John: 'Then there is an end to the matter. If the majority prefer to poison themselves, they have a perfect right to do so.'

No one backs Vogué up and so the window remains open.

'Like the ceiling raised any?' this from Buddy and the first words of a lasting friendship.

John describes Buddy thus:

> . . . a very small, clean-shaven man with a prominent nose and chin, a steel trap mouth, and a look of great determination and resolution. His eyes were very light grey, hard and penetrating, his hair straw-coloured and stubbly, his face lantern-jawed and tanned.
>
> 'How did you know I was English?'
>
> 'What else? Pink and white . . . own the earth . . . dude . . . "open all the windows now I've come! British".'

Next, John meets Buddy's friend, Hank:

> A huge man, he appeared to be some seven feet in length, four in breadth and two in depth. In face he greatly resembled the small man, having the same jutting chin, prominent nose, tight mouth and hard leathery face. His eyes were of a darker grey, however, and his hair black and silky. He also looked a hard case and a very bad enemy. Conversely though, I gained the impression that he might be a very good friend . . .

Prophetic words.

The language used in the repartee is interesting. Wren is fond of Americans. Some he holds superior to Britons and some inferior, but always they are brave men and true.

John realises at once that these two are down on their luck:

> 'Would you gentlemen lunch with me? Brothers in arms and all that . . .'
>
> 'He's calling you a gentleman, Hank. He don' mean no real harm though. He's talking English to you . . .'
>
> I made another effort.
>
> 'Say,' quoth I, 'I gotta hunch I wanta grub-stake you two hoboes to a blow-out. Guess I can cough up the dough, if yew ain't too all-fired proud to be pards with a dod-gasted Britisher.'

[One wonders what the Americans made of this speech. Do Americans, or did Americans, ever speak in this fashion?]

Be this as it may, the two Americans accept the invitation but before the three 'pards' can repair to the canteen, food arrives in the shape of *soupe*, the twice-daily ration which, from what Wren tells us, was standard fare in the French army, the Legion or otherwise.

John tells us that the *soupe* was 'a kind of stew, quite good and nourishing, sometimes with a little meat in it.' Also served was bread of a greyish colour, used to mop up the stew with as no cutlery was provided. Unsweetened milkless coffee, too, was served – no doubt with which to wash all down!

We now get a preview of the great strength and determination of Hank, the very much bigger of the two Americans. He and his friend Buddy, down on their luck, are just about starved. They take two bowls of soup each and so does John.

> I looked round. There appeared to be more bowls than people in the room. I snatched two . . . This disgusting exhibition of greed on my part cannot be excused, but may be condoned as it was not made in my own interests . . .

John offers a bowl to each of his new American friends and believes he has made them his friends for life.

> A large German lumbered up gesticulating, and assailed Hank: 'You eat dree! I only eat vun! Himmel! You damn dirty tief!'

Buddy, in the mischievous way we come to love, urges the German: 'Don't you stand for it! Beat him up!' And when the badly done by man shakes a useful fist under Hank's nose the latter raises a huge hand and the former finds himself flat on his back. End of argument.

After their first meal in a French barracks Hank and Buddy accept the offer, made earlier by John, of refreshment, but not food, wine.

Reaching the canteen Hank says: 'Drinks are on you pard. Set 'em up.'

> The wine was the national drink – good red wine at three-halfpence the bottle. It struck me as far better wine than one paid a good deal for at Oxford, and good enough to be set before one's guests anywhere.

Wren uses the canteen scene to highlight the differences between Hank and Buddy, on the one hand, and John on the other.

Hank:	'Gee! It's what they call wine. Got to get used to it with the other cruel deprivations and hardships . . .'
John:	'Quite good wine, but I can't say I like it as a drink between meals.'

> I found that my companions were of one mind with me, though perhaps for a different reason.
>
> *Buddy:* 'Yep! Guess they don't allow no intoxicatin' hard likkers in these furrin canteens.'
>
> *Hank:* 'Set 'em up again, Bo.'
>
> And I procured them each his third bottle.
>
> *Buddy:* 'You ain't drinking, pard.'
> *John:* 'Not thirsty.'
> *Hank:* 'Thirsty? Don't s'pose there's any water here if you was.'
>
> and feeling I had said the wrong thing, covered my confusion by turning away . . .

Perhaps we can agree that John has said the 'wrong thing'!

Observing the throng John sees a man, dressed in civilian clothes, entering the canteen.

> I had noticed him in the barrack-room . . . despite his shabby dress he looked like a soldier. Not that he had by any means the carriage of an English guardsman . . . his face was a soldier's, bronzed, hard, disciplined.

The newcomer is Boldini, of whom we will hear a lot more. He offers to trade information concerning life in the Legion for a bottle of wine. This John gladly supplies as he is anxious to learn as much as possible, and Boldini appears to be an educated man but down on his luck. Hank and Buddy are included in the quest for knowledge.

> *Hank:* 'I wants to know when we gits our next eats.'
> *Buddy:* 'An' if we can go out an' git a drink.'

The answer from Boldini is that they would get *soupe* at about four o'clock and that they would not be allowed to leave Fort St Jean under any circumstances whatsoever, until they were marched out to board the boat for Oran. It transpires that Boldini is an old legionnaire rejoining after his first five year term.

John (naively): 'Speaks well for the Legion.'

The reply that comes back is far from reassuring: 'Or ill for the chance of an ex-legionnaire to get a crust of bread.'

Then John does that which is never done – he asks: 'Why did you join the Legion?'

And the reply comes back: 'For the same reason as you did. For my health.' This statement is accompanied by a cold stare.

However Boldini is of a forgiving nature – especially as he senses there is more money in John's reserves. At first John and Hank take to Boldini. Buddy, however, is wary of this Italian, who speaks English, Hindustani and French.

Later in the evening, after the four o'clock *soupe*, John finds himself entertaining the bulk of his barrack-room mates. Even those who had objected to him opening the window are charmed to accept his hospitality!

> It is quite easy to be lavishly hospitable with wine at about a penny a pint . . .
>
> Fun grew fast and furious, and I soon found I was entertaining a considerable section of the French army, as well as the Legion's recruits. I thoroughly enjoyed the evening, and was smitten upon the back, poked in the ribs, wrung by the hand, embraced about the neck, and, alas, kissed on both cheeks by Turco, Zouave, Tirailleur, Artilleur, Marsouin, and Spahi . . .

Boldini's manners degenerate as the evening wears on; he cannot hold his drink and becomes more and more familiar. John begins to regret that he has given him ten francs as a 'retainer'.

When John checked into his hotel in London he had ten pounds sterling in his pocket. This sum of money enabled him to pay for: his London hotel; his Oxford Street barber; his trip from London to Paris (train, steamer, train); his hotel and barber in Paris; and numerous drinks in the canteen in Marseilles. These were the days when value could be obtained for money. The same excursion would, today, cost several hundred pounds!

Wren obviously enjoyed the canteen scene. It is repeated in *Beau Sabreur* when Henri de Beaujolais entertains his barrack-room companions to an evening of drinks.

> Meanwhile, Hank and Buddy, those taciturn, observant, non-conmmittal, and austerely-tolerant Americans, made hay while the sun of prosperity shone, drank more than any two of the others, said nothing and seemed to wonder what all the excitement was about, and what made the 'pore furriners' noisy.

Buddy, breaking a long silence of his own: 'Ennyboddy 'ud think the boobs had bin drinkin'.'

To which Hank replies: 'They gotta pretend this yer wine-stuff is a hard drink, an' act like they got a whisky-jag an' was off the water-wagon . . .'

John had been extremely disappointed not to find Michael and Digby at Fort St Jean. Boldini, though, assures him that anyone joining the Legion would go from Fort St Jean to Fort Thérèse in Oran, and from there to either Saida or Sidi-bel-Abbès.

This information somewhat allays John's fears that he might have committed himself to five years in the Legion only to discover that his brothers have not joined that regiment, but are elsewhere in the wide world.

A look at John's character and background, at this stage, would do no harm. He is twenty years old and what in those days was termed a 'gentleman'; he is a student at Oxford holding a boxing blue. He is in love with Isobel Rivers, who is eighteen years old.

John could not be one hundred per cent certain that his brothers had joined the French Foreign Legion – perhaps he was entitled to be ninety per cent certain. There was really no need for him to have absconded when in so doing doubt was cast on his integrity. He could have remained in England and finished his university career. But no, he felt compelled to follow his brothers.

John does not appear to have been cast in the soldier's mould. No doubt he has served in a cadet corps and knows the rudiments of drill on a parade ground. He displays naivety and yet is, in some respects, mature beyond his twenty years.

In Paris, John has fallen out with the recruiting sergeant-major and yet when he leaves he adds two francs to the three handed him by the sergeant-major (being his travel subsistence allowance) and hands five francs back, stating: 'Let us part friends, Sergeant-Major, for I hate leaving ill-feeling behind me . . .'

When in Marseilles the escorting sergeant asks John whether he has any money left, John feels a pang of disappointment, as he has judged the man to be honourable, and says, 'Yes.' The sergeant who was about to hand John back the change from the money John had given him for the purchase of refreshment whilst he had breakfasted on rolls and coffee, says that if it is indeed the case that John has cash over, he will keep the change. John immediately feels better disposed towards this sergeant. Could it be that John is one of those people, met with so frequently in life, who are incapable of saying 'no'?

When Boldini asks if he may finish the wine in John's glass ('as it would be a pity to waste it'). John replies, 'Pray do,' and then reminds himself that he is no longer at Oxford. One cannot help getting the feeling that Michael and Digby would have disported themselves in different fashion.

Back in the barrack-room, after having entertained a considerable section of the French African Army, Buddy asks:

'Got any money left, pard?'

John: 'Why, yes, certainly. You're most welcome to . . .'

Buddy, cutting in: 'Welcome nix. If you got any left shove it inside yer piller an' tie the end up.'

John: 'Hardly necessary, surely? Looks rather unkind and suspicious, you know . . .'

Buddy: 'Please yerself, pard, o' course, and let Mister Cascara Sagrada [Boldini] get it.'

As things turn out Boldini does make a try for the money but Buddy has got in first and taken it from under John's pillow. The next morning:

> I partly dressed, and then felt beneath my pillow for my money. It was not there. I felt savage and sick . . . Robbed . . . the beastly curs . . .
>
> *Buddy:* 'Here it is. Thought I'd better mind it when I aheered your nose-sighs . . . Shore enuff, about four this morning, over comes Mister Cascara Sagrada to see how youse a gettin' on . . . 'all right, Bo,' says I, speaking innercent in me slumbers, "I'm a mindin' of it".'
>
> *John:* 'No! Not really?'
>
> *Buddy*: 'You betcha. An' Mister Cascara Sagrada says, "Oh, I thought somebody might try and rob him." "So did I", I says "and I was right too" I says, and the skunk scoots back to his hole.'

One can imagine how foolish John must have felt, especially as worldly-wise Buddy had warned him of the possibility of theft. Wren paints a picture of a gentleman in the Legion. Capable of looking after himself, physically, but a child in such matters as parting with his cash to all and sundry and an innocent belief in the honesty of his fellow recruits.

CHAPTER 3

North Africa

EARLY NEXT MORNING, as predicted by Boldini, the recruits are marched to the dockside (*bassin*), where they embark on the SS *General Negrier* for Oran.

On the voyage to Oran there is trouble with the cook who refuses to feed the recruits, his policy being to sell the rations rightly belonging to the troops. But his plans go awry on this voyage as he has to reckon with Boldini, the old soldier, and above all, with Hank and Buddy. Once Boldini has made it clear to the latter what their rights are Hank decides to see to it that they receive 'our doo and lawful eats'.

Pressure is applied to the cook; more specifically to the cook's throat, by Hank. After being nearly choked to death the cook produces the rations, and Hank and Buddy's hunger, to say nothing of that of the other prospective legionnaires, is assuaged.

During the fracas with the cook we have another glimpse at John's character:

> A sort of quartermaster, followed by a sailor came up, and I feared trouble. Visions of us all in irons, awaiting a court-martial at Oran, floated before my eyes.
>
> 'Assaulting the cook?' quoth the man in uniform. 'Good! Kill the thrice-accursed thieving food-spoiler, and may *le bon Dieu* assist you.'

During the altercation with the cook Buddy has promised to fight him after they had been fed. Buddy is a small man, the cook, large and fat.

> ... the cook rushed to his doom. I fancy myself as an amateur boxer. Buddy was no amateur and the cook was no boxer. It was not a fight so much as an execution. Buddy was a dynamic ferocity, and the thieving scoundrel was very badly damaged.

The landing at Oran and the march to the barracks finds Wren guilty of one of his few lapses in geographical accuracy.

> On through the wide streets to narrow slums and alleys we went, till at length

the town was behind us and the desert in front. For an hour or more we marched by a fine road across the desert.

Anyone who has been to Oran will be aware of the fact that the town is surrounded by vineyards and wheat fields – the desert is many miles to the south. Wren, believing that most people associate North Africa with the Sahara and the French Foreign Legion with the desert, thought, perhaps, that he should introduce his readers to the desert as soon as possible.

It is at Fort St Thérèse that John meets up with his brothers. As John enters the barrack-room Digby, who is sitting on his bed with Beau, remarks, 'Enter the third robber.' This is a significant remark and plays a role in the ensuing story – especially as the remark is overheard by Boldini.

> Boldini was deeply interested: 'Third robber!' he said on a note of mingled contempt and enquiry to Glock.

Beau's greeting of his younger brother is somewhat different to Digby's: 'Good God! You unutterable young fool! God help us . . .'

Wren, who liked Americans and believed that he was familiar with American slang, has John introduce Hank and Buddy to his brothers as follows:

> 'Beau and Dig, let me introduce two shore-enough blowed-in-the-glass, dyed-in-the-wool, whole-piece White Men from God's Own Country – Hank and Buddy . . . My brothers Michael and Digby.'
> 'Americans possibly,' said Digby!
> 'Shake,' said Hank and Buddy as one man, and the four shook hands gravely.

When Boldini's turn comes things go rather differently: *John*: 'Mr Francesco Boldini.' – and neither Michael nor Digby offers his hand . . . until that gentleman reaches for it effusively.

Wren goes into more detail now concerning the rations served to the army in North Africa: half a pound of meat, three sous' worth of vegetables served as a stew. A pound and a half of bread, half an ounce of coffee and half an ounce of sugar. Being French these victuals were no doubt served up in a most appetising manner.

The recruits assembled at Fort St Thérèse, as seen by Wren through John's eyes are: . . . men from France, Belgium, Germany (chiefly Alsace and Lorraine), Spain, Austria and Switzerland. They look like labourers, artisans, soldiers in mufti, newspaper sellers, shop-boys, clerks and the usual sort of men of all ages whom one would see in the poorer streets of any town, or in a Rowton House.

[Rowton Houses, or 'doss houses' as they are colloquially termed, are registered lodging houses where bachelor working men, at a nominal inclusive charge a night, can obtain a night's lodging and the use of a reading-room. Founded by Lord Rowton in 1892. Ref. *Everyman's Encyclopaedia*. Do they still exist?]

Thus the impression John gains is that these men are not criminals and rogues. This is quite a different impression from the one that is usually held; that the Legion is a haven for criminals from most of the races of the world.

At Fort St Thérèse Jean St André is introduced into the story. John describes him as having 'soldier' stamped all over him, well dressed, smart, dapper and soigné, well educated with charming manners; we hear more of him.

That evening, the brothers three, having stood all recruits, plus many old hands, to drinks in the canteen, decide to leave the barrack-room and doss down in the open courtyard of the Fort. Propped against the wall of the courtyard they prepare for a night under the 'wonderful African stars'.

Michael admonishes John in the following manner: 'Well, my poor, dear, idiotic, mad pup – and what the devil do you think you're doing here?'

John has no valid answer, other than that he wishes to be with his brothers.

The three then go on to discuss plans for informing those at home as to their whereabouts. They feel, and rightly so, that they owe some sort of explanation to their aunt Patricia, who had, after all, brought them up.

As discussion flows freely between them as to who stole the 'Blue Water' and what each intends doing with the proceeds when the gem comes to be sold, little do they know that Boldini is ensconced around the corner and taking the light banter in the most serious vein.

The following dialogue ensues:

Michael: 'It's rough on Claudia.'

Digby: 'Deuced lucky for young Gussie that Isobel was able to clear him.'

Michael: 'That's what makes it hard on Claudia – or would have done, if we hadn't bolted. Gussie and Isobel being out of it – it was she or one of us.'

In the silence which follows John becomes aware of a sound, close by, where a buttress of the wall projects. Probably a rat or some nocturnal bird: possibly a dog. It was, of course, a rat – Boldini!

On the following day the recruits learn that they are to be assigned to one of the two Foreign Legion depôts – Saida, the depôt of the Second Regiment or Sidi-bel-Abbès, the depôt of the First Regiment.

There is the very real possibility that the three brothers could be parted or that Hank and Buddy could be sent elsewhere. However they need not have feared.

> To us came Boldini as we strolled around the court-yard.
>
> 'Let's stick together, we four,' quoth he. 'I'm going to the First, and you'd better come too. I know all the ropes there . . . get you in right with the corporals . . . Sergeant Lejaune's a friend of mine . . .'
>
> 'We three are certainly going together,' said Michael, 'and we want the two Americans to come with us, and we prefer the First on the whole. Have we any say in the matter?'
>
> 'Ten francs would have a say,' replied Boldini . . . 'but why bother about the Americans? They are uncultured people.'
>
> *Michael*: 'We are going to cultivate them!'

Despite their general dislike for Boldini, the three brothers are prepared to pay ten francs to go along with him. Perhaps they reason that ten francs is a cheap price to pay in order to remain together. Whether Boldini is responsible for Hank and Buddy being included in the draft for Sidi-bel-Abbès is not clear. It would have been in his own interest to have had them sent off to Saida. It could be that he did nothing, either way, concerning the Americans, and that it is pure luck that they were sent to Sidi-bel-Abbès.

> As we 'fell in' to march to the station, St André and I stood behind Michael and Digby, while Boldini and an English-speaking Swiss, named Maris, stood behind Hank and Buddy, who were next to Michael and Digby.

Maris is described thus:

> . . . he seemed an excellent person. He had been a travelling valet and courier, and had all the experience, address, linguistic knowledge, and general ability to be expected of a person who could earn his living in that capacity.

He attached himself to the Geste boys because he was 'fond of gentlemen'.

CHAPTER 4

Sidi-bel-Abbès

THE TRAIN FROM ORAN to Sidi-bel-Abbès passes through country which is far more accurately depicted by Wren than his placing of Fort St Thérèse (outside Oran) in the desert.

> . . . cultivated country fields, farms, orchards, and gardens . . . [but again lapses, by stating] . . . it was not until we were approaching our destination that sand-hills and desert encroached . . .

Unfortunately this is not correct as the desert lies well to the south of Sidi-bel-Abbès beyond the Saharan Atlas.

> Entering the town itself, through a great gate in the huge ramparts, we were in a curiously hybrid Oriental-European atmosphere in which moved stately Arabs, smart French ladies, omnibuses, camels, half-naked Negroes, dapper officers, poor working folk, soldiers by the hundred, grissettes, pig-tailed European girls, Spaniards, Frenchmen, and Levantines. Men and women straight from the Bible, and others straight from the Boulevards, Spahis, Turcos, Zouaves, and Chasseurs d'Afrique, made up the throng.

Both in *Beau Geste* and in *Beau Sabreur* Wren states that a 'lane' divided the barracks of the Spahi cavalry from those of the Foreign Legion. When the writer visited Sidi-bel-Abbès, however, before the Legion left Algeria, he was unable to discover this 'lane'. The great gates of the Legion's parade-ground opened out onto the street and there was no sign of the Spahi barracks. That famous regiment could, however, by that time, have been disbanded. An attempt to take photographs of the famous gates was frustrated by a colour-sergeant shouting *'Interdit'* and brandishing his cane!

On filing through the gates and onto the parade ground, the recruits are met by the sergeant of the guard. Several legionnaires are standing nearby and one remarks:

> *'Mon dieu*! there's that blackguard Boldini back again. As big a fool as he is a knave, evidently.'
>
> Boldini affected deafness.

We are now introduced to Colour-Sergeant Lejaune:

> He came from the regimental offices, a fierce-looking, thick-set, dark man, with the face and figure of a prize-fighter, glaring and staring of eye, swarthily handsome, with the neck and jowl of a bulldog . . . a terrible and terrifying man . . . to his admiring superiors he was invaluable; to his despairing subordinates he was unspeakable . . . he took a delight in punishing, and nothing angered him more than to be unable to find a reason for doing it.

Lejaune receives the draft as follows:

> *Lejaune to Buddy:*   'An undersized cur!'
>
> *Buddy to Lejaune:*   'Guess I've seen better things than you dead on a sticky fly-paper.'

This remark, being made in English, was fortunately not understood by Lejaune. But a vile recruit had spoken back and from that moment Buddy was a marked man. And what was more his friends were marked men.

> *Lejaune to Hank:*   'A lazy hulk, I'll take my oath. I'll teach you to move quickly in a way that will surprise you.'
>
> *Hank:*   'Sure Bo. Spill another mouthful.'

Hank was what one might call a doubly-marked man.

When the blood-shot eye of Colour-Sergeant Lejaune fell on Boldini, it halted, and a long look passed between the two men. Neither spoke.

> *Lejaune to the Gestes:*   'Run away pimps. Show me your hands. I'll harden them for you, by God . . . Never done a stroke of work in your lives . . . I'll manicure you before you die . . . I'll make you wish you had gone to gaol instead.'

In the well-known book *The Legion of the Damned* by Bennett J. Doty, Doty, who had apparently read *Beau Geste*, states that at no time during his sojourn in the Legion did he meet a character who resembled Lejaune, or who treated legionnaires as he did.

This ordeal over, the draft is kitted out by the *fourrier-sergent* of the Seventh Company:

> . . . two cloth uniforms, white fatigue uniforms, linen spats, underclothing, the blue woollen sash or cumberband, cleaning materials, soap and towels, but no socks, for the Legion does not wear them.

The author has not been able to check this statement concerning socks. After the Second World War socks were issued (see *The Making of a Legionnaire* by Peter Macdonald).

Soap played an important part in the everyday life of the legionnaire. In the *The Wages of Virtue* Wren tells us that John Bull (Sir Montague Merlin in real life) kept his soap in his mouth whilst he was rinsing his clothes, for fear that it would be lifted if put down even for a few seconds.

The uniform described by John and depicted on the dust-cover of the 1926 edition of *Beau Geste* appears to be similar to that worn by the Legion in the 1870s as illustrated in Martin Windrow's *Uniforms of the French Foreign Legion*. By the 1920s the classic French Foreign Legion uniform of blue great-coat, white trousers and spats, with white *kepi* and neck flap, had given way to khaki. The *kepi blanc* (and neck flap) were, however, retained and are *de rigueur* to this day.

It is thus difficult to determine exactly in what period of the Legion's history Wren sets his book.

The barrack-room occupied by the recruits is described thus:

> . . . a huge clean well-ventilated chamber in which were thirty beds. This is a great improvement on the barrack-rooms of either Fort St Jean or Fort St Thérèse. The recruits, or *bleus* were allotted beds between old legionnaires.
>
> The morning call was at 5.15 and by 5.30 the legionnaires were to be on the parade-ground in

Typical legionnaire

white uniform and sash, with knapsack, rifle, belts and bayonet. Before quitting the room the bedding of each man had to be folded and piled at the head of the bed, with hairbreadth accuracy, and the floor beneath the bed swept clean.

This near obsession with the cleanliness of the barracks is mentioned in numerous books on the Legion.

> Apparently this cleanliness need not extend to the person, for there were no washing facilities of any sort in the room, nor on the whole of that floor of the barracks, nor on the one below. An eccentric, in search of a morning wash, had to make his way down four flights of stairs to a rude and crude kind of lavatory on the ground-floor.

Wren, like a lot of authors, fails to mention such essentials as urinals or commodes.

During the fifteen minutes available for preparing for parade, coffee is served to each man, sitting up in bed, by the *guarde-chambre*. This must have been, and must still be to this day, the only army in which coffee was served to men in bed! After coffee, said by John to be 'hot, strong and good', the corporal in charge of the room shouts, '*Levez-vous! levez-vous!*'

Michael, Digby and John, no doubt being eccentrics, dash to the far-off lavatory, 'dashed our heads into water and fled back towelling.'

Arriving back in the barrack-room they find all three of their beds made, their kit folded and their boots brushed. All this is by courtesy of the old legionnaires who perform these chores for, 'a couple of sous'.

> An income of a halfpenny a day is one that will stand a good deal of augmenting . . .

Wren does not mention how Hank and Buddy fared; whether they washed or not; they certainly had no cash with which to pay for chores to be done. It seems as if none of the men in the room, other than the Gestes, wash themselves – perhaps this is done in the evenings; we are not told.

The barrack-room is then inspected by the Colour-Sergeant of the Company, Lejaune, and is found to be *klim bim*.

The rifle used by the French army of that time was the Lebel rifle. These were stowed in the racks of the barrack-room. The bayonet was a 'sword bayonet', somewhat longer than that used by the British army of the time.

Wren gives details of how discipline was enforced in the French army and especially describes that of the Legion. This is a common theme in all Wren's books concerning the Legion. It features, too, in books on the Legion by other authors.

Most of Wren's characters are, at one time or another, subjected to this discipline. The Geste brothers, however, appear to go through their period in the Legion without being punished, or if they are, as seems likely, we are not told about it.

> In the French army non-commissioned officers can, like prefects in our public schools, award punishments without reference to officers. They give the punishment, enter it in the *livre de punitions*, and there is an end to the matter – unless the officer, inspecting the book, increases the punishment by way of punishing the offender for getting punished.
>
> The system enhances the power and position of the non-com enormously, and undoubtedly makes for the tremendous discipline – and some injustice and tyranny.

This first morning at Side-bel-Abbès is dealt with here in some detail, as Wren does not repeat this routine in this or any other of the books of the trilogy.

The squad, complete with Lebel rifles and bayonets, is on parade at 5.30 a.m.

> The battalion marched away to field-exercises, and the recruits were formed up, told off by *escouades*, each under a corporal, and taken out to the 'plateau', a vast drill-ground near the *village nègre*, for physical training, which was simply steady running.
>
> It was nothing for athletes like us three, but a little cruel for half-starved or out-of-condition men, who had not run for some time.
>
> On other mornings the physical culture took the form of gymnastics, boxing or a long route-march . . .
>
> On our return to barracks, wet and warm, we had our morning meal of *soupe* and bread, and a quarter litre of good wine. [The French don't mind drinking liquor before mid-day!] There was meat as well as vegetables in my excellent stew, and the bread, though grey, was palatable, and more than sufficient in quantity.

In no other of the books of the trilogy is the victualling of the men dealt with in such detail as in *Beau Geste*. Food was important to the men, and with the French love of good food and wine one can well see that the victuals had to be of a fair standard.

John goes on to describe the rest of their day:

> After a rest the recruits had a lecture, and after that squad and company drill,

while the battalion did attack formation exercises on the plateau. After this we were set to work with brooms and wheel-barrows at tidying up around the barracks, and were then free to go to the *lavobo* to wash and dry our white uniforms.

At five o'clock we got our second meal, exactly like the first, and were then finished for the day, save in so far as we had to prepare for the next . . .

John is not shy in describing how he and his brothers became trained soldiers:

> We three soon became good soldiers, aided by our intelligence, strength, sobriety, athletic training, sense of discipline, knowledge of French, and a genuine desire to make good . . .
>
> More fortunate than most, we were well educated and had 'back-ground'; a little money (thanks to Michael's fore-thought) which was wealth in the Legion; good habits, self-control, and a public-school training; and we were inoffensive by reason of possessing the consideration, courtesy, and self-respecting respect for others proper to gentlemen . . .

Thus did a young man of good breeding regard himself in the early nineteen-hundreds, particularly so if he were a British Anglo-Saxon!

All, though, is not a bed of roses. There are plenty of 'cons' offsetting the 'pros' — these are:

> Less fortunate than most, we were accustomed to varied food, comfortable surroundings, leisure, a great deal of mental and physical recreation, spaciousness of life, and above all privacy . . .

John is saying they were 'less' fortunate than others, who presumably are used to monotonous food, uncomfortable surroundings and so on, and are thus far better able to cope with the dull monotony of barrack life.

As all drill and all lectures are given in French one wonders how men who came to the Legion knowing no French manage to cope. The Geste boys at least know a little.

By now the brothers feel that it is imperative that Aunt Patricia and the rest of the family at Brandon Abbas be advised as to their whereabouts. After a 'Council of War' it is decided that John write to Isobel:

> Legionnaire John Smith, No. 18896
> 7th Company, Premier Étrangère
> Sidi-bel-Abbès, Algeria
>
> Dear Isobel,
> A letter to the above address will find me. Michael and Digby know it also.

I can send them any messages, or news from Brandon Abbas. Neither of them is in England. Either of them will let me know if he changes his present address. I am in excellent health. I shall write again if I hear from you. I am so anxious to know what is happening at home . . .

                                                            John

Discreet enquiries have been made of Boldini (the wrong man!) as to whether the English police would take steps to pursue legionnaire John Smith. They are assured that they would not.

It is inevitable that John inserts a private letter to Isobel with a message of 'undying and unutterable love'.

A reply to John's letter is received a fortnight later. (Excellent postal service in those early days of the century.)

Aunt Patricia has done exactly nothing. She has reported the theft of the 'Blue Water' neither to the police nor anyone else. She has accepted the fact that one of the Gestes had stolen the 'Blue Water' and has decided to do nothing at all about it, but simply await her husband's (Uncle Hector's) return.

This seems strange indeed. Why is Aunt Patricia reluctant to inform Scotland Yard? Is it that she fears a scandal? Is it to protect the name of the Gestes?

Sitting on Michael's bed the brothers discuss Isobel's letter, Brandon Abbas, and the 'Blue Water' — none of them is aware of Boldini lying 'sleeping' on his cot, just behind them!

Thus the mystery of the 'Blue Water' builds up in the minds of the legionnaires most closely associated with the Gestes, principally in the mind of Boldini, who is in possession of enough verbal evidence to convince him that the three brothers are high-class jewel thieves.

Buddy warns John, time and again, about Boldini, calling him

    – a rattle snake with a silent rattle,

    – Lejaune's spy: opining,

    – He's on your trail for somethin' . . .

It is during this time of intense boredom in Sidi that Michael decrees that they, the three brothers, should learn Arabic. As put by John

> . . . for the good of our souls and with a view to future usefulness as such time we should be generals entrusted with diplomatic missions or military governorships . . .

Our Arabic proved useful before then!

Sidi-bel-Abbès

It is amusing to hear Buddy relate, through John, how he dissuaded Boldini from being part of their walking out, or canteen set:

> 'Get the hell outa this, Cascara Sagrada. Don' want ya. Go gnaw circles in the meadow and keep away from me with both feet . . .'

When challenged by Boldini, Buddy would invite him to come outside and 'bring his fists with him'. However, Boldini, who had witnessed the carve up of the cook by Buddy, always declines the invitation!

John's life in the Legion is made somewhat easier to bear as he hears from Isobel, by letter, regularly once a month. Though we know that he and Isobel are unofficially engaged, Wren now and again suggests that Digby might have honourable intentions in that direction.

When Isobel writes that she intends visiting Algeria it is Digby who reacts with, 'The little darling! I bet she comes to Sidi. Hope she comes before we go – or that we don't go before she comes.' And we are told that he bounces on his bed with glee.

In 'The Devil and Digby Geste', a short story from *Good Gestes*, when Digby is campaigning far to the south in the mule corps, we find the following:

> Ere he fell asleep the thoughts of Digby Geste wandered. First to Brandon Abbas, where dwelt the girl who had been his life's music, for a brief sight of whose face he would have given almost anything – certainly a year of his life. Darling Isobel.

Did his brother know of, or even suspect, a rival in his beloved brother?

A battalion of the Legion was about to move out of Sidi headed for the south in 'peaceful penetration', hence Digby's remark that he hoped Isobel came before they left. And John, certainly, and Digby, secretly, are torn between a visit to Sidi-bel-Abbès by Isobel and 'duty' with the battalion. John adds, however, that his longing to see Isobel is so great that he has at times contemplated 'going on pump', the Legion's term for deserting.

Desertion plays quite a big part in Wren's novels. Legionnaires continually discuss it and frequently attempt it. During the Indo-China war so many legionnaires jumped ship when their trooper passed through the Suez Canal that this route was abandoned and the troopships routed round the Cape of Good Hope. On rounding the Cape many legionnaires jumped overboard in an effort to reach land. Jumping into the ice-cold waters of the Benguela current, they did not long survive these attempts at 'going on pump'.

> . . . deserting generally consists in slow preparation and swift capture, or a few days of thirst-agony in the desert, and ignominious return, or else unspeakable torture and mutilation at the hands of the Arabs.

In 'What's in a Name', a story in *Good Gestes*, we read of Legionnaire Robinson who, when taken prisoner, has his cheeks slit perpendicularly and twigs and grass threaded through this lattice work. Likewise his forehead is sliced and threaded by his captors, who are about to go to work on his lips, nose and ears when a half-troop of Spahis come on the scene and rescue him.

John goes on:

> Several legionnaires, whom we knew, went off into the desert and were either found dead or mutilated or never heard of more; many were brought back running, or dragging on the ground, at the end of a cord tied to the saddle of an Arab *goum*.
>
> However, we had come here to make careers for ourselves as Soldiers of Fortune, and to become generals in the Army of France, as other foreigners had done, from the ranks of the Legion. And we did our utmost to achieve selection for the picked battalion that was to march south for the next forward leap of the apostles of pacific penetration of the Sahara and of the Soudan.

It seems as if all thoughts of Isobel have been placed in the discard.

Others such as Boldini, Schwartz and Bolidar make no effort whatsoever to 'achieve selection'; they are picked and sent off willy-nilly.

Before the march to the south takes place the matter of the 'Blue Water' again becomes a subject of focus. Maris, the Swiss ex-courier, invites the Geste brothers to meet him one evening at Mustapha's (a restaurant in Sidi) where he feels it would be safe for him to report a conversation he has overheard. The gist of his report is that one evening whilst sitting in the Tlemcen Gardens he has overheard Boldini, Colonna and Guantaio planning to rob 'le Beau' of the fabulous diamond which he carries, 'like the kangaroo keeps its young'. Boldini is proclaiming his friendship with Lejaune and urging them on, stressing his ability to shield them from higher authority if necessary. The brothers, except for John, treat the matter as a huge joke, thank Maris, fill him up with cous-cous and let it go at that.

John takes the matter to Buddy:

Sidi-bel-Abbès

I had the bright idea of getting the advice of an older, worldly-wiser, and far cleverer person than myself – and decided to appeal to Buddy.

I accordingly walked out one evening with Hank and Buddy, 'set the drinks up' at the Bar de Madagascar and told them . . . about Boldini and his gang.

'Of course my brother can look after himself . . . but would they stick a knife into him whilst he slept? That's the only thing that worries me . . .'

Worldly-wise Buddy opines:

'Fergit it, son. Those slobs would never do that. Don't trust each other enough for one thing. Far too risky for another. Why, one drop of blood on his hands or shirt, or one yell out of your brother, an' he'd be taken red-handed.'

Hank agreed.

'Shore. Not in the barracks they wouldn't. Get him up a side street and bash him on the head, more like . . .'

However John pretends to remain unconvinced and continues to worry the problem, arguing against himself as much as against his two friends.

'I don't know so much. Suppose Guantaio and Colonna simply crept to his bed and drove a bayonet through his blankets and through his heart. There'd be no blood stains on the murderer . . .'

But Hank will not agree,

'Look at here, Bo. Figger it was you agoin' to stick me. How'd you know where my heart was, me curled up under the blankets, and nearly dark an' all? How'd you know that everybody was asleep all right? Nope, these legendaries don't stand for murder in the barrack-room, still less for robbery, and least of all for being woke up at night outa their due and lawful sleep . . .'

Buddy supports his friend,

'See, boy, that barrack-room is just your brothers' safest place . . .'

Hank and Buddy are right about murder. Robbery is another matter. That very night there is an attempt made to rob Michael. The barrack-room is awakened by a crash and a shout. When the lights come on Michael is seen to be on top of someone and holding him by the throat.

Buddy: 'Wring the sneakin' cayote's neck, Bo.'

Digby: 'Learn him to be a toad, Beau.'

When Michael arises the person that surfaces is neither Guantaio nor Colonna, neither Gotto nor Vogue. Boldini is sound asleep in his bed (or so it would seem), as is Corporal du Preez, his face to the wall! Legion law is about to be administered. Schwartz, Brandt, Haff and others, throw the offender onto the table with yells of 'Crucify the swine!' Hank and Buddy try to intervene, Hank shouting, 'Give the guy a fair trial.'

Michael (shouting in French): 'He belongs to me . . . he's had enough.'

'I lost my way,' screams the prisoner.

'And found it to the bed of a man who has money,' laughs a voice.

And the mob screams, 'Legion law. On the table with him.'

The miserable offender is flung onto the table and, not pretty to relate, bayonets are driven through the palms of his hands and through the flaps of his ears. Try as they will the Geste boys cannot stop the grizzly work. Hank restrains John:

> 'Let be, Johnny. It's the salootery custom of the country . . . But I wish it was Boldini they was lynchin'.'

As Michael is tackling Schwartz 'like a tiger', there is a sudden cry of 'Guard!' and when the Guard tramps in it finds a roomful of silent and sleeping men – except for the Geste boys who are pulling bayonets out of the whimpering man's body.

In the film, 'Beau Geste', Colour-Sergeant Lejaune is in command of the Guard and he admonishes the Geste boys: 'Save the first-aid for yourselves – you'll need it!' In the book the mutilated man is merely taken away to the infirmary and no one is punished. Thus is robbery frowned on in the Legion.

The potential thief turns out to be one Bolidar, 'a wharf-rat docker from Lisbon'. He features later in the saga!

> As all the old *legionnaires* prophesied would be the case, we heard nothing whatsoever from the authorities about the riot and the assault upon the thief. Clearly it was thought best to let the men enforce their own laws as they thought fit . . .

CHAPTER 5

The Desert

WREN NOW INDULGES in the romanticism of the Legion. Departure from Sidi-bel-Abbès, as seen through John's eyes, goes as follows:

> We left the depôt of Sidi-bel-Abbès in the spirit in which boys leave school at the half . . .
>
> . . . with a hundred rounds of ammunition in our pouches, joy in our hearts, and a terrible load upon our backs, we swung out of the gates to the music of our magnificent band, playing the March of the Legion, never heard save when the Legion goes on active service . . .
>
> . . . we had insufficient water, insufficient rice and macaroni, no meat nor vegetables, and insufficient bread and were perfectly fit and healthy. We had no helmets and no spine pads, we wore heavy overcoats, we had only a linen flap hanging from our caps to protect our necks, and we had no cases of sunstroke nor heat apoplexy.

The battalion's goal is Ain-Safra and near to this location it fights the battle of El Rasa. The half-company in which were the Geste boys is set to bait the trap for a huge *harka* of Touareg. Lejaune, who has been promoted to Sergeant-Major, is in command and John's praise for him is fulsome:

> To watch him conducting operations that day was to watch a highly skilled artisan using his tools with a deftness and certainty of a genius . . .
>
> I would have liked to admire him as much as I admired his military skill . . .

Lejaune sends out scouts who draw the enemy towards the main body of men as they, the scouts, retreat in good order under covering fire from each other. When within fifty yards of the concealed *escouade* Lejaune gives the order to fire and the advancing Arabs are cut down by the withering volleys. The Lebel rifles used by the French at that time were magazine guns, loaded by operating the bolt by hand – they were not fully automatic.

After several volleys in rapid succession Lejaune orders, *'Baionnettes au canon'* and the half-company execute a bayonet charge in classical fashion.

The mule company to which Digby Geste, Hank and Buddy were drafted

Mentioned in this skirmish are Boldini (now a corporal), Gontran, promoted to corporal after the action, and Rastignac, both of whom we will hear more of. Lejaune is promoted to *adjudant*.

John describes his first kill with the bayonet:

> I drove at his chest with all my strength, and the curved hilt of my Lebel bayonet touched his breast-bone as he fell staggering back . . .

Digby has his coat torn under the armpit by a spear and Michael is reported as excelling with the bayonet and also with his ability to use the butt of his rifle as a club.

The bayonet charge over, Lejaune's men retreat to the oasis of El Rasa where a pitched battle is fought. John has no 'adventures' to relate – merely lying under a palm-tree and shooting whenever he has something to shoot at: 'I might as well have spent the day on a rifle-range . . .'

After what John calls the 'signal victory of El Rasa' the battalion is split up and the brothers are parted. Digby is ordered to Tanout-Azzal and becomes a member of the mounted infantry school which is stationed there – the mounts being mules; Hank and Buddy go with him. Michael and John are sent, with many of the original recruits, to garrison Fort Zinderneuf, described by John as 'the ultimate furthest desert outpost'.

The separation of John and Michael from Digby, Hank and Buddy is germane to Wren's overall plot.

If any reader has seen Fort Mirabel, well to the south of El Golea, he or she will have a good idea of what Fort Zinderneuf looked like. The writer passed by Fort Mirabel in 1960. There it stood, near an oasis, crenellated in typical fashion but now heavily sand-bagged as well, as the insurgents of the sixties possessed weapons of far heavier calibre than those used against Lejaune and his men.

Life is hell at Zinderneuf: confined, hot and boring. Furthermore, after a month, the kindly commandant, Captain Renouf, shoots himself. It is rumoured that he has contracted a 'horrible disease', the nature of which we are not told.

In *Beau Geste* the demise of Corporal Gontran is glossed over – Corporal Gontran shoots himself; he was a good corporal and thus a loss to the men of the garrison. In *Good Gestes* Wren devotes a chapter entitled 'Dreams come True' to the death of Gontran.

In *Beau Geste* John states: 'What Corporal Gontran's grievance against the Sergeant was I do not know . . .'

In fact he does know. Gontran has told both Michael and John of an incident that had taken place in civilian life. Gontran has followed Sergeant Heintz to the Legion in order to exact retribution for the latter having murdered his wife (and perhaps lover). When Gontran tells the story no names are mentioned but it is obvious that Sergeant Heintz is involved, as he persecutes Gontran even after he is promoted to corporal. Gontran has told the story by way of relating a dream and as Michael and John witness the assassination they are able to piece together some of the background:

> That night, a night so unbearably and dangerously hot that but few could sleep, Beau Geste and his brother John sat side by side beneath the desert stars, and talked of Digby, away at Tokotu, of Brandon Abbas, and of old, happy, far-off things . . .
>
> *Beau:* 'Who's that with Boldini?'
>
> *John:* 'Bolidar . . . They're very thick these days . . . .'
>
> As he spoke Sergeant Heintz approached, Bolidar slunk away. Heintz gave Boldini a sharp order, and as he hurried off to fulfil it, another man, descending steps that led down from the roof, approached.
>
> *John:* 'The Lover and the Husband . . . Which is which?'
>
> *Beau:* 'Neither of them knows much of love, I think.'
>
> Corporal Gontran and Sergeant Heintz met in front of the brothers and a few yards from where they were sitting:
> 'Get to your room and dream, you dog,' growled Sergeant Heintz. 'Dream while you have time. Dream you're on the scaffold and . . .'
> 'I'm dreaming now, Sergeant Heintz. I'm dreaming now, you cesspool of sin,' and drawing his sword-bayonet he stabbed Sergeant Heintz in the left breast.
> '*Lisette!*' he shouted, and as the stricken man staggered back, sagged to the knees and fell to the ground, Corporal Gontran struck again, driving the bayonet through the Sergeant's throat.
> '*Lisette!*' he cried a second time, and as the astonished brothers sprang forward, he whipped out an automatic pistol . . . placing the muzzle to his temple, his last words were,
> '*Je viens, ma Lisette.*'

Wren was a great lover of this type of melodrama. The betrayer and the betrayed figure repeatedly in his works, the just and the good usually triumphing over the evil and the bad.

John maintains that he does not know the reasons for Gontran murdering Heintz. It can only be that in the much later work, *Good Gestes* (1929), did Wren realise that he had an opportunity of working up a good story based on this murder of a sergeant by a corporal.

Soon after this event, Lieutenant Debussy, who has taken command after Captain Renouf's death, sickens and dies.

His place is taken by Adjutant Lejaune.

CHAPTER 6

Of the Strange Events at Zinderneuf

. . . AS TOLD BY MAJOR HENRI DE BEAUJOLAIS to George Lawrence Esq CGM, of the Nigerian Civil Service.

We first learn of the fort at Zinderneuf from Major Henri de Beaujolais of the Spahis – an officer dubbed 'Beau Sabreur'. He is on leave after campaigning in the Sahara north of Zinder, having relieved the Foreign Legion fort at Zinderneuf. Being a practical Frenchman (albeit with an English mother) he opts for the shortest and most comfortable route home to France. He travels by camel-train south from Zinder to Kano, and from there by railway train to Lagos.

By coincidence de Beaujolais meets one George Lawrence of the Nigerian Civil Service, an old school friend, on the railway station at Kano. Lawrence, too, is due leave and is making the train trip south to Lagos. Nothing remarkable in this meeting! Wren justifies it thus:

> With de Beaujolais, Lawrence had been at Ainger's House at Eton; and the two occasionally met, as thus, on the Northern Nigerian Railway; on the ships of Messrs Elder, Dempster; at Lords; at Longchamps; at Auteuil; and, once or twice, at the house of their mutual admired friend, Lady Brandon at Brandon Abbas in Devonshire.

Nothing remarkable in this – except that George Lawrence had proposed marriage to Patricia Rivers and she had turned him down in favour of Sir Hector Brandon.

We have Lawrence's opinion of de Beaujolais. This could be said to be a 'typically English' view that was prevalent before the Great War:

> For de Beaujolais, Lawrence had a great respect and liking. Frequently he paid him the remarkable English compliment, 'One would hardly take you for a Frenchman, Jolly, you might almost be English.'
> De Beaujolais smiled inwardly – his mother had been a Devonshire Carey.

Lawrence saw de Beaujolais as,

> . . . a French soldier of the finest type, keen as mustard, hard as nails, a

thorough sportsman, and a gentleman according to the exacting English standard.

Major Henri de Beaujolais has a tale to tell and he could have found no better victim on which to inflict this tale than his friend George Lawrence. De Beaujolais, though, tells it in his own fashion – slowly and deliberately: starting at the beginning and finishing at the end. There is no jumping the gun for him.

> 'I tell you my dear George, that it is the most extraordinary and inexplicable thing that ever happened. I shall think of nothing else until I have solved the mystery, and you must help me. You, with your trained official mind, detached and calm; your *phlegm Britannique.*
>
> 'Yes – You shall be my Sherlock Holmes, and I will be your wonder-stricken little Watson . . .'
>
> 'Quite,' replied Lawrence. 'But suppose you give me the facts first?'
>
> 'It was like this, my dear Holmes . . . As you are aware I am literally buried alive in my present job at Tokotu. But yes, with a burial-alive such as you of the Nigerian Civil Service have no faintest possible conception . . . You, with your Maiduguri Polo Club! Yes, interred living, in the southernmost outpost of the *Territoire Militaire* of the Sahara . . .
>
> 'Seconded from my beloved regiment, far from a boulevard, a café, a club, far, indeed, from everything that makes life supportable to an intelligent man, am I entombed . . .'
>
> 'I've had some,' interrupted Lawrence unsympathetically. 'Get on with the Dark Mystery.'
>
> 'I see the sun rise and set; I see the sky above, the desert below; I see my handful of *cafard*-stricken men in my mud fort . . .'
>
> 'I shall weep in a minute,' murmured Lawrence. 'What about the Dark Mystery?'

The Major ignores the remark:

> 'If I am lucky and God is good, a slave-caravan from Lake Chad. A band of veiled Touaregs led by a Targui bandit-chief, thirsting for the blood of the hated white *Roumi* – and I bless them even as I open fire or lead the attack of my mule-cavalry-playing-at-Spahis . . .'
>
> 'The Dark Mystery must have been a perfect godsend, my dear Jolly,' smiled Lawrence.
>
> 'A godsend indeed,' replied the Frenchman. 'Sent of God, surely to save my reason and life. But I doubt if the price were not a little high, even for that! The deaths of so many brave men . . . And one of those deaths a dastardly cold-blooded murder! The vile assassination of a gallant *sous-officier* . . . And

by one of his own men. In the very hour of glorious victory . . . *One of his own men* – I am certain of it. But why? *Why*? I ask myself night and day. And now I ask you my friend . . .

'Have you heard of our little post of Zinderneuf – far far north of Zinder, north of your Nigeria? No? Well you will hear of it now, and it is where this incomprehensible tragedy took place.

'Behold me then, one devilish hot morning, yawning in my pyjamas over a *gamelle* of coffee, while from the *caserne* of my *legionnaires* comes the cries of "*Au jus, Au jus,*" as one carries round the jug of coffee from bed to bed, and arouses the sleepers to another day in Hell. As I wearily light a cigarette there comes running my orderly, babbling I know not what of a dying Arab *goum* – they are always dying of fatigue these fellows, if they have hurried a few miles – on a dying camel, who cries at the gate that he is from Zinderneuf, and that there is siege and massacre, battle, murder and sudden death. All slain and expecting to be killed. All dead and the buglers blowing the Regimental Call, the rally, the charge . . .

'I leap into my belts and boots, and rush to the door and shout "*Aux armes! Aux armes!*" to my splendid fellows and wish that they were my Spahis. And then to my orderly:

'"And tell the Sergeant-Major that an advance party of the Foreign Legion on camels marches *en tenue de campagne d'Afrique* in nine minutes from when I shouted '*Aux Armes.*' The rest of them on mules."

'You know the sort of thing my friend. You have turned out your guard of Haussas of the West African Frontier Force nearly as quickly and smartly at times, no doubt.'

'Oh, nearly, nearly, perhaps. *Toujours la politesse,*' murmured Lawrence.

'As we rode out of the gate of my fort, I gathered from the *goum*, that a couple of days before, a large force of Touaregs had been sighted from the look-out platform of Zinderneuf fort. Promptly the wise *sous-officier*, in charge and command since the lamented death of Captain Renouf, had turned the *goum* loose on his fast *mahari* camel, with strict orders not to be caught by the Touaregs if they invested the fort, but to clear out and trek with all speed for help. The *goum* estimated a force of ten thousand rifles, so I feared there must be at least five hundred . . .

'Anyhow, I was away with the advance-party on swift *mahari* camels, a mule-squadron was following, and a company of Senegalese would do fifty kilometres a day on foot till they reached Zinderneuf. Yes, and in what I flatter myself is the unbreakable record time between Tokotu and Zinderneuf, we arrived – and, riding far on in advance of my men, I listened for the sound of firing or of bugle-calls.

'I heard no sound whatever, and suddenly topping a ridge I came in sight of the fort – there below me on the desert plain, near the tiny oasis.

'There was no fighting, no sign of Touaregs, no trace of battle or siege. No blackened ruins strewn with mutilated corpses there. The *Tri-couleur* flew merrily from the flag-staff, the fort looked absolutely normal – a square grey block of high, thick mud walls, flat castellated roof, flanking towers, and lofty look-out platform. The honour of the Flag of France had been defended. I waved my *kepi* above my head and shouted aloud in my glee.

'I, Henri de Beaujolais of the Spahis, had brought relief, the danger was over and the Flag safe. I fired my revolver half a dozen times in the air. And then I was aware of a small but remarkable fact. The high look-out platform at the top of its long ladder was empty. I must offer the *sous-officier* my congratulations on the excellence of his look-out, as soon as I had embraced and commended him! A pretty state of affairs in time of actual war. No, there must be something wrong in spite of the peaceful look of things . . . I pulled out my field-glasses to see if they would reveal anything missed by the naked eye. Yes, there were good European faces of the men at the embrasures, bronzed and bearded, but unmistakably not Arab . . .

'And yet again that was strange. At every embrasure of the breast-high parapet round the flat roof stood a soldier, staring out across the desert, and most of them staring along their levelled rifles too; some of them straight at me. Why? There was no enemy about. Why were they not below in the cots in the *caserne*, while sentries watched from the high look-out platform. And why did no man move; no man turn to call out that a French officer approached!'

MAJOR HENRI DE BEAUJOLAIS

Perhaps this is a good point to examine de Beaujolais' character, if only briefly. He is full of enthusiasm, does not like sitting still, does his job well, trains his men well but is bored by inactivity. War is his game and when the news of the attack on Zinderneuf is brought to him he springs into action. Arriving at the fort he is about, as we have seen, to dress down the commandant – yet he himself is guilty of military imprudence. It is very unlikely not to say unusual for a commanding officer to leave his men and ride far in advance of them. He could have been ambushed, waylaid or could have lost his way. Nevertheless Henri de Beaujolais comes over as a man full of life.

'As I lowered my glasses and urged my camel forward, I came to the conclusion that I was expected, and that the officer in charge was indulging in a little natural and excusable *fantaisie*, showing off – what you call "putting on the dog", eh?

'He was going to let me find everything as the Arabs found it when they made their foolish attack – every man at his post and everything *klim-bim*. Yes, that must be it . . . Even as I watched, a couple of shots were fired from the wall. They had seen me . . . The fellow, in his joy, was almost shooting at me in fact!

'And yet – nobody on the look-out platform! How I would prick that good fellow's little bubble of swank! And I smiled to myself as I rode under the trees of the oasis to approach the gates of the fort. It was the last time I smiled for quite a little while.

'Among the palm trees were little pools of dried and blackened blood where men had fallen, or wounded men had been laid, showing that, however intact the garrison of the fort might be, their assailants had paid the toll to the good Lebel rifles . . . And then I rode out from the shade of the oasis and up to the gate.

'Half a dozen or so kept watch, looking out over the wall above, as they leant in the embrasures of the parapet. The nearest was a huge fellow, with a great bushy grey moustache, from beneath which protruded a short wooden pipe. His *kepi* was cocked rakishly over one eye, as he stared hard at me with the other, half closed and leering, while he kept his rifle pointed straight at my head.

'"Congratulations, my children," I cried. "France and I are proud to salute you," and raised my *kepi* in homage to their courage and their victory. Not one of them answered. Not one of them stirred. Not a finger or an eyelid moved. I was annoyed. If this was "making *fantaisie*", as they call it in the Legion, it was making it at the wrong moment and in the wrong manner.

'"Have you of the Foreign Legion no manners," I shouted. "Go one of you at once, and call your officer." Not a finger nor an eyelid moved.

'I then addressed myself particularly to old Grey-Moustache. "You," I said, pointing up straight at his face, "go at once and tell your Commandant that Major de Beaujolais of the Spahis has arrived from Tokotu with a relieving force – and take that pipe out of your face and step smartly, do you hear?"

'And then, my friend, I grew a little uncomfortable . . . Why did the fellow remain like a graven image, silent, remote – like an Egyptian god on a temple wall . . . ? Why were they all like stone statues? Why was the fort so utterly and horribly silent? Why this tomb-like, charnel-house, inhuman silence and immobility?

'Where were the usual sounds of an occupied post? Why had no sentry seen me from afar and cried the news aloud? Why had there been no clang and clatter at the gate? Why no voice or footstep in the place?

'When, as in a dream, I rode right round the place, and beheld more and more of these motionless silent forms, with their fixed unwinking eyes, I clearly saw that one of them, whose *kepi* had fallen from his head, had a hole in the centre of his forehead and was dead – although at his post, with chest and elbows leaning on the parapet, and looking as though about to fire his rifle!

'"Why were they not sleeping the sleep of tired victors?" I had asked myself a few minutes before. They were, yes, all of them, *Mort sur le champ d'honneur*!

'My friend, I rode back to where Grey-Moustache kept his last watch, and, baring my head, I made my apologies to him, and the tears came to my eyes. Yes, and I, Henri de Beaujolais of the Spahis, admit it without shame. I said, "Forgive me, my friend." What would you, an Englishman, have said?'

'What about a spot of tea?' quoth Mr George Lawrence, reaching beneath the seat for his tiffin-basket.

GEORGE LAWRENCE

George Lawrence now starts to take an interest. No longer does he exude bored indifference.

'But, of course, it soon occurred to me,' continued the Major, 'that someone must be alive . . . shots had been fired to welcome me . . . Those corpses had not themselves taken up those incredibly life-like attitudes. Whoever had propped them up and arranged them and their rifles in position, must be alive. For naturally, not all had been struck by Arab bullets and remained standing in the embrasures. Nine times out of ten, as you know, a man staggers back and falls, when shot standing.

'Besides, what about the wounded? There is always a far bigger percentage of wounded than of killed in any engagement. Yes, there must be survivors, possibly all more or less wounded, below in the *caserne*.

'The problem would soon be solved. My troop was approaching. I was glad to note that my Sergeant-Major, on coming in sight of the fort, had opened out and skirmished up in extended order . . . On arrival of the men I had my trumpeter sound the '*rouse*', the '*alarm*', [the Regimental Call] – fully expecting that after each blast the gates would open. Not a sound nor a movement! Sending for the *Chef*, as we call the Sergeant-Major, I ordered a rope be found or made, and set an active fellow to climb from the back of a camel, into an embrasure, and give me a hoist up.'

[In the Paramount production the troop was well prepared and carried the necessary rope and grapnel with them!]

'That Sergeant-Major is one of the bravest and coolest men I have ever known, and his collection of *ferblanterie* includes the Croix and the Medaille given on the field, for valour.

"'It is a trap, *mon Commandant*," said he. "Do not walk into it. Let me go." Brave words – but he looked queer, and I knew that though he feared nothing living, he was afraid.

"'The dead keep good watch, *Chef*," said I, and I think he shivered.

"'They would warn us, *mon Commandant*," said he. "Let me go."

"'Neither of us will go. We will have the courage to remain in our proper place, with our men.'"

[De Beaujolais had not thought of remaining with his men when he so blithely rode ahead from Tokotu!]

"'Send me that drunken *mauvais sujet*, Rastignac," said I.

"'May I go, *mon Commandant?*" said the trumpeter, saluting.

"'Silence,' said I. My nerves were getting a little on edge.'

Rastignac refuses point blank to enter the fort.

'Not I, *mon Officier*. Let me go to Hell dead, not living. I don't mind joining the corpses as a corpse. You can shoot me.'

De Beaujolais draws his revolver and orders Rastignac to ride his camel up to the fort and climb in and open the gates.

Rastignac: 'Not I, *mon Officier*. I have a dislike for intruding upon a dead Company that stands to arms and keeps watch.'

The major aims his revolver at Rastignac's head and pulls the trigger. There is a click – de Beaujolais had emptied the revolver when he had fired it into the air on his approach to Zinderneuf.

[This seems very careless and negligent.]

De Beaujolais then orders the *Chef* to arrest Rastignac:

'You can live – to be court-martialled and join the ranks of the *Bat d'Af*, the *Joyeux*.'

Turning to the trumpeter, he orders him to enter the fort. In next to no time the trumpeter is inside the fort and de Beaujolais mutters to his *Chef*, '*Un brave.*'

Now they watch and wait. Two minutes pass, five and then seven . . . no sign of the trumpeter.

'That one won't return,' cries Rastignac loudly, and receives a blow on the mouth from the corporal guarding him. *The corporal:* 'What about a little *crapaudine* and a little mouthful of sand, my friend?' (Crapaudine is a form of torture where the hands and feet are tied together in a bunch in the middle of the back.)

'At the end of ten minutes, a very *mauvais quart d'heure*, I beckoned the Sergeant-Major. I could stand the strain no longer. "I am going in," I said. "I cannot send another man . . . take command . . . if you do not see me within ten minutes, and nothing happens, assault the place. Burn down the gates and let a party climb the walls, while another charges in. Keep a half-troop under the corporal, in reserve."

'"Let me go, *mon Commandant*," begged the *Chef*, "if you will not send another soldier. Or call for a volunteer to go."'

'"Silence, *Chef*," I replied, "I am going," and I rode to the fort. Was I right, George?'

'Dunno,' replied George Lawrence.

'I remember thinking, as I rode back, what a pernicious fool I should look if, under the eyes of all – the living and the dead – I failed to accomplish that by no means easy scramble, and to fail to climb where the trumpeter had gone. However all went well . . . and I scrambled up and crawled into an embrasure.

'And there I stood astounded and dumbfounded, *tout bouleversé*, unable to believe my eyes. There, as in life, stood the garrison, their backs to me, their faces to the foe whom they had driven off, their feet in dried pools of their own blood – watching, watching . . . And soon I forgot what might be waiting me below, I forgot my vanished trumpeter, I forgot my troop waiting without – *for there was something else.*

'Lying on his back, his sightless eyes out-staring the sun – lay the Commandant, and through his heart, a bayonet, one of our long, thin French sword-bayonets with its single-curved hilt! No – he had not been shot, he was absolutely untouched elsewhere, and there he lay with a French bayonet through his heart. What would you say to that my friend?'

'Suicide,' replied Lawrence.

'And so did I, until I realised that he had a loaded revolver in one hand, one chamber fired, and a crushed letter in the other! Does a man drive a bayonet through his heart, and then take a revolver in one hand and a sheet of paper in the other? I think not.

'Have you ever seen a man drive a bayonet through his heart, my friend? Believe me, he does not fumble for letters, nor draw a revolver and fire it. No. In any case, does a man commit suicide with a bayonet when he has a loaded revolver?

'Was it any wonder that my jaw dropped and I forgot all else, as I stared.... *Voyez donc*! What had become of my trumpeter? These Watchers, as I have termed them, I felt certain, had been compelled by this dead man, who lay before me, to continue as defenders of the fort after their deaths. He was evidently a *man*. A bold, resourceful, undaunted hero, sardonic, of a macabre humour, as the Legion always is.

'As each man fell, throughout that long and awful day, he had propped him up, wounded or dead, set the rifle in its place, fired it, and bluffed the Arabs that every wall, every embrasure and loophole of every wall was fully manned. He must, at last, have run from point to point, firing a rifle from behind his dead defender.

'No wonder the Arabs never charged the fort.

'All this passed through my mind in a few seconds – and as I realised what he had done, and how he had died in the hour of victory, *murdered*, my throat swelled and my blood boiled – and I ventured to give myself the proud privilege of kneeling beside him and pinning my own Croix upon his breast. I thought of how France should ring with the news of his heroism, resource, and last glorious fight, and how every Frenchman should clamour for the blood of his murderer.

'Only a poor *sous-officier* of the Legion. But a hero for France to honour . . . and I would avenge him!

'Such were my thoughts, my friend, as I realised the truth – what are yours?'

'Time for a spot of dinner,' said George Lawrence.

Now de Beaujolais relates to Lawrence how he checked the Watchers to see that all had their bayonets; how he loaded his revolver; how he descended the stairway into the *caserne*.

'. . . into the sinister stillness that had swallowed up my trumpeter. And what do you think I found there my friend?'

'Dunno,' said George Lawrence.

'*Nothing*. No one and nothing. Not even the man who had fired the two shots of welcome! The *caserne* was as orderly and as tidy as when the men left it and stood to arms – the *paquetages* on the shelves, the table apparatus in the hanging cupboards, the *gamelles* and cleaning-bags at the heads of the beds, the bedding folded and straight.'

[Here de Beaujolais could be describing the barrack room at Sidi-bel-Abbès – the Legionnaires had certainly carried their training with them to the remoter parts of the Sahara!]

'No, not a thing was missing or awry. The stores were untouched – the rice, the biscuits, bread, coffee, wine, nothing was missing . . .'

'Except a rifle,' grunted Lawrence.

'My friend, you've said it! Where was the rifle belonging to the bayonet that was driven through the heart of the murdered officer up above? Had an Arab – expert in throwing knife or bayonet as in throwing the *matrak* – possessed himself of a French bayonet, after some desert-massacre of one of our tiny expeditionary columns? And had it by chance, or skill of the thrower, penetrated the heart of the Commandant of the garrison?'

'Possibly,' said Lawrence.

'So I thought, for a moment,' replied de Beaujolais, 'though why a man armed with a breech-loading rifle should leave the cover of his sand-hill, trench, or palm tree, and go about throwing bayonets, I don't know. And then I remembered that the bayonet went through the breast of the *sous-officier* in a slightly *upward* direction from front to back. Could a bayonet be thrown thus into the middle of a wide roof?'

'Sold again,' murmured Lawrence.

'No, I had to abandon that idea. And I was driven, against common sense, to conclude that the officer had been bayoneted by one of his own men, the sole survivor, who had then detached the rifle from the bayonet and fled from the fort. But why?

'*Why*? If such was the explanation of the officer's death – why had not the murderer shot him and *calmly awaited the arrival of the relieving force*?

'Naturally all would have supposed that the brave Commandant had been shot, like all the rest, by the Arabs.'

De Beaujolais suggests to George that the sole survivor would have been showered with honours, a reward and promotion. He feels certain that the murderer, nursing some real or imagined wrong, would have shot the officer, *not* bayoneted him. He puts this to Lawrence who states that he certainly would have shot rather than bayoneted.

Then de Beaujolais remembers that one chamber in the officer's revolver was empty. He speculates as to why this chamber is empty. He tells Lawrence that no one would use a revolver in defence of the fort.

'Does a man who is conducting the defence of a block-house, against tremendous odds, waste time in taking pot-shots *with a revolver* at concealed enemies, two or three hundred yards distant?'

[Here de Beaujolais differs from the Hollywood producers of 'Beau Geste', as they have Lejaune dashing from one loophole to the next firing off his revolver. This is of course in true Hollywood Cowboy style.]

Henri de Beaujolais then suggests that the commandant might have been murdered *before* the Arab attack and that his murderer might have conducted the defence but asks himself,

'. . . who propped the last man up? He did not do it himself, that was certain – for every single corpse on that roof had been *arranged* before *rigor mortis* set in.'

Now de Beaujolais remembers a man who was lying on his back near the commandant, the only man who was not 'to the life'. Was he about to be set up when the final tragedy, whatever it was, occurred? The truth is coming ever closer. De Beaujolais now avers:

> 'It may have been that the brave *sous-officier* was going to arrange this very corpse when he was attacked. Or, as I say, the officer may have been dead the whole time, or part of it, and the last survivor may have had this last work cut short by a bullet, before he had put the man in position. But if so, where was he?.. . . Was it the man who had fired the two shots in answer to mine – and if so, what had become of him? *Why had he fired if he wished to hide or escape?*
>
> 'My head spun. I felt I was going mad. And then I said to myself, *Courage, mon brave*! Go calmly up to that terrible roof again, and just quietly and clearly make certain of two points. First: Is there any one of those standing corpses who has not quite obviously been arranged, propped up, fixed in position? If so – *that* is the man who killed his officer and was afterwards shot by the Arabs. Secondly: Has anyone of those dead men been shot point-blank by a revolver? That I should be able to tell at a glance. If so, *that* is the man who killed his officer – who lived long enough to thrust his assailant into an embrasure . . .'

'After himself being bayoneted through the heart?' enquired Lawrence.

'Exactly what I said to myself – and groaned aloud as I said it,' replied Henri.

'Anyhow,' he continued, 'I would go up and see if any man had been shot by a revolver, and if any man lay *naturally* against the slope of an embrasure . . . I turned to ascend the stair, and then, George, and not until then, I got the *real* shock of that awful day of shocks. For, *where was my trumpeter?*

'I had made a quick but complete tour of the place and now realised in a flash that I had seen no living thing and heard no sound.

'"*Trompette! Trompette!*" I shouted. I rushed to the door leading to the courtyard, the little interior, high-walled parade ground.

'"*Trompette!*" I shouted and yelled again and again . . .

'Not a sound, not a movement. And then I rushed to the gates, lifted down the great bars, pulled the heavy bolts, turned the great key, and dragged them open – just as the mule-squadron arrived and my good Sergeant-Major was giving them the signal to join the assault!

'It was not that I had suddenly remembered that the time I had allowed him must be up, but that I needed to see a human being again, to hear a human voice, after a quarter of an hour in that House of Death, that sinister abode of tragic mysteries. I felt an urgent and unconquerable yearning for some . . .'

'Breakfast,' said George Lawrence.

Bathed, full-fed and at peace with the world the two *compagnons de voyage* lie smoking the cheroot of digestion. Not for long, though. Soon 'the impulsive and eloquent *beau sabreur* of the Spahis' returns to what is uppermost in his mind.

De Beaujolais describes to Lawrence how he attended to matters military, instructing Sergeant-Major Dufour to let the men fall-out, to post vedettes, water the animals, make fires and prepare *soupe*. As de Beaujolais planned to re-enter the fort, this time accompanied by Dufour, he instructed that Sergeant Labaudy be placed in command. [We meet this man again: said to have the loudest voice in the French army.] After an hour's rest a grave-digging party was to assemble. Labaudy was to report as soon as the mule-scouts, riding in advance of Lieutenant St André's Senegalese, were sighted. [St André's brother was among the dead.] Meanwhile de Beaujolais and Dufour partook of chocolate and cognac.

Continuing to impart his thoughts to his friend, George Lawrence, de Beaujolais tells of how he now began to take an interest in the man lying next to the commandant, the man who had been laid out 'reverently'; his eyes had been closed, his head propped up on a pouch and his hands folded upon his chest.

> 'As I glanced at their *kepis* lying there, I noticed something peculiar. One had been wrenched and torn from within. The lining, newly ripped, was protruding, and the inner leather band was turned down and outward. It was as though something had recently been torn violently out of the cap – something concealed in the lining perhaps? . . . "Now what is this?" I thought. "A man shot through the brain does not remove his cap and tear the lining out."
>
> 'Bullets play funny tricks, I know, but not upon things they do not touch..The bullet had entered the head below the cap. There was no hole in that what-so-ever. To which of these two men did the cap belong?'

De Beaujolais apologises, half to himself and half to Lawrence, for not having noticed this cap before. He puts it down to the fact that there had been too much else on his mind. However, now his eyes go from the torn cap to the crushed piece of paper in the hand of the *sous-officier*. He is about to take the piece of paper from the hand of the dead officer, when he thinks: 'No! Everything shall be done in order and with correctness.' And so he awaits the return of the Sergeant-Major, so that there can be a witness.

> 'But without touching the paper, I could see, and I saw with surprise – though

the *bon Dieu* knows I had not much capacity for surprise left in my stunned mind – that the writing was in English!

'Why should that be added to my conundrums? . . . A paper with English writing on it, in the hand of a dead French officer in a block-house in the heart of the *Territoire Militaire* of the Sahara!'

Lawrence suggests that the man might have been English: 'I have heard that there are some in the Legion.'

'No,' was the immediate reply. 'That he was most certainly not. A typical Frenchman of the Midi – a stoutish, florid, blue-jowled fellow . . . Perhaps a Provençal. Conceivably a Belgian . . . but certainly not an Englishman.'

'And the recumbent bareheaded chap?' asked Lawrence.

'Ah – quite another affair, that! He might very well have been English. A Northerner, English most probably. What you are thinking is exactly what occurred to me. English writing on the paper; an English-looking legionnaire; his cap lying near the man who held the paper crushed in his hand; the lining just torn out of the cap! Ha! Here was a little glimmer of light, a possible clue. I was just reconstructing the scene when I heard the Sergeant-Major ascending the stairs . . .

'Had the Englishman killed the *sous-officier* while the latter tore some document from the lining of the man's cap? Obviously not. The poor fellow's bayonet was in its sheath at his side.'

'Might have been shot afterwards,' said Lawrence.

'No. He was *arranged* as I mentioned to you. As I awaited the arrival of the *Chef* a thought crossed my mind: "one bayonet more than there were soldiers or rifles!" As I pondered I heard the bull voice of Sergeant Lebaudy, down at the oasis, roar: "*Formez les faisceaux*" and '"*Sac à terre.*" I came back to facts as the Sergeant-Major approached and saluted.

'As I have said, my *Chef* was of the bravest of the brave, yet he on looking around muttered: "*The fallen were not allowed to fall – the dead forbidden to die.*" Then – "*but where in the name of God is Jean the Trumpeter?*"

'"*Tell me that, Chef,* and I will fill your *kepi* with twenty-franc pieces . . . ," said I.'

De Beaujolais and his *chef* then have a long argument as to the whereabouts of Jean the trumpeter but can come up with no solution. We learn later, of course, if we have not already suspected, that Jean the trumpeter was none other than Digby Geste. He had hidden, either in the cells or by taking his place with the dead at the embrasures and 'playing dead'.

The major now tells Dufour, 'We will reconstruct this crime, first reading what is on this paper.' And to Lawrence, 'I opened the stiffened fingers and took the paper. There was a dirty crumpled envelope there too. Now *Georges, mon vieux*, prepare yourself. You are going to show a little emotion, my frozen Englishman!'

Lawrence smiled faintly.

'It was a most extraordinary document,' continued de Beaujolais. 'I'll show it you when we get on board the ship. It was something like this: On the envelope was, "*To the Chief of Police, of Scotland Yard and all whom it may concern.*" And on the paper, "*Confession. Important. Urgent. Please publish.*"

"'*For fear that any innocent person may be suspected, I hereby fully and freely confess that it was I, and I alone, who stole the great sapphire known as 'Blue Water'.*"'

'What!' shouted George Lawrence, jumping up. 'What? What are you saying, de Beaujolais?'

'Aha! my little George,' smiled the Frenchman, gloating. 'And where is the *phlegm Britannique* now, may I ask? That made you sit up, quite literally, didn't it? We do not yawn now, my little George, do we?'

George Lawrence stared at his friend, incredulous, open-mouthed.

'*But that is Lady Brandon's jewel!* . . . What on earth . . .' stammered Lawrence, sitting down heavily. 'Are you romancing, de Beaujolais?'

'I am telling you what was written on this paper – which I will show you when I can get my dispatch-case, my friend,' was the reply.

Never had his friend seen this reserved, taciturn, and unemotional man so affected.

'I don't get you. I don't take it in. Lady Brandon's stone! *Our* Lady Brandon? The "Blue Water" that we were allowed to look at sometimes? Stolen! And you have found it?'

'I have found nothing, my friend, but a crumpled and bloodstained piece of paper in a dead man's hand.'

Lawrence sat down. 'Go on, old chap,' he begged. 'I sincerely apologise for my recent manners. Please tell me everything and then let us thrash it out.'

'No need to apologise, my dear George,' smiled his friend. 'If you seemed a little unimpressed and bored at times, it only gave me the greater zest for the *dénouement*, when you should hear your . . . our . . . friend's name come into this extraordinary story.'

'You're a wily and patient old devil, Jolly. I salute you, Sir. A logical old cuss, too! Fancy keeping *that* back until now, and telling the yarn neatly, in proper sequence and due order, until the right point in the story was reached, and then . . .'

'Aha! Wonderful how the volatile and impetuous Frenchman could do it, wasn't it? And there is something else to come my friend. All in "logical proper sequence and due order" there comes another little surprise.'

By now it is obvious that George Lawrence has more than a passing interest in Lady Brandon. But more of that later. Readers, are you wondering what Lady Brandon is like? How old is she and what does she look like? Remember she is Aunt Patricia to the Geste boys and their fair cousins.

> 'Then, for God's sake get on with it, old chap! . . . More about Lady Brandon, is it?' replied Lawrence, now all animation and interest.
> 'Indirectly, *mon cher Georges*. For that paper was signed – *by whom?*' asked the Frenchman, leaning forward, tapping his friend's knee, staring impressively with narrowed eyes into those of that bewildered gentleman.
> And into the ensuing silence he slowly and deliberately dropped the words, '*By Michael Geste!*'
> 'By *Michael Geste*! Her nephew! You don't mean to tell me *Michael Geste* stole her sapphire and slunk off to the Legion? "Beau" Geste! *Get* out . . .' came the reply from George Lawrence.
> 'I don't mean to tell you anything, my friend, except that the paper was signed "Michael Geste".'

Major Henri de Beaujolais then tells Lawrence how, many years ago, on a visit to Brandon Abbas, he had met 'two or three boys and two beautiful girls'. The bare headed man lying with folded arms could have been one of those boys, the age would fit, but then again he may have had nothing to do with the signed paper in the hands of the *sous-officier*, who was most certainly not Michael Geste, being a man of forty or forty-five years old.

We now learn from Lawrence that Michael 'Beau' Geste 'would have been about twenty or so'. This seems an extremely young age for a man who exercised such command over hardened legionnaires, as we will see.

Then Lawrence throws in this classic, 'But, my dear Jolly, the Gestes don't *steal!*'

Here de Beaujolais mildly interjects with, 'What too of the murdered *sous-officier* and the vanished trumpeter?'

From Lawrence, 'Damn them.' Then another apology to his friend. He can think only of Lady Brandon. 'The only woman in the world.'

We must now return to the fort at Zinderneuf where we left Major de Beaujolais and his *Chef* standing on the roof of the fort – the Major holding the confession paper.

> 'What is in the paper, might one respectfully enquire, *mon Commandant*,' asked

the Sergeant-Major.

'The confessions of a thief – that he stole a famous jewel,' I replied.

De Beaujolais now outlines his plan of action:
- one more search,
- *déjeuner*,
- a quiet, sensible discussion of the facts,
- burial of the dead, and
- a new *escouade* to garrison Fort Zinderneuf.

After the last search, which reveals nothing new, he and the sergeant-major quit the fort and prepare to muster the men once they have lunched. Dufour, however, warns of danger, the possibility of mutiny. The legionnaires, brave in battle against live foes, are painfully frightened of the 'House of Death with its Watchers'. Rastignac began it. Rastignac, the fearless, refused to enter the fort, and Jean, the trumpeter who entered, has not returned.

Sergeant-Major Dufour and Sergeant Lebaudy have formed the men up and the *escouade* to garrison the fort has been drawn from the worst men, 'all *mauvais sujets*', of the Company.

Before the order to occupy the fort is given, the Major urges his men to give the fallen heroes of France an honourable military funeral, worthy of the Flag. Ever emotional, he concludes by quoting:

> '*Soldats de la Légion,*
> *De la Légion Étrangère,*
> *N'ayant pas de nation,*
> *La France est votre mère.*'

The selected new garrison receives the order, '*Par files de quatre. En avant. Marche,*' but instead of obeying, as trained soldiers of France, they, with precision, stoop as one man, and lay their rifles on the ground. A grizzled veteran of Madagascar, Tonquin, and Dahomy states that he and his friends would rather die with Rastignac than enter the fort.

De Beaujolais to Lawrence, 'This was flat disobedience and rank mutiny. I had hardly expected this.'

And here de Beaujolais shows his courage and his training,

> 'But Rastignac is not going to die. He is going to live – long years, I hope – in the *Joyeux* [the terrible penal battalions of North Africa] You, however, who are but cowardly sheep, led astray by him, shall have the better fate. You shall die now, or enter Zinderneuf fort and do your duty . . . Sergeant-

Major, have those rifles collected. Let the remainder of the Company right form, and on the order '*Attention pour les feux de salve*,' the front rank will kneel, and on the order '*Feu*,' every man will do his duty.'

To Lawrence,

'But I knew better. That is precisely what they wouldn't do.'

The Sergeant-Major, Dufour, intervenes. He explains to his commandant that the men are rotten with *cafard* (the dreaded desert madness), and over-fatigue. That they will, in all probability, shoot the officers and non-commissioned officers, and desert *en masse* into the desert.

One can sense the struggle that goes on in de Beaujolais' mind – his military conscience and his private conscience in conflict with one another. In the years to come his sharp sense of 'right' and 'wrong' will again conflict and Dufour will be one of the players.

Dufour urges that a 'holiday' be granted. Allow the men a break of four hours and he reminds de Beaujolais that St André and the Senegalese were expected to come up by midnight.

The Commandant, then, in a loud voice to his Sergeant-Major: 'You are too merciful, Sergeant-Major. We don't do things thus in the Spahis. But these are not Spahis' – and he goes on to grant the 'holiday' finishing with, 'At moon-rise our motto is work or die.'

The order *Rompez* is given.

Major Henri de Beaujolais now tries a different tactic. He asks Dufour to send him all the influential men of the *escouade*. Previously he has banked on the *mauvais sujets*, now he wants men who are regarded as 'leaders' in their different cliques. From these men he calls for volunteers willing to enter the fort with him. Only two men step forward:

> They were in extraordinary contrast in body, for the one was a giant and the other not more than five feet in height, while both had clean-shaven, leathery countenances, lean hatchet faces, biggish noses, mouths like a straight gash and big chins. By their grey eyes they were northerners, and by their speech Americans.

We have seen that in the French army the men are far removed from their officers, who leave the daily routine to the *sous-officiers*. In *Good Gestes* there is an incident in which Digby is left behind when his patrol makes a hasty retreat – being in the act of rescuing a brother legionnaire. Hank and Buddy gallop back on their mules to assist him and come under heavy fire, along with Digby and the wounded man. Major de Beaujolais is in command of this patrol and one can only think that Hank and Buddy's action would have come to his attention. At Zinderneuf he talks as if it is the first time he has seen these two men – so extraordinarily contrasted!

Hank and Buddy having volunteered to enter the fort, the herd instinct now manifests itself, and others of the 'influential' group, one by one, volunteer, until de Beaujolais has six good men to accompany him into the fort.

> *To George Lawrence:*   'And then I suddenly remembered . . .'
>
> *Lawrence:*   'The murdered *sous-officier!*'

'Exactly, George! These fellows must not see him lying there with a French bayonet through him! I must go in first, alone, and give myself the pleasant task of removing the bayonet.'

Whilst the *Chef* musters the loyal men, de Beaujolais mounts his mule and rides quickly to the fort; dismounting he hurries to the roof so as to perform the distasteful duty of removing the bayonet from the *sous-officier's* heart.

> 'And there I stood and stared and stared and rubbed my eyes – and then for a moment felt just a little faint and just a little in sympathy with those poor suspicious fools of the *escouade* . . . For, my dear George, *the body of the sous-officier was no longer there!* Nor was that of the bareheaded recumbent man!'
>
> *Lawrence:*   'Good God!'

The thought now occurs to the Major that a living man could be shamming dead and pretending to be one of the corpses. Whilst hurriedly checking the dead the *Chef* and the six loyal men arrive on the roof. The Sergeant-Major is dumb-struck at the disappearance of the body of the *sous-officier*, but manages to hold his peace. De Beaujolais notes that the Americans appear to be looking for comrades amongst the dead. At any moment he expects the question: 'Where is their officer?' or, 'Where is Jean, the trumpeter?' But these questions do not come and Dufour marches the men back to the oasis and then hurries back to the fort.

'Did you move it?' Both Major and Sergeant-Major put the question simultaneously!

Dufour and his commandant make their way back to the oasis, too nonplussed to discuss the affair, although Dufour does produce some of the finest oaths, '. . . in length and originality, remarkable even for the Legion.'

There is a weakness here. Why did not de Beaujolais and Dufour together search the barrack-room and the *caserne*? One can only conclude that they had had enough for that day.

> 'Well, George, *mon vieux*, what do you think happened? Did the *escouade* obey and enter the fort like lambs, or did they refuse and successfully defy me, secure in the knowledge that the others would not fire on them?'
> 'You are alive to tell the tale, Jolly . . .'
> 'But tell me – what do you think happened? Did they refuse or obey?'
> 'I give up Jolly – I can only feel sure that one of the two happened.'
> 'And that is where you are wrong, for neither happened. They neither obeyed nor entered, nor disobeyed and stayed out!'
> 'Good Lord! What then!' from George Lawrence.

And this time it is the Frenchman who suggests a spot of refreshment.

The last act of what de Beaujolais terms an 'event' is about to take place.

The Major bids Dufour parade the men in front of the fort with their backs to it and the *escouade* detailed to garrison the fort placed on the right of the line.

Sergeant-Major Dufour to Major Henri de Beaujolais:

> '*Bien, mon Commandant*, might I presume to make a request and a suggestion? May I stand by you, and Rastignac stand by me – with the muzzle of my revolver against his liver – it being clear that, at the slightest threat to you, Rastignac's digestion is impaired?'

The Major will have none of this. Matters will proceed normally. De Beaujolais is pinning his faith on the loyal men, as well as on the imminent arrival of St André and his Senegalese. At that juncture he has the choice of commanding the parade from the back of either a mule or a camel. In choosing the mule we learn a little more about de Beaujolais:

> I am a cavalry man and the *arme blanche* is my weapon. Cold steel and cut and thrust, for me, if I had to go down fighting. You can't charge, and use a sword on a camel, so I compromised on the mule – but how I longed for my Arab charger and a few of my Spahis behind me! It would have been a fight then, instead of a murder. . .

And that which George Lawrence declined to hazard a guess at happens: The fort goes up in flames and the 'Touareg' renew their attack. De Beaujolais' men retreat to the shelter of the oasis, and that officer, ever mindful of the safety of the relief force, orders that two legionnaires be sent to warn St André.

It is interesting to note that the two men selected for this task do not volunteer, they act under orders. The Sergeant-Major passes the word for the two Americans: 'He recommended them as men who could use the stars, good scouts, brave, resourceful, and very determined.'

[Furthermore these two legionnaires, having been into the fort, knew that John Geste was not amongst the dead.]

CHAPTER 7

How George Lawrence takes de Beaujolais' Story to Lady Brandon

WREN DESCRIBES George Lawrence as follows: a tall, bronzed, lean man, taciturn, forbidding and grim, who never used two words where one would suffice. This then is the man who volunteers to relieve de Beaujolais of the duty of taking the story of the confession concerning the 'Blue Water' to Brandon Abbas.

We do not have to look far for the reason. Lawrence is in love with Lady Brandon. He has been in love with her ever since she was Patricia Rivers and had his love rejected by her and she married Hector Brandon, and his title, instead. He had taken her refusal like the man he was, and had sought an outlet in his work in Central Africa.

It is difficult to conjure up a picture of Lady Brandon (Patricia Rivers), aunt of Beau Geste and his brothers. One gets the feeling that she is a severe and, even though married, a spinsterish – or great-aunt – type of woman. We learn, however, that she has wide grey eyes, beautiful teeth and a soft deep contralto voice and that she is a woman of forty years. That she has an aristocratic bearing goes without saying. On meeting George she allows him to kiss her hands. George Lawrence comes straight to the point in telling Lady Brandon that he has a longish story to impart but that it can be cut short if she can assure him that Beau Geste is alive and well and that the 'Blue Water' is safe and sound.

As can be expected Lady Brandon is taken somewhat aback at this direct line of attack. She parries the thrust by asking whether George has seen Michael, and the answer comes back in the negative. Lawrence realises that he will have to begin at the beginning and goes through his meeting with de Beaujolais and the events at Zinderneuf.

Patricia merely asks, '*Our* Henri de Beaujolais . . . Rose Carey's son?'

The love of George Lawrence's life will not admit to the loss of the 'Blue Water'; neither will she admit or deny that the writing on the confession paper is that of Michael Geste!

But Patricia Rivers, being a lady in both senses of the word, does, at least, grant George a hearing and he goes through the details as given him by de Beaujolais with a fine-tooth comb, but with a difference. The difference is that whereas de Beaujolais has looked at events with a soldier's eye, Lawrence is concerned more with the piece of paper, and how it reached the hand of a dead man on the roof of a desert outpost in the Sahara.

George Lawrence finds though that he is doing all the talking and Patricia contributing nothing but an occasional question. Realising that this cannot go on, Lawrence again resorts to a frontal attack:

> 'My dear – I think everything has now been said, except one thing – your instructions to me. All I want now is to be told exactly what you want me to do.'
>
> 'Listen, my dear. This is what I want you to do for me. Just *nothing at all*. The 'Blue Water' is not at Zinderneuf, nor anywhere else in Africa. Where Michael is I do not know. What the paper means I cannot tell. And thank you so much for wanting to help me, and for asking no questions. And now, good-bye, my dear, dear friend . . .'

George Lawrence departs a 'sadder but *not* a wiser man!'

It is easy, in hindsight, to suggest that had Michael not instructed John to get the private letter to Aunt Patricia, that letter would have been found by de Beaujolais on Michael's body and the mystery of the 'Blue Water' would have been cleared up so much sooner. Then of course the story would have been spoiled and the foundations of the trilogy cut away.

CHAPTER 8

The Fall of the Fort at Zinderneuf

WE LEAVE DE BEAUJOLAIS astride his mule confronting his *cafard* stricken and mutinous troops before the fort at Zinderneuf.

From the moment Lejaune takes command at Zinderneuf life in the fort becomes hell. Not so much life but the avoidance of death from sun-stroke, heat-stroke, monotony, madness, or Adjutant Lejaune . . .

Cafard is rampant, but Lejaune is not considered mad by his superiors. He can hold the fort and maintain discipline, and to this end he is invaluable.

Michael and John have each other to help keep one another sane. They plead with one another to do nothing foolish to provoke Lejaune. Both brothers agree that it is almost a blessing that Digby is not with them – they feel that Digby is liable to back-chat Lejaune. Even more so they felt that Hank and Buddy are best out of the clutches of Lejaune, who has not forgotten, nor forgiven their first meeting!

MUTINY

As matters grow progressively worse mutiny is plotted. That there is a 'priceless' gem in the fort complicates matters. Factions form: on the one hand Schwartz heads up those men most pliable and therefore most likely to mutiny; Boldini and his Italian friends are more concerned with the 'Blue Water', and form a 'cell'. John and Michael, along with Cordier, Maris and St André, decide that they had best stand together.

Those of the garrison supporting Lejaune are termed '*cochon*' and those supporting Schwartz are termed '*charcutier*'. All, at various times and by various plotters, are approached and asked into which category they fall.

John is approached by Schwartz.

'Are you enjoying life, Smith?'
'Quite as much as you are, Schwartz.'
'Would you like a change?'
'I am fond of change.'

'Have you ever seen a pig die?'

'No.'

'Well you will. You are going to see a big pig die. Yes. *Monsieur le cochon* is going to become *Monsieur Porc.*'

'And are you going to become *Monsieur charcutier*, Mr Pork-butcher, so to speak?'

'Aha! my friend, that remains to be seen. So many want a *cotelette de porc* or a *savouret de porc* . . . We shall have to cast lots. Do you want a chance to be *charcutier*?'

'I have no experience in pig-killing.'

'Look you, you will have the experience shortly, either as pig or butcher, for all here will be *cochon* or *charcutier* – in a day or two. Choose whether you will be a pig or a butcher, and tell your brother to choose . . . .'

That night John tells Michael of this conversation, but before the brothers can communicate with Schwartz a side plot surfaces.

Guantaio approaches John. He is unable to make up his mind whether or not to join the mutiny and seeks John's advice. Before John can give it Guantaio discloses that an 'Italian' faction has formed, the members of which are Boldini (now corporal, and the most hated man in the garrison, after Lejaune), Guantaio, Colonna and Gotto. The 'Blue Water' weighs heavily on the collective mind of this putative faction. Guantaio advises that if John and his brother do not join in the mutiny they are to be shot by one of the mutineers and be relieved of the jewel, it ending, in all probability, in the hands of Schwartz. Guantaio's faction has to hedge its bets. Discussion between John and this worthy ends on a very English note:

> Well – I shall decide tonight. And now please go away. I want to think – and also I'm not extraordinarily fond of you, Guantaio, really . . .

In due course Michael is informed of these conversations and he calls a meeting of what he terms the 'loyal' men, who are St André, Maris, Glock, Dobroff, Marigny, Blanc and Cordier. These men are what Wren, through John, terms, 'fundamentally decent and honest men of brains and character . . .'

Michael addresses the meeting,

> As you know there is a plot to murder Lejaune and the non-coms, to desert and abandon the fort. Schwartz is the ring-leader and says that those who do not declare themselves supporters will be considered as enemies – and treated as such. Personally I do not do things because Schwartz says I must, nor do

I approve of shooting men in their beds. Supposing I did, I still should disapprove of being led out into the desert by Schwartz, to die of thirst. Therefore I am against the plot – and I invite you all to join me and to tell Schwartz so. We'll tell him plainly that unless he gives up this mad scheme of murder and mutiny, we shall warn Lejaune.

Here we have something of the real Beau Geste. It is sad that Wren gives us all too little of him.

The 'loyal and decent men' do not all turn out to be such. Several cannot agree that Lejaune be warned. This, they feel, would be betrayal of legionnaires to officers. These men elect to join Schwartz.

Cordier: Fancy fighting to protect Lejaune . . . !
St André: We are fighting to protect the Flag. Lejaune is incidental . . .
Cordier: Who'll tell Schwartz?
Michael: I will.

But before Schwartz can be confronted Michael and John are intercepted by Bolidar, the thief who had been 'crucified' in the barrack-room in Sidi-bel-Abbès.

It transpires that Bolidar is a man in the 'middle'. He has been ordered by Lejaune to 'get the diamond'; and he has been ordered by Boldini to 'get the diamond'. He is a man in a state of severe shock and on the point of a nervous breakdown. Michael attempts to calm him down by inviting him to join the 'loyal' party, and advising him that he (Michael) is about to tell Schwartz that Lejaune is to be warned of what is afoot.

Bolidar merely shrieked with mirthless laughter,

'He knows! He knows! He knows all about it – and when it is to be – and every word that is said in the barrack-room!'

When asked by Michael who it is that informs, the shameless answer from Bolidar is, 'I do, and when he has got your diamond he will kill me.' Bolidar goes on to explain that Lejaune is waiting to find out which faction the Geste brothers join before he acts against Schwartz. And if they don't join Schwartz they are to be killed in the attack by the loyal men on Schwartz, so says Bolidar. In either case, no matter which faction Michael is party to, Bolidar is to shoot him dead and then rob him. The scenario is as follows:

If Michael joins Lejaune, Bolidar is to remain in the Schwartz faction and shoot Michael as he enters the barrack-room with Lejaune; if Michael joins Schwartz Bolidar will join Lejaune and shoot Michael as he (Bolidar) enters the barrack-room with Lejaune. In either case Bolidar is to rob the dead body of Beau Geste and hand the diamond to Lejaune.

Bolidar: 'Guantaio tells me that Boldini intends to get the diamond for himself . . . but I don't wholly trust him . . .'

Michael: 'Don't you really?'

Bolidar: 'No, I don't think he's absolutely honest . . .'

Michael: 'You surprise me – the dirty dog!'

Bolidar, having made it indubitably clear that he trusts none of the conspirators, proposes that the three of them, Michael, John and himself, form a syndicate and divide the proceeds received from the sale of the 'diamond'.

Michael: 'Why should you trust us any more than you do Boldini and Guantaio?'

Bolidar: 'Because you are English. In Brazil we say, "word of an Englishman" and, "word of an American"! when we are swearing to keep faith.'

[One hopes that this sentiment, as expressed by Bolidar, prevails today! Does it?]

Michael: 'This is very touching. But suppose I give you my word that I haven't got a diamond and never possessed a diamond in my life?'

Bolidar refuses to buy this one: 'One knows of the little parcel in your belt-pouch!'

When asked, by Bolidar, to swear, by 'all that's holy' that he has not a diamond, Michael merely replies: I have not a diamond – 'word of an Englishman'.

This somewhat flummoxes Bolidar and that worthy, grasping at any straw, concludes that Michael is telling the truth: he has not got a diamond 'on him', the diamond has been left at Sidi-bel-Abbès; and he takes himself off to impart this piece of news to Lejaune.

Michael and John then decide between themselves that they will 'cover' one another as follows:

Michael is to shoot Bolidar before Bolidar can shoot him; John will cover Lejaune and shoot him should he draw on Michael once Bolidar has been disposed of. To complete their plan it is further decided to tell Schwartz, as soon as possible, that they will not join his mutinous gang, and advise him that Lejaune is already privy to the plot and is certain to act before Schwartz can act. It is agreed, though, that John will not shoot Lejaune in cold blood, but only in the event of him acting against Michael.

Back in the barrack-room the brothers do not have to wait long before being confronted by Schwartz who demands to know from them whose side they are on.

Michael comes out directly: 'He knows all about it . . .'

Schwartz seizes his bayonet but Michael coolly outfaces him, saying that it would be most unlikely that he would report the mutiny to Lejaune and then tell Schwartz he had done so – what would be the point!

No, he is not the traitor – but by looking lengthily at Guantaio Michael shifts suspicion from himself to that unfortunate, even though Michael knows that Bolidar is the culprit. The more the mutineers can be provoked into distrusting one another the better chance of survival the loyal men stand.

It is a lucky thing for both Michael and John that they have boxed at university level. Had they not there is no way they could stand up to the murderous mutineers. Wren is very keen on the 'noble art' and his book *Soldiers of Misfortune* is almost entirely devoted to boxing.

It seems fairly certain to the brothers that Schwartz and his gang will act that night so as to surprise Lejaune. The picture emerging is that Lejaune is to be murdered; Schwartz and his co-conspirators march off into the desert; Michael, John, St André, Cordier and Maris are left in the fort. Someone will have to assume command and Michael proposes that that someone be St André – a former French officer. John feels that a vote would go Michael's way. But before this stage is reached Michael and Schwartz stage a final confrontation:

Schwartz:	'What are you going to do if someone kills Lejaune without doing himself the honour of consulting your lordships?'
Michael:	'Nothing. We shall continue in our duty as soldiers. We shall obey the orders of the senior person remaining true to his salt and the Flag.'
Schwartz:	'The devil burn their filthy Flag. I spit on it!'
Michael:	'A pity you came under it if that's what you think.'
Schwartz:	'Then you and your gang of cowards and blacklegs will not interfere?'
Michael:	'If you will desert, you will desert. That is not our affair.

	As for deserting – I should say the Legion will be well rid of you!'
Schwartz:	'Mr Preacher, you and your brother look to yourselves.'
Michael to John	'They will do it tonight. We must secure our rifles and we must keep awake.'

John manages one more meeting with Bolidar, who has, in the meantime, had discussions with both Lejaune and Schwartz.

'Lejaune does not believe a word about the diamond not being here and the mutineers are going to shoot him and all the non-coms on morning parade tomorrow instead of at night. They think he will be expecting it at night, as some informer must have told him that is the plan. He'll be off his guard..They are going to kill Dupré and Boldini simultaneously with Lejaune. If your party is a big one they are going to leave you alone, if you leave them alone. They will load themselves with water, wine, food and ammunition and march out at sunset.

'Blanc, who has been a sailor, is going to lead them straight over the desert to Morocco, by Lejaune's compass. Schwartz is to be captain; Brandt and Haff, lieutenants; Delarey and Vogué, sergeants; and Glock and Hartz, corporals. There will be twenty privates . . .

'They are going to court-martial Guantaio, and if he is found guilty they are going to hang him . . . I know enough to get him hanged, the dirty traitor . . .

'I am to shoot Lejaune to prove my sincerity and good faith. If I don't I am to be shot myself . . . Guantaio has been maligning me to Schwartz . . .

'I am just going off to tell all this to Lejaune now.'

And he does. Bolidar reports all to Lejaune, and he, Lejaune, trained soldier that he is, fearless and ruthless, acts.

That night Lejaune stands at the door of the barrack-room, totally alone, with only his revolver in his hand. Looking from bed to bed he discovers that John Geste is awake or has been awakened by his presence. In fact John has hardly slept as he turns over and over in his mind the situation that he and his brother are in. Lejaune, placing his finger to his lips to indicate silence, signals John to follow him.

It is a strange fact that no other man in that turbulent barrack-room is awake, or is awakened – not even by the sounds John must make, as he struggles into his trousers and tunic. Perhaps some are awake or are awakened, but think it expedient to pretend sleep.

Lejaune leads the way to his quarters – a small room – almost bare except for table and bunk. We are given another picture of Lejaune by Wren, through John's eyes.

> Lejaune stared at me in silence, his hot arrogant eyes glaring beneath heavy eyebrows contracted in a fierce evil frown.
>
> *Lejaune:* 'Do you and your miserable brother want to live? Answer me, you dog.'
>
> *John (trying to strike a note between defiant impudence and cringing servility):* 'On the whole, I think so, *mon Adjudant.*'

The ensuing conversation, very much a one-sided affair, illustrates the vast gap between the French non-commissioned officer of the day and a private soldier.

> *Lejaune:* 'Oh – on the whole, you do, do you? Well – if you do, you'd better listen carefully to what I say, for only I can save you. D'you understand? Answer me, you swine.'
>
> *John:* 'Yes, *mon Adjudant.*'

Now we have Lajaune's version of the impending mutiny:

> 'See here then, you infection, there's some talk among those dogs, of a jewel. A diamond your gang of jewel-thieves got away with in London. Also there is a plot among them to murder you both and steal it, and desert with it.'
>
> *John (mildly):* 'Is that so, *mon Adjudant.*'
>
> *Lejaune:* 'Don't answer me! God smite you, you unspeakable corruption! Yes, it is so and I know all about it, as I know everything else that is done and said and *thought* too – in this place . . . Now I don't care a curse what you stole and I don't care a curse what becomes of you and that anointed thief, your brother; but I won't have plots and plans and murders in any force under my command . . . Do you hear me, sacred animal?'
>
> *John:* 'I hear you, *mon Adjudant.*'

Lejaune goes on to tell John that he will detail him and his brother Michael, St André, Cordier and Maris to form a 'Corporals Guard' and arrest the mutineers. The members of this guard are to shoot down any man that Lejaune orders them to. Lejaune has, no doubt, lost faith in his regular corporals and Sergeant Dupré.

Lejaune finishes thus:

'... your brother will hand over this diamond to me. I'll put it where no plots and plans will trouble it ... You and your cursed jewels! Wrecking discipline and causing trouble! You ought to be doing twenty years in gaol, the pair of you ... It was your brother I wanted, but you happened to be awake and I saw no point in entering that cage of treacherous hyenas ... As soon as I have the diamond locked for safety in the Company treasure-chest, I'll give you a chance to save your worthless lives ...'

Two points arise – What would have been the outcome had Beau been awake and Lejaune had demanded the diamond from him? And one can only wonder at the reason for Beau carrying the diamond on him or with him.

John re-enters the barrack-room and wakes Beau and the two, in turn, wake Maris, Cordier and St André. The loyal men then join Lejaune.

It seems most improbable, almost impossible, that four men could be awakened, semi-dress themselves, take their rifles from the rifle-rack and quit the barrack-room without disturbing or awakening a single mutineer. It may have been that some of the mutineers were awake but deemed it prudent to pretend to be asleep, especially as Lejaune was standing at the doorway to the barrack-room, his loaded 'forty-five' in his hand.

Leaving St André and Cordier to stand guard over the barrack-room, Lejaune takes Michael and John with him to his office, leaving Maris outside the office guarding the doorway to the office.

Once inside the office, the following exchange ensues:

Lejaune (to Michael): 'Give me the wretched diamond which is the cause of all this trouble.'

Michael: 'Diamond, *Monsieur l'Adjudant*? I have no diamond.'

John backs his brother in this asseveration, and:

Words failed Lejaune. It appeared that he was going to have an apoplectic fit. His red face went purple and his eyes bulged yet more. He raised and pointed his revolver. Michael did not turn a hair – a movement would have been mutiny and probably death with Michael's body being searched for the 'diamond'.

The position is precarious. At any moment the mutineers might rush St André and Cordier. Lejaune is a brave man. Yet were he to dispose of the Geste boys he would be down to three loyal men – perhaps without the fire-power to hold down the mutineers. Furthermore, were he to shoot

Beau and John the 'loyal' men might turn out to be not so loyal at the murder and loss of their highly respected comrades.

> And then without thought, I did what would have been the bravest thing in my life if it had been done consciously, and with intent. I defied, insulted and outfaced Lejaune! 'Look here Lejaune,' I said coolly, and in the manner of an Oxford undergraduate addressing a cabman, 'don't be a silly fool. Can't you understand that in about two minutes you may be hanging on that wall with bayonets through your hands – and left there in a burning fort to die? Or pinned out on the roof with the sun in your face? Don't be such an ass. We've got no diamond and you've got five good men to fight for you, more's the pity! Stop gibbering about jewels and be thankful that we five know our duty . . .'

This speech was delivered in French as Lejaune had no English. One wonders how it 'came over' in French. Beau understood the content, and murmured,

'Very Stout Fella. Order of *Michael* for you, John.'

Lejaune reacted somewhat differently. He sprang to his feet, his face suffused with hate and anger, but before he could pick up his revolver, which he had foolishly placed on the table in front of him, Michael swept it off the table to the floor. As it clattered to the ground Lejaune found John's bayonet, backed by his Lebel rifle, at his throat.

Lejaune:	'So you *are* mutineers, you beautiful loyal lying grandsons of Gadarene swine, are you?'
Michael:	'Not at all. We wish to help you put down a mutiny – not babble about diamonds.'

After threats and curses Lejaune agrees to postpone the argument over the diamond to a later date:

'If you don't both die *en crapaudine*, you shall live *en crapaudine!*

Michael:	'Reward for saving your valuable life, I suppose.'
Lejaune:	'You'll do that as your simple duty, my friend. Oh! you love your duty.'

Exercising supreme control of his emotions Lejaune pulls himself together and takes Michael, John and Maris (who, standing guard outside Lejaune's office, has been wondering just what was taking place within), back to the barrack-room to join Cordier and St André. Whilst these two remain on guard, joined now by Lejaune, Michael, John and Maris proceed to empty the arms-rack of the Lebel rifles. During this operation various of the mutineers awake but, seeing Lejaune at the doorway, immediately pretend sleep. None sleep so deeply as Corporal Boldini!

ATTACK

Next the sentries, on duty on the roof of the fort, and at the gate, have to be disarmed. Going with Lejaune to the parapet, John easily disarms Sergeant Dupré, who surrenders tamely, along with Gronou. Dupré and Gronou are ordered to relieve the sentries at the gate of their rifles and bring these up onto the roof, to where Lejaune and John will be waiting. As Gronou reaches the top of the stairway connecting the courtyard to the roof, he will, for a moment, be looking *out* of the fort, across the desert, towards the oasis.

A dramatic turn of events now takes place.

> Gronou released the muzzles of the rifles; they crashed down on the parapet, and he stood, pointing, staring, his mouth wide open. So obviously was he stricken by some strange vision that Lejaune, instead of knocking him down, turned to look in the direction of his pointing hand -
> *The oasis was swarming with Arabs, swiftly and silently advancing to attack.*

Lejaune shows his mettle instantly.

'Run like hell,' he barks at Gronou. 'Back with those rifles, send Sergeant Dupré here quick.'

To John: 'Down to the barrack-room. Give the alarm . . . send me the bugler.'

Lejaune then proceeds to open fire on the advancing Arabs with his own rifle.

John's cry goes up, '*Aux arms! Aux arms! Les Arbis! Les Arbis! – Aux arms! Aux arms! Les Arbis!*'

The delighted men, forgetting their mutinous intent, snatch at their clothes. There is nothing like the smell of action and the sound of fire to galvanise bored soldiers into action.

> Lejaune worked like a fiend, for within a few minutes of Gronou's dropping the rifles, every man in the fort was on the roof, and from every embrasure rifles poured their magazine fire upon the yelling, swarming attackers.
>
> A large band of Arabs attacked the gate with stones, axes, heavy swords and bundles of kindling-wood to burn it down.
>
> Here Lejaune exposed himself fearlessly and led the defence, controlling a rapid volley-fire that had a terrible effect. The whole attack ceased as suddenly

as it had begun, and the Touareg, as the sun rose, completely vanished from sight, to turn the assault into a siege.

Did Lejaune err in not having a look-out posted on the high platform? Had there been one on that high vantage point the approaching Touareg force would have been observed very much sooner. It must be that Lejaune could not afford to have a possible mutineer up on the platform from where he could command the courtyard below.

The culmination of the mutiny is handled somewhat differently in the 1940 movie, 'Beau Geste' by Paramount. In many ways the movie version is more convincing. Here there is a look-out posted. The mutineers are marched into the courtyard by Lejaune and the loyal men, lined up and Lejaune orders Michael and John to commence shooting them. This the Geste brothers refuse to do and just as Lejaune is on the point of declaring them mutineers as well the look-out sentry sounds the alarm – '*Aux armes . . .*'

In the first skirmish, in which the Touareg have suffered sufficiently to decide on withdrawing, the Legion has lost one man only – the seaman, Blanc.

> Lejaune strode over from his place in the middle of the roof, and shouted,
> 'No room nor time, yet, for shirkers,' and putting his arms around the man, dragged him from the ground and jerked him heavily into the embrasure. There he posed the body, chest on the upward sloping parapet, and elbows wedged against the outer edges of the massive uprights of the crenellation. Lejaune then placed the rifle on the flat top of the embrasure, a dead hand under it, a dead hand clasped around the small of the butt, the heel-plate against the dead shoulder, a dead cheek leaning against the butt.
> 'Continue to look useful, if you can't be useful. Perhaps you'll see the route to Morocco if you stare hard enough.'

Then come orders to Boldini to take every third man below to the *caserne* to get them fed and properly dressed, *klim-bim*, within thirty minutes. Maris and St André fetch up more ammunition; Cordier brings pails of water onto the roof and places them above the gate in case the Touareg attempt another bonfire. Sergeant Dupré is detailed to bring the medical panniers to the roof, as Lejaune decrees that no wounded would be permitted to go below. The wounded are to be treated where they fall but even so Lejaune is not above thrusting a wounded man back into an embrasure without treatment. No one dares to disobey, as this would be mutiny in the face of the enemy and Lejaune could, and indeed would shoot the offender dead on the spot.

The Arabs, now dug-in on the crests of the sand-dunes, keep up a sporadic fire on the fort. The first of the mutineers is sent to his death by Lejaune. Schwartz is ordered up onto the look-out platform: 'It was the post of danger.'

> *Lejaune to Schwartz:* 'Watch the oasis – till the Arabs get you . . . .You'll have a little while up there for thinking out more plots.'

Lejaune, at this point, is described by John who, although hating him, is never-the-less forced to concede that he is 'a competent, energetic and courageous soldier . . .'

Down below in the *caserne* while having *soupe* and wine, St André tells his friends that Lejaune's *goumiers*, who had been patrolling outside the fort, have made off to Tokotu to summon the relief. [We know this from de Beaujolais' narrative.] Cordier makes a toast with his ration of wine! *'Madame la République – morituri te salutant!'*

Schwartz does not last long on the high platform but before he dies he is able to raise the alarm once more. The Arabs are climbing the palm trees and firing down into the fort from them. Lejaune at once directs rapid fire at the palm-trees bringing men from the other three sides of the roof to deal with this menace and overcome it as quickly as possible.

> 'Brandt, up with you to the look-out platform, quick.'
> Brandt looked at the platform and then at Lejaune. Lejaune's hand went to the revolver in the holster at his belt, and Brandt climbed the ladder, and started firing as quickly as he could work the bolt of his rifle . . .

Mutineer Brandt does not long survive on the exposed look-out tower. Soon picked off by an Arab marksman he comes crashing down onto the roof of the fort. Lejaune orders Dupré to prop up the 'carrion'.

Haff is next to climb the ladder to the platform of almost certain death. He survives somewhat longer than his predecessors, as a lull settles over the fighting. During this lull it is ascertained that a good half of the garrison is either dead or dying. Sergeant Dupré and Corporal Boldini fail to answer the muster roll. Cordier has his self-fulfilling prediction come true. Maris, too, has fought his last fight.

St André is promoted corporal and throughout the long day the fallen are propped up in the embrasures they had occupied whilst living. Lejaune never leaves the roof, his bread, *soupe* and wine being brought to him.

During the lull, too, Michael has a chance to converse with John whilst they are below in the *caserne*:

> 'There's some letters. A funny public sort of letter, a letter for Claudia, and one for you, and one for Digby, in my belt – and there's a letter and a tiny package for Aunt Patricia. If you possibly can, old chap, get that letter and packet to Aunt. No hurry about it – *but get it to her*. See? *Especially the letter*. The packet doesn't much matter, and it contains nothing of any value, but I'd die a lot more comfortable if I knew that Aunt Patricia was going to get that letter after my death.'

The brothers then discuss the very real possibility of them both being killed in the action. In this event Beau expresses the hope that the effects of a dead soldier would be forwarded to his next of kin. These effects would, however, have to survive both the Arabs and Lejaune.

John's wishes are simply that he wishes to be remembered to Digby and to Isobel.

Michael: 'I'll say the right things about you to Isobel, old son.'

The besieged garrison now await a dawn rush – much depends on the *goums*. St André, now a corporal, has had converse with Lejaune:

> 'Lejaune is certain that one of the *goums* got away. The Arabs couldn't get them both, he says, as they were at opposite sides of the fort, and half a mile apart, always at night.'

In the early dawn Lejaune addresses the diminished garrison:

> 'Now my merry birds you are going to sing, and sing like the happy joyous larks you are. We'll let our Arab friends know that we are not only awake, but are also merry and bright. Now then, the Marching Song of the Legion first. All together you warbling water-rats . . .'

Lejaune then takes them through the Legion's extensive repertoire, and between songs the bugler blows every call he knows.

> 'Now laugh, you merry, happy, jolly, care-free, humorous swine. You there, Vogué (who had replaced Haff on the look-out platform), roar with laughter or I'll make you roar with pain . . .'
>
> A wretched laugh, like that of a hungry hyena came down from the look-out platform. It was so mirthless a miserable cackle that the men below all laughed genuinely.

[In the Paramount production this scene was extremely well enacted and proved to be one of the memorable scenes of the film. However the producers had Boldini up on the platform laughing like an hyena. In fact in the film production Boldini and Bolidar are one and the same character.]

Then Lejaune causes the survivors, one by one, to laugh, urging each man to surpass the previous one's laughter in volume.

Whatever one may think of Lejaune the man, his tactics as a soldier pay off. There is no dawn rush, and when the sun comes up the Touareg merely resume sniping from the sand-dunes.

Men, though, continue steadily to fall and are just as steadily, by order of Lejaune, propped up back into an embrasure.

Lejaune then, with his own rifle, crouches behind each dead man in turn and fires several shots, adding to the illusion that the dead are alive. Later still he sets one man to each wall to do the same thing – to fire from behind the dead. By midday the Arabs cease their firing and the bugler sounds first the 'Cease Fire' and then the 'Stand Easy'.

Ten men only, including Michael and John, remain alive. Most of those who sprang from their beds the previous morning with cries of joy at the shout of *'Aux armes!'* are dead. The end is inevitable, unless relief comes from Tokotu. Ten men cannot continue to hold the fort. If, on the other hand, they can hold out until the relief arrives, it will have been the dead men who saved them.

St André now takes half the survivors down to the *caserne* for *soupe*. Michael and John are in this small contingent.

> 'Last lap! Last cigarette! Last bowl of *soupe*! Last mug of coffee. Last swig of wine! Well, well! It's as good an end as any – if a bit early. Look out for the letter, Johnny.'

Thus spoke Beau Geste, as he patted the front of his sash.

John: 'Oh, come off it. Last nothing – the relief is half-way here by now.'

'Hope so, but I don't greatly care, old son. So long as you see about the letter for me.'

'Why I, rather than you Beau? Just as likely you do my posting for me . . .'

'Don't know, Johnny. Just feel it in my bones. I feel I'm in for it and you're not, and thank the Lord for the latter, old chap.'

And here he gives John's arm a little squeeze above the elbow. And on the way up the steps back onto the roof:

> 'Well, good-bye, dear old Johnny. I wish to God I hadn't dragged you into this – but I think you'll come out all right. Give my love to Dig.'

Lejaune, who has purposely sent men to their deaths on the look-out platform, climbs to that death-spot, and with his field glasses searches the terrain towards Tokotu, looking for signs of the relief column.

Again there is sporadic fire from the Touareg lines, and once it ceases, the ranks of the defenders have been thinned out by three more fatal casualties and St André has been wounded.

Lejaune, whom we either love or hate, now takes over the duties of the bugler and sounds the 'Cease Fire' and the 'Stand to' alternatively. Between lulls he walks up and down the roof humming '*C'est la reine Pomare*'.

The next 'stand to' sees the Arabs advancing on the fort *en tirailleur*. The defenders are down to John, the wounded St André and Lejaune – Michael has fallen, soon to be followed by St André, and John and Lejaune are left to defend the fort – two walls apiece.

John thinks that now he and Lejaune are the sole survivors the latter might relax his stern disciplinary attitude. But Lejaune neither softens nor relents:

> 'Both walls, damn you! To and fro, curse you! Shoot like hell, blast you!'
> And so Lejaune and I held Fort Zinderneuf for a while . . .

Lejaune might not have softened his attitude, but he is still very much concerned with his and John's bodily welfare and needs. He sends John below for coffee and *soupe* to be brought up onto the roof to be consumed there. 'Hurry, you swine!'

Before going down to the *caserne* John has seen his brother lying face down in a pool of blood. Whilst preparing the food it suddenly occurs to him that Lejaune will prop Michael up in an embrasure, and this he, John, cannot, will not, stand for – especially as he feels that Michael might only be wounded. He concludes that he might be about to mutiny after all. But first he would say to Lejaune:

> 'I'll fight till I drop, and I'll obey you implicitly – but leave my brother's body alone, leave it to me.'
> After all, things were a little different now. Lejaune and I were the only survivors . . . We had kept the flag flying. Surely he would be decent now, unbend a little, and behave as a man and a comrade . . .

On regaining the roof John finds Lejaune bending over Michael:

> He had unfastened my brother's tunic, torn the lining out of his *kepi*, removed his sash, and opened the flat pouch that formed part of the money-belt that Michael wore.
>
> Lying beside Lejaune were three or four letters, and a torn envelope. In his hands were a tiny packet, bound up in string and sealing-wax, and an open letter.
>
> I sprang towards him seeing red, my whole soul ablaze with indignant rage that this foul vulturous thief should rob the dead, rob a soldier who had fought beside him thus – a brave man who had probably saved his life before the fight began.
>
> 'So he *had no diamond?* Didn't know what I meant?'

John, who had admired Lejaune's qualities as a fighting man is now horribly disillusioned.

> 'You damned thief! You foul pariah dog.'
> – and in a second his revolver was at my face . . .

But despite this menacing threat, John continues,

> 'I didn't know that *men* crept around robbing the dead after a fight, Lejaune. I thought that was left to Arab women . . . You dirty thieving cur – you should be picking over dust-bins in the Paris gutters . . .'

John might as well have saved his breath for all the impression these insults make on a man now obviously mad.

> 'A fine funeral oration from a jewel thief! Any more grand sentiments before I blow out what brains you have? The Arabs won't attack again today, and they've settled my mutineers nicely for me . . . The relief column will arrive at dawn . . . and I shall get the Cross of the Legion of Honour, a Captain's commission, and a trip to Paris to receive thanks and the decoration . . . and in Paris, my chatty young friend, I shall dispose of this trifle that your gang so kindly brought to the Legion for me. A rich man, thanks to you, and this . . .'
>
> – he actually kicked Michael's body!
>
> Even as I snatched my sword-bayonet, and leapt forward – in the instant that my dazed and weary mind took in the incredible fact of this brutal kick – it also took in another fact even more incredible . . .
>
> *Michael's eyes were open and he turned to me.*

Meanwhile Lejaune, ever ready to seize on an excuse to mete out what he feels is justice, ejaculates,

'Good! Armed attack on a superior officer – and in the face of the enemy! Excellent! I court-martial you myself. I find you guilty and sentence you to death . . . I also carry out the sentence myself – thus . . .'

And he places the revolver muzzle in the pit of John's stomach.

> As Lejaune had spoken, Michael's right hand moved. As the last word was uttered he had seized Lejaune's foot, jerking him off balance, as he pulled the trigger in the act of looking down and stumbling.
>
> I leapt and lunged with all my strength and drove my bayonet through Lejaune . . . he lay on his back, twitching, the blade of the bayonet through his heart.
>
> Lejaune was dead, and *I* was the mutineer and murderer after all!

Many years will pass before Major Henri de Beaujolais learns the true facts of the murder of 'the valiant *sous-officier*'.

The battle of Zinderneuf is of interest in that it is the only battle that the author can recall that was won by dead men. The annals of the French Foreign Legion record some great and bloody encounters and battles but none feature the 'ploy' used by Adjutant Lejaune.

Is it feasible – is it possible? Could dead men really fool a *harka* of Touareg? A newly dead man could, in fact, be thrust back into the embrasure he had recently vacated and once rigor mortis had set in he would remain in place. Arabs, from a distance, would not be able to determine whether a man was dead or alive, even though he remained motionless.

De Beaujolais tells us that the Arabs did not possess field-glasses. This seems strange in view of the fact that many of them owned modern magazine rifles. It is unlikely that an attacking force would have time enough on its hands to observe a particular man for any length of time, and take note of whether he moved or not.

Henri de Beaujolais was fooled and he had had a close-up view of the dead defenders. Furthermore each man, during the battle, appeared to be firing from his embrasure, even if only intermittently.

Luck, no doubt, was on Lejaune's side in the battle. He was able to hold out just long enough to bring it home to the attackers that their losses were too punishing. Their scouts, too, would have alerted the main body to the approach of the relieving force.

The battle is over and the fort temporarily secured; but where does this leave John? He is alive in a fort in the middle of the Sahara, surrounded by hostile Arabs, and he has a mission to fulfil. He has to get a letter back to his Aunt Patricia and above all his own natural desire is to get home to Isobel.

Although Beau Geste had been mortally wounded, there was sufficient life in him left to enable him to save his brother's life by upsetting Lejaune's balance. But Michael Geste is fast sinking.

> 'Got the letters, Johnny?'
> I told him I would deliver them in person. That we were the sole survivors. That the relief would come soon and we would be promoted and decorated.

John knows that this is not true as he has already determined that he is the sole survivor. His words are those that would be spoken to a dying man, giving him comfort.

> 'For stabbing Lejaune? Listen, Johnny, I'm in for it . . . Bled white . . . Listen, I never stole anything in my life . . . Tell Dig I said so and *do* get the letter to Aunt Patricia. You mustn't wait for the relief . . . They'd shoot you . . . Get a camel and save yourself . . . If you can't get away say I killed Lejaune . . . I helped to anyhow . . .'
> Within two minutes of seizing Lejaune's foot and saving my life, my brother was dead . . . My splendid, noble, great-hearted Beau . . .

Michael must have had great faith in the ability of his younger brother to carry out his far from easy wishes. To expect him to get a letter back to England was something of a forlorn hope. Yet was it not better for him to possess this faith in his brother and to die happily, than to die full of doubts and fears?

Wren does not tell us why John does not choose to sit tight in the fort, await the arrival of the relief column, assign the blame for Lejaune's murder to Michael and then get the letters to England through the mail.

John is not to know that a family friend, Major Henri de Beaujolais, is in command of the relief column, and that if he were to explain matters to this ever sympathetic officer, he would be believed and perhaps even decorated and promoted.

[We have touched on the fact that Digby, de Beaujolais' trumpeter, who on occasions spoke directly to de Beaujolais, was not recognised by him. But Digby did not ever say, *'Mon Commandant,* I am Digby Geste from Brandon Abbas.']

John, however, in the very delicate situation he finds himself in, may have no alternative but to reveal his true identity to de Beaujolais. He does not know, cannot even imagine, that de Beaujolais would be in command and far and beyond this he, being John, could never bring himself to lay the blame for the murder of a superior on his brother Michael. Conjecture is all that is left.

The obstacles in John's way appear insurmountable. Firstly, the Arabs that invested the fort might still be in the vicinity, next, the vast Sahara Desert lies in wait for him. Then, too, he must determine his route and ensure adequate provisions.

Desertions from the Legion are related in several of the P.C. Wren books: mostly well planned by a small select body of men. One such desertion is described in *The Wages of Virtue* which takes place from the barracks in Sidi-bel-Abbès, which is not in the desert. In *Stepsons of France* ten men desert from a desert fort where life has become intolerable under Sergeant-Major 'Suicide Maker', a forerunner to Lejaune!

FLIGHT

John's preparations for leaving Zinderneuf for his desert ordeal consist of filling his water-bottle and three wine-skins with water, his knapsack and haversack with bread and coffee, and slinging an extra pair of boots about himself.

The rush by the Touareg which had found John and Lejaune alone defending the fort, was, as predicted by Lejaune, their final attack – but John cannot be sure of this. His immediate plan is to reconnoitre the Arab camp that night, in the hopes of stealing a camel, but before he can do much beyond seeing to his provisions he falls asleep. Who can blame him. He has not slept since battle was joined two days ago.

Awakened by small-arms fire, he looks out and sees:

> . . . a man on a camel, a man in uniform, waving his arms above his head and firing his revolver in the air.
> It was a French officer.

The relief has arrived from Tokotu and here is a French officer riding straight into an ambush (or so John thinks). John's instincts are to warn him so that he and the following column will not fall victims to the supposedly lurking Touareg. It is at this point that John fires the warning shots which, some months later, de Beaujolais tells Lawrence of.

After firing the warning shots John remarks to himself:

'If he walks into an ambush now, he is no officer of the Nineteenth Army Corps of Africa'; and then:

> Rushing across to the side of the roof furthest from the line of approach, I dropped my rifle over, climbed the parapet, hung by my hands and then dropped, thanking God that my feet would encounter sand . . . Snatching up my rifle I ran as hard as I could go, to the nearest sand-hill. If this were occupied I would die fighting, and the sounds of rifle-fire would further warn the relief column.

But the sand-hill shelters no one and John decides to shelter there himself, hiding in an Arab trench. From this vantage point he will be able to observe the movements of the relief force and plan his next moves. He is thus in a position to watch the relieving force advance *en tirailleur*, preceded by scouts and guarded by flankers,

> Slowly and carefully the French force advanced, well handled by somebody more prudent than the officer who had arrived first . . .

It becomes abundantly clear to John that the siege has been lifted and that the Arabs have departed. He wonders to himself whether this is due to Lejaune's ruse and the fort's apparently undiminishing garrison, or of news, brought in by Targui scouts, of the approach of a strong mounted force of French troops.

Soon John realises that his position is fast becoming untenable. The legionnaires move off to the oasis, '*campez*' is sounded and he realises that, soon, vedettes will be posted at all four corners of the fort.

John decides that his best course of action is to make for a small rocky hill about a mile from the fort, lie in the shade of the rocks and wait until evening:

> . . . on my fairly hopeless journey . . . Fairly hopeless? . . . Absolutely hopeless unless I could secure a camel . . . I firmly rejected the idea that entered my mind of killing a vedette to get his beast. That I could regard as nothing better than cold-blooded murder.

Watching from his hill and waiting for nightfall John observes the troops assemble before the fort. This is the assembly at which de Beaujolais was determined the force detailed as the new garrison would enter the fort or be shot; either this or he, and the loyal men and *sous officiers* would die.

The destruction by fire of Fort Zinderneuf, as seen by John Geste:

> The fort was on fire! . . . What might *this* mean? Surely it was not 'by order'?
> And as I stared, in doubt and wonder, I was aware of a movement on the roof of the fort!
> Carefully keeping the gate-tower between himself and the paraded troops,

a man was doing precisely what I myself had done! . . .

And who could he be, this legionary who had set fire to the fort of Zinderneuf?

In a flash John makes up his mind to warn this man of the vedettes and perhaps join with him in a potential alliance. He notes, too, the trumpet or bugle carried by the man and remembers that a trumpeter had been first to enter the fort.

> As I came closer to the man, I was conscious of that strange contraction of the scalp muscles which has given rise to the expression 'his hair stood on end' . . .
>
> I grew cold with a kind of horrified wonder as I saw what I took to be the ghost or astral form *of my brother* there before me, looking perfectly normal, alive and natural.
>
> It *was* my brother – my brother Digby, Michael's twin . . .

The meeting is described, somewhat, in the classical Stanley-Livingstone meeting:

> 'Hello, John. I thought you'd be knocking about somewhere round here.'
>
> For all his casual manner and debonair bearing, he looked white and drawn, sick to death . . . his face a ghastly mask of pain.
>
> *John:*   'Wounded?'
>
> *Digby (biting his lip):* 'Er – not physically . . . I have just been giving Michael a "Viking's Funeral".'
>
> Poor Digby! He loved Michael as much as I did, and he was further bound to him by those strange ties that unite twins – psychic spiritual bonds . . .

It is now that the attack, which sends de Beaujolais' force which was parading before the fort scurrying back to the oasis, takes place.

Digby plans this fake attack. He is not to know that de Beaujolais has no intention of attempting to extinguish the flames now gutting the fort. His concerns are that he does not wish the 'Viking's Funeral' to be aborted or the evidence of Lejaune's murder to survive the flames.

So what de Beaujolais took for a renewal of the Arab attack was in fact Digby and John executing rapid fire over the heads of the legionnaires, in which the vedettes took part. De Beaujolais feels that the Arab force could be between himself and St André and his Senegalese, who are coming up from Tokotu on foot.

Having thrown de Beaujolais' relieving force into disarray, the brothers now have a few hours, before sunset, to bring one another up to date regarding their respective movements.

Digby's *escouade* had been ordered, after Tonout-Azzal, to Tokotu, where he had found to his amazement, that they fell under the command of Major Henri de Beaujolais – the Spahi officer who had visited Brandon Abbas and who was now engaged in training legionnaires in the art of mobile desert warfare.

> The Major had not recognised Digby, nor Digby the Major, until he had heard his name and that he was a Spahi.
>
> And it was him that I had been shooting at . . . this very friend of boyhood's days . . . Time's whirligig . . .
>
> *Digby:* 'Well, you know what I saw when I got on the roof . . . I dashed around to see if you were among the wounded, and then I realised there *were* no wounded . . . That meant that you had cleared out, and that it was your bayonet ornamenting Lejaune's chest, and that it was you who had composed Michael's body and closed his eyes . . . Who else but you would have treated Michael's body differently from the others? As I told you, I was mighty anxious, coming along, as to how you and Michael were getting on . . . and I had been itching to get up on to the roof while de Beaujolais was being dramatic with Rastignac. "*Anyhow – he shall have a 'Viking's Funeral'*", I swore. And then de Beaujolais came over the wall and proceeded to yell and shout for me. I hid in the cells. Dufour joined de Beaujolais and they actually looked into the cells, but I was behind the door. Presently they departed and I had to act swiftly.'

Digby left the cells and went back onto the roof, lifted Beau up in his arms, carried him down to his bed in the barrack-room and placed him on the bed. He laid piles of wood from the cook-house, around Beau's cot and drenched the wood with lamp oil:

> 'I did my best to make it a real "Viking's Funeral"; my chief regret was that I had no Union Jack to drape over him . . .
>
> *Oh! Beau! Beau! . . . I did my best for you, old chap . . . There was no horse, no spear, nor shield to lay beside you . . . But I put a dog at your feet though . . . And your rifle and bayonet were for sword and spear . . .*'
>
> He must be going mad. 'A dog? You are not getting it right, you know . . .'
>
> 'Yes, a dog. I did not carry it down, as I carried Beau. I took it by one foot and dragged it down.'
>
> 'Lejaune?'

'Yes, John, Lejaune – with your bayonet through his heart. And Beau had his "Viking's Funeral" with a dog at his feet. . .'

The brothers, realising that escape through the endless wastes of the Sahara, without some sort of transport, is out of the question, decide that their best plan of action is for Digby to rejoin his *escouade* and commandeer a camel or preferably two camels. As long as Digby does not encounter de Beaujolais or Dufour he will be safe from the accusation of 'desertion in the face of the enemy'. His comrades will merely suspect that he has gone *en promenade* – taken a smoke break. Even the corporals or even that epitome of military virtue, Sergeant Labaudy, would overlook the matter now that he was safely back in the ranks.

Digby is however, spared the test, as two legionnaires mounted on camels head from the oasis towards where they lie concealed.

To be fair to Wren, and his penchant for 'coincidence', these two legionnaires have not volunteered for this duty. They have been ordered to undertake this mission – but why them? The answer lies in the fact that Sergeant-Major Dufour knew his men.

It must be taken into account, though, that the warning emissaries, Hank and Buddy, knew that Michael and John had been posted to Zinderneuf; they have seen Digby enter the fort ; he has not reappeared. Furthermore, they themselves entered the fort with de Beaujolais; it did not take them long to conclude that neither Digby nor John were in the fort. The absence of Michael, whom they know as Beau, but whose pseudonym is Brown, no doubt puzzles them; but then it is impossible to recognise someone whose face might have been shot away.

Thus if Digby and John are not in the fort they have to be somewhere in the vicinity of that fort. Hence a little detour *en route* to St André's advancing column will hurt no one.

If they can locate, or stumble on by accident, the Geste brothers and also warn the Senegalese contingent they will have certainly achieved a creditable double. Things turn out, though, somewhat differently.

Seeing two legionnaires mounted on camels, John moves towards them, determined to bargain with them for the camels and, if need be, take the camels from them by force (without killing their owners).

The meeting:

Hank: 'Here's *one* of the mystery boys . . . I allowed as how you'd be around somewheres when we see you all three gone missin' from the old home . . .'

In a valley between two sand-hills, Hank and Buddy brought their camels to their knees and dismounted.

[In the Paramount picture Hank and Buddy were riding thoroughbred Arab horses – not even mules.]

Buddy: 'No offence, and excusin' a personal and dellikit question, Bo, but was it you as had the accident with the cigar-lighter an' kinder caused arsonical proceedins?'

Hank: 'Sort of 'arson about' with matches like?'

John replies that, regrettably, it was not he, but Digby who had caused the conflagration, and Hank rejoins,

'Then I would shore like to shake him by the hand . . .'

John then relates his part in the defence of Zinderneuf, explaining how he killed Lejaune. On learning of Michael's death, Hank remarks:

'He was shore a white man pard. 'Nuff said,' and Buddy, 'He was all-wool-an'-a-yard-wide.'

John feels that Michael might have had worse epitaphs.

Digby and John suggest to the two Americans that they give up their camels to them in a sham fight: they can tell de Beaujolais that they have fought their way back to the oasis against heavy odds, after being robbed of their beasts.

But Hank, deadpan, says no, 'We want them ourselves.' The brothers' disappointment is obvious so Hank goes on to insist that he and Buddy will team up with them and accompany them on their effort at 'going on pump'.

'Why, what did you figure? That we'd leave two innercent children to wander about . . . on their lone?'

So the upshot is that a little band of four plus two camels sets out to put as much distance between themselves and Zinderneuf as possible and ultimately to make good their total escape. It is agreed that they head south towards Nigeria, which country, being British territory, would afford them shelter from the long arm of the Legion.

Hank and Buddy, on being advised by John that it was he and Digby who had 'played at being Arab' by opening fire at, although shooting well over the heads of, de Beaujolais' squad, and that St André's Senegalese are in no danger of ambush, are relieved of the duty of warning the approaching troops.

Hank immediately takes command and the first part of his plan is that they turn 'Injun', by which he means 'native' or 'Arab'.

The story of the flight from Zinderneuf takes on the proportions of a saga. It is important as it lays part of the foundations of the second book of the trilogy, *Beau Sabreur*. It deals, also, with Digby's death.

CHAPTER 9

The Journey Home

*'Greater love hath no man than this,
That a man lay down his life for his friends.'*

THIS EPIC TREK TO SAFETY can be divided into episodes, some under which they prosper and others under which they suffer.

Hank's idea is that their small party should not be passive. They are well armed, have plenty of ammunition and two camels. He advocates an active role. Arab dress is essential and additional camels desirable.

They are doubly anxious to procure the disguise on learning that, in the south, towards Nigeria, there are numerous forts and outposts of the French Niger Territory, garrisoned by Senegalese, and that between these posts, numerous patrols will carefully watch the caravan-routes, and visit such Arab towns and settlements as exist.

It would certainly be better to encounter a patrol in the role of Arabs than in that of runaway soldiers from the Foreign Legion.

Accordingly Hank decrees that they must push on, only enough time being spent for the camels to eat and drink their fill, wherever water and grazing can be found.

The first episode is a lucky one – a break, much needed if they are to make progress. Hank's party come across a village recently raided by Touaregs. The village has been ransacked and put to the torch. The band is now encamped nearby and is busy enjoying the plunder. Hank plans, with the help of some of the survivors of the raid, to stage a counter-raid and recover camels and capture rifles, if all goes well.

The plan is fairly simple. The Touareg are camped in a ravine and if attacked at one end can only retreat through the other end. Thus, with the aid of Digby's bugle and much firing from behind rocks the Touareg are persuaded that a unit of the French army is upon them, and they flee.

The upshot of the business was that we left the village each riding a splendid *mehari* camel, and each clad in the complete outfit of a Touareg raider. A spare camel, laden with food and water was also supplied.

Wren states that this was perhaps the longest and most arduous ride ever achieved by Europeans in the Sahara.

> As I have said, an account of our *katabasis* would fill a volume, but a description of a few typical incidents will suffice:
> One day we rode over a long ridge of sand-covered rock – straight into a band of armed men.

Hank's band is taken prisoner and taken to a mountainous region but are well treated and sent on their way, in due course. This true desert hospitality contrasts markedly with the treatment they receive in Agades where they are imprisoned and their rifles taken from them.

The ruler of Agades at this time is one Tegama, and he does not believe the story that Digby and John are telling: that they have come with messages from El Senussi, and that Hank and Buddy are pious men under an oath of silence. (Both Digby and John can speak Arabic, which they learned during the long and boring days at Sidi-bel-Abbès.)

They escape from Agades one night before what they feel certain is fated for them, execution by impalement. They escape mounted on camels, thanks to a maiden that Buddy has befriended, but without their rifles.

Wren writes that the first Europeans to set foot in Agades were members of the French Military Mission which came in the great annual salt caravan from the south in 1904. In this piece of intelligence Wren might err as some historians hold that Scipio Africanus crossed the Sahara from the *north*, with his legion, and discovered Lake Chad. If this is corect he would more than likely have passed through Agades.

> . . . I could tell of a fair-bearded man who stared at us with blazing *grey* eyes, a man whose tongue had been cut out, whose ears and fingers had been cut off, and who was employed as a beast of burden.
> I could tell of a Thing that sat always at the Sôk, swaying to and fro as it crooned. Its lips, eyelids, ears, hands and feet had been cut off, it was blind and it crooned in *German*. . .
> I should like to tell of Tegama's executioners, four negroes who were the most animal creatures I ever saw in human form, and not one of whom was less than seven feet in height. The speciality of their leader was the clean, neat flicking-off of a head or any required limb, from a finger to a leg, with one

stroke of a great sword; while that of another was the infliction of the maximum number of wounds and injuries without causing the death of the victim.

Tegama grows more and more suspicious and truculent. Hank and Buddy who are 'under a vow of silence' have been overheard talking fluently to one another! It is time for the party to leave and they go, aided by a young person of magnificent physique, magnificent courage, and negroid ancestry – probably the daughter of a negro slave-woman from Lake Chad – (Buddy's friend!).

Being mounted on fresh camels was one thing, having a fresh supply of food was a plus, but without rifles or water Hank and his party cannot hope to get far, especially as they have to avoid the regular camel routes so as to avoid capture.

> A couple of days later we were riding in a line, just within sight of each other, and scouting for signs of human beings and water.
>
> Hank was on the right of the line, I next to him and half a mile away, having Buddy on my left with Digby at the far end. Looking to my right I saw Hank, topping a little undulation, suddenly wheel towards me, urging his camel to its top-most speed.
>
> As I looked, a crowd of riders swarmed over the skyline, and two or three of them, halting their camels, opened fire on us. Buddy rode at full speed towards me and Hank. Digby was cut off from view by a tor of rocks.
>
> Hank rode up shouting, 'Dismount and form squar'.' I knew what he meant. We brought our camels to their knees, made a pretence of getting out rifles from under the saddles, crouched behind the camels, and levelled our sticks as though they were guns, across the backs of the animals, and awaited death.
>
> *Buddy:*   'This is whar we gits what's comin' to us.'
>
> I could have wept that we had no rifles. The feeling of utter impotence was horrible. Could Digby possibly escape? There was an excellent chance that they would pass straight on without seeing his trail.
>
> And then from somewhere, there rang out loud, clear, and to our attackers, a terrible bugle-call. That portentous bugle-call, menacing and fateful, the bugle-call that announced the closing of a trap . . .
>
> The effect was instant . . . The band swerved to their right, wheeled and fled. As the bugle-calls died away Hank roared orders in French at the top of his enormous voice.

Digby, the better to get his bugle-calls to carry has climbed up onto one of the rocks of the tor. He stands there exposed and is observed by a member of the fleeing robber band. As this rider closes with him Digby poises himself in the attitude of a javelin-thrower.

> As the Arab raised his great sword, Digby's arm shot forward and the Arab reeled receiving the stone [which Digby had picked up] full in his face.
>
> Digby sprang at the man's leg and pulled him down, the two falling together. They rose simultaneously, the Arab's sword went up, Digby's fist shot out, and we heard the smack as the man reeled backwards and fell, his sword dropping from his hand.
>
> And then we heard another sound. A rifle was fired and Digby swayed and fell. An Arab had wheeled from the tail of the fleeing band, fired this shot, and fled again. Digby was dead before I got to him, shot through the head with an expanding bullet.
>
> *Digby was dead. Michael was dead.*
>
> *Hank, chewing his lips:* 'He shore gave his life for ourn.'
>
> Buddy wept.

There is not much they can do with their captive. He has no rifle, only his sword and camel. He is left by the now diminished band at the first water-hole they come to. Now a series of disasters overtake them.

[The scene of Digby's death is extremely well acted in the Paramount production of 'Beau Geste'.]

Sand storms, the loss of their camels from eating poisonous weed owing to their near starvation, and water supplies down to a bare minimum, leave the three in a parlous state.

Hank makes a sacrifice equivalent to that of Oates of Antarctic fame. A few days after losing the camels, John and Buddy wake up to find Hank gone, and a note left:

> 'Pards, drink up the water slow and push on quick. Good old Buddy, we bin good pards. Hank'
>
> Hank was gone . . .

As luck would have it, John and Buddy come across a small village where the inhabitants are friendly and here they rest for a while, hoping against hope that Hank will rejoin them.

> *Buddy:* 'Nobody could kill Hank . . . He's what you call ondestructable . . .'

After some months a caravan comes from the north, heading south to Zinder, headquarters of the French *Territoire Militaire*. Buddy and John join this caravan as fighting men, one dumb, the other talking Arabic. As the caravan nears Zinder they leave it for fear of being recognised by some military men of the garrison.

> Our adventures between Zinder and the British border at Barbera, where we first saw Haussas in the uniform of the West African Field Force, were numerous. But Fate had done its worst – and now that I had lost Digby, and Buddy had lost Hank, and neither of us cared very much what happened, our luck changed and all went fairly well.

John and Buddy arrive in Kano and introduce themselves to an official named Mordaunt who is a friend of a certain Mr George Lawrence, who in turn is a friend of a certain Aunt Patricia.

Buddy however will go no further than Kano. Having seen John to safety he turns round and goes back to find Hank. He does not go alone, though. Mordaunt arranges for a guide to go with him, a Haussa ex-soldier, plus a fine camel, a small tent, a rifle, ammunition and provisions. Lawrence agrees to pay for the equipment, plus the guide's salary and agrees that John should reimburse him at some future date. John cannot talk Buddy out of this venture.

> 'Would you go if your brother was lost, pard? Nope, Hank gave his life for us . . .'
>
> I hated parting with the staunch, brave, great-hearted little Buddy, and I felt he would never return to Kano unless it was with Hank, and I had no hope whatever of his doing that . . .

John was right. Buddy does not return to Kano, neither does Hank. But this is the basis of another part of the saga. Wren planned well.

The meeting between John and George Lawrence deserves attention. They recognise one another immediately and Lawrence wastes no time in taking up the mystery of the 'Blue Water'.

> *Lawrence:* 'And now I have something to tell *you*. Your Major de Beaulolais was sent down to Zinder and from there he went home on leave via Kano – and on Kano railway station I met him, and he told me the whole story of Zinderneuf Fort from *his* side of the business, and about finding your brother's 'confession'. I went on to Brandon Abbas and told Lady Brandon what he had told me – and really it did not seem to interest her enormously!'

It was incredible to sit there in a hammock-chair under the African stars, outside this man's tents, a whisky-and-soda in my hand and a cheroot in my mouth, and hear him tell how *he* had taken our Zinderneuf story to *Brandon Abbas*!

George Lawrence completes the Zinderneuf incident as told to him by Major Henri de Beaujolais.

'And so you see, my dear young friend, our Major de Beaujolais was not murdered by his mutinous men, neither did his men enter the fort. In fact no one ever again entered the fort. You yourself saw, from your vantage point in the sand-hills, the fort go up in smoke, burning like a tinder box.

'The Major had Dufour stand the men at ease and watch the flames consume the dreaded death-house.

'Then rifle-fire broke out (which you know about) and the legionnaires retreated to the oasis, *au pas gymnastique*, as our friend would have it, and may I say he added,

'"They are grand soldiers, those Legionnaires, George. No better troops in our army!"

'Reconstructing events from what you have told me, your friends, the two Americans were sent out to warn St André and his Senegalese and found you and Digby. Realising that there was no need to warn the Senegalese they joined you and your brother and the four of you set out, and here you are with me. Of course the Major knows nothing of this. He surmised that he had sent the Americans to their deaths as when St André's and his troops came up they reported that they had encountered no messengers of any description.'

But I must complete the Major's side of the story. The Major had a great respect for Lieutenant St André, stating that he was,

'. . . a man with a brain, ambitious and a real soldier and although he has private means, he serves France where duty is the hardest.'

Did Lieutenant St André know that his brother had been killed in action in the battle? His body had been consumed in the fire and so could not be identified.

'No matter what theories St André advanced, our Major was able to discredit them. Our friend could do no more than leave a detail to bury the dead, the charred remains of the legionnaires, and clean up as much as possible so that the French authorities could, in due course, rebuild the fort. He himself returned to Tokotu, and I well recall that he told me that to every stride of his camel a little tune throbbed through his head:

'*Who killed the Commandant, and why, why, why?*'

Lawrence is not the only person to be puzzled about Aunt Patricia's indifference to the fate of the 'Blue Water'; John, too, is a puzzled young man. It seems as if she does not want the wretched jewel back!

Other news imparted to John by Lawrence:

Sir Hector Brandon was dead. He had died of cholera in Kashmir; the Chaplain had died of a paralytic stroke; Claudia had married one of the richest men in England, nearly old enough to be her grandfather; Augustus had fallen off his hunter and been dragged until he was very dead; but 'Isobel was well and unmarried!'

Why did Wren find it necessary to have Digby killed? Apart from the drama of the occasion, 'Greater love hath no man . . .' there seems to be no valid reason. Michael (Beau) Geste, supposedly the principal character in the trilogy, was dead – why his twin? Could not two brothers together have taken the news of the 'Blue Water' to Brandon Abbas? Why only John? Hank's sacrificial act of going off on his own and leaving the balance of the small quantity of water to Buddy and John fits the 'Greater love hath no man . . .' parable as closely as Digby's act of bravery. Digby though must have thought he stood a chance – Hank must have known that his chance of survival was extremely thin.

Could it be that Wren, having told us that Digby was in love with Isobel, as was John, did not want Digby to return and suffer at seeing Isobel bestow her love on John? Michael certainly knew that Isobel loved John, as we have seen.

Digby was sent by Wren to Tokotu, separating him from his brother and his twin. This was necessary as it enabled him to fulfil the promise he had given Michael, when as a boy, he had promised his brother a 'Viking's Funeral'.

It is clear that Wren was planning well in advance. John, Hank and Buddy have to survive to carry the story into the second and third books.

Michael (Beau) Geste's spirit, only, survives as a golden thread.

CHAPTER 10

John's Return Home

THE NEWS of Michael's and Digby's deaths have preceded John, having been wired to Brandon Abbas by George Lawrence. Isobel and Aunt Patricia have been advised that John is coming home and that he, George Lawrence, would accompany him. All that remains is for John to regain his health during the sea voyage home, and to curb his impatience to see his beloved Isobel.

And so, one day, I found myself on the deck of a steamer, breathing glorious sea air, and looking back on the receding coast of horrible Africa, and almost too weak to keep my eyes from watering and my throat from swelling, as I realized I was leaving behind me all that was mortal of two of the best and finest that ever lived – my brothers, Michael and Digby. Also two more of the finest men of a different kind, Hank and Buddy, possibly alive, probably dead – and but for Isobel, I should have wished that I were dead too. . .

I will not write of my meeting with her. Those who love, or ever have loved, can imagine something of what I felt as I walked to the Bower, which she had elected to be our meeting place . . .

Aunt Patricia was coldly kind, at first. After lunch, in the drawing-room, the room from which the 'Blue Water' had disappeared, I gave her, in the presence of Isobel and George Lawrence, the letter and packet that had been Michael's charge to me.

She opened the letter first and read it, and then read aloud in a clear and steady voice:

'*My most dear and admired Aunt Patricia,*

When you get this, I shall be dead, and when you have read it I shall be forgiven, I hope, for I did what I thought was best, and what would, in a small measure, repay you for some of your great goodness to me and my brothers.

My dear Aunt, I knew you had sold the 'Blue Water' to the Maharajah (for the benefit of the tenants and the estate), and I knew you must dread the return of Sir Hector, and his discovery of the fact, sooner or later.

I was inside one of the suits of armour when you handed the 'Blue Water' over to the vizier or agent of the Maharajah. I heard everything, and once you had said what you said and I had heard it – it was pointless for me to confess that I knew – but when

I found you had had a duplicate made, I thought what a splendid thing it would be if only we had a burglary and the 'Blue Water' substitute was stolen! The thieves would be nicely done in the eye, and your sale of the stone would never be discovered by Sir Hector.

Had I known how to get into the Priest's Hole and open the safe, I would have burgled it for you.

Then Sir Hector's letter came, announcing his return, and I knew that things were desperate and the matter urgent. So I spirited away that clever piece of glass or quartz or whatever it is, and I herewith return it (with apologies). I nearly put it back after all, the same night, but I'm glad I didn't. (Tell John this.)

Now I do beg and pray you to let Sir Hector go on thinking that I am a common thief and stole the 'Blue Water' – or all this bother that everybody has had will be all for nothing, and I shall have failed to shield you from trouble and annoyance.

If it is not impertinent, may I say that I think you were absolutely right to sell it, and that the value is a jolly sight better applied to the health and happiness of the tenants and villagers and to the productiveness of the farms, than locked up in a safe in the form of a shining stone that is of no earthly benefit to anyone.

It nearly made me regret what I had done, when those asses, Digby and John, had the cheek to bolt too. Honestly it never occurred to me that they would do anything so silly. But I suppose it is selfish of me to want all the blame and all the fun and pleasure of doing a little job for you.

I do hope that all has gone well and turned out as I planned. I bet Uncle Hector was sick!

Well, my dear Aunt, I can only pray that I have helped you a little.

With sincerest gratitude for all you have done for us,

Your loving and admiring nephew,

    'Beau' Geste.

'A beau geste, indeed,' said Aunt Patricia. And for the only time in my life, I saw her put her handkerchief to her eyes.

Michael (Beau) Geste's letter is an admirable confession – it is, nevertheless, in the nature of a 'white lie'. A long period of time will elapse before the mystery of the 'Blue Water' is finally solved and the truth is revealed.

Extract from a letter from George Lawrence Esq., CMG of His Majesty's Nigeria Civil Service to Colonel Henri de Beaujolais, Colonel of Spahis, XIXth (African) Army Corps:

> '. . . and so that is the other side of the story, my friend. Alas for those two splendid boys, Michael and Digby Geste. . . And the remaining piece of news is that I sincerely hope that you will be able to come over to England in June. You are the best man I know, Jolly, and I want you to be my Best Man, a desire heartily shared by Lady Brandon.
>
> Fancy, after more than thirty years of devotion! I feel like a boy.
>
> And that fine boy, John, is going to marry the 'so beautiful child' whom you remembered. Lady Brandon is being a fairy godmother to them, indeed. I think she feels that she is somehow doing something for Michael by smoothing their path.

And should we, assiduous reader, forgive P.C. Wren one of his oh so very few chronological lapses?

John and Isobel marry 'more or less' at the same time that George Lawrence marries his childhood sweetheart, Patricia Rivers (Lady Brandon). Wren refers to 'Major' de Beaujolais, some years after John and Isobel are man and wife; when they are on a visit to the Vanbrugh ranch in Wyoming.

Thus Lawrence (or Wren) promoted de Beaujolais 'colonel' prematurely. Does it matter? only the purists will cavil!

BOOK ONE ENDS

The Second Book
Beau Sabreur

Beau Sabreur

Foreword taken from a note in the 1928 edition

THE AUTHOR would like to anticipate certain of the objections which may be raised by some of the kindly critics and reviewers who gave so friendly and encouraging a chorus of praise to *Beau Geste*, *The Wages of Virtue*, and *The Stepsons of France*.

Certain of the events chronicled in these books were objected to, as being impossible.

They were impossible.

The only defence that the Author can offer is that, although perfectly impossible, they actually happened.

In reviewing *The Wages of Virtue*, for example, a very distinguished literary critic remarked that the incident of a girl being found in the French Foreign Legion was absurd, and merely added an impossibility to a number of improbabilities.

The Author admitted the justice of the criticism, and then, as now, put forth the same feeble defence that, although perfectly impossible, it was the simple truth . . .

The reader may rest assured that the deeds narrated, and the scenes and personalities pictured, in this book, are not the vain outpourings of a film-fed imagination, but the re-arrangement of actual happenings and the assembling of real people who have actually lived, loved, fought and suffered . . .

Truth *is* stranger than fiction.

P. C. Wren

PART I — FAILURE

Out of the unfinished Memoirs
of
Major Henri de Beaujolais
of the Spahis and the French Secret Service

> To set the cause above renown,
> To love the game beyond the prize,
> To honour, while you strike him down,
> The foe that comes with fearless eyes;
> To count the life of battle good,
> And dear the land that gave you birth,
> And dearer yet the brotherhood
> That binds the brave of all the earth . . .
> *Sir Henry Newbolt*

The Making of a Beau Sabreur

CHAPTER I

Out of the Depths I Rise

I WILL START at the very nadir of my fortunes, at the very lowest depths, and you shall see them rise to their zenith, that highest point where they are crowned by Failure.

Behold me, then, clad in a dirty canvas stable-suit and wooden clogs, stretched upon a broad sloping shelf; my head near the wall, resting on a wooden ledge, a foot wide and two inches thick, meant for a pillow.

Between my pampered person and the wooden bed, polished by the rubbing of many vile bodies, is nothing. Covering for me is a canvas 'bread-bag'. As a substitute for sheets, blankets or eider-down quilt, it is inadequate.

The night is bitterly cold, and, beneath my canvas stable-suit, I am wearing my entire wardrobe of under-clothes, in spite of which my teeth are chattering and I shiver from head to foot as though stricken with ague.

I am not allowed to wear my warm regimentals and cloak or overcoat, for, alas, I am in prison.

Some of my fellow troopers pride themselves on being men of intelligence and reason, and therefore believe only in what they can see. I cannot see the insects, but I, intelligent or not, believe in them firmly.

Henri de Beaujolais goes on to describe the prison as:

... a reeking, damp and verminous cellar, some thirty feet square, ventilated only by a single grated aperture, high up in one of the walls, and it is an unfit habitation for a horse or a dog.

In fact, Colonel Du Plessis, our Commanding Officer, would not have one of the horses here for more than an hour. But I am here for fifteen days ... and serve me jolly well right.

For I have *tirée une bordée* – absented myself, without leave for five days – the longest period that one can be absent without becoming a deserter and getting three years' hard labour as such.

So why is this Beau Sabreur in the making in prison? As is not unusual there is a 'Lady' in the case. Also a man; de Beaujolais' superior officer, in fact. As the story unfolds we will read of de Lannec and Véronique

Vaux. The latter had sent a letter to de Beaujolais requesting him to come to Paris with all haste. He had obliged and had paid the penalty.

> Soon the cruel cold, the clammy damp, the wicked flea, the furtive rat, the odour, and the proud stomach combine with the hard bench and aching bones to make me wish I were not a sick and dirty man starving in prison.
> And a few months ago I was at Eton! . . . It is all very amusing . . .

How and when did P. C. Wren decide to make Henri de Beaujolais a main character in the trilogy? In *Beau Geste* de Beaujolais' part is vital. It was he who, as a French officer seconded to the Legion, entered the doomed fort at Zinderneuf. A fort, defended in part by nephews of a friend (Isobel Rivers – now Lady Brandon); men he had known as boys.

Having played his part in the first book, Wren could have thrown him in the discard. But he did not. De Beaujolais becomes one of the most engaging of the characters of the *Beau Geste* trilogy.

That a trilogy, or at the very least a sequel, to *Beau Geste* must have been in Wren's mind from the very beginning is evident from the fact that the thief who stole the 'Blue Water' is not exposed until the third and final volume of the trilogy was published.

Readers of *Beau Geste* who fail to read on to the end of the trilogy are left thinking that Michael Geste had purloined that priceless gem, the 'Blue Water'.

As a young man, de Beaujolais found many things 'amusing.' In later life this is not the case as he is subjected, by Wren, to tests and ordeals which would have taxed the fibre of the staunchest of men.

We return now to de Beaujolais' account of how he became a trooper in the distinguished regiment – The Blue Hussars.

Doubtless you will wonder how a man may be an Etonian one year and a trooper in a French Hussar Regiment the next.

> I am a Frenchman, I am proud to say; but my dear mother, God rest her soul, was an Englishwoman; and my father, like myself, was a great admirer of England and of English institutions. Hence my being sent to school at Eton.
> On my father's death, soon after I had left school, my uncle sent for me.

He was even then a general, the youngest in the French Army, and his wife the sister of an extremely prominent and powerful politician, at that time Minister of State for War.

[Thus we see that young Henri de Beaujolais is very well connected – he has relations in high places.]

My uncle is fanatically patriotic, and *La France* is his goddess. For her he would love to die, and for her he would see everybody else die – even so agreeable a person as myself. When his last moments come, he will be frightfully sick if circumstances are not appropriate for him to say, '*I die – that France may live*,' – a difficult statement to make if you are sitting in a bathchair at ninety.

[It is already apparent that de Beaujolais has a streak of facetiousness in him!]

De Beaujolais now tells us that he left his mother in Devonshire, and hurried to Paris to present himself to his uncle at the War Office.

My uncle eyed me keenly and greeted me coldly, and observed – 'Since your father is spilt milk, as the English say, it is useless to cry over him. You are a Frenchman, the son of a Frenchman. Are you going to renounce your glorious birthright and live in England, or are you going to be worthy of your honoured name?'

I replied that I had been born a Frenchman, and that I should live and die a Frenchman.

'Good,' said my uncle. 'In that case you will do your military service. Do it at once and do it as I shall direct.

'Someday I am going to be the master-builder in consolidating an African empire for France, and I shall need tools *that will not turn in my hand*. Tools on which I can rely absolutely. If you have ambition, if you are a man, obey and follow me. Help me, and I will make you . . . Fail me, and I will break you . . .'

Henri tells us that he could only gape at his uncle and look imbecilic, which was something he chose now and again to do. His uncle expands on his African dream, outlining the territories held in Africa by the British and expressing the view that France should have a share, a rightful share, of the African 'spoils'.

Henri, who is a very intelligent young man, now discards his imbecilic look and tries to look intelligent and pay attention to what his uncle is saying.

'Now boy,' concluded my uncle, impaling me with a penetrating stare. 'I will try you, and I will give you a chance to become a Marshall of France as falls to few. Go to the headquarters of the military division of the *arrondissement* in which you were born, show your papers and enlist as a *Volontaire*. You will then have to serve for only one year instead of the three compulsory for the ordinary conscript. I will see that you are posted to the Blue Hussars, and you will do a year in the ranks. You will never mention my name to a soul, and you will be treated precisely as any other private soldier.

'If you pass out with high marks at the end of the period, come to me, and I will see that you go to Africa with a commission in the Spahis. There, learn Arabic until you know it better than your mother tongue; and learn to know the Arab better than you know yourself. *Then* I can use you! But mind, boy, you will have to *ride alone!*'

As for 'riding alone,' – excellent . . . I was not the sort of man that allows his career to be hampered by a woman.

The General now suggests 'lunch,' a proposal to which Henri gives his unconditional consent.

After lunch, and on his own once again, de Beaujolais concludes:

All 'very amusing!

There are on record several opinions of de Beaujolais; his looks, his character and general demeanour:

George Lawrence:	[He was] a fine type of French soldier, suave, courtly and polished, ruddy of face and brown of eye and hair.
Otis Vanbrugh:	I liked the handsome, hard, clean-cut Major Henri de Beaujolais from the first; and he attracted me enormously. To the simplicity and directness of the soldier he added the cleverness and knowledge of the trained specialist; the charm, urbanity and grace of the experienced man of the world; and the inevitable attractiveness of a loveable and modest character.
De Beaujolais (of himself):	I had won the Public Schools Championship for boxing (Middleweight) and for fencing as well. I was a fine gymnast, I had ridden from childhood, and I possessed perfect health and strength . . .

CHAPTER 2

The Blue Hussar

ONE FINE MORNING, the necessary strings having been pulled by his uncle, the General, Henri de Beaujolais presents himself at the great gates of the barracks of the famous Blue Hussars.

> I beheld an enormous parade ground, about a quarter of a mile square, with the Riding School in the middle of it, and beyond it a huge barracks for men and horses. The horses occupied the ground floor and the men the floors above – not a nice arrangement I thought. I continued to think it, when I lived just above the horses, in a room that held a hundred and twenty unwashed men, a hundred and twenty pairs of stable-boots, a hundred and twenty pairs of never-cleaned blankets – and windows that had been kept shut for a hundred and twenty years, to exclude the exaltations from the stable, because more than enough came up through the floor!

[That an Old-Etonian could suffer these barracks for a year says quite a lot for his character.]

On presenting his papers to the Sergeant of the Guard, de Beaujolais is greeted in the following manner:

> One of those anointed *Volontaires*, are you? Well, my fine gentleman, I don't like them, d'you understand? And I don't like you . . . I don't like your face, nor your voice, nor your clothes, nor anything about you. D'you see?

De Beaujolais saw, and held his peace! He had been well-briefed by the mentor, later his friend, whom his uncle had appointed to guide him – Lieutenant de Lannec.

Getting no rise out of the *Voluntaire*, the Sergeant instructs a trooper to escort Henri to the sergeant-major in charge of recruits.

The guide:	'Come on, you gaping pig. Hurry yourself, or I'll chuck you into the manure-heap.'
de Beaujolais:	'Friend and brother-in-arms, let us go to the manure-heap at once, and we'll see who goes on it . . . I don't know why you ever left it . . .'

The guide: 'Oh! You're one of those beastly bullies, are you?'

Henri had made his point – *he* was not there to be bullied.

The guide leaves Henri in the office of the Squadron Sergeant-Major; a person altogether different to the Sergeant of the Guard. A dog that never barked, but bit hard was Sergeant-Major Martin. De Beaujolais' particulars are entered in the *livret*, or regimental-book, which accompanies every French soldier for the duration of his service.

Next comes the *peleton* Sergeant – a Sergeant de Poncey who, realising at once that de Beaujolais is a 'gentleman', proclaims himself one too, but down on his luck. He immediately attempts to borrow twenty francs from Henri:

> 'No, Sergeant,' I said, and his face darkened with pain and annoyance. 'I am going to *give* you a hundred, if I may . . .'

De Beaujolais has made a friend and matters go further, for Sergeant de Poncey tells Corporal Lepage that, although a *Volontaire*, he is a good fellow, 'friend of mine, see?' Corporal Lepage 'sees' and invites Henri to be a friend of his too!

The morning ends with de Beaujolais sitting astride his narrow bed, eating *soupe* from a tin plate and thinking:

> An amusing morning.
>
> I shall never forget being tailored by the *Sergeant-Fourrier* that afternoon. I was given a pair of red trousers to try on 'for size'. They were not riding breeches but huge trousers, the legs being each as big round as my waist. The Sergeant-Tailor bade me get into them – I got. The heavy leather ends rested on the ground and the tops cut me under the arm-pits.
>
> 'Excellent,' declared the tailor, and handed me a blue tunic to try on, 'for size!'

The tunic is so large that Henri is able to pull the collar over his head and his hands are invisible, tucked somewhere near the elbow joints.

'Yes, you go into that nicely too,' said the Sergeant-Tailor.

Henri barely manages to stagger to the store which houses the Sergeant-Bootmaker. This worthy is reputed to have 'an entire range of boots of all sizes'. The 'entire range' consists of four pairs, none of which fits de Beaujolais.

'You've got deformed feet, oh, *espèce d'imbécile.*'

Not at a loss, the bootmaker makes Henri put on the largest pair, a pair fully five inches too long in the feet. The bootmaker's solution to the problem of 'fit' is to suggest that the toes of the boots be stuffed with straw: 'and is straw so dear in a cavalry regiment that you cannot stuff the toes with it, Most Complete Idiot?'

Henri knows that once he has quit the barracks this ill-fitting uniform will not much matter as he has a perfectly tailored uniform awaiting him at his hotel, and boots bespoke by the best bootmaker in Paris.

His immediate problems are twofold: He has to pass the Captain of the Week, and the Sergeant of the Guard, who inspects all troopers leaving the barracks. Once safely in his hotel, de Beaujolais will be fairly comfortable and he blesses de Lannec for having suggested such a haven to him.

De Beaujolais presents himself before the Captain of the Week:

> I do not know what I expected him to do. He did not faint, nor call upon Heaven for strength. He eyed me as one does a horse offered for sale. He was of the younger school – smart, cool, and efficient.
> 'Take off that tunic.'
> I obeyed with alacrity.
> 'Yes, the trousers are too short. Are you a natural fool to come before me with trousers that are too short? And look at your boots. Each is big enough to contain both your feet. Are you an *un*natural fool to come before me in such boots?'
> '*Oui, mon Capitaine,*' I replied, and felt both a natural and an unnatural fool.
> 'Have the goodness to go, and return in trousers twice as large and boots half as big. You may tell the *Sergeant-Fourrier* that he will shortly hear something to his disadvantage . . . it will interest him in you . . .'

De Beaujolais is shuttled between the *Sergent-Fourrier* and the Captain of the Week. The game is played to the full.

The boots are either too small or too large; the trousers too small or too large and the tunic too large or too small. The end comes when, on the fourth presentation, de Beaujolais finds that the Captain has gone to dinner and that he can return to the *Sergent-Fourrier* and truthfully say that the Captain had found no fault with him!

The full uniform is detailed as:

> . . . an extra tunic, an extra pair of incredible trousers, an extra pair of impossible boots, a drill-jacket, a *kepi,* two canvas stable-suits, an overcoat, a

Soldat Premier Classe and Officier

huge cape, two pairs of thick white leather gauntlets, two terrible shirts, two pairs of pants, a huge pair of clogs, and no socks at all.

This is a far greater quantity of kit than that which was issued to the Gestes when they joined the Foreign Legion. The non-issue of socks is again made mention of (as it is in *Beau Geste*). Peter MacDonald, however, in his authoritative book, *The Making of a Legionnaire*, assures his readers that the modern Legion recruit is indeed issued with socks!

Wren now introduces three characters into the trilogy: Dufour, Becque and de Redon. Dufour features in all three books of the trilogy, and you may remember him in *Beau Geste*. Becque, under both his own and an assumed name, features in two of the books and is made mention of in the third book.

In need of help in straightening out his newly issued kit Henri asks a trooper who is sitting on his bed close to Henri's bed whether he would care to earn a franc or two. The trooper, who is, at that juncture, suffering from 'old French' (a shortage of money), was nothing loath to volunteer his services.

Henri de Beaujolais tells us about him:

> I found that his name was Dufour, that he was the son of a horse-dealer, and had had to do with both horses and gentlemen . . .
>
> From that hour he became my friend and servant, to the day when he gave his life for France and for me, nearly twenty years later. He was very clever, honest and extremely brave; a faithful, loyal and noble soul.

Becque, the second of the three characters mentioned, is an 'agent', a 'Man with a Message', a 'propagandist', and an 'agitator'. He appears to have plenty of money and plenty of ideas and he has formed a 'society' which meets in a room above a wine shop.

Dufour has been invited to attend one of these 'society' meetings and out of curiosity he has gone along. What he hears at the meeting disturbs him and he reports the proceedings to de Beaujolais. It is then and there decided that Dufour will take de Beaujolais to the next meeting.

> Becque's talk interested me. He was clearly a monomaniac whose whole mental content was hate – hate for France; hate for all who had what he had not; hate of control, discipline and government . . . the perfect *agent provocateur*.

Becque persuades both Dufour and de Beaujolais to swear an Oath of Initiation, principally to the effect that they will never divulge the secrets of the Society nor give any account of its proceedings.

It is strange that Henri takes such an oath, but, in fact, he has to, to enable him to learn more about Becque and his Society. Very much to his credit, de Beaujolais keeps his oath.

In the early years of the twentieth century both France and Germany were preparing for war; the Franco-Prussian war of 1870 was still fresh in memory.

De Beaujolais puts the question to Becque, 'And what happens to France when her army has disbanded itself? What about Germany?'

Becque: 'The German army will do the same, my young friend. Our German brothers will join hands with us. So will our Italian and Austrian and Russian brothers . . . All shall own all, and none shall oppress any. There will be no rich, no police, no prisons, no law, no poor . . .'

And from a trooper, who has imbibed freely, 'And no work.'

The meeting breaks up, and:

> taking my sword, I dragged myself from his foul presence, lest I be tempted to take him by the throat and kill him . . .

Duelling in the French army at that time was not merely permitted, but, under certain circumstances, was compulsory. The use of fists in the French cavalry was regarded as vulgar, ruffianly and low. Under no circumstances would two troopers be allowed to 'settle it' behind the Riding School in the Anglo-Saxon way. If they fought at all they fought with swords, under supervision. But troopers were encouraged to avoid fighting one another altogether.

Henri and Dufour plan a 'set-up' and provoke Becque into attacking Henri. This takes place in the stables and Becque attempts to set about Henri with a broom. Unfortunately for Becque, de Beaujolais wrests the broom from his hands and slaps his face, whereupon Becque spits at him. Very soon higher authority appears and:

> . . . the excellent Dufour gabbled a most untruthful version of the affair, and the sergeant took notes. Trooper Becque had publicly spat upon *volontaire* de Beaujolais, who had then knocked him down . . .

The Colonel, in due course, receives the Sergeant's report and orders that a duel be fought:

> The successful combatant in this duel will receive fifteen days imprisonment, and the loser will receive thirty days . . .

Thus ordered the Colonel.

The duel takes place in the Riding School and is witnessed by the Colonel and various of the officers. The combatants fight with heavy cavalry swords and an umpire stands ready to knock up any sword that ventures too near an opponent. But Henri has not gone to the trouble of getting Becque into a situation where he can hand out severe punishment only to see his efforts frustrated by a clumsy sergeant umpire.

Becque fights at a furious pace and then suddenly retreats, thrusting his sword point into the ground:

'I am satisfied,' he states.

'Well I'm not,' says the Colonel in an icy voice, 'fight on.'

There can be no doubt that Henri is by far the better duellist and he wins the encounter, wounding Becque severely in the right breast.

> France, my beautiful France, my second Mother, had one active enemy less for quite a good while . . .
>
> 'I'll do that for you again, when you come out of hospital, friend Becque.'

The upshot of this is that there is a tremendous row, as the *maître d'armes* has not prevented the severe wounding of Becque – but as nothing irregular has occurred the *Conseil de discipline* refuses to act beyond the fifteen days imprisonment decreed before the duel took place.

The duel, however, leads to de Beaujolais' first meeting with the third of the characters mentioned, *Sous-Lieutenant* Raoul d'Auray de Redon. After serving his fifteen days in the cells, not to be confused with the fifteen days confinement he received for absenting himself without leave, de Beaujolais is ordered to appear before de Redon in the latter's quarters.

> I had noted this young gentleman, and had been struck by his beauty. I do not mean prettiness nor handsomeness, but *beauty*. It shone from within him, and illuminated a perfectly formed face . . . He radiated friendliness, kindness, helpfulness, and was yet the best disciplinarian in the Regiment – because he had no need to 'keep' discipline. It kept itself where he was concerned. And with all his gentle goodness of heart he was a strong man. Nay, he was a lion of strength and courage . . .

De Redon was soon to the point:

> 'Why did you want to fight this Becque?'
>   I was somewhat taken aback:
> 'He has dirty finger-nails, *mon Lieutenant*.'
>   *De Redon*: 'Quite probably . . . but so do other troopers in the Blue Hussars.

Why Becque in particular out of a few hundred?'

'Oh! – he eats garlic – and sometimes has a cast in his eye – and he jerks his horse's mouth – and has a German mother – and wipes his nose with the back of his hand . . .'

De Redon (drily):   'You supply one with interesting information. Now I will supply you with some, though it won't be so interesting because you already know it . . . In addition to your list of dislikes, he is a seditious scoundrel and a hireling spy and agitator . . . you have attended his meetings and taken the oath of secrecy to his Society.'

De Beaujolais can only stare at de Redon in astonishment.

De Redon now orders de Beaujolais to tell him what happened at the meetings, just what was said, and the names of the troopers who were present.

De Beaujolais refuses, pleading that he has taken an oath of secrecy – a fact de Redon appears to be aware of.

> Sub-Lieutenant Raoul d'Auray de Redon rose from his chair, and came around to where I was standing. Was he – a gentleman – going to demand with threats and menaces that I break my word – even to a rat as Becque!
>
> 'Stand at ease, Trooper Henri de Beaujolais, and shake hands with a brother of the Service! Oh, yes, I know all about you . . . from de Lannec . . .'
>
> I took the proffered hand and stammered my thanks at this honour from my superior officer.
>
> 'Oh, nonsense. You'll be my 'superior officer' someday. I must say I admire your pluck in coming to *us* by way of the ranks.'

How did de Redon know about Becque and his Society? Had someone denounced Becque to de Redon? A trooper, too drunk to take the oath at the last meeting; a trooper, who in his cups had slurred the words, 'And no work.' That man, de Redon!

De Beaujolais now hears from his mentor, de Lannec, who writes that:

> His very soul was dead within him, and his life 'but dust and ashes, a vale of woe and mourning, a desert of grief and despair in which was no oasis of joy or hope . . .' For he had lost his adored Véronique Vaux . . . she had transferred her affections to a colonel of Chasseurs d'Afrique and departed with him to Fez!

De Beaujolais had met this Véronique Vaux and had, in fact, visited her in Paris, bringing down on his head fifteen days in the cells for being absent without leave. We hear of her again.

CHAPTER 3

Africa

At the end of his year in the Blue Hussars de Beaujolais receives his commission and is posted to Algeria where he is to report to the Quartier des Spahis at Sidi-bel-Abbès.

A note: Henri de Beaujolais was never a member of the French Foreign Legion. As we have seen (in *Beau Geste*) he was seconded to the Legion for a short period, but he at no time served in their ranks.

> I stood at the great gates in the lane which separates the Spahis' barracks from those of the Foreign Legion – and knew that I had arrived.

[The author visited the Foreign Legion barracks in 1960. The Spahis' barracks had gone.]

> Standing at the big open window of the *Salle de Rapport*, was a strikingly smart and masculine figure – that of an officer in a gold-frogged white tunic, which fitted his wide shoulders and narrow waist as paper fits the walls of a room. Beneath a high red *tarbush* smiled one of the handsomest faces I have ever seen.

Here Wren again deals with the love one man can have for another. There are many such relationships in the trilogy – Hank and Buddy; Otis Vanbrugh and John Geste; not to mention the brotherly love that existed between the Geste brothers.

> I know that one man *can* really love another with the love that is described as existing between David and Jonathan . . . I do not believe in 'love at first sight', but tremendous attraction, and the strongest liking at first sight, soon came, in this case, to be a case of love at second sight . . . To this day I can never look upon the portrait of Raoul d'Auray de Redon, of whom more anon, without a pang of bitter-sweet pain, and a half-conscious prayer . . .

De Beaujolais sends, as we shall see, many men to their deaths. He does not send de Redon directly to *his* death, but may be the indirect agent which causes de Redon to die a comparatively young man.

De Beaujolais soon admits to boredom in the barracks at Sidi-bel-

Abbès. There is insufficient in a small garrison-town to amuse him. The study of Arabic does, however, help him to pass the time away.

Dufour duly arrives in the ranks of the Spahis. Henri, through the influence of his uncle, is able to pull the necessary strings.

Soon, for de Beaujolais, comes promotion to Captain, and a transfer to Morocco. With him goes Dufour. The battle of M'karto (see Martin Windrow – *Uniforms of the French Foreign Legion*), took place in 1907. De Beaujolais' squadron took part in this action:

> I am charging a great *harka* of very brave and fanatical Moors, at the head of my squadron . . . We do not charge in line as the English do, but every man for himself, hell-for-leather, at the most tremendous pace to which he can spur his horse . . . being the best mounted, I am naturally well ahead . . . The earth seems to tremble beneath the thundering onrush of the finest squadron in the world . . . I am wildly happy . . . I wave my sabre and shout for joy. . . As we are about to close with the enemy I lower my point, and straighten my arm. The Moors are cunning as they are brave. Hundreds of infantry drop behind rocks and big stones . . . level their long guns and European rifles, and blaze into the brown of us, hundreds of cavalry swerve off to the right and the left, to take us in flank and surround us, when the shock of our impact on the main body has broken our charge and brought us to a halt. They do not know that we shall go through them like a knife through cheese, re-form and charge back again – and even if we do not scatter them like chaff, we will effectively prevent their charging and capturing our guns . . .
>
> I am into them with a mighty crash . . . A big Moor and his Barbary stallion go head-over-heels, as my good horse and I strike them amidships.

We are now treated to a description of the fight in terms such as cut and parry; slash, parry and cut; thrust and strike; hack and hew . . .

> And then I know that my horse is hit and going down, and that I am flying over his head and that the earth rises up and smashes my face, and strikes my chest so cruel a blow that the breath is driven from my body, and I am a living pain . . . my right arm broken . . . And, oh! the torture of my dead horse's weight on my broken leg and ankle . . .
>
> And why is my throat not being cut? Why no spears being driven through my back? Why my skull not being battered in?
>
> I was the centre of a terrific 'dog fight' and standing across me, leaping over me, whirling round and round . . . a grand athlete and great hero – was Dufour . . . Sick and shattered as I was, I could still admire his wonderful swordsmanship . . . Soon I realized I could do more than admire him. I could

help, although pinned to the ground by my horse . . . With infinite pain I dragged my revolver from its holster, and rejoiced that I had made myself as good a shot with my left hand as with my right.

Then lying on my right side . . . I fired at a man whose spear was driving at Dufour's back; at another whose great sword was swung up to cleave him; at a third whose long gun was presented at him; and then into the very face of one who had sprung past him and was in the act of driving his big curved dagger into my breast . . .

As I aimed my last shot – at a man whose sword was clashing on Dufour's sabre – the squadron came thundering back, headed by Lieutenant d'Auray de Redon . . .

For his part in this skirmish, Dufour is awarded the *médaille militaire*. Quite rightly so. But it is distressing to note that de Redon is still a lieutenant, while de Beaujolais has advanced to captain.

De Beaujolais enters a period of his life when he becomes more and more involved in secret service work. His uncle, the general, has come out to North Africa, and is close at hand to pull the strings.

I was able to join his Staff as an officer who knew more than a little about the country and its fascinating towns and people; an officer who could speak Arabic and its Moorish variant like a native; and who could wander through *suq* and street and bazaar as a beggar; a pedlar; a swaggering Riffian *askari* of the *bled* [backveld]; a nervous, cringing Jew of the *mellah*; a fanatic of Mulai Idris [Lybia]; a camel-man or donkey-driver – without the least fear of discovery.

In making use of what in today's world would be termed 'pejorative' references to race, terms that might offend modern day susceptibilities, Wren does not mean to be cruel to any of the categories of people mentioned. Wren was a writer of his times. It was the fashion of the day. It was taken for granted that people from Europe were superior to people from the East – and this was so, until proved otherwise, later in the twentieth century. In any event Wren loved his eastern characters and produced brave men from many climes.

Soon de Beaujolais is promoted the youngest major (Commandant) in the French army and, 'disappears from human ken to watch the affairs in Zaguig . . .'

. . . Not quite from 'human ken', as in Zaguig he meets de Redon, who has taken on the guise of a camel-driver. De Redon has interesting, if not important, intelligence to impart to his friend (and now superior).

De Redon has come across a man, a heavily bearded fanatic, who is preaching against the infidel, especially the *Franzawi* who have conquered Algeria and penetrated Tunisia and Morocco, and intend to come to Zaguig.

De Redon detects something not quite right with the bearded one's Arabic accent and, his suspicions aroused, he follows him. The bearded one composes himself on a bench in the town gardens and de Redon approaches him from behind and delivers a blow to the man's head with his long camel stick. Taken completely by surprise the man utters but one exclamation and then recovers himself: 'Himmel!'

> 'Henri, do you remember a man who – let me see – had dirty finger nails, jerked his horse's mouth, had a German mother, revealed a long dog-tooth when he grinned sideways . . . ?'
>
> 'Becque!' exclaimed de Beaujolais.

Yes, indeed. Becque has been discovered and his disguise penetrated but, being a clever agent, the blow to his head, seemingly without any good reason, alerts him to possible danger, and he quits Zaguig almost immediately. We know, though, of his future movements: he surfaces in the Foreign Legion as . . . Rastignac.

As for de Redon, he receivs his orders from de Beaujolais and departs for Lake Tchad and Timbucto.

Captain de Lannec relieves de Beaujolais in Zaguig, the latter departing for the south . . .

> . . . ostensibly to organise Mounted Infantry Companies out of mules and the Foreign Legion, but really to do a little finding out and a little intelligence-organising in the direction of the territories of our various southern neighbours, and to travel from Senegal to Wadai, with peeps into Nigeria and the Cameroons . . .
>
> Here I had some very instructive experiences and a very weird one at a place called Zinderneuf, whence I went on leave via Nigeria, actually travelling home with a most excellent Briton named George Lawrence . . . It is a queer little world and very amusing . . .

Thus is the Zinderneuf incident dismissed by de Beaujolais. The time scale, or chronological order, is perfect.

CHAPTER 4

Zaguig

MAJOR HENRI DE BEAUJOLAIS now tells us that Fate, and his uncle, bring him to the greatest adventure of his life, and what he believes to be the supreme failure that rewards his labours at the crisis of his career.

His orders come: 'Return forthwith to Zaguig and await instructions.'

Zaguig was a 'holy' city and, like most holy cities in Wren's opinion, was tenanted by some of the unholiest scum of mankind. The Arab proverb speaks for itself: 'The holier the city, the wickeder the citizens.'

Holy or unholy, Zaguig proves to be a turning point in de Beaujolais' life. Up until now we have seen him admiring handsome young men. In Zaguig he meets Miss Mary Hankinson Vanbrugh. Wren describes her as 'extremely beautiful' – de Beaujolais refers to her as a 'young girl'. How did such a woman come to be in a town such as Zaguig?

At the time of de Beaujolais' second visit to Zaguig it has been occupied by a small French force. Colonel Levasseur of the Zouaves is in command and de Beaujolais at once realises that the troops garrisoned there are hopelessly inadequate for the policing mission they are carrying out.

Mary Vanbrugh's brother Otis is 'an honorary ornament' at the American Embassy in Paris. To show his sister, who wishes the experience, the '*real* desert and Empire in the making', he has prevailed on Colonel Levasseur to allow them to accompany him to Algeria. In due course they arrive in Zaguig from Bousen (the latter town being, at that time, the terminal of the desert railway line which ran south).

De Beaujolais does not like the pair, helpless civilians, being in Zaguig at all. Levasseur, in turn, does not like de Beaujolais. He is both suspicious and jealous of the Secret Service. In addition, he fears de Beaujolais, seeing in the younger man a rival for the hand of Mary Vanbrugh. He is, however, de Beaujolais' superior in rank and can issue orders which the junior man is obliged to carry out.

Initially de Beaujolais dislikes Mary Vanbrugh. His dislike is prompted by her attitude towards him and his utter inability to understand her.

The said attitude was one of fairly mocking mild amusement, and I had not been accustomed to regarding myself as an unintentionally amusing person . . .

Mary has bestowed on de Beaujolais the nickname of *Ivan* and then *Major Ivan*. When asked by him, 'Why Ivan?'

> . . . her half suppressed provoking smile would dimple her very beautiful cheeks as she replied:
> 'But surely? . . . You are really Ivan Whats-his-name in disguise aren't you? Colonel Levasseur told me you are a most distinguished Intelligence Officer on Secret Service, and I think that must be one of the Secrets . . .'

And when de Beaujolais resignedly shrugs his shoulders Mary exclaims:

> 'Oh, *do* do that again Major Ivan. It was so delightfully French and expressive . . .'
> 'Yes – we are amusing little funny foreigners, Mademoiselle . . .'

De Beaujolais may have replied in that vein, but his thoughts were otherwise:

> Level-eyed, slow-spoken, unhurried, she was something new and strange to me, and she intrigued me in spite of myself.

It is possible to calculate from Wren's writings that de Beaujolais was about thirty-eight or thirty-nine years old at this stage of his career. His rival, Colonel Levasseur, would have been about fifty years old, and he regarded de Beaujolais as 'the younger man'. Mary Vanbrugh was twenty-three or twenty-four years old.

As if to cement the annoyance (and the intrigue) Mary Vanbrugh takes to humming a tune and singing the words of a song:

> And the boldest of all
> and the bravest by far
> was Ivan Skivinsky Skivar

The song, well known at the turn of the century is still, every now and then, heard these days.

Before the breaking of the political storm and general uprising of the townspeople, assisted by the rural tribes who will pour into the town in search of loot, de Beaujolais and Dufour, who know what is coming, make their preparations to act immediately on receipt of secret orders. They are greatly assisted by Sidi Ibrahim Maghruf, a self-made merchant of the town and a friend of the French, whom he sees as a provider of protection to his caravans.

De Beaujolais describes Ibrahim Maghruf as someone in whom he has complete faith. His money is in French banks. He exports dates to France and imports cotton goods from Manchester. He is in fact a merchant prince of Islam. His motto (or dictum): 'A man should not sleep on silk until he has walked on sand.'

In Maghruf's house de Beaujolais feels safe. His equipment is stored there and his camels are stabled there. His camels are:

> . . . of the finest breed, brindled, grey-and-white, bluish-eyed, lean, slender greyhounds of the desert, good for a steady ten kilometres an hour.

It is time now to meet Miss Maud Atkinson, Mary Vanbrugh's personal maid. She is 'pretty' and 'piquant'. De Beaujolais, who seems to carry more red blood in his veins than some other of Wren's characters, wonders whether 'she was as flirtatious as she looked'. Maudie is a Cockney and is treated by Mary Vanbrugh as a maid-companion, in the democratic American manner. She has a penchant for 'sheikhs'. 'They are such lovely men' – she has read of them in fiction:

> 'Oh, Miss, they catches you up into their saddles and gallops off with you into the sunset! No good smacking their faces neither, for they don't take "no" for an answer, when they're looking out for a wife.'
>
> *Miss Vanbrugh:*   'Or wives.'
>
> 'Not if you're the first, Miss. They're true to you. And they fair burn your lips with hot kisses.'

Maud Atkinson's view of 'sheikhs' plays an important part in de Beaujolais' adventures in the days to come.

Colonel Levasseur, in order to impress the townspeople, decrees a formal and full-dress parade of his entire garrison, set for an hour before sunset, to salute the Flag. De Beaujolais is of the opinion that the only impression this parade will have on the populus will be to leave them in no doubt as to the inadequacy of the French force. He makes his view known to Levasseur, who responds, officially, by ordering him to be present at the parade.

> The good Levasseur did not like me, and I wondered whether it was on account of Miss Vanbrugh or the fact that he was twenty years my senior and but one grade my superior in rank. Nor did I greatly love the good Levasseur, but I must be just to the brave colonel – for he died in Zaguig with a reddened

sword in one hand and an emptied revolver in the other, at the head of his splendid Zouaves.

De Beaujolais, having been ordered to be on parade, leaves his billet in full dress-uniform, booted and spurred and armed with sword and revolver. As he enters the street at the doorway to his billet, he sees a big horse, ridden by a female, being pursued by a group of Arabs, one of whom is running beside the horse, holding on to a stirrup leather. De Beaujolais knows that there is only one woman in Zaguig who would ride astride and on an officer's charger – Mary Vanbrugh! He gives chase and is in time to see the horse collapse, having been stabbed through the heart by the man running alongside it.

Dismounting, Mary runs up an outside flight of stairs that leads to the flat roof of a compound type of building, hotly pursued by the Arabs shouting: 'Hack the . . . in pieces and throw her to the dogs!' De Beaujolais follows, and on reaching the roof-top, springs into action, plying his trade. Mary, however, has not been idle. She is in a corner defending herself with her riding crop and her attackers have their backs to de Beaujolais. Deciding against making a 'fair' fight of it, he runs his sword through the back of a man who appears to be the leader, and then, withdrawing the steel, he lays about him with what, in the days of King Arthur, would have been called 'right good will'.

Mary assists by staging what could be called a side-show – laying in with her riding crop and in one instance taking an attacker, who is concentrating on de Beaujolais, around the neck from behind, and half choking him, before he is dispatched by de Beaujolais.

Rescue effected, skirmish won, de Beaujolais realises that he cannot take Mary back to the military compound and he quickly decides she will be safest in his billet until he can get her, and Maudie, whom he plans to bring to his billet, to Ibrahim Maghruf's house.

A remark made by Mary after the skirmish, supposedly illustrating the coolness of the all-American girl, is worth recording:

'The boys seem a little fresh. Some dog-fight, Major Ivan.' 'Major Ivan' has just dispatched seven tribesman, and an eighth is crawling away, deeply wounded.

Returning to his billet with Mary, he leaves her in the care of Achmet, his personal attendant, and goes off to bring Maudie away. This he accomplishes and then, leaving the two women, he proceeds to the 'safe' house.

The house, however, save for an ancient retainer, and Djikki, the Soudanese in charge of de Beaujolais' camels, is deserted. A message, left for de Beaujolais and given him by the retainer, is as follows:

'Jackals and hyenas enter the cave of the absent lion to steal his meat . . .'

The wily Ibrahim has cleared out, taking his family with him. He will not return until after the tiny garrison has been massacred and the subsequent looting has abated and a new and stronger garrison installed.

This is clearly no place for Mary and Maudie. Fortunately Maghruf's women have left a quantity of clothing behind which will come in useful for purposes of disguise.

De Beaujolais is now forced to join the parade (and warn Levasseur that the insurrection will take place that night).

Colonel Levasseur is holding what de Beaujolais describes as 'his futile' parade in the market square:

> a poor handful consisting of his 3rd Zouaves, a company of *Tirailleurs Algériens* – possibly none too loyal when the cry of the Faith went up – and a half-squadron of *Chasseurs d'Afrique*. What were these against a hundred thousand fanatics each anxious to attain remission of sins, and Paradise, by slaying an Infidel?
>
> The old story of the work of the soldier ruined by the hand of the politician.

[Rudyard Kipling would have agreed.]

De Beaujolais reaches the market-square through strangely empty streets – in itself an ominous sign. A dense and silent throng is watching the Review. Rooftops are crowded with onlookers, all eyes turned towards the minaret from where the expectant call of 'Kill! Kill!' is awaited.

De Beaujolais describes the scene thus:

> The Governor sat on his horse, his *officier d'ordonnance* behind him, with a bugler and a four of Zouave drummers. The band of the 3rd Zouaves was playing the *Marseillaise*.

The Governor (accusingly and offensively):	'You are late, Major.'
Henri:	'I am, Colonel, but I am alive. Which none of us will be in a few hours unless you take my advice and expect to be attacked at odds of a hundred to one, in an hour's time.'

The Major then tells Levasseur of the attack on Miss Mary Vanbrugh, and receives the following reply:

> 'Oh, you Intelligence people and your mares-nests! A gang of rude little street boys I expect!'
> . . . ten minutes later he dismissed the parade – the men marching off in five detachments, to the four gates of the city and to the Colonel's own headquarters respectively. As the troops left the Square, the mob, still silent, closed in, and every eye was turned unwaveringly to the minaret of the mosque . . .

Two points present themselves, neither of which Wren addresses:

Why does the mob not attack when Levasseur has his men in the open of the market-square – why wait until some of them have gained the shelter of the Residency?

What does Henri de Beaujolais expect his superior to do?

The answer to the first must be that the muezzin is cleverer than given credit for; he wants the troops scattered.

The answer to the second is that Levasseur can do nothing. It is too late to send for reinforcements and all he can do is deploy his limited troops as he thinks best, and await events. Having detachments at the city gates enables him to control entry to the city, at least.

Thus it seems that de Beaujolais is a little hard on him whom he called 'the good Colonel'!

Major Henri de Beaujolais is about to be put to the test, not for the last time. His dilemma is what to do with the two women and the ever-present possibility of orders which will take him away from Zaguig. Ibrahim Maghruf's house is no longer a proposition. He feels that it were best that the women remain in his quarters, even though they are known as the habitation of a *Franzawi* officer, disguised as Arab women, under the protection of Achmet. It is certainly not his inclination to cower in an upper back room with two women while his comrades fight their last fight.

CHAPTER 5

Raoul d'Auray de Redon and Others

O N HIS ARRIVAL in Zaguig, Major Henri de Beaujolais had found a sealed letter awaiting him. The letter, containing orders, gives as well a very clear picture of the French government's intentions in what has now come to be known as 'The scramble for Africa'.

Extracts from the letter from Henri's uncle, the General:

'. . . and so, my dear Henri, comes your chance – the work for which the tool has been fashioned . . . you will have to be as swift and silent as you will have to be clever, and you must stand or fall absolutely alone. If they fillet you and boil you in oil – you will have to boil unavenged . . .

'A desert column operating in that direction would rouse such a howl in the German Press, and in one or two others, as would do infinite harm at home, and would hamper and hinder my work here for years . . .

'I am expecting the sanction of a million francs which will subsidise the Federation as long as it remains in alliance with France and rejects all overtures to Pan-Islamism. That (Pan-Islamism) is the fear and the danger . . . to our young and growing African Empire . . .

'What makes me anxious, is the possibility of this new and and remarkable Emir el Hamel el Kebir announcing himself to be that very Mahdi whom the Bedouin tribes of that part are always expecting – a sort of Messiah.

'As you know, the Senussi Sidi el Mahdi, the holiest prophet since Mohommet, is supposed to be still alive. He disappeared at Garu on the way to Wadai, and an empty coffin was buried with tremendous pomp and religious fervour at holy Kufara.

'If this Emir el Hamel el Kebir takes it into his head to announce that he is the Mahdi, we shall get precisely what the British got from their Mahdi at Khartoum – for he has got the strongest tribal confederation yet known . . .

'Well – I hope you won't be a Gordon, nor I a Wolseley-Kitchener . . .

'You get a treaty made with this Emir . . . and you will have created a buffer-state just where France needs it most . . .

'When you get word, be gone in the same hour, and let nothing whatsoever delay you for a minute. D'Auray de Redon came through from Kufara with one of Ibrahim Maghruf's

> *caravans and saw this Mahdi or Prophet himself . . . he takes a very serious view and thinks it means a jehad sooner or later.'*

[We are not told of de Redon's visit to el Hamel, but we are told of how he falls in with a disaffected Arab who fled from el Hamel's forces after the battle of the Pass of Bab-el Hoggar. This man, we later learn that his name is Suleiman the Strong, is to be de Beaujolais' guide in his quest to find Emir el Hamel el Kebir.]

> *'In conclusion – regard this as the most important thing in the world – to yourself, to me, and to France . . .'*

There is a post-script to this letter and de Beaujolais feels that it is intended to convey more than just 'Service news'.

> *'By the way, I have broken Captain de Lannec, as I promised him (and you too) that I would do to anyone, who in any way failed me . . . A woman, of course . . .'*

De Lannec had strayed from his orders. He had been sent to relieve a certain Captain St André and instead had gone off into the mountains where rumour had it that a Frenchwoman was being held captive by tribesmen.

[Captain St André was killed in the defence of Zinderneuf. He had left the Secret Service and signed on as a legionnaire.]

> *'It seems as if de Lannec had known her in Paris . . . ..One Véronique Vaux . . . Loved her, perhaps . . . He turned aside from his duty; he wasted a week in getting the woman; another in placing her in safety; and then he was so good as to attend to the affairs of his General, his Service and his Country! Exit de Lannec!'*

[Exit de Lannac! The general may have dismissed him – but Wren had not.]

De Beaujolais can only reflect.

> Serve him right of course! . . . Yes, of course . . . A little hard? . . . Very, very sad – for he was a most promising officer, a tiger in battle, and a fox on Secret Service; no braver, cleverer, finer fellow in the French army . . . But yes, it served him right, certainly . . . He had acted very wrongly – putting personal feelings and the fate of a *woman* before the welfare of France, before the orders of his Commander . . . He deserved his punishment . . . Yes . . . He had actually put a mere woman before *Duty. Exit de Lannec.*
>
> Serve him right, poor devil . . .
>
> And then the Imp that dwells at the back of my mind said to the Angel that dwells at the front of my mind:

> 'Suppose the captured woman, dwelling in that unthinkable slavery of pollution and torture, had been that beautiful, queenly and adored lady, the noble wife of the stern General Bertrand de Beaujolais himself?'
> Silence, vile Imp! *No one* comes before Duty. Duty is a Jealous God.
> I was to think more about de Lannec ere long.

At the start de Beaujolais does not like the beautiful Mary Vanbrugh. She ribs him – gets under his skin – calls him 'Major Ivan', a veiled reference to that great warrior of song, 'Ivan Skavinsky Skavar', a tune she is not averse to humming whenever he is around.

De Beaujolais does not like the fact that she and her brother Otis are in Zaguig at all. He, Dufour and de Redon know that an uprising is imminent. The great friend of the French, Ibrahim Maghruf, has warned him, and is himself about to depart for healthier climes.

On quitting the parade, at which Colonel Levasseur has displayed his hopelessly inadequate garrison to the populous, de Beaujolais returns to his billet, all the while racking his brains as to what he should do about the two women hiding there in disguise.

> As I swung down from my horse in the lane at the back of my house, I was conscious of a very filthy and ragged Arab, squatting against the wall, his staff, begging bowl and rosary beside him . . . He muttered in Arabic and then in French, 'Start at once . . .'

It is none other than Captain Raoul d'Auray de Redon, and it is he who had brought the long awaited orders.

De Beaujolais can think only of his uncle's last words in the letter, 'Begone in the same hour.'

> This was ghastly! I should be *escaping in disguise* from Zaguig, at the very time my brothers-in-arms were fighting for their lives . . . I should be leaving Mary Vanbrugh to death or worse than death . . .

[Yet if Henri knew that he must fulfil his duty to France and his uncle, his superior officer, there was no point in his staying in Zaguig to perish with the garrison. He himself has stated quite clearly that there will be no survivors. In this he is wrong as we learn later.]

Acting rapidly, de Beaujolais dons his disguise – that of a good-class Bedouin. Whilst robing himself he sends Achmet to fetch Otis Vanbrugh from the Governor's house. He then attends to de Redon, who informs him that the uprising will start that night:

'The tribes are up, all around the north-west and are hurrying in. It's for sunset this evening.'

De Beaujolais then informs de Redon of the presence of the two European girls.

De Redon: 'God help them. They'll be alone in an hour.'

De Beaujolais then asks de Redon if he is to ride south with him to meet the Emir, and conclude, if possible, the desired treaty:

> 'No – the General does not want us both killed by this Emir lad. He thinks that you're the man to pull it off, now that poor de Lannec's gone. I begged him to let me go, as it was I who brought him confirmation of the existence of this upstart Emir. Said it was such almost certain death too, that he'd prefer to send his nephew. I shall join the mob here and lead them all over the shop on false scents – confuse and start rumours – then I'll get back with the news of what's happened here!'

Achmet returns from the Residency with Otis Vanbrugh. On being offered the option of hiding out in de Beaujolais' rooms with his sister and Maudie, Vanbrugh responds:

'Hide nothing, sir! I shall fight alongside my host and his men.'

'*Un brave*,' from de Redon.

> He was – and yet he was a gentle, refined and scholarly person. I thought of James Love Allen and 'Kentucky Cardinals'. He had the eyes and forehead of a dreaming philosopher – but he had the mouth and chin of a *man*.

The first of the many conflicts and verbal exchanges between Mary Vanbrugh and de Beaujolais, over their differing notions of 'duty', now takes place:

Henri:	'I am leaving Zaguig at once!'
Mary:	'Not escaping?'
De Redon:	'Major de Beaujolais has just received dispatches, and has to go.'
Mary:	'How very convenient for the major. And' (indicating de Redon) 'who is this nobleman, anyway, one may ask?'
Henri:	'Let me present Captain Raoul d'Auray de Redon', (indicating the filthy beggar).
Mary:	'Don't present him too close! You escaping too?'
De Redon:	'*Non*, Mademoiselle, I am not escaping. Neither is Major de Beaujolais. He is going on duty, infinitely against his will at such a

time. But he's going to dangers quite as great as those in Zaguig at this moment.'

I could have embraced my friend! (No de Lannec follies for Henri de Beaujolais!)

Inevitably, in the end, de Beaujolais sets out on his mission accompanied by Mary and Maudie and his extremely small troop. He cannot bring himself to abandon these two women to what he knows will be a frightful and fatal end.

De Redon it is, though, who plays the trump card: 'Take the two girls in a *bassourab*. It would add to your plausibility in a way to have a *hareem* with you. You might be able to hand them over to a north-bound caravan.'

De Beaujolais makes one last effort (to de Redon): 'Wouldn't you . . .?'

'Stop it, Henri. I'm not de Lannec. My job's here, and you know it.'

De Beaujolais relents, as he must, as he is already, although he does not know it, in love with one of the girls. But it is no meek submission on his part – he lays down the rules, the law, and reads the riot act:

'I take no responsibility for Miss Vanbrugh, that she realises what she is doing, and that I shall not deviate a hair's breadth from what I consider my duty.'

'Oh, Major! You *are* so pressing!'

I turned away as Vanbrugh crushed his sister to his breast.

That poor unworthy fool, de Lannec!

CHAPTER 6

Abandoned

MAJOR HENRI DE BEAUJOLAIS' destination is the Great Oasis, ruled over by the Emir Sheikh el Hamel el Kebir and his Vizier, Sheikh el Habibka; a treaty with this powerful despot is his aim.

The party that leaves Zaguig is a small but well-equipped one and is made up of de Beaujolais, Dufour, Achmet, Djikki, and a guide, by name Suleiman the Strong. In addition to the fighting men there are Mary Vanbrugh and her personal maid, Maud Atkinson. The camel which these two ride on is equipped with a *bassourab* (a small hooped tent rigged over the camel-saddle). The whole party are mounted on excellent camels and the baggage is carried by strong baggage-camels.

De Redon: 'Better go, Major. It's begun!'

> As he spoke, a growing murmur of which I had been subconsciously aware of for some minutes – a murmur like the sound of a distant sea breaking on a pebble beach – rose swiftly to a roar, menacing and dreadful, a roar above which individual yells leapt clear like leaping spray above the waves. Rifles banged irregularly and then came crash after crash of steady volley-firing.
>
> '*En avant – marche!*'

Quitting the town presents no great problem. Most tribesmen not engaged in the siege of the Government Residency are busy looting and take no notice of de Beaujolais' small band. On the one occasion that a small band, hurrying in from the district and taking de Beaujolais' party for one laden with loot, attempts to despoil them, Henri promptly shoots its leader through the head.

'A bell-ringer for Major Ivan,' from Mary. [This is an Americanism with which the author is unfamiliar.]

Once clear of the town the journey south proceeds without undue incident. Mary, dressed as a man, is now riding her own camel. Maudie, who has never ridden in her life, is slowly settling into the rhythm of a camel and occupies the *bassourab* on her own.

When bivouacked Mary and Henri continue their discussion on 'duty' and the light in which both see it.

De Beaujolais:	'Do you know, the devil tried to tempt me last night to give the order to saddle-up and ride north, and put you in a place of safety.'
Mary:	'Did you fall, Major?'
De Beaujolais:	'I did not even listen to the tempter. But I'm feeling horribly worried and frightened and anxious about you.'
Mary:	'Business down yonder urgent, Major?'
De Beaujolais:	'Very.'
Mary:	'Then defy the devil and all his works, Major, and don't let my welfare interfere with yours. And don't play Joseph's Brethren with me by handing me over to a north-bound caravan. I'm coming right along with you – to share and share alike.'

A Targui scout, motionless on his *mehara* camel, on a high sandhill, one evening, is the first sign of trouble. The scout will report back to the main body of Touareg and soon de Beaujolais and his party will know that they are being followed.

Soon a small skirmish, by way of a pipe-opener, takes place with the vanguard of the Touareg. In this skirmish de Beaujolais is wounded in his left arm. Although only a flesh wound it makes matters such as fighting, and there is to be fighting, difficult for him. It does, however, place him in the nursing care of Mary, where he is more than happy to be!

Dufour, who has been talking to Suleiman, discloses to his chief that a few miles to the south-east there is a *shott* that extends to the base of a range of mountains. The strip of land between the *shott* and the mountain base being very narrow, it seems a good place to make for, and there attempt to fight off the Touareg.

Dufour:	'That will be the place for us, Sir.'

'Yes, this is the place for us, and this is where I will "abandon my children",' I thought to myself.

And this is the truth of it. Major Henri de Beaujolais makes a run for it, taking Mary (much against her will) and Maudie with him, leaving Dufour to hold the pass, in what Wren refers to as an 'African Thermopolae'.

> It would be a very miserable and heart-breaking duty – to ride on and leave my men to hold that pass – that I might escape and fulfil my mission.
>
> However it is useless to attempt to serve one's country in the Secret Service, if one's private feelings, loves, desires, sorrows, are allowed to come between

one and one's country's good. Poor de Lannec!

There was one grain of comfort – nothing would be gained by my staying and dying with my followers. It would profit them nothing at all. They would die just the same. If the Touareg, by dint of numbers, could overcome four, they could overcome five. I could not save them by staying with them.

The pass appears to be an excellent defensive position: it is narrow and rock-strewn, not more than a hundred yards in width.

De Beaujolais to Dufour:	'You'll hold this pass while there is a man of you alive.'
	'*Oui, mon Commandant.*'
	'Should the Touareg abandon the attempt, any survivor is to ride due south-east until he reaches the Great Oasis.'
	'*Oui, mon Commandant.*'
	'But I fear there won't be any survivors – four against a *harka*, say a hundred to one . . . but you must hold them up until I'm well away . . . they won't charge while your shooting is quick and accurate . . . when they do they'll get you, of course . . . don't ride for it at the last moment . . . see it through here, to give the impression that you are the whole party. I must not be pursued. Die here.'
	'*Oui, mon Commandant.*'
Mary Vanbrugh (icily cold and incisive):	'Excuse me, Major de Beaujolais, is it possible that you are talking about *deserting your men*? Leaving them to die here while you escape? *Ordering* them to remain here to increase your own chance of safety in fact.'
	'I was giving instructions to my subordinate. Would you be good enough to refrain from interrupting.'

My uncle's words burned before my eyes! '*A woman, of course!* . . . *He turned aside from his duty . . . Exit de Lannec.*'

There is no doubt that these must have been terrible orders to issue. One can only pity, and feel for Henri de Beaujolais. He *is* deserting his friends.

A battle of wills ensues. Mary refuses to leave the defending party. Henri must, and will go – and yet he cannot bring himself to leave two women, doomed to certain death, behind.

Suleiman, standing watch, calls that a rider is approaching on the horizon:

'It is Djikki, the black slave.'

'Djikki, the French Soudanese soldier, you dog.'

And here Wren commits one of those small and rare errors. The party was a Bedouin party – they were all dressed as Arabs. Not on any account would de Beaujolais have admitted to Djikki being a 'French' soldier.

Djikki's intelligence is that the Touareg are an hour's ride away and that the *harka* numbers 'a battalion'.

Ultimately de Beaujolais' point, that if four could not prevail against the Touareg, five could not, convinces Mary; but she insists on a temporary compromise. Before riding away from the action they are to show that there are six rifles, not four, making the stand.

De Beaujolais is thus there to conduct the opening stages of the battle: '*Fixe. Feux de salve. En joue. Feu!*'

After several volleys he gives the order, *feu de joie* (rapid fire), and then he pulls Mary away from her firing position, and he, Mary and Maudie, ride away to the south.

During the ride south de Beaujolais tells Mary of his deep attachment to the men he has deserted. All of them, Suleiman excepted, have, at one time or another, saved his life. Not only have they saved his life and served him faithfully, they are his friends. Dufour has been with him from the day he joined the Blue Hussars and in his French way de Beaujolais refers to them as his 'children'.

Dufour, who is left in command of the small defending garrison, is indeed a man amongst men. He accepts his orders, orders to die, without a murmur of dissent. At Zinderneuf he proved to be a normal man, a man with normal fears as well as fears of the supernatural. And here, at the pass of the salt-lake, he accepts his fate without a murmur.

> Indeed, and indeed, ours is a hard Service, a Service for hard men, but a noble Service. And – duty is indeed a jealous God.

CHAPTER 7

The Great Oasis

A ND, ONE WEARY DAY, as we topped a long hill, we saw a sight that made me rub my eyes.

The sight is that of a troop of camels and their riders, deploying as would a Camel Corps trained by western drill sergeants. De Beaujolais likens the manoeuvring of this Camel Corps to that of a troop of Spahis. He could pay no greater compliment.

There is no escape. They can neither flee nor fight – surrender, and hope for decent treatment, is the only choice. Riding towards the Corps, de Beaujolais gives the universally accepted sign of surrender – he holds his hands above his head.

The commander of the Corps, a powerful dwarf, introduces himself as Marbruk ben Hassan, 'Commander of a hundred in the army of my Lord the Emir el Hamel el Kebir'.

> We rode on, prisoner-guests of this fierce, rough, but fairly courteous Arab, in a hollow-square of riflemen whose equipment, bearing and discipline I could not but admire. And what if this Emir had an army of such – and chose to preach a *jehad*, a Holy War for the establishment of a Pan-Islamic Empire and the overthrow of the power of the Infidel in Africa?

The *Jehad* or Holy War was very much in the mind of western statesmen at the beginning of the twentieth century – perhaps it still is.

The small captive-guest party is escorted to the guest tent, which it finds to be divided in two, one section for men, the other for females. Thus de Beaujolais occupies one half of the tent and Mary and Maudie, who are presumed to be his wives, the other.

'Our Lord, the Emir el Hamel el Kebir offers you the three days' hospitality, due by Koranic Law – and by the generosity of his heart – to all travellers. All that he has is yours.'

This was the message brought them from the Emir, and de Beaujolais wonders whether this might not include 'the edge of his sword'!

Wasting no time de Beaujolais washes, shaves and dons his uniform, that of a French field officer, and thus arrayed he is presented to the Emir.

De Beaujolais' years of training in the Secret Service, should now, hopefully, pay off. He has to assess the Emir and his Vizier and his assessment must be accurate so that he can gauge how far to go and how far not to go in the negotiations which will ensue.

> Seated on dyed camel-hair rugs piled on a carpet, were the Emir el Hamel el Kebir and his Vizier, the Sheikh el Habibka, stately men in fine raiment.
>
> I saw at a glance that the Emir, whatever he might claim to be, was no member of the family of El Sayed Yussef Haroun el Sayed el Mahdi el Senussi, and that if he pretended to be the expected 'Messiah', el Mahdi el Senussi, he was an imposter.
>
> For he was most unmistakably of Touareg stock, and from nowhere else could he have got the grey eyes of Vandal origin, which are fairly common among the Touareg, many of whom are blue-eyed and ruddy-haired.
>
> I liked his face immediately. This black-bearded, black-browed, hawk-faced Arab was a man of character, force and power. But I wished I could see the mouth hidden beneath the mass of moustache and beard.
>
> The Vizier, whose favour might be most important, I took to be of Touareg or Berber-Bedouin stock, he too being somewhat fair for a desert Arab. He was obviously a distaff blood-relation of the Emir.
>
> These two men removed the mouth-pieces of their long-stemmed *narghilehs* from their lips and stared *and* stared at me in petrified astonishment – to which they were too stoical or too well-bred to give other expression.
>
> [Any desert Arab, seeing before him a man in a full uniform of the French army would, naturally, be stupefied.]
>
> Had not the idea been too absurd, I could almost have thought that I saw a look of fear in their eyes. Perhaps they thought for a moment that I was the herald of a French army that was even then getting into position round the oasis!
>
> Fear is the father of cruelty . . .

De Beaujolais then greets the Emir in accepted terms and the Emir replies: 'in an accent with which I was not familiar', and then de Beaujolais, wastes no time in telling the Emir of the defence of the pass at the salt lakes and of his fears for his men.

The Emir summons Marbruk ben Hassan, the powerful cripple, and soon his commander of a hundred is, with his men, on his way to investigate the scene of the battle and to scout out the whereabouts of the Touareg. It is not in the Emir's interests to have Touareg too close to his domains.

As de Beaujolais has shed his Arab disguise it is time too for Mary and Maudie to do likewise.

> *The Emir:* 'I am informed that wives of the *Roumis* eat with their lords in the presence of other men.' And goes on to request that the *Sitts* 'grace his tent'.

De Beaujolais explains that the two females are not his wives and proceeds to give an account of the massacre at Zaguig and his flight therefrom.

> *The Emir:* 'You will receive no such treatment here as they of Zaguig meted out to you. They who come in peace remain in peace. They who come in war remain in peace also – the peace of Death. Do you come in peace or in war, *Roumi*?'

On receiving the reply that he comes in peace, de Beaujolais feels that both the Emir and the Vizier look relieved and he again wonders if the two are thinking of the presence of a French army in the neighbourhood!

The introduction of Mary and Maudie to the two Arab rulers proves interesting. They enter the Emir's tent in Arab dress and then discard their *barracans,* thus exposing two Paris frocks which Mary, far-sighted woman, has packed into the portmanteau in Zaguig. The effect on the Emir and the Vizier is 'electrical,' and de Beaujolais supposes that neither man has ever seen a white woman before.

The impact of meeting 'Sheikhs' was most pronounced on Maudie. All she can utter was, 'real Sheikhs' and 'Oh, sir, isn't the big one a lovely man!'

An imposing introduction is then made by de Beaujolais:

'The Lady Sitt Miriyam Hankinson el Vanbrugh, and the Sitt Maud el Atkinson.'

Mary, in her inimitable way, cannot resist indulging in a bit of Americanism:

'Well, well, Major! Arn't they sure-enough genuine Parlour Sheikhs of song and story.' And before de Beaujolais can stop her, she offers her hand to the Emir.

> Probably neither the Emir nor the Vizier had ever 'shaken hands' before. Both made a good showing at this new ceremonial of the strange *Roumis* and their somewhat brazen, unveiled females. Indeed, the Vizier seemed to know more about holding Mary's hand than releasing it . . .

As the meal progressed and the sense of shyness and strangeness wore off, I was glad that the Sheikh and his Vizier could not possibly know a word of English, for Miss Vanburgh's criticisms were pungent and Maudie's admiration fulsome.

Mary, on top form, determines to sing a song, instructing the Major to tell their hosts that it is the custom of westerners to sing after-dinner songs, and before de Beaujolais can express his objections she launches into:

> The sons of the Prophet are hardy and bold,
>   and quite unaccustomed to fear:
> But of all the most reckless of life and of limb,
>   Was Abdul the Bul-bul Emir!

These are new words to de Beaujolais, but the tune is that same niggling one he has so often heard.

As the Arabs sat there almost open-mouthed I felt that if the worst came to the worst Maudie would be imprisoned in the Emir's *hareem* and Mary in that of Sheikh el Habibka – unless the Emir took them both . . .

The banquet drags on and Mary, tiring of the proceedings, declares in a loud voice,

'Well, Major, it's time you went to bed. Remember you're a sick man.'

And when de Beaujolais, thanking the powers that be that neither sheikh can speak English, explains that they cannot leave until the Emir decrees they may, Mary goes on,

'Well, I wish he'd do it, the old coot . . . he's not the perfect little gentleman he thinks he is.'

Shortly after these remarks the Emir ends the proceedings with a protracted leave-taking which involves the much shaking of hands!

On entering the guest-tent de Beaujolais remarks: 'Scream if there's any trouble in the night.'

To which remark Mary makes reply: 'Scream? I shall shoot. Let the *trouble* do the screaming.'

Such is the independence of Mary Vanbrugh!

The following day de Beaujolais outlines the terms of the Treaty to the Emir and his Vizier, dwelling on the blessings of civilisation which would flow from the Treaty.

The Emir muses: 'Blessings of civilisation! Drink . . . Disease . . . Unrest . . . Machine-guns . . .'

But press as he may de Beaujolais finds that the two Arab rulers are timeless men – they are in no hurry to sign anything, and put de Beaujolais off with one excuse after another. He must wait.

In the meantime riding parties are organised, sometimes on horse-back and sometimes on camels; the Emir riding out with Mary and returning with Maudie and the Vizier at the other end of this exchange of riding partners. As for de Beaujolais, he is compelled to ride along with minor sheikhs, councillors or plain 'hangers-on'.

As the days pass de Beaujolais is forced to conclude that the Emir and the Vizier are planning to hold the two women captive, each taking the one he fancies into his *hareem*, or the Emir, being the more powerful, taking both.

When the Treaty is mentioned the reply is always the same: 'We will talk of it tomorrow, *In Shallah*.'

But tomorrow never comes.

CHAPTER 8

Fears Confirmed

THE RETURN of Marbruk ben Hassan and his camel-squadron brought me news that depressed me to the depths.

Evidently my heroes had fought to their last cartridge and had then been overwhelmed. Beneath a great cairn of stones Marbruk and his men had buried the remains of Dufour, Achmet and Djikki. There was a track of a single camel fleeing south-eastward from the spot; Suleiman had deserted.

We are now introduced to the future Sheikh of the tribe, a young boy, Yussuf Latif Fetata, and his sister, 'a most lovely girl', by name the Sitt Leila Hakhla. Two things are clear from the introduction to the scene of these two characters. Firstly, the line of succession of ruler of the tribe has been ordained – the Emir el Hamel el Kebir is in fact a Sheikh-regent, holding the tribe together until such time as the young boy becomes of age to rule in his own right.

Next, we learn that Sitt Leila Hakhla, though still a young girl, worships the Emir el Hamel (and detests Maudie, 'from whose face the Emir's eye roved but seldom').

Major de Beaujolais now treats us to a homily on the amorous natures of the darker races:

> An amorous Arab is something very amorous indeed. With these desert despots, the desire is to take, and if I were an obstacle it would be very easy to remove me. And what of the girls then . . .?

The out-rides now become an almost daily occurrence. It is clear that the Emir is falling in love with Maudie, and she with him (dreaming of Sheikhs!). Sheikh el Habibka, the Vizier, it is clear too, is falling in love with Mary Vanbrugh. De Beaujolais notes that Mary does not exactly 'flirt' with el Habibka, but she undoubtedly enjoys his company – but then she enjoys that of the Emir as well.

Musing on these rides, de Beaujolais comes to the conclusion that they must have been 'silent rides – with a strange dumb alphabet!' And he feels that 'any love-making would have to be done in dumb-show . . .'

For a Frenchman, the gallant Major appears somewhat naive!

Henri speaks to Mary of his fears for her and Maudie's safety, and receives the following reply:

> 'Don't you worry, Major de Beaujolais. I tell you they are *all right*. Yes, *both* of them. I am just as safe with them as I am with you . . . and I'm *awfully* safe with you, Major, am I not?'
> Women always know better than men – until they find they know nothing about the matter at all.

The testing time for Henri de Beaujolais has come.

> Then to me, one night, came the Emir and the Vizier, clearly on business bent.

They are willing to sign the Treaty but on certain additional terms. By now we should have a shrewd idea as to the nature of these 'additional terms'. Apparently de Beaujolais has no idea as to what they could be, and so when they are put:

'That you take the treaty, signed and sealed by me, and witnessed by my Vizier and twelve Ekhwan – *and leave the two Sitts whom you brought here;*' de Beaujolais for once loses what we would today term 'his cool'. Duty and love and honour do battle in his mind, and suddenly he is clear in his mind:

> *'Damn your black face and blacker soul, you filthy hound! Get out of my tent before I throw you out, you bestial swine!* WHITE WOMEN! *You black dogs and sons of dogs . . .!'*
> . . . and shaking with rage, I pointed to the doorway of my tent. They rose and went – and with them, all my hopes of success.

Strange words which could have issued from the mouth of a later twentieth century apartheid-minded person. The stressing of white women would not find much favour these days in our so-called emancipated society.

> *Oh, splendid de Lannec! He was right, of course.*

From the other side of the felt wall that divided the guest-tent:
'Your language certainly sounded bad, Major! I'm glad I don't understand Arabic!'

> It was the next morning that Miss Vanbrugh greeted me with the words:
> 'Major, you haven't congratulated me yet. I had an honest-to-God offer of marriage from a leading citizen of this burg yesterday . . . I'm blushing still . . . Inwardly . . .'

I was horrified. What next? And I could only ask 'who from' knowing that the offer could have come only from one of two persons.

In reply to Henri's question, 'who from?', Mary replies, 'From the Sheikh El Habibka.'

De Beaujolais: 'But how did he make the proposal? No one here can speak English or French and I was not around to interpret.'

Mary: 'By signs and wonders – he certainly made himself clear.'

I stammered, hardly knowing how to ask if the ruffian had seized her in his hot, amorous embrace and made fierce love to her. My blood boiled, though my heart sank, and I knew that depth of trembling apprehension that is the true fear – the fear for another, whom we esteem.

'Miss Vanbrugh, we shall have to walk very delicately,' I said.

Mary: 'So will the Sheikh-lad. But don't go prying heavy-hoofed into a young thing's first love affair, Major – for I won't stand for it.'

De Beaujolais knows that Mary Vanbrugh always carries a revolver with her. The fact that el Habibka is still alive leads him to believe that there has been no violence.

Wren's hero is sadly missing the point. Mary is a tease!

De Beaujolais is now put under virtual 'house arrest', a big Soudanese sentry being posted at the door of his tent. Life for him is further complicated by the fact that he is advised that Suleiman the Strong has arrived at the Great Oasis. The intelligence is brought to him by the chief *marabout* of the tribe, Hadji Abdul Salam. This holy man is not only a schemer, he is a potential murderer and assassin as well. Not only does he put certain facts before de Beaujolais, he also makes certain proposals.

These are:

That de Beaujolais escapes, with his help, and in return for this help he asks de Beaujolais to return with a French army, defeat the Emir, and make him, the Hadji, ruler of the Great Oasis, or

That Suleiman the Strong be assisted in the assassination of the Emir, and de Beaujolais then uses his influence to place the Hadji in the seat of power. And what of Suleiman after he has put paid to the Emir? The Hadji would see to it that he was poisoned!

De Beaujolais sounds the Hadji out on the possibility of an escape organised to include the women. This is impossible – the two girls are guarded even more closely than de Beaujolais himself is guarded, not so much against escaping, but against penetration of their quarters by undesirables of the tribe.

The Hadji then makes it clear that de Beaujolais is to go alone (and return with the price of the Treaty and a French army) or not at all. And here he places a second set of facts before de Beaujolais:

'. . . *there are other messengers from another Power, here, in the Great Oasis* . . .'

The Hadji goes on:

'It is a small caravan, but very well equipped. There is plenty of money behind it . . . I never saw better camels nor weapons, and their hired camel-men are well paid and content. Our fair Lord gives them audience daily in their camp.'

Of all the double dealers this holy Hadji must be the worst. He is openly playing de Beaujolais off against the party from another Power. He has been promised much gold if he will poison de Beaujolais and the two *Sitts*.

After much bargaining de Beaujolais persuades the Hadji to take him to the *sharab* (camp) of the rival players in the game.

Entering their principal tent de Beaujolais finds two men asleep on rugs. One is an obvious Oriental and the other is of lighter complexion, with an enormous black beard.

If, reader, you have not guessed who this man with an enormous black beard is, you are about to learn.

> I struck the sleeper heavily on the chest:
> 'Bonjour, mon cher Monsieur Becque!'
> '*Himmel*,' he exclaimed [just as he had done in Zaguig when de Redon had struck him on the head with his camel stick].

It is strange, but nevertheless, the story runs in such a fashion, that we find the Emir and Vizier are also on a visit to the emissaries of the Second Power. Have they been informed of de Beaujolais' visit? Or is it one of their regular visits, as told by the Hadji? We are never to learn – but they arrive at a most opportune time – just as Becque's companion gets the 'drop' on de Beaujolais.

> Like a fool, I had absolutely forgotten the second man in my excitement at discovering that it was indeed *Becque* . . . ..My old friend, *Becque*!

[A trained soldier, such as de Beaujolais, should not overlook these matters, even in excitement.]

On enquiring from the Emir the reasons for his presence in Becque's tent, de Beaujolais explains that Becque is a traitor to France, that he has been plotting (with the Hadji) to poison the two women who had accompanied him to the Great Oasis and that he is plotting to have the Emir murdered. He further tells the Emir of his first duel with Becque and proposes a second one, now.

Becque and de Beaujolais have been speaking to one another in French. How is it possible that the Emir understood what was being said? This thought flashes through de Beaujolais' mind and he concludes that actions speak louder than words!

> I ask you to let me meet him face to face and foot to foot and sword to sword – that I may punish him and rid my country of a matricidal renegade . . .
>
> *The Emir:*   'And what says our other honoured guest?'
>
> *Becque (ever game):*   'Oh, I'll fight him. It will give me great pleasure to kill this chatter-box . . . the bright *de Beaujolais* . . . de Beaujolais – the Beau Sabreur of the Blue Hussars! de Beaujolais, the Beau Sabreur of the Spahis and the Secret Service! de Beaujolais, the hero of Zinderneuf.'

De Beaujolais is somewhat taken aback at the mention of Zinderneuf:

> But how in the name of his father the Devil did he know anything of the affair at Zinderneuf?
>
> 'You will fight at dawn and with . . . swords,' said the Emir.
>
> Half an hour later, Becque and I stood face to face. We were stripped to the waist, and wore only baggy Arab trousers and soft boots.
>
> Each held a noble two-edged sword, pliant as cane, sharp as a razor, exact model of those brought to the country by Louis the Good and his Crusaders. I verily believe they were Crusaders' swords, for there are many such in that dry desert where nothing rusts and a good sword is more prized, cared for, and treasured, than a good woman.

De Beaujolais tells us that Becque 'peeled well'. He is finely muscled and in splendid condition. As in the first duel, when Becque and de Beaujolais were troopers in the Blue Hussars, Becque rushes his opponent, fighting furiously and tiring himself out.

De Beaujolais describes the duel:

> He rushed me like a tiger, his sword moving like forked lightning, and I gave my whole mind and body to parry and defence . . .
>
> All critics of my 'form' have praised my foot-work, and I used my feet and brain to save my arm, for the swords were heavy . . .

[Much thrusting and parrying]

Suddenly his sword went up and back, as to smite straight down upon my skull, and, judging that I had time for the manoeuvre, I did not parry – but sprang to my left and slashed in a smart *coup de flanc* that took him across the ribs beneath the raised right arm; a gash that would mean a nice little blood-letting . . . In the same second, his sword fell perpendicularly on my right thigh, merely slicing off an inconsiderable – shall I say 'rasher' . . .

I had drawn first blood and I had inflicted a wound and received a graze.

'Mary Vanbrugh,' I whispered.

He began to retreat; he retreated quickly; he almost ran backwards for a few paces – and, as I swiftly followed, he ducked, most cleverly and swiftly, below my sword and lunged splendidly at my breast. A side step only just saved me, for his point and edge cut my upper arm as it rested for a moment against my body . . . But the quick *riposte* has always been my strong point, and before his sword returned on guard, I cut him heavily across the head.

'Mary Vanbrugh.'

And then my opponent changed his tactics and used his sword two-handed. One successful stroke delivered thus would lop off a limb or sever a head from a body.

It was rhinoceros against leopard now . . .

Hitherto we had crossed swords point downward, as in 'sabres', now I held my point upward as in 'foils', and dodged and danced on my toes, feinting for a thrust.

Cut or thrust?

A cut from Becque would be death for de Beaujolais . . . a thrust from de Beaujolais would be death for Becque.

My foe forced the pace again . . . He rushed like a bull, and I dodged like a matador. A hundred times his sword swept past my head like a mighty scythe, and so swift was he that never had I a chance for the matador's stroke – the *coup de grâce*. We were both panting, our breath whistling through parched throats and mouths, our bare chests heaving like bellows . . . We were streaming with sweat and blood.

'Mary Vanbrugh.'

Becque, with a look of devilish hate and rage upon his contorted face, swept his sword once more above his head, and this time swept it up too far! It was well above his head – and pointing downward behind him – for a stroke that should cleave me to the chin, when I dropped my point and lunged with all my strength and speed . . .

'Mary Vanbrugh.'

I had won. My sword stood out a foot behind him . . .

Becque was not dead but being far from hospitals and surgeons it was not likely that he would survive.

Mary Vanbrugh and her first aid kit are sent for. She arrives, accompanied by El R'Orab the Crow carrying the medicines.

De Beaujolais, who has been fighting for her, now receives a jolt to his ego:

Mary, in a voice of ice and steel: 'Your work? More *Duty*? [Bitter and scathing] Oh! You killer, you professional paid hireling *Slayer*. Oh, you *Murderer* in the sacred name of your *Duty*!'

Once Becque's wounds have been dressed he is removed to the guest-tents and laid on de Beaujolais' bed, the better for Mary to attend to his wounds.

Then turning to de Beaujolais: 'I'll attend to *you* now, Killer.'

Henri avers that he can attend to himself and if need be he will summon the holy Hadji Abdul Salam to assist him.

What looks like a nasty case of pettyness developing between our two heroes is averted by de Beaujolais doing the correct thing – he goes down in a dead faint. Rest and bandages and cognac soon put him to rights but Mary in her obstinate manner insists on calling him 'Killer'.

Then Henri says something that he regrets for ever afterwards:

'It is not so long since you were fairly glad of the killing-powers of a Killer . . . On a certain roof in Zaguig, the Killer against eight, and your life in the balance . . . I apologize for reminding you . . . I am ashamed . . .'

[And he really is ashamed of himself. He feels in that lovely old-fashioned phrase, *a cad*.]

> 'I am ashamed . . . I apologize – humbly, Major de Beaujolais,' she replied, and her eyes were slightly suffused as I took her hand and pressed it to my lips . . . 'But oh! why do you . . . why must you . . . all these fine men . . . Dufour, Achmet, Djikki, and now this poor mangled butchered creature . . . Can you find no Duty that is help and kindness and love, instead of this Duty of killing, maiming, hurting . . . ?'
>
> Yes – I was beginning to think that I could find a Duty that was Love . . .

The last action involving Becque is played out that night.

Becque: 'So you win, de Beaujolais.'

> 'I win, Becque.' I would not rejoice over a fallen foe, and I would not express regret to a villainous renegade and a treacherous cur – who, moreover, had plotted the death, mutilation and dishonour of two white girls (and one of them Mary Vanbrugh).

[Again the Edwardian age's accent on 'white' girls!]

Becque goes on in what de Beaujolais construes as semi-delirious wanderings. He recalls the day when de Beaujolais nearly shot him and he nearly had de Beaujolais hanged from the flagstaff of the fort at Zinderneuf. *'Another mutiny in the discontented and rotten French army!'*

But de Beaujolais cannot recall this incident. At the mention of Zinderneuf, thoughts flash through his mind. Dufour was there, Sergeant Lebaudy was there, Corporal Brille was there, but not Becque. The trumpeter, who volunteered to enter the fort, where 'the Dead were forbidden to die – the Fallen were not allowed to fall'. The trumpeter – yes – one of the three Gestes of Brandon Abbas. He had found this out some years later when he had attended George Lawrence's wedding. But no Becque.

Two Americans – he remembered he had spoken to them in English and he had sent them to their deaths in an attempt to warn St André and his Senegalese – but no Becque.

Then Becque plays his last card . . .

He tells de Beaujolais how he is suffering – the pain being unbearable, he feels nothing can save him and asks de Beaujolais to shoot him so putting him out of his misery. De Beaujolais can't.

> *Becque:* 'De Beaujolais, I make a last appeal as a soldier to a soldier . . . Don't keep me alive, in agony, for days . . . If you cannot bring yourself to shoot me put your pistol near me – and let Becque die as he lived, with a weapon in his hand . . .'
>
> I put the pistol beside his right hand.
>
> 'Good-bye Becque. In the name of France and Mary Vanbrugh I forgive the evil you tried to do them both . . .'
>
> And I touched his hand and turned my back.

De Beaujolais' cavalier attitude, his faith in other people's characters, his naivety, all conspire to place him in great danger or, if not great danger, in tight spots.

> The bullet cut my ear.
>
> I sprang round and knocked the pistol from Becque's hand:
>
> 'You treacherous *devil*!'

'You poor gullible *fool*. You win again, you dog. What a fool I was to aim at your head – with a shaking hand . . . But I did want to see those poor brains you are so proud of.'

CHAPTER 9

For My Lady

BECQUE HAS PLAYED HIS LAST CARD, and with, 'I'll get you, my Beau Sabreur,' he falls back dead.

Mary Vanbrugh, very naturally, is curious about the shot. She thinks that the Major might have fired it at Becque, 'in the name of Duty'. Despite himself, de Beaujolais has to confess that it was Becque who had fired at him. This in no way mollifies Mary's attitude towards him. 'Duty' is playing a prominent part in both their lives at this stage.

De Beaujolais:	'A man's duty is his duty.'
Mary:	'Oh, quite. I would not have you deviate a hair's breadth from your splendid path . . . But since the day you informed me that you would have left me to the mercies of the Touareg – had there been but one camel – I have been thinking a good deal . . . Yes, 'a man's duty is his *duty*,' and – if I might venture to speak so presumptuously – a woman's duty is *her* duty too . . . '
De Beaujolais:	'Surely.'
Mary:	'And so I find it *my* duty to hinder you no further, and to remain in the Oasis . . . *under the protection of the Emir el Hamel el Kebir* . . . I think too that I prefer the standards and ideals of this Emir. Somehow, I do not think that *anything* would have induced *him* to leave a woman to certain death or worse . . . not even a *treaty*. Good-bye, Major de Beaujolais.'

I sat for hours with my pistol in my hand, and I think I may now claim to know what suffering is.

Major Henri de Beaujolais cannot do what he thought Becque would do – blow his brains out.

The holy Hadji Abdul Salam pays de Beaujolais another visit – his last. After hearing out further proposals de Beaujolais sends him on his way:

'And now Holy One, depart in peace, before I commit an impiety. In other words – get out, you villainous, filthy, treacherous dog, before I shoot you . . .'

The Hadji went and ran straight into the arms of Sheikh El Habibka – and I saw him no more in this life, and do not expect to see him in the next.

A piece of luck, el Habibka waiting outside the guest-tents!

I lay awake till dawn.
Mary Vanbrugh . . . France . . . My Service . . . My uncle . . . My Duty . . . An outraged, unforgivably insulted despot . . . and in whose hands lay the fate of the two women for whose safety I was responsible.

That night things come to a head. The Emir and Vizier visit de Beaujolais' tent; they act as if nothing is wrong and they are on the friendliest of terms.

The Emir establishes the fact that de Beaujolais has the welfare and happiness of 'Sitt Miriyam' much at heart – that he, de Beaujolais, values it more than the Treaty. Once this is established, they prepare to test him. He has a choice – he can have the signed Treaty immediately and he can leave with it. If this course is chosen the 'Sitt Miriyam' enters the Vizier's *hareem*, and the 'Sitt Moadi' enters the Emir's *hareem*. Or de Beaujolais can commit suicide in the sure and certain knowledge that the two Sitts will be set free and conveyed to any point as they may wish.

| *De Beaujolais:* | 'What proof and assurances have I that you would keep your word, Emir?' |
| *The Emir:* | 'None whatever – save that I have given it. It is known to all men that I have never broken faith . . . *If you die by your own hand to-night, your white women are as free as air.* I, the Emir el Hamel el Kebir, swear upon the Holy Q'ran and by the Beard of the Profit and the Sacred Names of God that I will deliver the two Sitts, in perfect safety, wheresoever they would be.' |

De Beaujolais realises that he has to accept this promise. The choice is now stark: the treaty (and loss of Mary) or Mary's freedom (and his death).

In either case he loses Mary, but in making the second choice he ensures her safe return to her own people, along with her companion, Maudie.

A dog, a pariah cur, is then brought into the tent and given a white liquid to drink. Within minutes it is writhing in its death throes (perhaps better out of its misery).

De Beaujolais now attempts a ploy. He produces the Treaty:
Sign the Treaty and let me go . . .

Smiling scornfully the Emir signs (with de Beaujolais' pen) and seals the document with his great seal bearing cabalistic designs and Arabic lettering. The Vizier adds his 'mark' as a witness.

Indicating the remainder of the poison cup the Emir says:

'We would have drunk together, you drinking that cup (indicating the poisoned cup) – and we would have wished prosperity and happiness to the Sitts. "*May each marry the man she loves,*" we would have said, and you would have died like a brave man. Now, O Seller of Women, take the other cup . . . drink tea with us – to the prosperity of our alliance with France instead.'

(Now all through these proceedings the Emir was stern and scornful of de Beaujolais; yet the Vizier was smiling and pleased with himself.)

> I said in Arabic: '*The Treaty is signed and witnessed, Emir,*' and in my mother tongue I cried: '*Happiness to my Lady, and success to my country,*' and rising to my feet, I drank of the poisoned cup . . . blind, and dying, I heard a woman scream . . . I . . .

PART II — SUCCESS

INTRODUCTION TO PART II

It is at this point necessary to quote in full from Wren's 'NOTE' in *Beau Sabreur*, and examine its plausibility.

> *Thus abruptly ends the autobiography of Major Henri de Beaujolais – which he begun long after leaving the Great Oasis and the society of the Emir el Hamil el Kebir and his Vizier.*
>
> *The abrupt ending of his literary labours, at the point of so dramatic a crisis in his affairs, was not due to his skill as a cunning writer, so much as to the skill of a Riffian tribesman as a cunning sniper.*
>
> *Major de Beaujolais, being guilty of the rashness of writing in a tent, by the light of a lamp, paid the penalty, and the said tribesman's bullet found its billet in his wrist-watch and arm, distributing the works of the former throughout the latter, and rendering him incapable of wielding either pen or sword for a considerable period . . .*
>
> *It happens, however, that the compiler of this book is in a position to augment the memoirs of his friend . . . and to shed some light on the puzzling situation. Paradoxically, the light came from dark places – the hearts and mouths of two Bad Men. Their wicked lips completed the story, and it is hereinafter set forth.*
>
> *The narrative which follows opens at a date a few years previous to the visit of Major Henri de Beaujolais to the Great Oasis.*

Two points arise from this 'Note'. The first is that we learn that Major Henri de Beaujolais did not succumb to the poison and die (which might spoil the story for some by anticipating the aftermath of the *coup de résistance*). The second is that we know for certain that Major Henri de Beaujolais is right-handed. Very few right-handed people wear a wristwatch on the *right* wrist. Thus the ploy to silence de Beaujolais by having his writing hand put out of action is a bit thin.

Nevertheless, Wren's tactic in moving the story away from de Beaujolais to the mouths of two others is a good one, as we see the story 'from the other side'.

The Making of a Monarch

CHAPTER I

El Hamel

A LARGE SEMI-NOMAD DESERT CARAVAN is moving slowly in the tracks of a Touareg *harka*. It moves slowly as it does not wish to run into the tail-end of the Touareg. A semi-nomadic caravan such as this was well armed and consisted of fast *mehara* camels and slower baggage camels, as well as women and children.

Wren uses the ploy of fugitives and caravans following up a robber band as being one of the safest places to be in, in the desert.

Anon the caravan comes across the body of a man, almost lifeless, lying on the slope of a sand-hill. The body is little less than a bag of bones and rags.

'The old Sheikh', leader of the caravan, is a gentle and honourable man, who attempts to live by the tenets of the Khoran; his Vizier, Suleiman the Strong, is the opposite – ruthless, cruel and scheming. The Hadji of the group is Abdul Salam, and it is he the old Sheikh orders to examine the bag of bones. The Hadji finds that not only is the body almost devoid of life owing to starvation and thirst, but there is also a bullet wound in the shoulder region, the result of having been shot, no doubt, by the Blue-veiled devils they were shadowing.

The Hadji pronounces the body lifeless but the old Sheikh is not convinced and bringing his camel to its knees he administers a few drops of water to the open and blackened lips of the near-dead man. At the feel of the cool liquid the eyelids of the wounded man flicker and the Hadji is quick to proclaim that it is he that has brought him back to life!

The old Sheikh gives orders that the foundling be strapped to the back of a baggage-camel and gives strict orders to Abdullah (the camel-man) that he be well-cared for, that praise may be given to Allah for his survival.

Suleiman, on the other hand, has 'a feeling against him, inexplicable but powerful,' and orders Abdullah to 'squeeze his throat', at the same time stroking his dagger to make his meaning quite clear. Abdullah is caught between what we might now call a rock and a hard place. On reflection he concludes that it would be in his best interest to obey the more powerful of the two, for the time being, the Sheikh!

The caravan progresses and one fine day it arrives at its destination – a small, settled oasis. During the trek the foundling's health had improved to the extent that he is able to ride his camel and Suleiman eyes Abdullah and sharpens his dagger.

The old Sheikh now declares that the name of his new found friend is to be 'El Hamel', which means 'foundling'. The Tribe watches and waits for the old Sheikh to tire of his protégé.

El Hamel, for his part, befriends one El R'Orab the Crow, who becomes his personal servant and bodyguard. One of his duties is to shadow Suleiman and his partner in crime, the Hadji Abdul Salam. Both men fear committing outright murder owing to the fact that as El Hamel's health improves, so his great strength manifests itself. There can be no food poisoning attempt either, as El Orab serves as a 'food-taster' to his new master and it is pointless attempting to poison a person who has a food-taster at hand.

Though El Hamel gains in health and strength, he is, much to the old Sheikh's distress, dumb; he is devoid of all speech. Despite this handicap he is a man of many talents, being skilful with a rifle and the throwing-knife. He is also incredibly strong and a remarkable horseman and horse-master.

But to cap all these talents he is a magician! And the day is fast approaching when he will work his first miracle. It comes about thus:

The Sheikh has 'lost' his *djedouel*, a silver box which contains a Hair of the Beard of the Prophet, purchased in Mecca for a considerable sum of money. Now it is the wont of the old Sheikh to go to El Hamel's tent in the evenings, where he finds El Hamel sitting before the door, silent and inscrutable. He loves the company of his protégé as he can do all the *faddhling* (talking and gossiping); his protégé, being dumb, is an attentive listener.

Some weeks after the Sheikh's terrible loss, still grieving, he visits El Hamel. As they talk others draw near – Suleiman, Hadji Abdul Salam, Marbruk ben Hassan, and other prominent citizens.

The sun is about to set, and the moon rise, when the members of the *faddhling* party notice a strange trance come over El Hamel. He begins to foam at the mouth, raise his clenched fists to the moon, and roll his eyes until only the whites show. His eyes, once back in focus, fix on a spot on the ground before his tent. All eyes follow his, but there is nothing to see . . . nothing but flat trodden sand.

The dumb man then makes passes with his hands above the spot at which he stares and then, taking up his water jug, pours water on the spot:

> . . . did their eyes deceive them? For even as the man sat, with eyes and hands strained beseechingly aloft, did a gleam of silver show through the sand, *and did the lost box of the Sheikh rise through the earth at their very feet*, before their very eyes, as they stared and stared incredulous? It did.

The old Sheikh's joy knows no bounds. He confers the title of 'Sidi' on El Hamel and gives him a reward of Turkish *medjidlies*.

But Suleiman and the Hadji are far from pleased and they are more determined than ever to murder El Hamel (but neither fully trusts the other).

> . . . there are those, who having beheld a similar miracle in other parts of the world, say that the miracle-worker excavates a hole at the required spot and then fills it with some material that expands rapidly when made wet – some substance, for example, as yeast, sawdust, grain or bran.

Neither Suleiman nor the Hadji appears to possess the prescience to inspect the ground under the silver box!

A factor weighing heavily on Suleiman's mind is that he, as Vizier, has until now been the automatic choice of Regent, to rule in place of the Sheikh's young son on the death of the old Sheikh. As El Hamel waxes in favour with the old man it appears more and more likely that the Regency will fall to El Hamel until the boy comes of age. As Regent, Suleiman would have no difficulty in disposing of a young boy and proclaiming himself Sheikh ruler. With El Hamel holding the Regency matters would look different. A confrontation between the Sheikh and Suleiman is inevitable.

When the confrontation comes it is brief and violent. Suleiman enters into argument with his leader, abusing and denegrating El Hamel. The old Sheikh is incensed and orders Suleiman to leave the settlement. With that Suleiman seizes the Sheikh by his venerable grey beard and shakes him to and fro, at the same time hurling insults directly at his face. This is unforgivable behaviour and Suleiman is driven from the oasis with blows and curses, like a pariah dog.

In the normal course of events such behaviour would have merited an immediate death sentence. But Wren is not yet through with Suleiman, and as El Hamel intercedes in the altercation, we have the spectacle of Suleiman being driven out, under a hail of stones.

With the departure of so mean and treacherous a character as Suleiman, El Hamel is free to busy himself in the training of riflemen, horsemen and, above all, the camel corps – commanded by Marbruk ben Hassan.

As a far sighted move he establishes the nucleus of a 'Desert Intelligence Department', consisting of Yakoub-who-goes-without-water and his three ancient brothers. These four are famous for the gift of living when others died, if lost in the waterless desert, or finding the water-hole dried up, at the end of a long trek. These men El Hamel sends out to oases, *douars*, and desert camps, to bring in information – a forerunner of the 'early warning' system. There is another reason as well which becomes obvious later in the narrative.

The time for El Hamel to be vested with the Regency comes. The old Sheikh, placing his ring and seal upon El Hamel's hand, pronounces the words: '*Rahmat ullahi Allahim* – the peace of God be upon him.'

Soon after this ceremony the kind, gentle, and compassionate Sheikh (leader of the Tribe), is gathered to his fathers.

Not long after, El Hamel works another miracle – this time on himself. Whilst waiting for the crescent moon to appear after the great feast of Ramazan, we find El Hamel standing before the Tribe, arms outstretched to the horizon. The moon rises and in that instant the miracle is worked:

'*As hadu illa Illaha ill Allah wa as hadu inna Mahommed an rasul Allah.*' The Dumb has spoken.

The people fall to the ground. After the working of this miracle, the Sheikh speaks seldom, and when he does, it is briefly, uttering only short orders and curt replies.

Yakoub-who-goes-without-water arrives one night on foot, his camel having collapsed and died a day's march from the oasis. He brings news of a great Touareg band to the north.

In the past the Tribe have adopted passive resistance tactics, some only of the women, young girls and boys being sent off into the desert with only some of the livestock. Evacuation of all women, children and livestock would cause the Touareg not only to come looking for them, but as well to torture those remaining in the camp. Wholesale flight is out of the question. Once the chosen people have gone off into the desert the *douar* is left to the Touareg to plunder at will (those remaining looking on and praying that they will not be tortured) – the reasoning being that the sooner the 'Forgotten of God, the Blue-veiled Silent Ones' get what they want, the sooner they will depart.

[In 1960 the author saw a tribe of the 'Blue-veiled Ones' at the oasis of In Guissam. They were very peaceful.]

El Hamel has other ideas. After much discussion he unveils a plan of attack:

'We will go and find our enemy and fall upon him and destroy him utterly.'

And in this he receives the support of Marbruk ben Hassan *'Hamdulillah! It shall be so. Inshallah!'*

The fight is a short, sharp one. The Touareg custom has always been that of a dawn attack and thus would in turn expect to be attacked at dawn, if at all. El Hamel decrees a dusk attack, when the raiding party will be preparing to cook the evening meal, water their camels and bed down for the night.

The plan is a simple one – surround the encampment with two rings of attackers; one ring firing and the other crawling forward to be the next line of shooters, whilst the first line of shooters passes through them to become the next line to pour in the withering rifle fire. The camp becomes a shambles. Some of the Targui warriors attempt to break out of the ring, attacking the perimeter with swords and spears. These attackers are gunned down without mercy. El Hamel gives the impression of being everywhere – urging his men on, emptying his own rifle with devastating effect, and generally supervising the tightening of the human noose about the enemy camp.

> And so the net drew tighter, the end came in sight, and the cool brain of El Hamel triumphed over the hot courage and tradition-bolstered invincibility of the terrible Touareg.
>
> Not till the battle was fairly won and the victory inevitable, did human nature triumph over discipline, and his followers, with a wild yell, rise as one man and rush upon the doomed remnants of their foe.

CHAPTER 2

El Habibka

In the camp of the defeated enemy El Hamel's men come across a Touareg prisoner, trussed and awaiting torture – the sudden attack has deferred this imminent event. The man is an emaciated scarecrow, almost dead from thirst and depravation.

[Hardly, one would think, a victim worthy of torture.]

This man El Hamel takes into his own special care – thinking perhaps how the old Sheikh cared for him when he was found at death's door.

> The Sheikh (El Hamel) laid his finger on the bloodless lips, sent all men away, and remained long alone with this piece of human salvage from the ocean of the desert, and its storm of war . . .

Apparently the men of the Tribe are so pleased with their leader and the victory ensured by him that they do not question this rather strange behaviour. In fact they confer on him the title El Kebir (the Lion).

In due course the new foundling is named El Habibka, the Friend, and indeed he becomes the chosen friend of El Hamel el Kebir.

Although small in stature in comparison with El Hamel, the newcomer, when he has recovered from the ordeal he has suffered in the desert and at the hands of the Touareg, proves to have many of the attributes possessed by his protector.

He can ride as well as El Hamel. He can shoot as well as El Hamel. He is particularly skilled with the 'little gun' (revolver), and the knife. He, too, possesses some of the powers of the magician which El Hamel possesses. Like the Sheikh he is skilled in a special form of *rabah* in which the empty hand is clenched, the thumb upon the first and second fingers, and a blow is delivered by shooting forward the hand in a straight line from the shoulder. And, like El Hamel when first found, El Habibka is dumb.

The Sheikh (Regent), El Hamel el Kebir, explains to his inner circle, his *ekhwan*, that El Habibka is from his own tribe, from the south, and that it is his intention to cure him of his dumbness as soon as Allah wills it.

El Habibka

Before this comes about El Habibka has occasion to speak, and at this time three words only. It comes about thus:

The Sheikh is, one evening, passing the tents of Sitt Leila Nakhla (the old Sheikh's daughter) and her brother. The young boy runs up to embrace the Sheikh and play with his great silver-hilted dagger. El Habibka watches the scene from the door of his tent, and suddenly he shouts the three words, in a strange tongue, as an almost naked man bounds from the shadows of the palm-trees, straight at the back of the kneeling Sheikh – a long knife in his right hand.

At the sound of El Habibka's cry the Sheikh turns, still kneeling, but keeping his body between the assassin and the young boy. As the assassin's knife flashes up, the Sheikh's great fist shoots out and catches him a terrible blow beneath the breast bone. In the same instant El Habibka's pistol rings out twice, crippling the man, but not killing him. A crowd immediately gathers and are about to dispatch the would-be assassin, but the Sheikh shouts that the man be damaged no further and El Habibka is in time to seize the wrist of Hadji Abdul Salam, just as the knife, held by that worthy, is about to enter the assassin's neck in the vicinity of the jugular vein. It is surprising with what force the Hadji struggles to execute justice – as if he does not want the man taken alive. But El Habibka, with a remarkable twist to the wrist holding the knife, causes the Hadji to drop the weapon and yelp in pain.

The assassination attempt, assassinations being fairly common in those parts, does not evoke as much comment as the other happening of the evening. And when people learn that there is to be no torture they turn their attention to that other event, the far more wonderful event, the fact that El Habibka has spoken, and that the Sheikh has understood the strange tongue. The afflicted of Allah was the object of the Mercy of Allah, and was given speech that he might save his master. As the days pass El Hamel slowly and patiently extracts from the potential assassin the intelligence that he has been sent on his dastardly work by a powerful sheikh to the north, one Emir Mohammed Bishari bin Mustapha Korayim abd Rabu, whose Vizier is none other than Suleiman the Strong (the friend of the Hadji).

El Hamel learns, moreover, that assassination is not all that was contemplated by the Emir Rabu. Once El Hamel is out of the way, he, Rabu, plans to attack and conquer the Tribe and add it to the confederation which is growing up around what would become known as the Great Oasis.

Many are the councils held by the Sheikh, El Habibka, wise old Dawad Fetata, Marburk ben Hassan, and the elect of the *ekhwan*, and the fighting men. After a decision had been reached, a great *mejliss* is held, a great public meeting, which is harangued in turn by the wise men and the fighting men of the Inner Council . . .

It comes to pass that at one of these council meetings El Habibka finds his speech. Rusty from disuse he calls aloud:

'Hamdulillah! Hamdulillah! Ana Mabsut! Ana Mabsut!'
. . . and fell upon his face before the Sheikh, his body quivering with sobs, or the wild hysterical laughter of a joy too great to bear . . .

And the decision of the Inner Circle, approved by the *mejliss* was that at the coming season of the sowing, when all tribes scatter far and wide for the planting of barley for the next year's food-crop, the Tribe should migrate and travel steadily north-west toward that wonderful land where there was known to be an oasis, covering a hundred square miles, of palm trees and all things green – the Great Oasis.

Sheikh El Hamel sends out his scouts – Yakoub-who-goes-without-water and his three ancient brothers who presumably also go without water. They disappear into the blue, as it were, and are not seen again for many days.

The Tribe, on this of its many moves, will move in a manner decreed by El Hamel, and not as a straggling mob, as in past moves. El Hamel's plan is that it will move as an army which is accompanied by a baggage-and-sutler train. Four drilled Camel Corps will proceed as an advance guard; two flank guards and a powerful rear-guard form the sides of a huge oblong, inside which the Tribe and its animals will march.

Particular attention is paid to the camels, these marvellous beasts of the desert, without which no tribe could survive. A fighting man's date-fed trotting-camel can consume a sack of dates a day and provision has to be made for them, as El Hamel knows, as does his newly-appointed Commander-in-Chief of the fighting men, El Habibka, that a battle is inevitable.

CHAPTER 3

The Confederation

As we have learnt, it was the intention of the Emir Rabu, ruler of the Great Oasis. and his new Vizier, Suleiman the Strong, to ride south-east with his fighting-men to conquer El Hamel el Kebir and his tribe.

El Hamel has, however, pre-empted this gambit, by himself moving his Tribe north-west and, informed by his spies, he plans an ambush at the Pass of Bab-el-Haggar.

[Wren does not make it clear that this was the battle which Raoul d'Auray de Redon was involved in; the battle in which he met up with Suleiman, and whom he later introduced to Major Henri de Beaujolais, of the Spahis, to act as his guide to the Great Oasis.]

Wren does tell us, though, that the Pass is an ideal place for an ambush. The attacking *harka* have to pass:

> ... through the deep dunes, and loose sand, churned to fine dust by fifty centuries of caravan-traffic in a rainless land.

Emir Rabu and his *harka* stand no chance. As they enter the powdered sand the camels of the fighting-men slow to a walk, their broad feet sinking into the fine dust. Here they prove to be the proverbial sitting ducks, as a hail of rifle fire is poured in on them from the rocks that board and form the defile.

The Emir, riding ahead, is the first to fall. Suleiman brings his camel to its knees, and lies beside it, feigning death.

The defeat is utter. To the surprise of the vanquished not a throat is cut. But all rifles, swords, spears and camels are confiscated. Emir Rabu's fighting-men are now leaderless, and without weapons or transport. After taking the necessary and precautionary hostages, the sons and daughters of the sheikhs, El Hamel's Tribe move into and occupy the Great Oasis.

To celebrate El Hamel's victory and conquest, Dawad Fetata gives a great feast, or *diffa*. Here we learn that the old Sheikh's daughter, Sitt Leila Nakhla, is in love with El Hamel – who could blame her!

El Habibka, though, is not very pleased, as it was he who, during the period of his dumbness, cured Leila of an unbearable headache. Soon, however, El Habibka is to transfer his affections to another!

Under El Hamel's rule the Great Oasis settles down to a period of peace and prosperity surpassing even that of Emir Rabu. Other nomadic tribes begin to join the confederation. Some of these join as they see the potential for prosperity; some join out of fear of being eaten up.

The fame of El Hamel's Camel Corps and of its leader, Marbruk ben Hassan, spreads. It is rumoured that it drills and manoeuvres like the *Franzawi* and other *Roumi* soldiers.

> And, as unto him that hath shall be given, more and more power was given to the Emir el Hamel el Kebir, as more and more sheikhs sought his protection . . . and his Confederation waxed like Jonah's gourd, until its fame spread abroad in all the land, north, south, east and west.
>
> In the north and the west it attracted the attention of certain deeply-interested Great Ones . . .

CHAPTER 4

Voices from the Past

AT THIS POINT IN THE TRILOGY Wren begins to tie up some loose ends.

Emir el Hamel el Kebir and his Vizier, Sheikh El Habibka, we are told, sit apart from all men, so that they can converse on matters of State in complete privacy.

Sitting on rugs and cushions under a canopy, they are guarded by four Soudanese soldiers, forming an imaginary square one hundred yards apart, and one hundred yards distant from their Lords.

They are so seated one day, when the Emir's faithful body servant, El R'Orab the Crow, brings the chief scout, Yakoub-who-goes-without-water, to them.

Yakoub reports the approach of a small caravan. It is led by two strange men, one an Egyptian Arab; the other, although dressed as a Bedouin, is not what he seems to be, having strange ways. Yakoub reports, too, that the two talk to one another in a strange tongue.

Three days later two heavily bearded men sit and talk to the Emir and the Vizier. Their message is simple:

They have orders from Stamboul to preach a *jehad*, a Holy War; the overthrow of the *Franzawi* and all other *Roumi* in Africa would follow and a Pan-Islamic State in Africa would result.

The Emir's Confederation, based on the Great Oasis and astride the trade routes to the south, is an important part of the building block. They have come to gain the Emir's assistance in the great plan. Beside it being part of a natural desire on the part of the Emir to rid Africa of the infidel, the strangers make it clear that there is plenty of money to go as a reward to those who help in the creation of the new Pan-Islamic State.

After the strangers have departed to their camp the following conversation ensues:

The Emir: 'Do you place him, Bud?'

The Vizier: 'Search me, Hank Sheikh! But I cert'nly seen him before . . .'

The Emir:	'Remember a sure-enough real thug way back in Tokotu when we was in the Legion? . . . Came to us at Douargala with a draft from the Saida depôt. The boys allowed it was him, and him alone, started that big Saida mutiny . . . same game at Tokotu . . . Always had plenty of money and spent it gettin' popular . . . Reg'lar professional mutineer . . . but a real brave man . . . Get him?'
The Vizier:	'Nope.'
The Emir:	'He had been in the French Cavalry . . . got jailed for mutiny there too . . . later he joined the Legion . . . He was on the march with us from Tokotu to Zinderneuf – the place those two bright boys burnt out and killed old Lejaune – and Old Man Bojolly shot this guy with his empty revolver, and then put him under arrest for refusing to obey orders . . .'
The Vizier, (with a cry of exclamation):	'*Rastignac! Rastignac the Mutineer*! Good for you, Hank Sheikh!'

What they are to do to or with Rastignac is decided by Hank Sheikh merely stating that 'they will teach him to play poker!'

Yussuf Latif Fetata, grandson of High Sheikh, Sidi Dawad Fetata, is summoned and instructed to:

> . . . bivouac a company of the Camel Corps beside the camp of the strangers, for their honour and protection . . . see that their camels be 'minded' and their rifles taken away to be cleaned and also 'minded' . . .

Thus Rastignac and his companion are effectively prevented from leaving the Great Oasis.

But though they cannot leave their camp, others can enter it. When a certain soldier, Gharibeel Zarrug, rumoured to be the illegitimate son of the Hadji Abdul Salam, stands guard, the pious Hadji is able to visit these strangers without hindrance, and 'much curious and interesting conversation ensued'.

Wren's picture of Rastignac's travelling companion is of a man:

> . . . who affected patent leather dancing pumps, silk socks, scent, hair pomade and other European vices – and who yearned exceedingly for a high stiff collar, frock-coat, *tarbush* and the pavements of Paris.

Rastignac knows, too, that his partner has more the cunning of the fox than the courage of the lion. This man, whose name we are never to know, welcomes the Hadji's visits, and opines:

> ... Might do worse ... He'd be ours, body and soul, both for the money and because we should know too much ... If he killed the Emir and his jackal, or had them killed, he would be the power behind the throne – until he was the throne itself ...

The Hadji, as we already know, is playing more than a double game – he is playing a triple game as he has already tried to work his wiles on de Beaujolais and failing there has introduced de Beaujolais to Rastignac – the consequences of which introduction would be dire!

[But this is in the future!]

As the Great Oasis is increasingly becoming the objective of the 'Great Ones' it is not surprising that the Emir and his Vizier receive, with equanimity, the news that Marbruk ben Hassan has returned from a routine patrol, bringing with him a small caravan consisting of three persons. The Emir extends the usual hospitality, as laid down by the Khoran. Neither does the fact that there are two women and one man in the caravan, worry them. After all there were many men in that part of the world that had more than one wife.

The two wise rulers, the Emir and his Vizier, receive the shock of their lives, when they learn exactly who the newcomers are:

> Anon men approached, in the midst of whom walked a French officer in full uniform.

The Vizier (pushing his elbow into the Emir's side):	'Sunday pants of Holy Moses! *It's Old Man Bojolly*! Run us down at last!'
The Emir:	'Game's up Bud. This is where we get what's comin' to us.'

They never-the-less receive the officer with severe dignity and calm faces ... (de Beaujolais tells us that he detected a note of fear in their faces).

Wren now takes us behind the looking glass as it were. We see and learn of the happenings concerning the Treaty, the love life of the main players, de Beaujolais, Hank and Buddy, through the eyes of his most lovable characters – Hank Sheikh and Buddy Bashaw. We learn, too, how Mary Vanbrugh becomes involved with the Emir and more particularly with his Vizier: and what happens in the life of the romantic Maude Atkinson.

In plotting his trilogy Wren planned well ahead. When writing *Beau Geste* he must have worked out the futures of Hank and Buddy. Hank (in Oates fashion) left Buddy and John Geste to share the last of the water and Buddy, after seeing John Geste to safety, returned to find his friend. At what juncture, one muses, did Wren plan to create desert Sheikhs of these two 'men of the road'?

So ingrained is the belief in the power of the Legion that the two masquerading sheikhs do not for a minute doubt that Major de Beaujolais, far from bringing a 'great and peaceful message', has come to arrest them.

Buddy says: 'They always get you in the end. I wonder what force he's brought and where he's left it?'

This is when Hank Sheikh sends Marbruk ben Hassan to rescue Dufour and his party, if possible, and to scout out the land to determine whether or not de Beaujolais has a supporting force.

Buddy again: 'What will we do if he gets up in the *Mejliss* and says: "I rise to remark I've come to fetch you two hoboes outa this for deserters from the French Foreign Legion on reconnaissance duty in the face o' the enemy an' Lord ha' mercy on your sinful souls amen, and you'd better come quiet or I'll call up my Desert Column?"'

Argument between the two flows to and fro before they reach the conclusion that the only thing they can reasonably do is to bluff it out. Little do they know what is going through de Beaujolais' mind; he has already classified the Emir as being of 'unmistakable Touareg stock' and the Vizier as being of 'Touareg or Berber-Bedouin stock'.

At no time do these case-hardened men contemplate violence against de Beaujolais; and they have more than enough devoted armed followers who would do their bidding.

Buddy half-heartedly suggests that they 'turn the Injins loose on him' or turn him over to Rastignac, only to be met with:

'*Can* it, Buddy Bashaw. Cut it out. We don't turn the Injins on to a lone white man, Son . . . No, and we don't set 'em up against Christian machine-guns nor Civilised artillery either . . . Not after they elected us to Congress like this, and made me President an' all . . .'

Buddy again: 'Some tracking Ole Man Bojolly's done! He's a cute cuss and a fierce go-getter . . . He's got a nerve too, to ride straight in here like a Texas Ranger into a Mex village

– an' I hand it to him, an' no ill-will . . . But I'd certainly like to go an' paste him one . . .'

['Ole Man Bojolly' is about forty years old at this point in the story.]

CHAPTER 5

The Emir and the Vizier

HANK AND BUDDY have by no means shaken off their 'Americanisms'. They talk of Texas Rangers, sheriffs and cowboys and refer to the Arabs as 'Injins'.

The two discuss at length the presence of the two girls with de Beaujolais and come up with the reason: that being French he must have 'shocking morals' and that it is none of their business if 'Bojolly travels comfortable'.

Wren, in keeping with the times in which he is writing, stresses the fact that de Beaujolais is a 'white man' and as such is deserving of their protection.

Some of the loose ends of the trilogy are being tied; four characters, Hank, Buddy, de Beaujolais and Rastignac, are all in the Great Oasis.

That evening, the feast at which Mary sings Abdul the Bul Bul Emir is held, and it is at this feast that Buddy, forgetting Leila, transfers his affection to Mary Vanbrugh.

It becomes evident in due course that Mary, that very night, saw through the masquerade and began to use the term 'Parlour Sheikhs'. This term is well understood by the Emir and his Vizier. Mary's prescience is well founded, as is later learnt. Hank Sheikh felt it, and knew it, for a certain very good reason. And because of this he talks to his Vizier, Buddy, along the following lines:

His plan is to talk to Miss Vanbrugh and tell her quite openly that he and Buddy are imposters. He will outline their rise to power and their commitment to the Tribe. Having done this he will rely on her goodwill, as a fellow American, not to betray them to de Beaujolais. Here Hank is on firm ground. That Mary has more than a passing fondness for the Major is obvious and it will do his career no good if it is discovered by his superiors that he has been taken in by imposters.

As for his friend's intention to make Mary his wife, Hank Sheikh cautions that he feels 'Ole Man Bojolly' is in love with the 'lovely little Peach'.

The Vizier closed a useful looking fist and shook it above his head . . .

'What . . . he'd come here to arrest us an' get us shot – an' he'd steal our girls from under our very noses too! . . . He would? Ole Man Bojolly better git up an' git . . . Let's ride him out o' town . . . I'll paste him one tomorrow . . . Hank Sheikh, Son – I'm goin' to propose to that sweet and lovely American girl, and lay my heart and fortune at her feet . . .'

'That's the spirit, Son! Good-luck to you Buddy-boy – an' I'll back you up. You court her gentle and lovin' and respectful . . . But we sure got to tell her about ourselves . . . All about us, so there's no deception like . . .'

They then discuss Miss Maudie Atkinson:

The Vizier: 'Some looker – if Miss Mary Vanbrugh wasn't there. An' not bad for British . . . Yep, I'd surely have fallen for her, if the American girl hadn't been there . . .'

The Emir: 'You certainly would, Bud . . . Thou Fragrance of the Pitt! "*Oh, Sir, ain't the big one a lovely man!*" That's me, Buddy Bashaw – an' don't you forget it . . .'

The Vizier: '*Lovely man*! You ever see a g'rilla, Hank?'

After the first formal meeting with de Beaujolais, at which he outlines the benefits of the Treaty and tells them of the million francs that will back up the Treaty, the Emir and the Vizier come to the firm conclusion that de Beaujolais takes them for what they appear to be – Arab rulers of a Bedouin tribe.

Having come to this conclusion they plan an evening ride with the two girls. The Emir is to ride out with Maudie and return with Mary, the Vizier reversing the order and de Beaujolais is to be accompanied by Marbruk ben Hassan and other tribal dignitaries.

When riding alone with Mary Vanbrugh, the conversation between the Emir and her goes as follows:

Mary: 'And you are really perfectly certain that you can bluff it through to the end, and that Major de Beaujolais won't place you?'

The Emir: 'Certain sure. We've been bluffing Arabs with our lives depending on it, and got away with it . . . It'll take more than a Frenchman to . . .'

Mary: 'He's one of the cleverest men that ever lived.'

The Emir: 'Sure thing. But he isn't an Arab. Why should he suspect anything wrong when he sees the Bedouin taking us for Bedouin? There's another Frenchman here too, who has lived in the same barrack-room with us! He takes us for Arabs.'

Mary Vanbrugh then wishes to know all about his, the Emir's, and his friend, the Vizier's, rise to power. Hank tells her of how he became *lost* and of the Tribe finding him. How, after he became Regent, he sent out his desert scouts to look for Buddy. And how he was found a prisoner of the Touareg.

Why does the Emir, Hank Sheikh, open up to Mary Vanbrugh in this fashion? It seems illogical that he would place the safety of Buddy and himself in the hands of a woman who is obviously in love with the man who could cause their downfall.

The reason is revealed, later, in one of Wren's series of remarkable coincidences.

Mary would like to know more about the Vizier:

'What sort of a man is he? He has certainly got good taste, for he gives me the eye of warm approval . . . Virtuous?'

'No. He isn't what I'd call that. I allow he's broken all the Commandments and looks to do it again . . . No, he hasn't got any virtues I know of, 'cept courage, and loyalty, and gratitude, and reliability . . . braver than a lion . . . never did a mean thing in his life nor went back on his word to his pal . . . doesn't know the meaning of the words fear, despair, failure or selfishness . . . Just an "ornery cuss".'

'You want me to like him, I see . . . so you damn him with faint praise. He sounds very much like a man to me. What would happen if you two fell in love with the same girl?'

'Poor girl would be left a widow like, before she was married.'

In answer to further queries from Mary Vanbrugh, Hank tells her that he is committed to remain as Regent until the son of the old Sheikh is old enough and powerful enough to rule the Tribe; and that Buddy would remain his Vizier:

'Unless you take him away, Miss Mary Vanbrugh.'

'Keep a stout and hopeful heart, Mr Emir.'

> *The Emir:* 'Or unless Major D. Bojol*lay* takes us both away in the middle of a camel-corps of *goums* . . .'

'Why should he want to do that?'

'He wouldn't *want* to, but it would be his painful "duty".'

And here the Emir, Hank Sheikh, learns from Mary Vanbrugh that the last thing she would do would be to reveal the identity of the Emir and the Vizier to the Major. Why? Because this would ruin de Beaujolais' career. His days in the Bureau Afrique would be over – he would have been duped by two deserters from the Legion!

Mary Vanbrugh then enquires as to how he and Buddy came to know the Major:

'And you actually served under him? It must have been splendid!'

The Emir: 'We hid our joy . . . We even tore ourselves away.'

That evening, after the departure of the servants, Hank tells Buddy of his conversation with Miss Mary Vanbrugh and that this had been in English.

The dialogue concerning the future of Mary Vanbrugh, (whether with the Vizier or the Major) is of interest as it shows how two good friends can talk to one another:

Hank:	'I've told Miss Mary Vanbrugh that we're two genuine low-brow American stiffs, honest-to-God four-flushers and fakers . . . She says she can see that for herself.'
Buddy, interrupting:	'You speak for *yourself*, Hank Sheikh.'
Hank:	'I did, Son . . . Miss Mary spoke for *you*. She says, "*Where did you pick up that lill' 'ornery dead-beat that side-kicks with you, Mr Emir?* Did the cat bring it in" . . . or words to that effect, like.'

The Vizier's face falls.

The Emir continues: 'Then *I* spoke for you, Son. I said "*The poor guy ain't such a God-awful hoodlum as he looks*, Miss Mary", and she replies kindly – "No, Mr Emir, I'm sure he couldn't be!" and then I spoke up for you hearty, Bud, and I said there isn't your equal in Africa . . .'

And as the Vizier's face lit up, his friend added:

'. . . to cut the throat of a goat and skin it . . .'

Hank Sheikh goes on to tell his side-kick that the information he has gleaned from Mary is all to their good. De Beaujolais has no inkling as to their true identity; he has no knowledge of Rastignac being in the Great Oasis, and that he is serious about the Treaty and the money that will go with it:

'So we're on velvet again, Bud . . . All Old Man Bojolly wants to do, is to pass the dough on to us. All we gotta do is to sign this Treaty not to let the Senussi in on the ground floor, and to have no truck with low foreigners. That means all people that on earth do dwell who aren't French.

'Shall we boot Rastignac out an' tell him to go while the going's good . . . or keep him around and make a bit on the side? . . . But it's ole' Boje's Treaty we'll sign!'

And the Emir looks at the ring, worn on 'a slightly withered finger, of which the top joint was missing', with which he will seal the Treaty.

Buddy makes it quite plain that he intends to have Mary Vanbrugh as his wife. Hank knows that she is in love with de Beaujolais, and he has to get this fact across to his friend, without hurting him or without seeming to take the side of Mary and the Major. Too much encouragement, on his part, of Buddy's flights of marital fancy could result in a severe disappointment for his friend.

For a while the two talk about their old commander:

The Emir: 'Well – as I figure it – he's the golden-haired blue-eyed boy. Saved her life in Zaguig. Shot up some stiffs who were handing out the rough stuff. Then brought her safe out of Zaguig – where her own brother must have got *his* by now. Whole garrison shot up, and him with 'em . . .'

The Vizier: 'Old Man Boje must have been mighty set on paying us a call here if he lit out from Zaguig while they were fighting . . .'

The Emir: 'Sure thing, Son . . . Mary says it's *the* Big Thing of his Life . . . He wouldn't stop in Zaguig for anything . . . though his comrades and his life-long pard and chum were in the soup . . .'

The Vizier: 'Sure, Judge. But who are you calling "Mary" so free?'

We are shown, from a different angle, the sacrifice to his integrity made by de Beaujolais.

Buddy suggests that they sign the Treaty, tell de Beaujolais he can depart with it, but that he must leave the girls behind at the Oasis. Hank, anxious to please his friend, agrees that it could be worth a try, but opines that he does not believe that '. . . he would leave two white girls in the wigwams of a camp of Injuns . . . I believe he is a blowed-in-the-glass White Man.'

A bet is struck. Hank bets that de Beaujolais will refuse the Treaty if he cannot take the girls along with him, back to civilisation; Buddy takes odds that de Beaujolais will place the Treaty above all else, take it away with him and leave the girls behind, adding:

'. . . and – don't forget – *he left Dufour and Achmet and the others to die while he made his getaway!*'

CHAPTER 6

Maudie

Riding alone with Mary Vanbrugh on another evening, the Emir el Hamel el Kebir consults her regarding his chances of winning the hand of Miss Maude Atkinson. He is anxious to know whether Major de Beaujolais would leave her behind with 'us low Injuns'.

Miss Vanbrugh replies: 'Well, I think that Love is the only thing that matters. I think that Love is Heaven and Heaven is Love . . . and if Maudie really loved you, and you really loved Maudie, I'd say, "Go to it, and God bless you, for you couldn't do a wiser thing."'

Wren is gracious enough to add that Mary 'flushed warmly' while making this declaration.

She goes on to assure Hank Sheikh that in her opinion Maudie would be as happy as the day is long with a man that really loved her, 'for she is the most romantic soul that ever lived – and one of the staunchest . . .'

Hank takes the opportunity of sounding out Miss Vanbrugh on the likely outcome of his bet with Buddy – but he does not, of course, disclose the bet:

'Would he leave the pair of you in return for my signing the Treaty?'

'I don't think you quite understand a gentleman – if you talk like that!'

'No. Sure. I haven't had much truck with gentlemen . . . Only low common men like me and Buddy. 'Sides, to tell you the truth *I was thinking of Dufour and the others he left behind to die*, for the sake of his Treaty! I knew old Dufour. He was a man. He was Sergeant-Major with Major D. Bojol*lay* when he was mule-walloping at Tokotu . . . I knew Achmet too . . . He was a real fine he-man and some scrapper . . .'

'Yes, yes, but it was his *Duty*. Duty is his God.'

[This from Mary Vanbrugh, who has, on several occasions attempted to suborn de Beaujolais from his duty. It is also worth noting that Hank, in denying association with 'gentlemen' seems to have forgotten, perhaps for strategic reasons, his friendship with the Geste brothers, 'gentlemen' if ever there were!]

As we have read, Maudie Atkinson has been fed a romanticised version of desert sheikhs. Mary Vanbrugh knows this as Maudie has often quoted to her from a book she has read, and still dreamed of:

> With a thunderous rush of heavy hoofs, the Desert Sheikh was upon her, and ere she could do so much as scream, she found herself swung like a feather to his saddle-bow and whirled afar across the desert . . . On, on, into the setting sun – while his hot lips found hers and drank deep of her beauty the while they burnt her very flesh like fire . . .

Mary's hand is clearly seen in what is about to befall her serving maid and companion.

Dressed in her best Maudie is standing at eventide on a sandhill and gazing towards the setting sun. She is thinking, and dreaming of her book on sheikhs and of the one close at hand . . .

> the great and beautiful man, the lovely man, in whose presence she had thrice feasted . . .

And so it came to pass – but the 'heavy hoofs' were those of the Emir's Arab steed. And that which happened in the story, happened, and Maudie was a very happy woman!

The Emir: 'Lill' girl, will you marry me?'

The answer was a resounding, 'Yes,' and then: 'Why – you spoke *English*!'

The Emir (modestly):   'I learnt it since you come – so's to talk to you, Maudie . . .'

And then, after a few more embraces:

                     'But mind you, Maudie, Major D. Bojolly mustn't know I've learnt English or else he'd want to talk English all the time – and get me muddled in business . . .'

Maudie: 'Oh, him! He's only a Frenchie . . . '

Later, in the Guest-tent, Maudie to Mary:

                     'Oh, Miss, may I tell you something? I'm not going to be Miss Atkinson much longer.'

Mary: 'You've told me already, Maudie.'

                     'Oh, no, Miss.'

Mary: 'But you have! You've been mad, Maudie, ever since it happened. You don't know who you are or where you are: nor whether you are on your head or your heels . . . Now tell me *all* about it . . .'

Maudie told.

CHAPTER 7

Buddy and the Blues

During the days that follow the Emir notices a change in the temper of his trusty Vizier. Buddy no longer sings his cowboy songs. His grey eyes lose their humour, and worst of all, he over-rides his horse.

The Emir decides the time has come for him to have a down-to-earth talk to his Vizier, a real *faddhl*.

Hank draws from Buddy that he has been turned down by Mary Vanbrugh and this due solely to de Beaujolais:

'Put me in Dutch with Miss Vanbrugh. The Infiddle Dorg . . . She turned down my respeckful proposal of matrimony, an' I spoke rude to a lady an' showed myself the low-life bindle-stiff I am.'

The Emir:	'Then you fired up about Bojolly?'
The Vizier:	'Sure. I axed her if she was engaged to be married to a scent-smellin', nose-wipin', high-falutin' dude French officer . . .'
The Emir:	'She talked American at you all right this time, then? What did she say?'
The Vizier:	'She says, "It's a beautiful sunset tonight, Mr Man, and I thought I was riding with a decent and courteous American . . . . and thank you, I'd like to ride back to the Oasis alone".'

And so, because he was sore, and ashamed of himself, Buddy hurt two of the things he loved most, a good woman and a good horse. But, being Buddy, he would not let the matter rest. He proposed to Hank that he fight de Beaujolais for Mary's hand:

'He can shout his own fancy – knives, guns . . . rifles if he likes. P'raps he'd prefer to use that sword he's brought all this way to impress us and the girls . . . I'll back my Arab sword against it, if he likes.'

'What d'*you* like, Son?'

'Knives. I ain't had a knife fight since when.'

And here his friend the Emir has to talk seriously to his friend and Vizier. Talk to him like a father to a son or a God-father to a God-child:

'And Miss Vanbrugh . . . ? Miss Vanbrugh, who you love so much, and who thinks Major D. Bojol*lay* the finest an' noblest an' bravest man she ever saw? Didn't I tell you, right back at the very first? Didn't I say to you, '*Don't you go kidding yourself, you Bud – for she's going to be a spinster or Mrs Boje*'?'

The Vizier looked glum, and who could blame him?

His friend continued:

'Now I'll tell you something for your good, Buddy Bashaw . . . You aren't in love with anybody . . . You are just plumb jealous of a better man than yourself because he's got away with it . . . Because you can't take his girl away from him!'

'Spill some more, you oozin' molasses-bar'l. But look here Hank Sheikh . . . *I'm plumb jealous of a better man than me, am I?* Well – no objection to makin' *certain* who's the better man, is there?'

His friend won't budge as far as a fight between de Beaujolais and Buddy is concerned. He provides reasons. De Beaujolais is their guest. He's about to hand over a wad of 'jack'. And above all, Hank does not want a French army coming down to the Great Oasis to look for de Beaujolais.

To reinforce all that he has said to his pal, the Emir adds: 'Now look here, Son. Get this straight . . . See that hand o' mine, Boy?'

'Some! I could see it seven mile away, without a telescope neither – and then mistake it for a leg o' mutton!'

The Emir repeats:	'See that hand o' mine, Bud? God's my witness, I'd cut it off if that would make you and Miss Mary happy for life. I cert'nly would. I'd sooner see Mary marry you and live on goat's flesh and barley-bread in a tent, than marry the Major and live in High Sassiety. Provided she loved you. But she don't. And won't . . .'
The Vizier:	'Very well, Pastor, an' that's that . . . Now then! We're goin' to find out how much this French parlour-snake and lounge-lizard *does* love Miss Vanbrugh.' And he reminds his friend of their bet! 'We're goin' to knock him up in the dead o' night an' offer him the Treaty, signed, sealed and witnessed – *provided* he saddles up an' lights out tomorrow *without* the girls . . .'

Hank Sheikh cannot go back on his word.

They turn their thoughts to Rastignac and his future. Buddy suggests that he has his knife-fight with Rastignac now that he has been denied that pleasure with de Beaujolais.

Little does he know what is happening in the de Beaujolais, and Rastignac/Hadji camp.

But before the de Beaujolais-Rastignac duel, the Emir and his Vizier subject de Beaujolais to his first test and we know the result – they leave the guest tent with the abusive shouts of de Beaujolais ringing in their ears.

Having lost his first bet to Hank Sheikh, Buddy is determined to press ahead with his second bet or test; de Beaujolais must take the Treaty away, duly signed, or give up his life by taking poison. The two girls are to be left to the fate or honour of the Emir.

It is difficult to understand Buddy's persistence in this matter of de Beaujolais, Mary and himself. She has refused his offer of marriage and de Beaujolais has demonstrated his loyalty to her and Maudie by refusing to trade the Treaty for their safety. In fact de Beaujolais had gone very far down the line to placing his own life in jeopardy by insulting the Emir in no uncertain terms.

Perhaps Wren wishes to make it indubitably clear that his hero, his Beau Sabreur, is indeed a nonpareil.

The Emir, foolishly, has not told his Vizier and friend of his engagement to Maudie. Buddy, who has assured his friend Hank Sheikh that he has 'done with women', nevertheless tests the waters so far as Maude Atkinson is concerned.

When pressed by Hank as to why he is so insistent on putting de Beaujolais to the second test, even though, as they both know, the result will not change Mary's feelings towards Buddy, Buddy opines:

'Do some good if it saves Miss Vanbrugh from a fortune-huntin' French furriner, won't it? American girls should marry American men . . .'

The Emir: 'And American men should marry American girls, I s'pose?'

And Buddy, thinking of Maudie, changes his stance: 'Say, ain't that li'll Maudie girl some peach?'

And when Hank reminds him that American men should marry American girls, Buddy again shifts his position, stating:

'Well, Anglo-Saxon men oughta marry Anglo-Saxon girls . . . course they ought . . . No frills an' do-dahs about Maudie, if she *is* British . . . Make a fine plain wife fer a plain man.'

The Emir agrees: 'You certainly *are* a plain man, Bud!'

CHAPTER 8

Maudie and Buddy

BESIDE A LITTLE IRRIGATION-RUNLET Miss Maudie Atkinson sat and waited for her sheikh. She had thrown off her *barracan* and stood revealed in a nice cotton frock, white stockings and white shoes . . . Much more attractive, she felt, than shapeless swaddlings of night dress and baggy trousers . . . Silly clo'es for a girl with a nice figger.

The big sheikh was late – affairs of state no doubt. Who arrived? Not the Great Sheikh, but the 'little one'.

Buddy:	'Evening, Miss. Shall we go for a li'll stroll under the trees?'
Maudie:	'I don't mind if we do, sir.'
Buddy, as they strolled off:	'I been admiring you since you come, Miss.'
Maudie:	'No! Straight? Have you reely?'
Buddy:	'Sure. All the time. In fact I follered you to-night to say so – an' to ask you if you thought you an' me might hitch up an' be pards . . .'
Maudie:	'Fancy *you* speaking English, too . . .'
Buddy:	'I sent for a hand-book as soon as I saw you that night . . . But you must never let Major Bojolly know.'

Maudie has been through the part of not letting de Beaujolais know, before, and so this comes as no surprise to her. She does, however, want to know why they are keeping the Major a prisoner.

Buddy:	'Oh, we're just making sure he doesn't run off an' take you two ladies away from us. My heart would certainly break if he did . . . Miss Maudie, will you marry me?'
Maudie, blushing, and looking down:	'Oh, sir! If you'd only spoke sooner! I'm engaged to the other sheikh . . . It's reely very kind of you, sir, but as things are . . .'

And when she looks up the sheikh has gone. Later, that man of unrequited love sticks his head into the sleeping tent of the Emir, a horrible scowl on his face and hisses: 'Oh, you Rambunctious Ole Goat,' and withdraws his head.

There is nothing Buddy can do but to forgive his Lord, and being a man of forbearance and generosity he makes no further allusion to the 'frailties' of Hank Sheikh.

But Buddy is restless. The arrival of Mary and Maudie has upset his equilibrium. He feels he has to do something – something like marriage or moving on.

He tells Hank that he cannot get 'Idaho, Montana, Utah, Oregon . . .' out of his mind. 'Marry or move . . .' is coursing through his brain, too. And he tells Hank Sheikh that he has now set his sights on the young girl, the Sitt Leila Nakhla, sister of the future ruler of the Tribe.

Despite Hank telling him not to be a 'damn fool', Buddy goes off to see 'Daddy Pertater', in fact Sidi Dawad Fetata, Leila's guardian.

Poor Buddy! The intelligence he receives from Dawad Fetata is not promising.

Sidi Dawad Fetata: 'My heart is sore for her, Sidi. She is possessed of *djinns* . . . She cannot sleep . . . Every night she rises from her cushions and goes forth to walk beneath the stars. Old Bint Fatma follows her . . . Always, too, she stands near the tent of the Emir and calls the protection of the Prophet and the blessings of Allah upon him . . .'

'Marriage worketh wonders with women,' suggests the Vizier.

Dawad Fetata: 'Ya, Sidi. But the poor Leila's pale bridegroom will be Death . . . She will not live to marry my grandson – and he will pine for her and die also . . .'

Buddy, to himself, strolling back to his tent: 'And what do you know about *that* for a merry ole crape-hanger, my son?'

CHAPTER 9

A Mixed Bag

MAJOR DE BEAUJOLAIS, before decamping, with Mary and Maudie, from the battle-ground at the salt lake, commands Suleiman the Strong to remain there and fight alongside the small force regulars.

Marbruk ben Hassan, after inspecting the scene of the battle, and burying the dead, reports that a single track of a camel has been seen to be leading south-east. This, of course, is the track made by Suleiman's camel, and he is on its back!

Wren's narrative does not make it clear as to whether the identity of the deserter is revealed by de Beaujolais to the Emir or his advisors. It seems not to have been, and this is strange, as Suleiman has told de Beaujolais that the Emir is his sworn enemy and, if he has survived his flight, must be living somewhere in the Great Oasis. For once the Emir's Desert Intelligence has let him down.

We now hear from Hadji Abdul Salam, doctor and saint, who has still to meet his come-uppance:

'Often they sleep in the big pavilion where they have sat and *faddhled* till nearly dawn. More often they sleep each in his own tent . . . There is usually a Soudanese sentry on the beat between the Guest-Tent and those of the Emir and the Vizier.'

These remarks are addressed to Suleiman the Strong and one Abdullah el Jemmal, the Camel-man.

The plot is simple. They will await a night on which Gharibeel Zarruk is on sentry-go and both the Vizier and the Emir are in the pavilion tent. Abdullah will enter stealthily, discern how the intended victims are lying and report back to Suleiman.

Suleiman admonishes Abdullah regarding the necessity for absolute silence and Abdullah replies:

'Right through the heart, Sidi – or across the throat – a slash that all but takes the head off, according to how he lies in sleep. And if I do my part well, I have *medjidies* – to my heart's desire . . . ?'

The Hadji answers:

'Yea! Verily! After the dawn that sees the death of the Emir and the Vizier, thou wilt never work again, Abdullah – never sweat nor hunger, nor thirst again . . .'

Abdullah, apparently too thick to detect the *double entendre*, can only think of how splendid it will be to be a Person of Quality and a Man of Consequence!

Exactly why Abdullah will not be permitted to go on living is obscure. As a co-assassin he is deeply involved and therefore bound to keep his mouth closed. It is difficult to imagine that he could do much harm to Suleiman. But there it is – he is destined soon to die.

And we now learn a few more facts from the Hadji's mouth:

'. . . return to this tent no more, for it is dangerous to do so. At times they visit me, though not often, at night, and I have a fancy that the accursed El R'Orab the Crow spies upon me, and also the aged Yakoub . . . Go in peace and remain hidden with the caravan men in the *fondouk* of the lower suq . . . Gharibeel Zarruk will bring thee word . . . *Emshi besselema.*'

The Great Oasis does, after all, cover one hundred square miles, and it should not be impossible for a man of Suleiman's cunning to hide himself successfully.

The recent sword-fight between de Beaujolais and Rastignac, which de Beaujolais won, is discussed by the Emir and his Vizier:

The Emir: 'Well, son Bud, what you know about *that* for a fight?'

The Vizier: 'I allow it was the best sword-fight I ever seen. I never denied that Rastignac nor Boje was real *men* . . .'

The Emir: 'And I'll tell the world that if Boje gets Miss Mary, she gets a husband to be proud of.'

[The Emir is coming out more and more strongly on de Beaujolais' side – reasons for which we will see later.]

The Vizier: 'Yep – as a he-man that can hold up his end of a dog-fight, all right, Hank. But I tell you a woman wants a man that's something more than a bad man to fight . . . S'pose he loves fightin' better than he loves her – what then, Hank Sheikh? And s'pose his real views of women is that they're just a dead-weight on the sword arm or gun-hand, and a dead-weight on your hoss's back?'

Although committed to subjecting de Beaujolais to his second test, Hank Sheikh is trying desperately to avoid doing so, and argument between his friend and himself goes back and forth. At last Buddy, with a long and critical stare at his Lord, asks, 'What's biting you now, you old fool?'

We now begin to learn something more of the background of the Emir el Hamel el Kebir:

> 'Miss Mary Vanbrugh. Ever since she came here I sit and think of all the things I learnt at school – and how I used to talk pretty an' learn lessons . . . and recite poetry . . .'

But Buddy only pours scorn on these reminiscences. During the evening ride, Mary, unable to hide her curiosity, and no doubt wishing to justify her rather uncharitable verbal attack on de Beaujolais, enquires of the Emir 'Who *was* this poor creature whom Major de Beaujolais found it expedient to kill? He was a Frenchman too, so why was he treated as an enemy?'

The Emir: 'He wasn't treated as an enemy by *us*, though he soon would have been. We received him politely and listened to what he had to say . . . Listened too long for our comfort.'

Mary: 'And was it interesting?'

The Emir: 'Some of it certainly was. He got to know there was a French officer here, openly wearing his uniform, and accompanied by two white women . . . He told us exactly what I ought to do with the three of them, and offered me quite a lot of money to do it.'

Mary: 'What was it?'

The Emir: 'I won't put it in plain words. But you just think of the plumb horriblest thing that could happen to you, and then you double it – and you'll hardly be at the beginning of it, Miss Mary Vanbrugh.'

Mary: 'Oh! And was that why Major de Beaujolais fought him?'

The Emir 'Partly, I guess – along with other reasons. It certainly didn't help the man's chances any, that the Major knew what was proposed for *you* . . .'

Mary: 'How did he get to know?'

The Emir: 'That's what I've to find out. If I have to pretend he won't get his Treaty unless he tells me . . . He'd do *anything* to get that safely signed, sealed and delivered.'

Mary: 'Not *anything*.'

The Emir: 'Well – *that* we may discover, perhaps, all in good time. Life is very dear – and a life's ambition is something even dearer . . .'

A Mixed Bag

The Emir is speaking English, with the words, accent and intonation of a person of culture and refinement; and his companion eyes him thoughtfully, her face wistful and sad.

Buddy, the vizier, possesses the gift of light sleep; the ability to awake if anything 'different' occurs. He acquired this gift from his mother, who lived alone with him, as a baby, in a log cabin and slept with a loaded rifle at her bedside for fear of 'Indians, wolves, mountain lions, Bad Men, and worst of all bad men, her husband'. Thus Buddy became possessed of his 'sixth' sense.

> Someone had passed the tent with stealthy steps . . . The sentry had done that a hundred times, but this was different. The Vizier passed straight from deep dreams to the door of his tent. Nobody . . . He crept towards the Emir's pavilion . . . Nothing . . . Yes – a shadow beside the guest tent, cast by the sentry, a young recruit, one Gharibeel Zarrug.

And so the Vizier circles the guest tent and lies behind it listening to, of all people, the Hadji and de Beaujolais talking. And the Hadji does not come over at all well. He proposes 'Murder' which does not please the case-hardened Vizier. De Beaujolais, however, comes over well. 'Good ole Boge. He is certainly a "White Man".'

> The Vizier crept around to the front of the tent and the knees of Gharibeel Zarrug smote together, as a figure rose beside him, and the voice of the Sheikh el Habibka el Wazir gave him sarcastic greeting . . .
>
> A few minutes later, the Vizier also gave the Hadji Abdul Salam sarcastic greeting, and said he would see him safely home to his tent: he would take no refusal of the offer of his company, in fact . . .

When de Beaujolais sends the Hadji on his way and that worthy walks straight into the arms of the Vizier, one's inclination is to think, 'what a coincidence!' But now we see that it is no coincidence at all.

CHAPTER 10

The Parting of the Ways

BUDDY'S SECOND TEST fails miserably. As we have seen, de Beaujolais drinks what he believes to be poison – becomes the victim of auto-suggestion – chokes, as he has seen the dog do, and falls to the floor, writhing in agony.

Mary Vanbrugh, who must have been listening at the felt flap which served as door between the Guest-tent and the female quarters, bursts in and, taking in the scene, sends the Emir and the Vizier packing.

Later, the Emir sneaks back, and is able to report to Buddy that he found Mary and the Major:

'Cuddling – fit to burst! He was kissin' her face flat . . .'

The Emir goes on to suggest that as Buddy has been the unwitting catalyst, he should now be Best Man.

And so Buddy, the Vizier, loses his bet and de Beaujolais wins Mary Vanbrugh!

In the early hours of that same night, whilst the Emir and the Vizier are trying to catch up on their sleep in the Great Pavilion, Suleiman the Strong and Abdullah el Jemmal make their play.

Conveniently, one Gharibeel Zarrug stands sentry. Suleiman sends Abdullah ahead to reconnoitre. He enters the tent creeping under the heavy felt flap and, moving slowly, discovers the Emir and the Vizier asleep on their rugs, 'sleeping the deep sleep of the innocent and just'. The Vizier is sleeping closest to the felt doorway.

Abdullah considers two quick stabs but, taking the great strength of the Emir into account, thinks better of it. Abdullah has seen both these men in action; he must adhere to the plan. He departs the way he came and reports to Suleiman.

Meanwhile:

The Emir: 'He did that very neat and slick.'

The Vizier: 'Not bad – he's a bit slow though.'

The Emir: 'S'pose we'd better hang Mister Gharibeel Zarrug bright an' early tomorrow.'

The Parting of the Ways

On receiving Abdullah's report Suleiman instructs him to re-enter the tent by way of the flap and crouch above the Vizier, while he, Suleiman, will enter through the tent-wall, exactly adjacent to the place where the Emir is sleeping.

> Suleiman to Abdullah: 'Listen, and live, you dog. Crouch ready to strike El Habibka at the moment I strike El Hamel. Watch the tent-wall beyond him. I shall enter there . . . And our knives will fall at the same moment . . . As your knife goes through El Habibka's heart, clap your left hand over his mouth . . . They must die together and die silently . . . Then we go back to the *fondouk* – and tomorrow I will appear to my friends and proclaim myself Sheikh Regent of the Tribe . . .'

Kneeling beside the sleeping Vizier, Abdullah el Jemmal poised his long, lean knife above his head, and stared hard at the tent wall beyond the recumbent form of the Emir . . .

In his sleep the Emir rolled his heavy head round and lay snoring, his face toward the very spot at which Abdullah stared.

A bright blade silently penetrated the wall of the tent. Slowly it travelled downward and the head of Suleiman the Strong was thrust through the aperture as the knife completed the long cut and reached the ground.

Gently Suleiman edged his body forward until his arms and shoulders had followed his head. Abdullah lifted his knife a little higher, drew a deep breath, and waited for Suleiman's signal – it did not come; instead the silence was horribly rent by the dreadful piercing scream of a woman in mortal anguish . . . a rifle banged . . .

Abdullah, unnerved, struck with all his strength, and his wrist came up with a sharp smack into the hand of the waiting Vizier, whose other hand seized the throat of Abdullah with a grip of steel.

Suleiman, with oaths and struggles, backed from the tent, and the Emir, bounding across the struggling bodies of the Vizier and Abdullah, rushed from the tent . . . in time to see Suleiman the Strong drive his knife into the breast of a woman.

The woman is the Sitt Leila, she whose wont it is to rise in the early hours of the morning and walk to the Emir's tent and pray for blessings on him. On these early morning walks she is accompanied by Bint Fatma (nurse and chaperon), who relates how, when Leila saw the prone form of a man with his head inside the Emir's tent, she realised immediately what this meant, and threw herself on him and grappled with him.

As gently as any mother nursing her sick child, the big Emir holds the dying girl to his breast, her arms about his neck, her eyes turned to his as turn those of a devoted spaniel to its master – and if ever a woman died happily, it was the little Arab girl . . .

Several things happen:

Buddy has the fight he has been looking for. Abdullah puts up a surprisingly good show. It takes Buddy several minutes to get Abdullah where he wants him – clasped to his chest with his powerful right arm, whilst his equally powerful left forces the assassin's knife hand back and back until both arm and joint snap. Buddy then seizes him by the throat with two hands and proceeds to choke him:

'That'll learn you, Mr Thug,' grunts the Vizier as he releases the murderer's throat.

But the final lesson has come too late in the learning – Abdullah is indeed a camel-man no longer!

Then comes the turn of the Emir, Hank. He engages in the knife-fight that Buddy really wanted. Giving Suleiman, who has been held captive by El R'Orab the Crow and Yussef Latif Fetata, time to recover, and time for the early morning light to improve, the Emir hands Suleiman his knife and takes up his own.

Later, El R'Orab describes the fight to Marbruk ben Hassan, who, to his abiding grief, had been absent on patrol:

'It was the fight of two blood-mad desert-lions – and they whirled and sprang and struck as lions do . . .

'Time after time the point was at the eye and throat and heart of each, and caught even as it reached the skin. Time after time the left hand of each held the right hand of the other and they were still – still as graven images of men, iron muscle holding back iron muscle, and all their mighty strength enabled neither to move his knife an inch . . .

'Then Suleiman weakened a little and our Lord's right hand pressed Suleiman's left hand down, little by little, as his left hand held Suleiman's right hand far out from his body. Slowly, slowly, our Lord's knife came downward toward that dog's throat, inch by inch – and Suleiman sweated like a horse and his eyes started forth.

'Slowly, slowly; his left hand grew feeble, and the Emir's hand, which Suleiman held, came nearer, nearer to Suleiman's throat . . .

'There was not a sound in all the desert as that blade crept nearer and nearer, closer and closer – till Suleiman uttered a shriek, a scream – even as the poor Sitt Leila had done – for the Emir's point had pricked him, pricked him right in the centre of his foul throat . . .

'And then *we heard the voice of our Lord saying, 'Leila! Leila! Leila!*' and with each word he thrust and thrust and thrust, till Suleiman gave way, and we saw the knife-point appear at the base of the murderer's skull . . . Right through! *Wallahi!* Our Emir is a *man*! . . .'

And Wren has this to say about this grim and gruesome fight, a fight that would have made many a Hollywood scene pale into insignificance!

> And from the Sixteenth-Century atmosphere of primitive expression of primitive passion, which from time to time still dominated the Oasis, the Emir slowly returned to the Twentieth Century and received the concise approving comments of his Vizier . . .

It is recorded that when Leila screamed, 'the French officer came running, sword in hand . . .' Yet nowhere is it recorded that he watched the knife-fight. This seems a little strange. Was he ordered back to his tent? Did he retire, gracefully, to his tent, not wishing to intrude on what was plainly Tribal business? Wren does not tell us.

That neither Mary Vanbrugh nor Maudie watched the fight goes without saying, as no women were allowed to watch contests such as these.

We are about to say farewell, for the time being, to Mary and her Major. They surface, briefly, from time to time, in the final book of the trilogy. He who Wren regards as his 'Beau Sabreur', is about to be superseded by another, this time a 'Beau Ideal'.

After the dispatch of Suleiman the Strong, matters move swiftly to a finale.

Mary Vanbrugh, in a private interview, gives the Emir the sharp edge of her tongue, for the hoax played on de Beaujolais.

The Emir's subsequent account of the interview confirms the Vizier's preconceived notion that the interview was well worth missing:

'I told you I took the blame for that foolishness, Son, an' I cert'nly got it . . . I thought I knew the worst about my evil nature . . . I was wrong, Son . . . I hadn't begun to know myself till Mary put me wise to the facts . . .'

An imposing caravan and escort carried Mary Vanbrugh and Major Henri de Beaujolais away to the North and the Emir departed on his honeymoon and the Vizier was left alone, in a populous place, with a gentle sadness settling on his soul.

The Emir had caused a beautiful camp to be pitched in a beautiful place, far off in the desert and he and his bride would ride there alone after the ceremony and great wedding feast.

For Maudie (and her Sheikh) . . . Dreams come true!

Before this all comes to pass the Emir and the Vizier have sat alone for the last hour of the former's bachelor life:

> *The Vizier:* '. . . and I don't see why you couldn't ha' kept your heavy hoof outa my affair with Maudie, Hank Sheikh!'
>
> *The Emir:* 'But your poor heart was broke right then, Son. And I just thought I'd stake out a claim 'fore it mended. Maudie's the first an' only girl I ever kissed, and she'll be the last . . .'
>
> *The Vizier:* '*Wot* a dull life you had, Hank Sheikh!'
>
> *The Emir:* 'Won't be dull any more, Son . . .'
>
> *The Vizier:* 'Ah well! S'pose I'll die an ole bachelor.'
>
> *The Emir:* 'Sure, Bud . . . Girls is discerning critters . . . But you might not o' course. You might get hanged young like . . .'
>
> *The Vizier:* 'Women always come between men an' their friends, Hank, pard. I reckon I better hike before Maudie does it . . .'

The Emir cuts his friend short, vowing that their 'Saul and David' relationship will continue, and then adds:

'Son, I got something to tell you. Something about Miss Vanbrugh that I promised her most solemn I wouldn't tell anybody.'

'Wot you want to tell me for then, Hank?'

'Becos you *ain't* anybody, see? You know I said I'd give my hand for you an' her to marry, if you loved each other?'

'Yup. And why was that, Hank?'

'*Becos she's my li'll sister, Mary!*'

'What a horrible liar you are, Hank Sheikh! When did you recognise her?'

On receiving this intelligence it can well be imagined that the Vizier collapsed heavily!

'The moment the Major said, "*Meet the Sitt Miriyam Hankinson el Vanbrugh*". My moniker's Noel Hankinson Vanbrugh!'

> *The Vizier:* 'Sunday socks o' Sufferin Samuel! That's the first interestin' thing I come across in a dull an' quiet life. I surely thought you was born-in-the-bone an' bred-in-the-butter plain "Hank"!'

'I forgot it till Boje mentioned it, Bud. Tain't my fault!'

And to Buddy's question as to whether or not Mary would tell the Major, Hank replies:

'. . . she'd do any mortal thing rather than let Major D. Bojol*lay* know that he's been a victim of a really high-class leg-pull and bluff . . . He takes himself mighty serious . . . He's goin' to have me an' you come to Paris to meet the President of the French Republic if we keep the Treaty nicely . . .'

Buddy cannot resist being Buddy: 'We'll paint li'll ol' Paris red . . . Paris girls like coloured gents I'm told . . . We'll surely give the public a treat.'

And then, as an afterthought: 'How did she recognise *you*, Son?'

> 'She says she took one look at my big nose – got a li'll scar on it, as perhaps you may ha' noticed – an' my grey eyes an' thick black eyebrows, an' then looked for my busted finger . . . I got the top shot off'n that, when Pop an' me an' the boys were chasin' hoss-rustlers off the range. She was a bright li'll looker then, and thought she c'd stick the bit on! . . . She knew me most as quick as I did her . . .'
>
> 'Why you didn't tell me, Hank?'
>
> 'Because she made me swear not to tell a soul. She never told Maudie . . . She was scared stiff someone might make a slip an' old Boje come to know . . . She wants Boje to be the Big Noise of the French African Empire someday . . . Neither is she plumb anxious for it to come out that we're the two Americans that quitted the Legion unobtrusive-like, down Zinderneuf way . . . They'd get us, Son . . . And they'd put us against a wall at dawn too, and take over the Great Oasis as a going concern . . . All sorts of boot-leggers, thugs, rollers, high-jackers, gunmen, ward-heelers, plug-uglies, and four-flusher five-ace fakers would come into this li'll Garden of Eden then . . .'

Hank certainly knows his underworld and things have not changed in the world much since those days.

Hank tells his friend that although he, Buddy, has never been a *good* man he is going to be Best Man, unless he wants to be 'a bridesmaid in those gay petticoats'.

Buddy opines that he had better marry the four Arab Janes which he has always threatened he would do. But Hank merely advises that he quits Sheikhing and goes off to the South Seas: 'An' be king of the Cannubial Islands . . .'

Thus ends the second book of the trilogy. Why no producer saw fit to make this story into an epic film to rival 'Beau Geste', escapes me.

In many ways it offers more than *Beau Geste*. There is certainly more action involved. *Beau Geste* describes two minor battles leading up to the siege of the fort at Zinderneuf. *Beau Sabreur* features the skirmish between de Beaujolais and the Arabs (when they attack Mary Vanbrugh); the defence of the pass at the bitter lake; the Emir's attack on the Touareg holding Buddy prisoner; the battle in the pass between the migrating tribe and the Emir who took Suleiman the Strong under his wing.

Then there are the duels. The first is de Beaujolais' formal duel with Becque when both are serving in the Blue Hussars; then there is de Beaujolais' duel with Rastignac (alias Becque) at the Great Oasis and the knife fight between Hank and Suleiman.

The Paramount picture stuck honestly to depicting the Geste brothers as young English gentlemen – later productions turned the brothers into 'all American boys'. *Beau Sabreur* would have suited the American mentality as none of the main characters is English – there are two American men, one American woman and a Frenchman, the only person of English extraction, Maudie, playing a very small part.

Perhaps, though, in time to come, a British company will produce *Beau Sabreur* and make an honest job of it!

There can be no doubting the fact that Wren loved his American men turned Arab. We learn more of their amazing exploits in the final book of the trilogy, *Beau Ideal*.

BOOK TWO ENDS

The Third Book
Beau Ideal

Introduction

THE MAIN CHARACTER in *Beau Ideal* is so radically different from the main character in either *Beau Geste* or *Beau Sabreur*, that one can only come to the conclusion that P. C. Wren wished to demonstrate that he was capable of writing about characters other than military men and characters other than those of British or French nationality. For Otis Vanbrugh is pure American and far removed from Wren's military personnel. Vanbrugh, apart from a short spell in the French Foreign Legion, is certainly not an 'officer and a gentleman', but rather a 'scholar and a gentleman'.

Beau Ideal opens, as does *Beau Geste*, with a prologue. The prologue in *Beau Geste* tells of the strange events at Zinderneuf as related by Major Henri de Beaujolais to George Lawrence Esq. but dealt with differently by this author.

For reasons best known to himself, Wren dispenses with both prologue and epilogue in *Beau Sabreur*, merely making use of introductory notes.

The prologue to *Beau Ideal* is set in a silo, a grain pit, somewhere in French Sahara. The characters are an Englishman, an American, a Spaniard, a Jew, a Russian, a prince of noble blood but now a convict, and a Captain of Spahis, There are several other prisoners but we learn nothing of them as they are not 'characters'. They do, however, suffer the same fate as all the main characters, excepting two.

These men are all members of the Disciplinary Battalions, the *Compagnies de Discipline*, the *Joyeux*, the *Zeyphys*, in fact the *Bataillon d'Infanterie Legère d'Afrique* – convicted criminals sentenced to punishment beyond punishment.

The silo is a deep grain-pit, its walls sloping inward and upward to a narrow aperture, the mouth of the silo. The construction of these silos has not altered since the time Carthage was young. The inward sloping walls prevents the unfortunate inmate, a human being who under no circumstances should have been confined to such a hell-hole, from gaining a modicum of comfort by leaning against the wall.

It is stored now, not with grain, but with men.

[Wren by way of a footnote states that punishment by way of confinement in a silo is no longer legal in the French army. One would hope not.]

Lowered into the silo, along with the men, is a drum of water and a sack of bread. Whilst these meagre rations last there is hope.

To while away the time some of the inmates relate tales, some true, some exaggerations of the basic truth. Others listen, now and then interjecting or offering dry comment. But most 'break' and give up the ghost.

The first of the internees to break is the Spaniard, Ramon Gonzales. We do not know it now, but shortly we will learn that it was this same Gonzales who betrayed John Geste to the camel corps patrol north of Zinder, who pointed him out to the French commander of the patrol as a deserter from the Legion.

After exacting a promise from the Englishman that he 'will forgive him' and a further promise that he will prop him up on his knees so that he can die kneeling, he goes on to tell why.

His great fear is that God will mistake him for his brother and punish him accordingly, for his brother had sinned mightily: treated God as an enemy.

> It was the priest's fault. We were good enough boys, only mischievous. Fonder perhaps of the girls and the sunshine and the wine-skin and the bull-ring than of religion and work. My brother *was* a good boy – if a little quick with his knife – until that accursed and hell-doomed priest – No! No! No! I mean that holy man of God – cast his eyes upon Dolores. My brother killed that priest; God may mistake me for him.'
>
> 'God makes no mistakes,' said the Englishman.
>
> My brother caught the priest and Dolores in the priest's own church. My brother married them before the altar and their married life was brief.
>
> But of course, God knew my brother was mad, and as he left the desecrated church, he cried, '*Never will I enter the House of God again! Never kneel or make the sign of the cross again.*'
>
> And that very night the big earthquake came and shattered our village.

As is often the case, the villagers flocked to the church for safety and the brother, carrying his mother in his arms for safety, was with the throng that sought refuge in this traditional haven.

> Yes! He had entered the House of God once more!
>
> But he could not stay in Spain, and I, who was innocent, fled with my

brother to South America – to that El Dorado where so many of us go in search of what we never find.

But Ramon's brother went from bad to worse, defying God and slaying men and women. On one occasion, forced to flee and pursued by *guardias civiles*, Ramon and his brother had become lost in a rain-storm and their escape route led along a precipitous mountain pass –

> a flash of lightning lit up a ruined building and into this we dashed and hid. It may have been the rolling thunder, the steaming rain, or an avalanche of stones dislodged by the horses of the pursuers, passing along the path above – I do not know – but there was a terrible crash, a heavy blow, a blinding, suffocating dust – and my brother was trapped, held as in a giant fist . . .
>
> And when daylight came he saw he was in a ruined chapel of the old *conquistadores*, kneeling before the altar – a beam across his bowed shoulders and neck; another across his legs behind his knees – and there my brother *knelt* before the altar of God. And thus the soldiers found him and took him to the *calabozo*. (I was lucky and the soldiers overlooked my hiding place in the crypt).
>
> The annual revolution occurred on the eve of his garrotting, and he was saved, but he had to flee the country, and with me, he returned to Spain. Owing to a little smuggling problem, in which a *guardia civil* lost his life we crossed the Pyrenees into France and signed on for the Foreign Legion.
>
> In the Legion we made quite a name for ourselves – not so easy a thing to do in the Legion, as some of you may know. There they fear nothing. They fear no thing, but God is not a thing, my friends. They fear neither man nor the devil, neither death nor danger – but they fear God . . . When they come to die, anyhow.
>
> But my brother did not fear God, and his *escouade* of devils realised that he was much braver than they. In Africa there was little fear of him having to flee to a church for shelter, or be pinned on his knees before a chapel altar! We aren't much troubled with chaplains and church parades in the Legion!

[This is the sole mention of a church parade or a chaplain in Wren's trilogy, or, for that matter, in any other of his Legion books.]

> But one day my brother saw a lad, a boy from Provence, make the Sign of the Cross upon his breast, as we were preparing to die of thirst, lost in a desert sand-storm. '*Sangre de Christo*! If I see you make that sign again I'll do it upon you with a bayonet.'
>
> 'If we come through this *I will* make the Sign of the Cross *on you* with my bayonet,' gasped the boy. But my brother only laughed, 'Try, try it on me when I am asleep. Why your bayonet would melt. *God himself could not do it!*'

And the next day my brother was lost in that sand-storm and the Touareg band that found him took him to the Sultan of Zaggat . . . and the Sultan of Zaggat *crucified* him in the market-place, 'as an appropriate death for a good Christian!'

Now help me to my knees, Senor Smith, and keep each word of your promise, for I think I am dying.

And then the cry of '*Dios aparece,*' and Ramon died.

Jacob the Jew is a great adept at concealment and he now produces five matches, one of which he lights revealing the sad state of affairs on the silo floor.

'Too late,' says Jacob softly. 'But perhaps *le Bon Dieu* will let him off with eight days *salle de police* in Hell . . .'

However, ignoring Jacob, the Englishman, assisted by the American, lifts the dead Ramon to his knees, and reverently does all that had been promised.

Jacob:	'There are but five matches, but Ramon shall have two, as candles at his head and feet. It would please the poor Ramon.'
The Englishman:	'You're a good fellow, Jacob . . . if you'll excuse the insult!'
Jacob:	'Pray for the soul of Ramon Gonzales, who dies in the fear of God – or, at any rate, in the fear of what God might do to him.'

And here the Frenchman attempts to lend a hand, stating that he has conducted military funerals in his capacity as a field officer in the French army. Before he can bring the litany to memory, however, he collapses in a faint.

Prince Berchinsky, in civilian life, legionnaire Badineff before his demotion to the Zephyrs, is the next to succumb. He has fought with General Faraux and General Dodds against the bloodthirsty and genocidal king of Dahomey, King Behanzin.

The overthrow of King Behanzin, and the conquest and colonisation of Dahomey are well recorded in history. Whether the French had any right to interfere with the murderous carryings on of the king is not within the scope of this work. Perhaps he should have been left to continue with his blood-purges.

Wren has not only Badineff fighting against the 'Amazons,' but also John Bull (alias Sir Montague Merlin) come up against these 'ladies'. (See

Stepsons of France.) These 'Amazons', female warriors, have nothing whatsoever to do with the world's greatest river which bears that name.

Badineff was soon to join his ancestors of the 'blood royal'.

As an exercise in pure militarism, it is difficult to understand why the French army opted to attack Dahomey from the sea, landing an army, the Legion in the vanguard, on the coast. Infiltration overland from the north would appear to have been the sensible thing to do. And again, we must assume that the colonisation of Africa at the time was the 'in' thing.

Jacob the Jew: 'The lad we want here is the bright, bold Rastignac, . . . Rastignac, the Mutineer.'

The Englishman: 'Oh, did you know him?'

Jacob does not answer directly, but proceeds to tell how:

'Rastignac escaped from the Zephyrs by killing a sentry, donning the sentry's uniform, breaking into a Public Works Department shed . . . taking a pot of black paint, a pot of white, and paint brushes . . . He then walked to the nearest milestone and neatly touched up the black *kilometre* figures and their white border . . . and then to the next, . . . and the next.

When patrols passed he exchanged jokes and the latest news . . . visited several camps and made himself useful to the officers with his paint.

And so he painted his way, milestone by milestone to Oran, where he produced the dead sentry's *livret* and leave papers and shipped back to France.'

[Jacob does not know that Rastignac subsequently took service with the Sultan of Turkey.]

Having listened to Jacob relating the adventures of Rastignac the talk turns to how long they will remain abandoned and how long their supply of water can last.

The ex-officer is of the opinion that:

'We are forgotten. We are the Forgotten-of-Men, as distinguished from our friends the Touareg, the Forgotten-of-God.

As you are aware, *mes amis*, a list of *les honourés punis* is made out, by the clerk of the *Adjudant*, every morning, before the guard is changed. Our names are not on that list, and so we cannot be released. We are not in "prison" because we are not recorded as being in "prison" – and therefore we cannot be released from "prison" . . .'

and Jacob observes:

'Convincing and very cheering . . . Monsieur must have been a lawyer before he left the world.'

'No . . . an officer . . . Captain of Spahis and in the Secret Service . . . about to die and unashamed. *No!* I should say *Légionnaire* Rien of the Seventh Company of the Third Battalion of the First Regiment of the Foreign Legion . . . I was wandering in my mind.

Should any genlteman here survive, I wonder whether he would be so extremely obliging as to write to my mother.'

The Englishman and the American memorise an address in Paris, and each declare that he will not only write to Madame de Lannec, but will visit her.

Neither the American nor the Englishman, despite Rien's logic, would admit that he also was in his grave.

The American:	'I've been nearer death too. Been dead really in this same Zaguig.'
The Frenchman:	'An unpleasant place, Zaguig. I know it well. I too have occasionally been in danger . . . but I finish here!'
The American:	'Never say die. Personally I refuse to die. I've got a job to do and intend to live until it's done.'
The Englishman:	'Same here . . . I must be getting home to tea shortly . . . my wife . . .'
The Frenchman:	'Ah, *mes amis*, you wish to live . . . I on the contrary wish to die.'

The Frenchman goes on to rave about 'Véroniquc', of a Colonel of Chasseurs d'Afrique, of a Moor of the Zarhoun whom he killed with his bare hands, but chiefly of 'Véronique'.

Jacob the Jew (the Roumanian gypsy) needles the Englishman on British attitudes – wanting to know the reason for his sloppy 'kindness' to Ramon Gonzales,

'I am a philosopher and a student of that lowest of the animals, called Man . . . Was it to please your Christian God and so acquire merit? . . . Or to uphold your insolent British assumption of an inevitable and natural superiority?

'Ramon Gonzales betrayed you . . . I would have strangled him . . . Didn't he betray and denounce you after you had found him in the desert and saved his life? . . . Recognised you as one of the Zinderneuf men he knew at Sidi . . . and sold you for twenty-five pieces of silver . . . Consigned you to sudden death – or a lingering death – for twenty-five francs and a Sergeant's favour!

	. . . And here the Judas was, wondrously delivered into your hand – and you "forgave" him and comforted him! Now *why*? What *was* the game?'
The Englishman:	'No game, no motive, no reason. He acted according to his lights – I to mine.'
Jacob:	'And where do you get your "lights"? What flame lit them?'
The Englishman:	'Oh – I don't know . . . Home . . . Family . . . One's women-folk . . . School . . . Upbringing . . . Traditions . . . One unconsciously imbibes ideas of doing the decent thing . . . I've been extraordinarily lucky in life . . . Poor old Ramon wasn't . . . One does the decent thing if one is decent . . . one's *"beau idéal".'*
Jacob:	'You don't go about, then, consciously and definitely forgiving your enemies . . . ?'
	'No, of course not! Don't talk rot!'
	'Nor with a view to securing a firm option or a highly eligible and desirable mansion in the sky – suitable for English gentlemen . . .'
	'Not in the least . . . don't be an ass . . .'
	'You disappoint me. I was hoping to find, before I died, one of those rare animals, a Christian gentleman . . . this was positively my last chance . . . I shall die here . . . But, look here Christian, if I summoned up enough strength, and swung this chain with all my might against your right cheek, would you turn the other, also?'
	'No, I should punch you on the nose.'

Soon after, the ex-officer of Spahis begins to rave and beg for water. Jacob offers to give up his ration, and an expletive issues from the Englishman's lips, '*Stout fella.*' For a reason which becomes clear later, the American starts and exclaims, '*Say that again, will you?*'

'Stout fella!'

'Merciful God!'

Soon after this the Frenchman, ex-Spahi officer, dies.

Only three left – Jacob, the Englishman and the American.

Jacob decides that his time has come. Lack of food and water have taken its toll, but Jacob, being a rational man, deduces that they stand no chance of being rescued:

'Either the Company has moved on, and there are a few more miles of the Zaguig – Great Oasis road, marked, or else there was a sudden raid and the Company is obliterated . . . Anyhow – I've had enough . . .'

Both the American and Englishman plead with him to hang on for another day – but no:

'I have opened a vein . . . when you want it, you'll find the piece of steel in my right hand . . . razor-edge one side, saw-edge the other. Pluck up your courage and come along with me, both of you . . .'

THE STORY OF OTIS VANBRUGH

A lean man, silent, behind triple bars
Of pride, fastidiousness, and secret life.
His thought an austere commune with the stars,
His speech a probing with a surgeon's knife.

His style a chastity whose acid burns
All slack, false, formlessness in man or thing;
His face a record of the truth man learns
Fighting bare-knuckled Nature in the ring.

John Masefield

A man's place in the scale of civilization is shown by his attitude to women. There are men who regard a woman as something to live with. There are others who regard her as something to live for.

(*Unknown – but attributed to P. C. Wren*)

CHAPTER I

Isobel

WE MEET OTIS as a young lad on a visit to Brandon Regis, the house of his maternal grandmother. Brandon Regis is a few miles from Brandon Abbas and it is Otis' wont to walk in that direction.

On one of his morning walks he catches his first sight of Isobel Rivers:

> . . . the girl's face was the loveliest I had ever seen. It is still the loveliest I have ever seen.

With Isobel were characters we have met – Michael (Beau) Geste, his twin brother Digby and his younger brother John.

It transpires that this party, what we know as Beau Geste and his Band, are out looking for Isobel's lost dog. Isobel is certain that the 'nice American boy' will help in the search, and gives Otis a smile that goes: 'straight to my heart – and also to my head.'

Otis, naturally, volunteers to assist in the search. This is the first, but by no means the last, time he volunteers to serve Isobel.

As things turn out Otis does not find the dog; it finds him at his grandmother's house and he is able to return it to Brandon Abbas and so gain another glimpse of Isobel. He gains more than a glimpse – a huge hug and a warm kiss from Isobel is his reward. From Beau, a 'Stout Fella! Splendid! Good scout!' From Digby, (on extending his hand): 'Put it right there, Mr Daniel Boone – or are you Kit Carson? Or Buffalo Bill?'

The upshot of all this is that Otis is made an honorary member of 'Beau Geste's Band'.

> The more I saw of the three Gestes, the better I liked them, and I knew that I could never see too much, nor indeed enough, of Isobel Rivers . . .

We are about to see something of the Gestes through the eyes of Otis Vanbrugh:

> Of the boys, I liked John best; for, in addition to all the attributes which he possessed in common with his brilliant brothers, he was, to me, slightly pathetic

> in his dog-like devotion to the twins . . .
>
> Yet, at the same time, I liked Beau enormously; for his splendour – and it was nothing less – of mind, body and soul; his unselfish sweetness and gentleness, and his extraordinary 'niceness' to everybody, including myself . . .
>
> But, then again, I liked Digby as much; for his unfailing mirth and happiness . . . He was the most genuinely and spontaneously cheerful person I ever met . . .

There can be no doubt that Wren wishes Michael 'Beau' Geste to be his hero, hero without spot, his non-pareil. Yet he does not 'come alive' as does Major Henri de Beaujolais. Everyone praises Michael Geste, and yet, in the trilogy he lives so short a time. It is pointless to speculate on a meeting between Mary Vanbrugh and Beau Geste – but one cannot help wondering what the outcome would have been!

> I suppose Claudia was of an immaculately flawless beauty, charm, and grace of form and face, even as a young girl – but personally I never liked her. There was a slight hardness, a self-consciousness and an element of selfishness in her character, that was evident – to me at any rate, though not I think to the others. Certainly not to Michael Geste, for she was obviously his *beau ideal* of girlhood . . .

Michael Geste was to pay dearly for his love for this girl.

> Nor could I like Lady Brandon, fascinating as she was to most. She was kind, generous and hospitable to me, and I was grateful – but *like* her I could not. She was imperious, clever, hard, 'managing' and capable. She was very queenly in appearance and style, given to cherishing of favourites – Michael and Claudia especially – and extremely jealous.

Otis Vanbrugh then tells us that:

> 'I am very intuitive, as well as being a student of physiognomy, and possessed a distinct gift for reading character.'

At the time of this pronouncement he must be all of fifteen years old, and we know, from George Lawrence's narrative, that Lady Brandon is 'about forty years old'.

Wren is a master at weaving into his story fragments of casual contacts and meetings that surface later on.

> After spending a few days in London, I was scolded for my absence of several days . . . and told that I had missed the chance of a lifetime, and chance of seeing and hearing a veritable Hero of Romance, a French Officer of Spahis

Isobel

... who had forever endeared himself to the children, by his realistic and true tales of Desert warfare, and of adventures in mysterious and romantic Morocco.

Otis has missed meeting his future brother-in-law. He is soon to leave for America and prepare himself for Harvard. At the leave taking of the Band, Isobel puts her arms around him, kisses him and says, 'You *will* come back soon, nice American boy?'

The Vanbrugh ranch in Wyoming need not detain us. It is, no doubt, a beautiful ranch, and Otis loves the free, outdoor life there and the fact that he can live on horseback.

His father he describes thus:

> ... hard, overbearing, autocratic ... not a bad man ... He was a very 'good' one. He was not cruel, vicious or vindictive; but he was a terror and a tyrant. He crushed his wife and broke her spirit, and turned his children into rebels, or terrified 'suggestibles'. Noel and Mary were rebels. Janey and I were cowed and terrified.

Noel, the eldest child, has gone 'missing' and his father neither knows nor cares where he is. He had refused a college education and felt more at home on the range than in a class-room, bunking with the cowboys in the bunkhouse whenever possible.

For suggestions that Noah might have had trouble gathering up both the polar bears and the kangaroos, for the ark, Noel receives a sound thrashing from his father.

> This was after father's return from a trip to Europe to buy a twenty-thousand dollar Hereford bull, and the finest pure-bred Arab stallion that money could purchase.

Finally, Noel pulls a gun on his father, and realises that if that sort of thing happened it were best that he quit the ranch.

> Yes, father certainly spoilt Noel's life and made him the wanderer he became.
> Noel departed, and returned after a quarter of a century in such wise as I shall relate.

A long way back, Major Henri de Beaujolais gave us a fleeting glimpse of his opinion of Otis Vanbrugh; we should now look at him through his own eyes:

> I loved books, and desired above all things to become a fine scholar ... I

considered 'my mind to me a kingdom is,' to be a grand saying if one could say it (to oneself only, of course) with real truth.

So here we have the scholar – not the military men of *Beau Geste* and *Beau Sabreur*. The scholar will, however, undergo hardships equal to, if not greater than, those to which our earlier heroes were subjected.

And so to Harvard. Otis enjoys everything from books to baseball at 'glorious' Harvard. He confesses though that his heart is in England, and even if he does not moon around in a hopeless state of calf-love, he is glad when his three years at Harvard are over and he can return to England and more particularly to Brandon Regis, 'a pleasant walk from Brandon Abbas'.

We learn no more of Otis' Harvard days than:

> I filled my days with work, read hard and played hard, lived dangerously when living in the West . . . and earned the warm approval of my brave and hardy sister, Mary . . .

Wren now treats us to one of the amazing coincidences with which the trilogy is filled – coincidences which, however unlikely, ring true.

> As I stepped from the Southampton-London boat train at Waterloo, another train was in the act of departure from the opposite side of the same platform, and gliding forward with slowly increasing speed. At a window, waving a handkerchief to three young men, was a girl, and with a queer constriction of the heart, a rush of blood to the head . . . I realised that the girl was Isobel Rivers – the child Isobel, grown up to a most lovely girlhood . . .

Otis is swept away by emotion, in fact he takes leave of his senses; the sight of the lovely Isobel is too much for him.

Abandoning his luggage, ignoring the 'three young men' (the Gestes), he boards the moving train which is by now travelling at ever increasing speed, but has, aboard, as a passenger, to his certain knowledge, Isobel.

The train unfortunately is one of those quaint British trains which is corridorless and Otis is confined to his compartment and is unable to go in search of Isobel.

His reward for his folly comes when the train reaches Exeter and he meets Isobel, and Lady Brandon, on the station platform.

Isobel, with sparkling eyes, offers him both her hands; Lady Brandon offers him two fingers, but nevertheless invites him to share their compartment in the small branch-line train which takes them to Brandon Abbas. Neither of the ladies, in true British fashion, comments on his lack of luggage. From Brandon Abbas he is conveyed, by carriage, to the home of his grandmother, High Gables, Brandon Regis.

The sparkle in Isobel's eyes has raised his hopes, but bitter disappointment is lurking just around the corner. Isobel and Lady Brandon have been staying in London with the three boys (now young men), who were about to set out on a walking tour, and were themselves leaving for Wales the next day. Poor Otis – his frenzied dash appears to have been in vain, but:

> *I had seen Isobel* and received confirmation of the fact that not only was she the most marvellous thing in all the world, but that everything else in the world would be as nothing in the balance against her.

Such is young love! But Otis is man enough to admit that it was 'a trivial and foolish little incident'.

Having made this admission he goes on, though, to enunciate and proclaim the very foundation and basis of the book we are concerned with:

> . . . as I lay awake . . . there came to me the great, the very greatest, idea of my life – the idea that I might conceivably, with the help of God and every nerve and fibre of my being, some day, somehow, contrive to make myself worthy to love Isobel and then – incredibly to be loved by Isobel, and actually to devote my life to doing that of which I had thought when her eyes sparkled and shone at seeing me . . .

Wren certainly tests him in the crucible!

Otis vows that he will ask her, when next they meet, whether she loves him as he loves her:

> But the next time we met, I asked her something else.

What was it that Otis asked Isobel? To find out we must deal with Otis' next visit to Brandon Regis and Brandon Abbas.

On this visit to England Otis acts more rationally – taking the train, accompanied by his luggage, to Exeter and on to Brandon Abbas. He meets Isobel in the lane and is greeted by her, as before with 'Why! It's our nice American Boy come back! I am so glad . . . Otis . . .'

There is however something wrong. Otis finds her voice different, older. Her face, too, is different, older. He gains the distinct impression of unhappiness.

Isobel: 'John has gone . . . The boys have gone away . . .'
Otis: 'Let me help you, Isobel.'

There it is. Instead of asking Isobel for her hand, Otis asks her whether he can *help* her. His mission from now on will be one of service to Isobel, but before this becomes indubitably clear he receives the 'body blow', the words coming through to him as through a mist; barely comprehensible and difficult to grasp and believe:

> '*John and I are engaged to be married . . .*' and the statement was accompanied by the splash of large tears.

> '. . . and he has had to go away . . . and I am so miserable, Otis . . . We were engaged one evening, and he was gone the next morning!'

Otis spends a month at Brandon Regis. Every day he rides out with Isobel. They talk of nothing but John Geste . . . but she cannot, will not tell him where he and his brothers are, or why they left Brandon Abbas. Otis, his love overflowing, is forced to talk about the other man!

> It occurred to me though, that it must be a mighty strong inducement, an irresistible compulsion, that took John Geste from Brandon Abbas on the day after his declaration of his love for Isobel!

Mercifully for Otis, Isobel goes to stay with friends and he flees to Paris from where he returns home to his father's ranch in Wyoming.

Wren goes to great lengths in outlining the conflict in the Vanbrugh family. . . the tyrannical father, the departed Noel, the weak sister Janey, the rebellious sister Mary. We may spare ourselves this ordeal, the upshot of which is that Otis and Mary decide to take a lengthy leave of absence and depart for Paris. Janey refuses to accompany them as she feels her duty lies in remaining on the ranch to look after her father.

The trilogy has, however, to run its course and Paris, as a stepping-stone to North Africa, is a good enough place from which to mature the plot.

CHAPTER 2

The Angel of Death

MARY AND OTIS have what Otis describes as a 'wholly delightful' time in Paris, and it is at one of their many parties that Mary meets a Colonel of Zouaves, the much-decorated Levasseur. Unfortunately for him, he falls madly in love with Mary, whilst she is merely 'amused' by him, and he is soon forgotten – but only for a short while as their paths are to cross again.

Setting out on their 'grand' tour of Europe, Mary and Otis 'take in' London, Rome, Venice, Naples, Athens and then cross the Mediterranean and arrive in Algiers, where they re-encounter the brave Colonel.

Wren now tells us, through the mouth of Otis Vanbrugh, something of Zaguig, the town Levasseur is posted to:

> Colonel Levasseur was preparing to set forth, as the point of a lancet of 'peaceful penetration', to the fanatical city of Zaguig, a distant hotbed of sedition and centre of disaffection – wherein the leaders of every anti-French faction, from eastern Senussi to western Riffian, plotted together and tried to stem the tide of civilisation.

What was this civilisation? According to Wren it was:

> ... roads, railways, telegraphs, peace, order and cultivation of the soil ...

Against these benefits Wren ranges:

> ... savagery ... blind adherence to the dead letter of a creed outworn ... ferocious hatred of all that was not sealed in Islam ... for the administration of rapine, fire, and slaughter ...

It is not within the scope of this work to pass judgement on Wren's views or of the consequences of colonisation. However it seems that the French left Algeria better off than they found it and the religion of the people, Islam, intact.

Wishing to see more of the desert Mary and Otis travel south to the town of Bouzen, which is at the end of the railway-line.

To this garrison town, from Zaguig, comes Levasseur, ostensibly to confer with the commandant of the garrison, but in fact to court Mary, whose arrival in that town has spread abroad via the desert telegraph.

Otis tells us that Levasseur shows up to much better advantage in Bouzen than he did in Paris. Here, as a colonel, he can put junior officers in their place and devote time to his courtship, taking Mary riding on horse and camel. The wide open spaces of the desert suit him far better than the ballrooms of Paris.

The invitation is duly made by Levasseur to Otis to bring Mary to Zaguig. Otis fears that this must end in an invitation of marriage to Mary, to which she replies that:

> ... sufficient unto the day is the proposal thereof, and that if her brother did not take her to Zaguig, Colonel Levasseur would.

The invitation is accepted, but before setting out from Bouzen for Zaguig Levasseur takes it on himself to show Otis:

> ... 'life' in Bouzen, by night – *recherché* 'life' not seen by the tripper, but solely by the select ...

Mary is left behind and in fact not told of the expedition. Ladies in that day and age were not permitted to see 'life' and neither Otis nor Levasseur wish her to know of their proposed escapade.

Otis, who is something of a prude, refuses to enjoy the evening but it is a fateful one for him as he meets the 'Angel of Death', one destined to play an important part in his life (and in the trilogy).

The Angel of Death is an Ouled-Naïl dancing girl, and on this particular night her escort is one Selim ben Yussef. These dancing girls were schooled in their art in Djelfa and were flourishing there as late as 1960; it is almost impossible to discover whether or not they are still in business or even in demand, today.

Otis describes her thus:

> ... there was something indescribably arresting, fascinating, wonderful about the real and remarkable beauty of the girl ... She was at once pretty, lovely, beautiful and handsome ...
>
> To begin with she was so fair that you thought her European until you realised her blue-black hair.
>
> Of her figure I can but say it was worthy of her face. It was perfect.
>
> She was a human flower ... An orchid – a white orchid marked with scarlet and with black. And as these flowers always do, she looked wicked – an incarnate, though very lovely, potentiality for evil.

The Angel of Death

As the colonel and Otis are the only foreigners present the Angel of Death makes straight for them and cutting Levasseur, much to his chagrin, dead, she gives all her attention to Otis, he of the blue eyes and blond hair.

> With a deep, deep curtsy of mocking homage and genuine challenge, that broke her slow revolving dance at my very feet, she sank to the ground, and, rising like a swift-growing flower from the earth – like Aphrodite herself – she gazed straight into my eyes, smiled with all the allure of the sirens, Delilahs, Sapphos .. and Cleopatras that ever lived, and whispered to me – as if she and I were alone in all Africa . . . alone in the gracious night . . . alone together, she and I at the door of our silken tent .. she and I alone upon the silken cushions and the silken carpet . . .

Such was the Angel of Death's power to captivate.

> I struggled like a drowning man . . . I was a drowning man, sinking down . . . down . . . down . . . hypnotized . . .
> 'No! No!' I shouted. '*NO!*'
> The only flower for me was my English rose . . . What had I to do with orchids of Africa?

These protestations do not in any way deter the Angel of Death. In French and broken English she plies her wiles (or are they?):

> '*Beaux yeux bleus*! *Baisez-moi*! I lov' you so . . . *Je t'aime! Je t'adore.* Kiss me, sweetheart . . . Crush me in your arms, darling . . .'

Colonel Levasseur sits watching the scene, smiling cynically: 'You are favoured, my friend.'

Otis resists her wiles with all his strength of will. Can he be blamed? Not many men would take a night-club singer or dancer in their arms and kiss her. Certainly not in the company of others, unknown or known to him or not. Our old friend, Buddy might have! But not Otis.

Levasseur throws light on the Angel of Death's origins. Her mother was an Ouled-Naïl dancing girl, Zaza Blanchfleur, from the street of the dancing girls. Her father was rumoured to be an Englishman – hence the Angel of Death's pale complexion. It seems that the 'Englishman' took Zaza off into the desert on an elaborate 'honeymoon'. Even though, according to Levasseur, Zaza Blanchfleur had had many lovers, some of high rank, she fell in love with this 'Englishman,' and when let down by him – he had coolly left her after their 'honeymoon' – she inculcated a hatred in the child of the union, the Angel of Death, a hatred of all Europeans..

The amorous advances she makes to Otis barely spell 'hatred', but she would have been playing a deep game.

At the scene of the dancing is a character destined to play a part in the unfolding story – one Selim ben Yussuf – who is the son of a powerful, but elderly, Sheikh. Furthermore, he is madly in love with the Angel of Death.

[Wren sets the scene of the Ouled-Naïl dancing girls in Bouzen, 'at the end of the railway'. There is no such town as 'Bouzen' in North Africa. There are towns with similar names but no Bouzen. The town 'at the end of the railway' is Djelfa and it is from here that the Ouled-Naïl dancing girls came.]

On the way home to their hotel that night, Levasseur takes Otis to the Street of the Ouled-Naïls and tells Otis more of their history.

> 'Interesting people, those Ouled-Naïl dancing-girls. They've danced, and they've sat in Obis Street, for a couple of thousand years or so. They danced for Julius Caesar and Scipio Africanus as they danced for you and me . . . Roman generals took them to Rome, and French generals take them to Paris . . . There isn't much they don't know about the art of charming. A hundred generations of hereditary love . . . Most intriguing and attractive.'

Otis is not convinced, and although he has told us that he is no prude he makes the following point:

> 'A matter of taste. Personally I'd pay handsomely to be excused. I don't see how a bedizened, painted, probably unwashed, half-savage Jezebel is going to "interest, intrigue, and attract" a person of any taste and refinement.'

The colonel is rather put out by this short dissertation but comes back with:

> 'One of them attracted the "Englishman" to some purpose . . . He took her from this very street . . . I could show you the house . . . He treated her like a bride . . . And what about her daughter, the Angel of Death? She has interested a few people of taste and refinement, I can tell you . . . she sat in the street, at first, but she has walked in a few other streets since . . . Bond Street; Rue de la Paix; Unter den Linden . . . visited nearly all the capitals of Europe . . . She may marry a Sheikh and go out into the desert for good – or marry a rich Moor and go into his *hareem* in Fez – stay here and amass wealth – go to Paris, Marseilles or Algiers – she may die a princess on a silken bed in a Sultan's palace, or on the floor of a foul den in Port Said . . .

Both the 'Englishman' and the Angel of Death re-enter the story down the line of time. Can you guess the identity of the 'Englishman'? A clue: he is not an Englishman at all.

The Angel of Death plays a rather more important part in the story than does this masquerading Englishman but, sadly, we do not know her end. Wren does not tell us whether any of the scenarios suggested by Colonel Levasseur come to pass or are fulfilled. A pity.

Of Otis Vanbrugh's attitude towards this beautiful dancing-girl little can be said. He had his likes and dislikes, and perhaps, as we shall see, he is correct.

CHAPTER 3

Encore Zaguig

AND SO TO ZAGUIG. Mary, as with many tourists, wishes to see 'the native in the raw', and Levasseur obliges by taking her and her brother to Zaguig.

In due course a certain Major Henri de Beaujolais arrives in Zaguig. This is his second visit; the first he made disguised as an Arab – this time he comes in uniform, his disguise well concealed for possible future use.

Otis has this to say of him:

> I liked this handsome clean-cut Major Henri de Beaujolais from the first . . . To the simplicity and directness of the soldier he added the cleverness and knowledge of the trained specialist; the charm, urbanity and grace of the experienced man of the world; and the inevitable attractiveness of a lovable and modest character.

Otis may have found de Beaujolais 'modest'. De Beaujolais's own writings reflect nothing of modesty.

He goes on:

> He combined the best of two nations, with his English public-school upbringing, and his English home-life of gentle breeding, on the one hand, and his aristocratic French birth, breeding and traditions on the other . . .

[Wren was writing of a period when birth and upbringing still meant something in this world. De Beaujolais is, without a doubt, one of his favourite characters!]

The differences in opinion between Major Henri de Beaujolais and his superior, Colonel Levasseur, have been written of. We now see the picture of the departure from Zaguig of de Beaujolais, Mary, Maudie, Dufour and others, through the eyes of Otis Vanbrugh.

Threads that were left untied by de Beaujolais, in his version of the flight, are now tied.

Wren, writing *Beau Ideal* two years after *Beau Sabreur* (and four years after *Beau Geste*) makes no mistakes. The dialogue and the chronology fit snugly.

Much is made of the fact that de Beaujolais quit Zaguig as the fighting was about to commence. This could have been construed as 'desertion in the face of the enemy'. We are left in no doubt that in obeying his orders to quit the town and proceed to the Great Oasis de Beaujolais was conscious of the fact that he might be labelled 'deserter' and carry that stigma for the rest of his life. He would have preferred to stay and fight alongside his superior, Levasseur.

Otis is summoned by de Beaujolais to report to his quarters. The message is conveyed to him by a Spahi trooper known as Achmet. The two men pass through the empty streets to where de Beaujolais, Mary, Maudie and 'a dirty ruffian' (Capt. Raoul d'Auray de Redon) are conferring.

Once it has been established beyond doubt that Otis would not remain hidden with Mary and Maudie in de Beaujolais' billet, he is urged by the Major to return to the Residency as quickly as possible and advise Levasseur of his departure and warn him in the strongest possible terms that the uprising is scheduled for that night.

[The reader will remember that this intelligence had been imparted to de Beaujolais by de Redon.]

On leaving de Beaujolais' quarters, Otis has two strokes of luck. Firstly he comes across a dead horse (the one his sister had been riding), the finding of which leads him to a mound of dead bodies (the would be assassins that de Beaujolais killed). It occurs to him that he would be safer moving through the streets disguised as an Arab than moving through them in European garb. And so, acting on impulse, he dons the robes of one of the Arabs killed by de Beaujolais.

Next, he meets up with de Redon who is hurrying from the house of Ibrahim Maghruf where he said goodbye to de Beaujolais and his party.

It must be said, though, that Otis did not 'meet' de Redon merely on the street as it were. Once safely in his disguise he is proceeding towards the Residency when de Redon hurries past him without recognising him. Otis pretends to attack him and when de Redon turns to defend himself Otis merely says, 'This one's on you, Captain.' Otis' disguise was thus perfect.

De Redon then advises Otis of his best plan for regaining entrance to the Residency:

'You'll have to be careful. It would be bad luck to get through the mob safely and be shot by the Zouaves . . .'

Otis learns too that de Redon does not plan on rejoining Colonel Levasseur and his men inside the Residency. Instead:

> 'My job is outside. I'm going to play around with the lads of the village and speak that which is not true . . . Yell that a French army is around the corner . . . or accidentally drop this club on top of the head of the most prominent citizen . . .'

One of the small detachments of Zouaves, commanded by Lieutenant Bouchard, is endeavouring to fight its way into the Residency from the market square, where it had been stationed after Levasseur's parade.

> The Zouaves were charging at the double – stoned and shot at from the roofs, and followed by a howling mob, only kept at bay by the rear-guard tactics of a Sergeant, who every now and then halted the end squad of the little column, turned them about, fired a volley, and rushed back to the main body . . .
>
> Occasionally a soldier fell and was instantly the centre of a surging mob that slashed and tore and clubbed him almost out of semblance to the human form . . .

As the skirmish hots up, the young Lieutenant at the head of the column throws up his sword hand and shouts;

'*Halte!* . . . *Cessez le feu! Formez le carré!*'

And in an instant, the company is a square, bristling with bayonets, steady as a rock, front ranks kneeling, rear ranks standing close behind them, awaiting the next order as if at drill.

Wren is at his best, and very accurate, when describing a pitched battle.

Now de Redon's act comes into play. He flings himself between the mob and the Zouaves and shouts:

'Run! Run! The *Franzawi*! We shall be slain . . .'

The mob wavers, de Redon, and with him Otis, goes to ground, and the Zouave officer orders in a strong, clear voice:

'*Attention! Pour le feux de salve! Enjane! Feu! Enjane! Feu!*'

The mob, discouraged by de Redon and raked by volley-fire, withers, but not for long, as a new and bolder leader, a *hadji* wearing a green turban, ousts de Redon and renews the attack on the Zouave square, which is forced to give way, and make a fresh attempt to gain the Residency.

De Redon's efforts appear futile. He does however manage to cause diversion and delay which helps the troops, momentarily, in their dire plight. Otis, too, plays his part and on one occasion he kills a man who is attacking de Redon from behind by splitting his skull with the sword he has taken from the dead man whose clothes he donned.

Soon, however, the time for Otis to regain entry to the Residency comes, and de Redon wants this as he is anxious that Levasseur be advised that Bouchard is attempting, with his small troop of Zouaves, to fight his way in.

'Good luck, *mon ami*,'
And those were the last words spoken to me by Captain Raoul d'Auray de Redon of the French Secret Service.

On reaching the perimeter wall of the Residency, Otis finds it under siege:

> From every window, balcony, roof-top, wall, minaret, tower, doorway and street corner, a steady fusillade concentrated upon the Residency, while every now and then, a great company of wild death-seeking fanatics rushed at the low wall that surrounded its compound, only to break and wither beneath the blast of the steady rifle-fire of the defenders, and to find the death they sought . . .

Major Henri de Beaujolais has warned Otis that the garrison will under no circumstances be able to hold out. De Redon concurred. Yet Otis is determined to join his host and lend his support to the defending troops. 'Death was a fellow I was quite willing to meet whenever he came along.'

How can he possibly enter the besieged building and compound?

Joining the mob in its rushes at the low perimeter wall, he will fall to the ground just as he judges the next volley to be due. There he will be, feigning death, until the next surge, when he will repeat the process. In due course he finds himself lying within a few feet of the wall. So near to the wall is he that on looking up all he can see is where the bayonets with their gleaming tips project beyond the wall, and an occasional *kepi*.

How to attract the attention of the defenders? Otis shouts:

'*Hi! Monsieur! Je suis Americain! Je suis un ami!*'

Nothing happens.

He then sings some verses of the Marching Song of the Legion (taught to him by de Beaujolais).

This ploy attracts the attention of a Sergeant who looks over the wall of the compound,

'*Que le diable emportez-vous?*' (Who the devil are you and what the hell are you doing there?)

Otis tells him that he is a friend and guest of Colonel Levasseur, and that he has an important message for the colonel.

The head disappears and,

'Damn the thick-headed fool!'

But no –

'When I shout '*come*' jump over the wall and throw yourself on the ground,' from the quick-witted clever man.

And when the shout 'Come' came, Otis cleared that wall and fell at the feet of the Sergeant.

Soon Levasseur, cool as on parade, arrives, and his first question is, '*Where's your sister?*'

There is no record of his reaction to Otis' reply that she has gone with de Beaujolais and that de Redon has reported them clear of the town.

Levasseur's reaction to the news from de Redon concerning Bouchard's column is gallic,

'And you fought your way in here to bring them relief? You shall get the Cross of the Legion of Honour for that, my brave friend . . . you have offered your life for Frenchmen and for France . . .'

Otis feels, for one dreadful moment, that 'he was going to embrace and kiss me . . .'

However, the good colonel does nothing of the kind. He immediately applies his mind to Bouchard's predicament and advises Otis to put on a tunic and a *kepi* and, giving orders that he be given a rifle, sends him up onto the roof to attempt to quieten enemy snipers.

Levasseur's concern now is not only the defence of the Residency, but the seeing of Bouchard and his column safely in. To this end he places more and more troops on the perimeter wall opposite the Street of the Silversmiths from where Bouchard is expected to debouch.

Otis has mentioned de Redon to Levasseur and Levasseur must know that de Redon is in Zaguig. He does not know that he is dressed as a filthy beggar and that he will be in the forefront of the mob urging them back.

Thus it is that Levasseur directs the volley that shatters de Redon. Otis, from his vantage point on the roof, sees what is coming. He rushes to appraise Levasseur of the facts but arrives too late – de Redon's body lies riddled.

And his death results in Otis living. Having painstakingly gained the refuge of the Residency Otis now quits it, jumping back over the low wall, in a desperate attempt to pull de Redon to safety – he should have known that the man he was attempting to save was dead – but his great respect for de Redon causes him to lose both his head and his reason. His rash action does, though, save his own life.

Had he stayed within the walls of the Residency he would have perished with Levasseur and the garrison, for not a man amongst the defenders is spared when the final rush overwhelms them.

Bouchard's column, too, is over-run and wiped out.

In attempting to assist de Redon, already dead, Otis receives a near-fatal wound. He lies where he falls in a semi-conscious and finally an unconscious state until the French relief force arrives.

The men of the burial party notice his fair complexion and report to their superior who in turn discovers him to be alive – the only survivor of the massacre.

From Zaguig Otis is transferred to Algiers where he is questioned by the military authorities. He, in turn, questions them as to the whereabouts of de Beaujolais (not mentioning his sister or her maid), but the military feign ignorance.

> My informant professed absolute ignorance of de Beaujolais' destination even . . .

CHAPTER 4

The Mystery of the 'Blue Water' Solved

Otis is far from well. The near-fatal head-wound sustained by him in his attempt to assist de Redon causes him to suffer the most appalling headaches. At times he thinks a splinter of bone from his skull is pressing on his brain – but the French army surgeon assures him that this is not the case.

The headaches persist and Otis determines to visit 'Sir Herbert Menken, then considered the greatest consulting surgeon in the world.'

Whilst he is getting ready to leave Algiers,

> Mary arrived, well, smiling, radiantly happy, and engaged to marry Major Henri de Beaujolais.

Mary has learnt in Zaguig, on her return there with de Beaujolais, from the Great Oasis, that Otis was the sole survivor of the massacre, and:

> ... a black cloud had been lifted from Mary's mind – for the joy and happiness of her engagement to the man she had 'loved at first sight' had been darkened and damaged by her fear of my death ...

Otis attends his sister's marriage to Henri de Beaujolais, in Paris, and then leaves for London still nursing his unbearable headache.

Two coincidences now occur – both possible, both probable, but without which the trilogy could not have been completed.

Otis has returned to England with the express purpose of seeking treatment for his blinding headaches at the hands of Sir Herbert Menken. Having made an appointment to see the great surgeon he fails to keep it. The reason? He has a nervous breakdown. Luckily for him very near to Harley Street.

Whilst clinging to the rails separating a garden from the sidewalk Otis is confronted by a policeman. Wren, as we have seen, had a great admiration for policemen

One of those strong, quiet men, wise, calm, unarmed . . . the very embodiment of law . . . the wonder and admiration of Europe

[That was in the first half of the twentieth century.]

This upholder of the law attempts to help Otis – whom he realises is not drunk. He suggests taking him back to his hotel and when Otis will not agree he suggests taking him to the police station. But before they can set out a man appears on the scene – by coincidence, 'the greatest alienist and nerve specialist in England [Dr Hanley-Blythe]'. The question is posed, by Wren: Coincidence?

But no answer is given.

Dr Hanley-Blythe takes Otis to his rooms and from his consulting rooms to his nursing-home in Kent. Here Otis undergoes what we today would call psychoanalysis – Wren does not use the term.

The psychoanalysis deals mainly with the love-hate relationship between Otis and his father. The finer details need not concern us, but Dr Hanley-Blythe's prescriptions should:

> 'You are a bachelor? . . . Well you shouldn't be . . . no healthy man has a right to be a bachelor at your age . . . And you have always lived the celibate life in absolute chastity? We shall have to find you a wife, my boy!
>
> 'Go and see your father – smite him on the back . . . call him dear old dad . . .
>
> 'What do I think caused your breakdown? I don't "think" – I *know*. Your father, of whom you had too much, and your wife whom you never had at all . . . . Caused a neurosis, and when you got physically knocked out at Zaguig, it sprang up and choked you . . .'

The coincidence of Otis falling into the expert hands of Dr Hanley-Blythe is followed by an even greater coincidence – or is it? Would not another person suffering a nervous breakdown be a likely patient at Shillingford House (Dr Hanley-Blythe's nursing home)? Yes, of course! And that other patient is Isobel! They meet on the lawn on a golden summer's afternoon and Isobel tells Otis her story.

Isobel's Story

Isobel takes Otis right back to their early days and early friendships.

You, the reader, may remember that Otis last saw the Geste boys standing on the station at Waterloo at the time he ran to board the train on which he saw Isobel. He has no idea of the events that led up to their absconding nor of their subsequent service in the Legion.

[Major de Beaujolais would have had no idea that his brother-in-law knew the Gestes; he did not even know that Digby Geste served under him at Tanout. And he was not certain that the man lying dead on the roof of the Fort at Zinderneuf was Michael (Beau) Geste.]

To return to Isobel's story: she reminds Otis of Claudia – he has not forgotten that most beautiful of young women.

> 'Michael worshipped her . . . He would have died for her . . . He did die for her . . . Poor, wonderful noble Beau . . . It nearly broke John's heart . . . He came back so different . . . Michael and Digby both . . . Yes, John returned different in every way, except in his love for me . . .'

Otis is very much taken aback at this news and fights mentally to place in perspective his love for Isobel and his respect for John.

Isobel goes on:

> 'Claudia is dead too. She was Lady Frunkse . . . the wife of Sir Otto Frunkse, "the richest man in England". Killed in a motor-smash . . . blinded and terribly disfigured . . . she took three days to die and on the last day she asked for me . . . and whispered [her confession]:'
>
> 'Is that you Isobel? There is no-one else here, is there? Listen . . . Tell this to my mother – Aunt Patricia is my mother – and to John and Otto and George Lawrence, everybody – after I'm dead . . . I cannot tell my mother myself . . . Digby knows, now . . . And poor little Augustus . . . My father knows too. I think he knew at the time. The mad know things that the sane do not . . . Poor darling "Chaplain" – we all loved him, didn't we, Isobel?
>
> 'Didn't you love Beau too, Isobel? *Really* love him, I mean? I worshipped the ground he trod on . . . But I was only a girl – and bad. I was bad . . . Rotten. I loved money and myself. Yes, myself and money, more than I loved Beau or anything else . . . anyone else . . .
>
> 'And Otto had caught me . . . Trapped me nicely . . . It served me right . . . How I loathed him, and feared him too – I actually believed he would let me be disgraced – let me go to prison – if I did not either pay him or marry him! . . . It was more than two thousand pounds . . . it seemed like all the money in the world to me, a girl of eighteen . . .
>
> 'And if I married him I should be saved – and I should be the richest woman in England . . . I thought it was a choice between that and prison . . . Otto made me think it. I couldn't doubt it after he had sent his tame solicitor to see me . . . The awful publicity and disgrace and shame . . .
>
> 'But Michael saved me – for a time . . . He saved me from everything and

everyone – except myself . . . He couldn't save me from myself . . . And when he was gone, and Otto was tempting me and pestering me again, I gave way and married him – or his money.

'Isobel, it was I who stole the "Blue Water" – the mad fool and vile thief that I was . . . I thought I could sell it and pay what I owed Otto – and a dozen others – dressmakers and people; shops in London. I must have been mad – mad with fear and worry . . .

'Michael knew – before the lights came on again . . .'

Before continuing to relate Claudia's confession to Otis, Isobel explains the background to what Claudia means by the 'Blue Water'. The story of the last viewing of the priceless gem and its disappearance is retold and how, after no one put it back, nor owned up to having taken the gem, 'as a prank', Beau, then Digby, then John disappeared. They joined the French Foreign Legion. Beau was killed and then Digby was killed – both falling in action.

It will be remembered that at their last meeting Isobel, as she was bound by secrecy, was not able to tell Otis that the Geste boys had joined the Foreign Legion.

'Yes, Michael knew . . . He came to my bedroom that night . . . I was in bed, wide awake and in a dreadful state of mind . . . I felt awful . . . Filthy from head to foot . . . I was a thief, and I had robbed my aunt, my greatest benefactress . . . I did not then know that she was my mother – she only told me when the Chaplain died and she was broken hearted and distraught . . .

'Michael crept in like a ghost.

'"Claudia, give me the 'Blue Water'. Let me put it back."

'I pretended to be indignant. I ordered him out of the room, and said I'd ring the bell and scream, if he did not go at once.

'"Claudia, give it me, dear . . . it was only a joke, of course . . . Let me put it back, Claudia. No-one will dream that it was you who took it . . .

'"You brushed close to me as you moved to the table and as you returned to where you were standing . . . Your hair almost touched my face . . . Don't I know the fragrance of your hair, Claudia? Shouldn't I know you if I were blind and deaf – and you came within a mile of me? Have I worshipped you all these years, Claudia, without being able to read your thoughts? . . . I knew it was you, and I went and stood with my hand on the glass so that it would look as if I was in the joke too, if Isobel turned the lights on while you were putting it back . . . Give it to me quickly, dear – and the joke is finished . . ."

'And he begged and begged me to give it to him and the more certain he was that I had got it, the angrier I grew. Isn't it incredible – and isn't it exactly what a guilty person does? At last he said,

"'Look here, then, Claudia, I am going away to my room for an hour . . . During that time the 'Blue Water' is going to find its way back . . . Someone is going to put it in the drawing-room before, say, one o'clock . . . and Aunt will find it in the morning . . . Good-night darling Claudia . . ."

'I lay awake and lived through the worst night of my life. I could not go down and put it back – tacitly confessing to Michael that I was a thief . . . I loved him so, and I valued his good opinion of me more than anything – except my beastly self . . .

'At about four o'clock in the morning I weakened and grew afraid of what I had done . . . I saw myself arrested by policemen . . . taken to prison . . . in the dock . . . tried and sentenced to penal servitude . . .

'. . . And as the time wore on I got more and more frightened at what I had done . . . In the morning I got up and went out into the rose-garden and he came to me there,

"'Last chance, Claudia, dear. Give me the 'Blue Water' now, and there shan't be a breath of suspicion on you . . . If you don't it is absolutely *certain* that you'll get into the ghastliest trouble. Aunt is bound to get to the bottom of it . . . How could she ignore such a business – eight of us there? And suspicion will be on poor little Gus – at first . . . You can't possibly sell it . . . Give it to me and I will give you my word that nobody will ever dream that you . . ."

'I burst into tears and was filled with anger and fear and hatred – hatred of Michael and Otto and of all the men in the world – that I broke down . . . I nearly gave it to him. And after breakfast I did give it to him, too late, and I told him I loathed him utterly and I hoped I should never set eyes on him again! . . . I never did, Isobel, as you know . . . And I have never had a happy hour since . . .'

Isobel, continuing her story to Otis, tells him that Claudia died on the night of her confession and that Aunt Patricia, who blamed herself for the deaths of Beau and Digby, took the death of her daughter extremely badly – very nearly going insane.

Otis fails to understand why Aunt Patricia should blame herself for the deaths of Beau and Digby and Isobel decides that she must tell him everything.

'Michael knew that Aunt Patricia had sold the real "Blue Water" – sold it to the descendant of the Rajah from whom it had been – acquired – by her husband's ancestor in India . . . She had a right to sell it, I believe, as her husband gave it to her as a wedding-present . . . This man, Sir Hector Brandon, used to leave her for years at a time. He was a very bad man – a bad husband and a bad landlord . . . I know that she put nearly every penny

The Mystery of the 'Blue Water' Solved

of the money into the estate . . . She had a model of the "Blue Water" made before she parted with the original . . . Michael ran away with this model. He thought it would be a splendid way of covering up what Claudia had done, too – and Sir Hector was about to return to England . . . Poor darling Michael – it is just what he would do! It must have seemed such a simple solution to him, and the end of terrible and dangerous trouble for the two women he loved . . . It saved Claudia from shame and disgrace and from Aunt Patricia's anger, and it saved Aunt Patricia from her husband's. Sir Hector would simply think that Michael had stolen the "Blue Water", and Aunt Patricia would think that he had stolen the dummy – in ignorance of its worthlessness.'

Otis reacts:

This Beau Geste! It was an honour and a boast to have known him!

It is worthwhile looking back to Michael's letter, which John delivered to Aunt Patricia on his return from North Africa.

Michael takes the blame for the theft of the 'Blue Water' which in fact is a worthless piece of glass – that he knows this is made clear. In taking the weight of the blame on his shoulders, Beau protects Claudia to the end and dies not knowing that she, too, has died.

With regard to the fake 'Blue Water' the question must be asked, why? Why does Michael carry it with him to the Legion, where his possession of it causes all sorts of problems for him and his friends? In Lejaune's opinion it causes a near-mutiny!

Why does Michael give John the unenviable task of taking the stone and the letter home to Aunt Patricia? The letter confession is perhaps understandable. Michael does not want his aunt to know for certain that he is the 'thief' until after his death. There is a danger of the relieving force not finding the letter – it would, in all probability, have been destroyed by the Touareg had they gained entry to the fort at Zinderneuf – and so he entrusts the letter to John.

The worthless stone could, however, have been disposed of by him before he landed in France. Dropping it overboard in the English Channel would have been about the safest and surest way of getting rid of it.

Otis, having heard Claudia's confession, now encourages Isobel to talk freely about John and his brothers. Not only does he want to know about the husband of the woman he loves but he feels that if Isobel can unburden herself of her mental stress, by talking to him, it will do for her what Dr Hanley-Blythe's counselling did for him.

Isobel tells Otis that John had no doubt that Michael and Digby had joined the French Foreign Legion. She mentions de Beaujolais' visit to Brandon Abbas and the impression he had made on the Geste boys.

'You may have met him at Brandon Abbas.'

'No, I didn't see him at Brandon Abbas. But I saw him in Africa, in a place called Zaguig. My sister married him . . . I mean he married my sister.'

CHAPTER 5

John and Otis

CONTINUING, Isobel relates the Zinderneuf incidents, the escape of Digby, John, Hank and Buddy, Hank's sacrifice in going off into the desert and leaving John and Buddy with the balance of the water; Buddy's seeing John to safety and of his returning in an effort to find his pard, Hank. And finally, how through the good offices of George Lawrence, John returned home.

> And we were married . . . And I was the happiest woman in the whole world .. for a time . . . it did not last long . . . John did not recover properly. He simply did not get fit again . . . He had had a most terrible time . . . The deaths of Beau and Digby before his eyes, and the awful hardships he had suffered, ending up with enteric or typhus . . .

John's condition deteriorated steadily – he could not sleep and would not eat. Dr Hanley-Blythe visited him at Brandon Abbas as he flatly refused to go to Kent. And then one night Isobel overheard him,
'*I shall go mad if I don't go back!*'
Isobel made up her mind immediately,
'You must go back and find them . . . I shall come with you – as far as Kano, anyhow.'
From that moment John's condition improved. He was now able to explain to his wife his terrible dilemma and the burden on his conscience:

> 'You see, they may be alive . . . they may be slaves . . . they may be in some ghastly prison . . . they may be in some place where they will stay for the rest of their lives . . . Isobel – they offered their lives for Digby and me when they helped us away from Zinderneuf . . . Hank gave his life for Buddy and me when he went off in the night, and left us the water . . . Buddy saw me safely to Kano before he went back to look for Hank . . . And I left them there, and am living in safety and misery . . .'
> 'We'll start as soon as you like, John.'

Here Otis deems it wise to suggest a break, but Isobel wishes to continue her story.

John's health immediately began to improve. He slept well, singing in his bath and went about his daily tasks whistling.

George Lawrence now married to Lady Brandon could pull all sorts of strings.

On the voyage from Liverpool to Lagos John's health completely recovered and so he was fit and well for the task ahead of him.

Lawrence was able to procure the best guides, camels, camel-men, outfit and provisions. Money was no object. Messengers, too, were taken and word would be sent back to Kano at regular intervals.

The plan was that John would proceed to Zanout and no further. From there he would put out that there was a big reward awaiting anyone who would bring in genuine news of the two lost men. He would get in touch with important sheikhs and Touareg chiefs. He would tell the people of the great Bilma salt-caravan of the reward. He had high hopes that the 'desert telegraph' would work in his favour.

> 'Poor John! He was so hopeful. He was so happy again, now that he was, at any rate, trying to do something for his friends.'

John and his party journeyed northwards and reached the settlement where he and Buddy had parted, and here his plans were put into action. Messages of hope went south to Isobel and Lawrence. From Zanout came news that a man from that place might be able to throw light on Buddy. It seemed as if Buddy had been with a caravan that had been captured by Touareg.

Wren tells us that the Touareg of those parts knew the brandmarks and appearance of every camel, and the details of every raid in which the camels were taken . . . could survivors of the raid be traced?

> *Isobel:*   'And then . . . And then . . . news that *John himself had been captured*! Not by raiders . . . He had been recognised by a French patrol and had been arrested.'

George Lawrence went into action in an attempt to rescue the husband of his favourite 'niece'. He contacted the Foreign Office, the Colonial Office, Members of Parliament, and his friend Major de Beaujolais who knew all about John Geste. Isobel and Lawrence together travelled to Paris and Algiers, to no avail,

> *Nothing could be done . . . The law must take its course . . . We civilian officials cannot interfere with the military authorities . . . Fair trial, of course . . . Court martial*

John and Otis

> ... *Death penalty generally inflicted – very properly – in cases of desertion in the face of the enemy . . . Some very peculiar features about this case moreover . . .*

The full story of John's capture eventually came through to Mr Morduant, Lawrence's agent in northern Nigeria.

John's party had come across a French soldier who had strayed or deserted from the camel-corps, *peloton méhariste*. Befriending this man, they gave him food, water and a camel, and the man had returned to his unit and betrayed John.

Through the good offices of de Beaujolais Isobel at least knows that John is alive – sentenced to eight years in the Penal battalions of North Africa, after which, if he survived, he would have to complete his five years of Legion service.

> '*Eight years*! He couldn't survive eight months of that life . . . and here am I . . . and I can do *nothing* . . . *nothing* . . .'

But Otis feels he can, and instead of taking Dr Hanley-Blythe's advice and marrying, he decides that his life will be one of service to Isobel . . . rather like a celibate priest regarding the Church as his spouse.

> 'I can though,' I said, and arose to begin doing it.
>
> A week later I was in Sidi-bel-Abbès – an earnest and indefatigable student of Arabic and of all matters pertaining to the French Foreign Legion and to the French Penal Battalions of convicts, as well, known as the '*Zephyrs*' or '*Joyeux*'.
>
> A fortnight later I was an enlisted legionnaire of the French Foreign Legion, and secretly a candidate for membership of the Zephyrs.
>
> It was my intention to see the inside of Biribi, the famous, or infamous convict depôt of the Penal Battalions, and only by way of the Legion could I do so. Thence, and only thence, could I possibly find John Geste, and until I found him, neither I nor anybody else could rescue him.

[Wren advises that Biribic was demolished – circa 1928.]

Otis has thus dedicated his life to a quest – the reuniting of John Geste and Isobel, whom he, Otis, loves. Indeed a great sacrifice of love.

What is not clear, however, and we are not told, is whether Otis himself has any clear idea of how the rescue of John will be effected. To find him, an almost impossible task, is one thing, to rescue him quite another matter. Chance, lady-luck or heavenly providence will have to lend a hand.

CHAPTER 6

The Legion

It is doubtful if any man, other than Otis Vanbrugh, has joined the ranks of that famous regiment, the French Foreign Legion, with the express purpose of ending up in the ranks of the Penal Battalions of North Africa.

Otis Vanbrugh's life in the Legion is completely different to that of the lives of the Geste brothers in that Regiment. Through Otis' eyes we see the Legion in a different light.

Wren had after all experienced, if not all, certainly some of the vicissitudes offered by *la Légion Étrangère*, and was able to see both the good and the bad.

In *Beau Geste*, Wren wrote of the 'Gay Romantics'. The Gestes determined, as much as it lay within their power, to enjoy themselves in that Corps of hard-bitten men. So now in *Beau Ideal* he paints a far from romantic picture of the *cavalarie à pied*.

Otis has neither the Gestes nor Hank and Buddy to befriend or keep an eye on him. A naturally aloof and shy man, he is to know utter loneliness and depression until mercifully he comes to the notice of his sergeant, Sergeant Frederic.

Before the advent of Frederic, we meet legionnaire Schnell:

> One of my room-mates, a poor creature name Schnell . . . who appeared to me to be not only the butt and fool of the *escouade*, but also of Fate, attached himself to me . . . and made himself extremely useful.
>
> For some inexplicable reason, he developed a great admiration for me. He put himself under my protection and in return for that, and some base coin of the realm, he begged to remain my obedient servant and was permitted to do so.
>
> I was to meet the good Schnell again – in different circumstances.
>
> What I suffered from, most of all, was a lack of companionship. There wasn't a comrade to whom I could talk English, and none to whom I cared to talk French.
>
> Stout fellows all, no doubt, and good soldiers, but there was not one of

The Legion

them with whom I had an idea in common, or appeared to have a thought beyond wine, women and song . . .

There is, though, the *salle d'honneur* where Otis can pass some of the long hours of tedium. This museum was at one time famous, and perhaps it still exists at Legion headquarters in Castle Naudry.

Otis finds that the military trophies, and battle pictures and portraits of distinguished heroes 'thrilled him to the marrow of his bones'.

> The simple exhibit that thrilled me most was . . . the hand of Captain Danjou in its glass case beneath the picture that told the story of the historic fight of sixty-five [Legionnaires] against two thousand . . .

This battle took place in Mexico and is well recorded and well documented.

As Otis' sole reason for joining the Legion is to gain 'membership' of the Zephyrs he should not complain about his short spell in the Legion. Rather he should look upon it as a 'heaven' as opposed to the 'hell' to which he is bound. He makes the valid point, though, that getting to the Zephyrs is far more painful than being in them. The pain is to his pride and his soul, and the advent of Sergeant Frederic makes matters much more difficult.

After completing the recruits' course, Otis is drafted to a Company where he comes under the notice of Sergeant Frederic.

> I found that my Sergeant was an Englishman, and one of the best of good fellows . . .
>
> I never knew his real name, but he was a Public School man, had been through Sandhurst, and had served in a Dragoon regiment.

His fall from a British Cavalry regiment to the Legion is never explained and Otis dares not ask.

That Hankinson, the Legion name chosen by Otis, is a protégé of the Sergeant, soon filters through to the corporals and life becomes much more bearable for him.

The Legion is renowned in book and song for its marching prowess. This ability to cover long distances on foot is mentioned in every book ever written on the Legion. Wren says it was known as 'The Foot-Cavalry' of the xixth (African) Army Corps.

> At first I used to be obsessed with the awful fear that should I fail and fall

out, and share the terrible fate of so many who have fallen by the wayside in Algeria and Morocco . . .

This abandonment of men not able to keep up on the march is a point of contention in the annals of the Legion. Wren makes it here, but in *The Wages of Virtue* he describes how exhausted men are picked up by a mule-drawn vehicle following in the wake of the march.

> Time after time, in the early days, I was reduced to a queer condition wherein I was dead, not from 'the neck up', but from the neck down. My head was alive, my eyes could see, my ears hear, but I had no body. My head floated along on a Pain . . . I used to think I could be shot, when in that condition, without knowing it and without falling . . . and I should go on marching, marching, marching.

But even the Legion cannot march forever and eventually come the commands, '*Halte! Campez. Formez les faisceaux. Sac à terre.*'

And then it is over, until the next march.

As a sergeant cannot hobnob with a legionnaire Otis and Frederic can talk to one another only when on manoeuvres or patrols and it is during one of these intermittent reconnaissance patrols of the mule-*peloton* that Otis broaches the subject of the Zephyrs.

The problem of gaining admission to the ranks of the Zephyrs is one of 'stress'. If one overdoes things it is the firing squad and if one underdoes things it is a matter of endless punishments inflicted by the corporals, sergeants and captains. Finally the Colonel might take note and commit the culprit to the Zephyrs or just increase the punishments already thrust on the shoulders of the unfortunate victim.

In reply to Otis' question:

> How can a man who wishes to do so, make certain of getting sent to the Zephyrs? Just that and nothing worse – nor better . . . the happy medium between a death-sentence from a General Court-martial, and thirty days solitary confinement from the Colonel.

Sergeant Frederic answers:

> 'You're a queer chap, Hankinson. D'you mean you *want* to join the honourable *Compagnies de discipline*? Don't you get enough discipline here? I suppose you'd find yourself in the Zephyrs all right if you gave me a smack in the eye, on parade . . .
>
>   Better not risk it, though. It is much more likely you'd be shot, out of hand . . . It is the law, even in peace time, that the death-penalty be awarded for

striking any *supérieur*, no matter what the provocation . . . And you know the awkward rule of the French Army, "No man can appeal against a punishment until he has served the whole of it."'

When Otis presses the subject, Frederic states that perhaps the safest way to the Zephyrs is by way of continued insubordination and indiscipline. The Colonel could pass a six month sentence to the Zephyrs for these petty crimes.

Otis plans to take this route as he is averse to hitting this admirable sergeant in the eye or anywhere else. But little does he know that it will be through Sergeant Frederic that he eventually comes to wear the uniform of the African Penal Battalions.

> I hate to look back upon the period of my life which now began. It was, in a way, almost a worse time than that which I spent in the actual Penal Battalion . . . the misery of the constant punishment and imprisonment that I deliberately brought upon myself, was nothing in comparison with what I suffered in *earning* that punishment.

The Harvard man now has to appear insubordinate, dirty, untrustworthy, lazy and incompetent. What hurts Otis most is the disappointment evidenced by Sergeant Frederic – disappointment which turns to scorn and contempt.

> 'Look here, Hankinson, what's the game? You're in the Legion and you've got to stay in the Legion for five years, so why not make the best of it, and of yourself?. . .
> '. . . and I thought you were a decent chap . . . Come man, pull yourself together . . . for the credit of the Anglo-Saxon name, if nothing else . . . Dismiss!'

Eventually, though, it dawns on Frederic that Otis really does want to be sent to the Zephyrs,

> 'I've come to the conclusion, Hankinson, that for some reason, best known to yourself, you are deliberately trying to get into the Zephyrs! If so you're a damned fool – a mad fool . . . But I can understand a mad fool, if there's a woman in it . . . perhaps you'd better give me a smack in the eye, and get it over . . .'

What a pity Otis cannot confide in this admirable sergeant; cannot tell him that there is a woman 'in it'; and a man as well.

Mercifully for both Otis and Frederic, barrack-room life gives way to field service, and here Otis is obliged to conform or perish – the latter option being of no use to Isobel.

Otis' *escouade*, under Frederic, is made up almost entirely of Russians, with the exception of Rien (a Frenchman); Jacob the Jew (a Roumanian); a few Spaniards and, of course, Otis.

The Russians, with the exception of Badineff, have formed themselves into a clique. Badineff, who hates his fellow Russians, despising them as 'revolutionaries', is of royal blood and has held a command in a regiment of Cossacks. His boast is that his Cossacks could ride around a brigade of Spahis while it galloped, and then ride through it, and back. How would Major de Beaujolais have reacted to this boast? Badineff has no time for 'intellectuals', stamping them as political plotters, a loathsome gang, foul as hyenas and cowardly as village pariah-dogs.

> Fate was in a slightly ironical mood when all my painful efforts to deserve and attain a Court-martial, were rendered superfluous.
>
> A sand-storm – aided by a brief failure of the commissariat, over-fatigue, and frayed nerves – provided me, without effort on my part, with that for which I had schemed and suffered for months.
>
> The battalion formed part of a very large force engaged on some extensive manoeuvres, which were, I believe, partly a training exercise for field-officers, partly a demonstration for the benefit of certain tribes, and partly a reconnaissance in force.
>
> My Company was broken up into a chain of tiny outpost groups, widely scattered in a line parallel to the course of a dry river-bed which was believed by the more ignorant legionnaires to form a rough boundary between Algeria and Morocco.
>
> Small patrols kept up communication between the river-bed frontier lines and these groups, and one day I found myself a member of such a patrol.
>
> Our patrol started from bivouac, after a sleepless night, long before the red dawn of a very terrible day.
>
> By one of those unfortunate concatenations of untoward circumstances that render the operations of warfare an uncertain and overrated pastime, we had to start with almost nothing in our water bottles, less in our haversacks and least in our stomachs.
>
> Sergeant Frederic, however, comforted us with the information that our march was but a short one, and that the outpost to which we were going was based on a small oasis, and was properly provisioned.
>
> All we had to do was to step out smartly, arrive promptly, eat, drink and be merry . . .

But Sergeant Frederic has lied. The post is quite thirty kilometres away, and not the ten that Frederic has intimated. Distance is to mean little, however. Weather is to play a dominant role in what now overtakes Frederic's patrol.

> It began with a wind that seemed to have come straight out of the open mouth of Hell. As the wind increased to hurricane force, the dust was mingled with sand and small stones that cut the flesh, and before long, gloom became darkness.
>
> We staggered on, Sergeant Frederic leading, and in every mind was the thought, 'How can he know where he is going? We shall be lost in the desert and die of thirst.'

Frederic has decided that he must keep his men on the move. To lie down would be to be overwhelmed by sand. Thus in single file the patrol staggers on, each man holding on to the bayonet-scabbard of the man in front of him. If a man loses touch with the man in front of him he is to sound the alarm immediately. Frederic orders Hankinson to bring up the rear. But what difference would it make if death comes by exhaustion or by suffocation from the sand!

> I was jerked to a standstill by the halting of the man in front of me. A Russian legionnaire, Smolensky, appeared to have gone mad, and screamed that he would go no further; that Frederic was a murderer maliciously leading us to our deaths, and a scoundrel who merited instant death . . .
>
> A man threw himself to the ground . . . Another . . . Another. As Rien, Badineff and I pushed forward, Sergeant Frederic loomed up through the murk of this fantastic Hell.
>
> 'What's this?' he yelled into the wind.
>
> And Frederic drew his automatic as Smolensky loaded his rifle. Like a prairie fire the madness leaped from man to man and the unauthorised halt was rapidly developing into a free-for-all. The single-file column was becoming a crowd – a maddened crowd ripe for revolt and murder.

Sergeant Frederic has to do one of two things – keep his troop moving and face mutiny or call a halt and take a chance that the stationary troop will not be enveloped in sand; he chooses the latter course:

'*Halte! Campez!*'

> All instantly obeying the command the men crouched on knees and elbows, feet to the wind and heads tucked in.
>
> In this posture, such as the Arab assumes in the lee of his kneeling camel,

when caught in a sandstorm, one may hope to breathe, and by frequent movement avoid burial.

Finally, as is inevitable, the sandstorm blows itself out. The Russian element are now firmly convinced that they are lost. When Frederic gives to order, 'March,' Smernoff yells,

'March? Where to? You have lost us; you have killed us, you swine!'

And he promptly shoots Frederic through the chest.

Frederic falls, rolls over, gasping and coughing blood, draws his automatic, and with what must have been a tremendous concentration of will, shoots Smernoff dead.

'Hankinson, take command. Shoot any man who disobeys you. March straight into the wind – due south . . .'

The mutineers, being disinclined to obey Frederic, are in no mood to obey Otis, who is like them a mere private. Instead of obeying, rifles are loaded. But the last of Frederic has not been seen.

> 'Stand aside,' said the brave Frederic, who had struggled to a kneeling position, one hand pressed to his chest, the other holding the automatic steadily.
>
> 'Mirsky, return to your duty. Fall in instantly.'
>
> Mirsky laughed and Frederic shot him dead.
>
> 'Andrieff, return to your duty.'
>
> Andrieff flung his rifle forward and they both fired. Frederic fell back. There was a thunder of hoofs, and a troop of Spahis came down upon us at the charge.

Their officer calls on the mutineers to surrender, giving the order to ground arms. Striding to where Frederic lies bleeding to death, he kneels beside him,

'Tell me, *mon enfant*.'

'Mutiny, not their fault, *cafard*, no water, lost . . .'

And with his last gasp Frederic, pointing at Otis, says,

'This man is . . .'

One can hardly blame the Spahi officer for thinking that the sentence would have finished with the words, 'the ring-leader'. Not for a moment would it dawn on him, or cross his mind, that there could possibly have been just one word to be added and that word, 'innocent'.

> That evening, we found ourselves strictly guarded and segregated prisoners in the camp, and after a brief field Court-martial next day, at which our Spahi officer testified that he had caught the lot of us murdering our Sergeant, we

were dispatched to Oran for the General Court-martial to decide our fate. Out of the mass of perjury, false witness, contradictory statement and simple truth – the latter told by Rien, Badineff, Jacob the Jew, and myself – emerged the fact that the *escouade* had murdered its Sergeant, losing three of its number in the process . . . Further it was decided that if those three, as might be assumed, were the actual murderers, the remainder were certainly accessories, even if they did not include the actual slayers.

It was a near thing, and I believe that only one vote stood between the death-sentence, and that of the eight years penal servitude, *travaux forcés*, in the Disciplinary Battalions of France.

The President of the Oran General Court-martial was a Major de Beaujolais . . .

Thus it was that Otis came to the Zephyrs – the place where he thought he could best further his quest and so serve Isobel.

One cannot but wonder at his luck at having his brother-in-law sitting as President of the Court. Wren excels at these coincidences. We can only presume, Wren does not tell us, that de Beaujolais recognises legionnaire 'Hankinson' and thus the one dissenting vote!

CHAPTER 7

The Zephyrs (or Joyeux)

IF ONE JOINS THE RANKS, willingly or unwillingly, of the Penal Battalions of Madame la République, how does one, then, go about finding the person one is seeking?

Otis does not dwell on his 'search' for John Geste, known in the Penal Battalion as John Smith – rather he dwells on the hardships of that Corps and the punishments, legal and illegal, meted out by those in charge.

The officers and *sous officiers* in command have to be ruthless. They are, by and large, in charge of desperate men, even of sub-human men. Not all are of Otis' kidney – there because he wants to be there – but they have been sent there for failing to maintain army discipline.

It must be presumed that Otis relies on word-of-mouth messages to inform John Geste that he is in the Zephyrs and searching for him. If these convicts smell a reward they will be only too keen to locate ex-legionnaire 'Smith'.

Otis tells us something of the punishments inflicted on misbehaving convicts in the penal battalions. He refrains from comparing the French convict system with that of the American or British, stating, merely, that the French system is improving and the abolition of Biribi is a step forward, and that he looks forward to the abolition of the Devil's Island penal settlement (which came to pass). He mentions the terrible treatment meted out to convict labour in American coal mines and Charles Reade's condemnation of the British convict system, ending on a wry note – those exiled to penal servitude in Siberia have a poor opinion of Russian methods of punishment!

There are, in the Zephyrs, legal and illegal punishments. Some of these, deemed illegal, appear mild when described, but when endured by men already debilitated by poor food and overwork, they are diabolical.

La Planche is one such punishment. The victim is made sit on a plank twelve feet above the ground. The plank is of such size that a man cannot lie down on it, he can only sit. To fall twelve feet to a stone floor below could end in fractures to limbs, cracked skulls or even death. That the plank is placed in a prison yard with white-washed walls which catch the full glare of the sun's rays turns the torture into a cruel and dangerous one.

There are several other minor, but no less ingenuous, forms of torture that are inflicted, such as:

> standing facing the sun in the corner of the white washed prison yard from sunrise to sunset without food or water; of being chained to a wall with the hands above the head; of being chained to an iron bar and left to sleep on a hard stone floor.
>
> The *crapaudine*, already mentioned, was an extreme form of physical torture.
>
> Most, if not all of these tortures, were 'abolished' by the great French general, General de Négrier – but this is not to say that they were not practised illegally.
>
> I wish to repeat that, in my case, I am not complaining. What I got, I asked for.

History tells us that at this period, before the Great War, the French, in North Africa, were consolidating their policy of 'peaceful penetration' by the building of roads.

Road gang, to which John Geste and Otis Vanburgh were sentenced

The latest road – a Road of Destiny indeed for me – was to run from the city of Zaguig, of horrible memory, to a place called the Great Oasis, a spot now of the greatest strategic importance to France. *On this road were working a large proportion of the military convicts.*

So once again, to Zaguig I came, and from Zaguig marched out along the uncompleted highway that was miraculously to lead me to my goal.

The finding or discovery of John Geste comes quickly. The French are anxious to complete the road to the Great Oasis and so it is natural that all the able bodied men available from the Penal Battalions will be assigned to this work.

According to Otis,

> Each day was exactly like its terrible predecessor. Each night a blessed escape from Hell . . . Often I wondered how men of education and refinement, such as Badineff and Rien, were able to bear the horror . . .

The end of 'slavery' in the Zephyrs comes quickly. It ends in death for most of the players but in the finding of John Geste. What happens is this:

A sergeant, no doubt doing his duty as he sees it, knocks Otis' cap off with a stick. The prisoner's cap is an accepted place of concealment of forbidden goods. Otis inadvertently glares at the sergeant, who promptly knocks him down, as *glaring* in the ranks of *les Joyeux* can be an offence.

Badineff immediately raises his spade and fells the sergeant from behind, while Rien grabs the sergeant's automatic, shouting as he does so, in what Otis describes as irrelevantly 'ludicrous' tones, 'You insolent dog! How dare you strike a gentleman!' Ramon Gonzales, hoping to curry favour with the guards, then strikes down Rien. A corporal now joins the mêlée, kicking Otis in the face and firing his automatic at Badineff. The newcomer, in the shape of the corporal, is immediately felled by a man from another *escouade*.

> . . . and, even in the moment, I noticed the splendid straight left with which he took the corporal on the point of the jaw, and the fact (which should have astounded me) that he ejaculated in excellent English, 'Damn Swine!' as he did so.

The mêlée then develops into a free-for-all. Badineff retrieves the automatic dropped by Rien, and shoots the sergeant and another guard. But as always, discipline prevails and order is restored. All the bodies but two promptly come to life. Wise men have thrown themselves to the ground to escape the flying bullets and also to disassociate themselves with the mutiny.

Those who cannot possibly escape implication are Otis, Badineff, Rien, Jacob (the Roumanian gypsy), Ramon Gonzales (despite his efforts to assist the guards), three or four more and 'the man with the useful left who had knocked the corporal out'.

Chained together these men are marched off to the depôt which is located in a deserted Arab village. Here they are confined, for safekeeping, in a grain pit or silo.

Being confined below ground in the silo prevents the prisoners from knowing what is taking place above ground. Some time later Otis is able to piece together the salient facts but of immediate concern is that the garrison of the depôt is wiped out by a sudden Touareg, or Bedouin, attack, and those in the silo are forgotten and abandoned.

> What happened below ground may be quickly told, for the worst hours of my life, hours which seemed certain to be my last, hours during which I was completely to abandon hope of helping Isobel, ended in the greatest moment of my life, *the moment in which I found John Geste*, the moment in which I knew that I had against all probability, succeeded.

One by one the inmates of that dreadful silo die, until only two survive – Otis and John Geste – John Geste, the bearded man who felled the corporal with a perfectly timed straight left and has:

> ... used an expression that I had heard nowhere else but at Brandon Abbas, 'Stout Fella'.

Otis and John have survived but how are they to escape the vile silo? The answer lies in the marvellous construction of the trilogy by Wren and one of the many coincidences which abound in the trilogy.

They are lifted out of the silo, or rather hoisted out of it by a camel which is attached to a rope which in turn was attached to their bodies. On reaching the surface Otis finds

> myself to be in the company of three extremely decrepit-looking old men, and three remarkably fine riding-camels. I promptly named them 'the three wise men of Gotham.'

CHAPTER 8

Zaza

THINGS, especially in P. C. Wren books, do not always run smoothly and so, before 'the three wise men of Gotham' can complete their work, a 'live' spectre in the shape of Selim ben Yussuf intervenes – he who had been the Angel of Death's escort in Bouzen. He now comes between the 'men of Gotham' and the rescued.

> There was no mistaking the high-bridged aristocratic nose, the keen flashing eyes beneath the perfectly arched eyebrows . . . the small double tuft of beard.

Otis tells us that Selim utterly fails to recognise the 'wealthy tourist' who so attracted the Ouled Naïl dancing girl at the house of Abu Sheikh Ahmed at Bouzen.

> Otis: '*Salaam aleikoum, Sheikh.* I claim your hospitality for myself and my comrade . . . He is a great man in his own country, and his father would pay a ransom of a thousand camels . . .'

The reply is a contemptuous, 'Filthy convict dogs.' And Otis and John find themselves delivered up to Selim's *douar*, but the three wise men withdraw and vanish.

The method and mode of transportation is not that with which the hospitality of the desert Bedouin is renowned.

> . . . when I tried to carry John Geste to the miserable baggage camel provided for our transport, I was tripped up, kicked, struck, reviled and spat upon, by these well-armed braves; bitter haters, every one, of the Infidel, the *Roumi*, the invader of the sacred soil of Islam.

For every dark cloud there is a silver lining and this silver lining comes in the shape and form of Selim's father, the ruling Sheikh:

> . . . a real courteous, chivalrous Arab gentleman of the old school, a desert knight of the type of which one often reads, and which one rarely meets.

We are reminded here of the 'Old Sheikh' of the Tribe that formed the nucleus of the Great Oasis. There was no relationship but Wren likes to describe these archetypal North African 'pater familias'.

Thus, although the old Sheikh sits on the throne, Selim is the power behind it, and yet there is a third person to be reckoned with: '. . . another stronger power behind him . . .' And that third person is the Angel of Death:

> There between father and son, evidently beloved by both, sat the indescribably beautiful . . . Ouled-Naïl dancing girl . . .
> She knew me instantly . . .

Otis and John have fallen into the hands of those who hate France, and one, the girl, who hates non-believers in general.

Otis, though, is not slow in claiming:

> '. . . in the name of Allah and the Koranic Law the three days hospitality due to the 'guest of Allah, the Traveller in need'.

Selim will have none of this.

> 'Traveller . . . Convict, you mean . . . a Pariah dog that is condemned by its fellow dogs.'

The old Sheikh, the father, reasons that if these 'guests' are enemies of the *Roumi*, then surely these 'Travellers' are their friends.

And so, the three days of grace are granted.

During the 'three days' both Otis and John begin to regain their health and strength. They are fed, at the old Sheikh's command, on fresh milk, broth, cheese, curds, *cous-cous*, bread, sweetmeats, butter, eggs, lemons and vegetables – by the sound of it a far better diet than either enjoyed whilst in the ranks of the Foreign Legion.

The painful encounter between the two men has to be faced. Otis decides that he must tell John his story from the time he met Isobel in the waiting room of Dr Hanley-Blythe's surgery. All John can do, after listening to the recount, is to press Otis' hand.

> As became good Anglo-Saxons we were ashamed to express our feelings . . .
> Then John would hesitatingly venture,
> 'Do you really mean that you actually enlisted in the Legion in order to get sent to the Zephyrs on the off chance of finding me? What can one say? Isobel shouldn't have let you do that . . .'
> 'Isobel had no say in the matter. Entirely my own affair . . . Gave me something to do in life.'

Otis points out to John that he himself came back to Africa to look for a man (Buddy), and after a little verbal sparring, the inevitable question comes.

> 'God! How you must *love* Isobel – to have come,' and from the great hollow eyes the very soul of this true brother of Beau Geste probed into mine . . .
> 'Vanbrugh, you have done for Isobel what few men have ever done for any woman . . . will you now do something for me?'
> 'I will, John Geste . . .'
> '. . . Will you answer me a question with the most absolute, perfect and complete truth . . .
> 'Tell me then, does Isobel love you?'

Otis is literally struck dumb by the question, even though he must have known it was coming. He cannot answer.

'I could not speak.' He wants to shout 'No! No! No!' and he feels he is wrestling with death.

Poor John stares at him with hollow eyes, and coughs slightly,

> 'Then what I ask of you, Vanbrugh, is this. Get you back safely to England . . . And with this message . . . That I died in Africa – for die I shall – and that the very last words I said were . . . that my one wish was that you and she would be happier together than ever man and woman had been before . . .'

Otis, as befits his love for Isobel and his loyalty to John, is now perforce blessed with the return of speech and in no uncertain terms disillusions John. Realising that Otis is telling the truth when declaring it is he, John, that Isobel loves, John replies:

'Isobel could only love once . . . How could I doubt her . . .'

And then, before he collapses from exhaustion, brought on, amongst other hardships, by this exchange, he mutters,

'Stout fella!'

Yes, the Gestes could *accept* generously, as well as give generously – which is not a thing all generous people can do.

The three days of hospitality come and go and with their passing a change in attitude of their hosts-captors. Instead of servants bearing food Selim himself comes, accompanied by half a dozen young burly and truculent followers.

He finds, to his surprise, not men dirty, unshaven and in prison garb, but two gentlemen of leisure, shaven and clean. Recognising Otis at once, he exclaims,

> '*Allah kermi*! Our blue-eyed tourist of Bouzen! The contemptuous *Nazarani* dog,

who had not the good breeding to accept the kiss with which the Angel of Death would have honoured him! She shall be the Angel of Death for you indeed, this time . . .'

Unfortunately for Otis and John, Selim's father, the ruling Sheikh, is away from the encampment, and Selim, acting quickly and in accordance with his tenets, drives them from the guest tent into a tent used to house goat-herds. They find their state greatly altered.

Otis concludes that their fate lies in one of two directions – death at the hand of Selim, or return to the French authorities, for the reward offered. He reasons:

> Any Bedouin tribe grazing its flocks in the neighbourhood of the Zaguig Great Oasis Road, would act wisely in giving every possible proof of innocence, virtue and correct attitude towards the French, in view of the recent attack on the road gangs.

[Which had resulted in the silo incident.]

Having found John Geste, Otis is soon to lose him. He is not to know this but their ways are soon to part, if only temporarily.

Otis falls seriously ill during the first night of their banishment to the goat-herd tent and when he recovers he finds himself back in the guest-tent, but without John.

His enquiries after his 'brother' are met with a simple answer, 'Gone!' Plunged into a state of shock at the apparent loss of the man he had found, Otis once again succumbs to a state of shock followed by deep sleep.

When he awakes he finds that the Angel of Death, if not exactly hovering over him, is sitting beside him regarding him with a look which is anything but inimical.

> She smiled, and while the smile was on her face she was utterly and truly beautiful, more beautiful than any woman I have ever seen, save one.

The Angel of Death now has Otis at her mercy, and it is mercy she exudes but mercy which demands love in return, his love. To all his demands and entreaties to his question, 'where is my 'brother?', she turns a deaf ear, feigns ignorance or even laughs mischieviously.

'He is only a man! But *I* am a *woman!*'

On attempting to leave the tent, it is made quite clear that he is a prisoner and although not manhandled, he is firmly restrained.

Otis is, however, not without resources. To the *hakim* attending him, he makes it quite clear that by 'the Ninety-nine Names of Allah' he will die, and so bring down the wrath of the Angel of Death on his, the *hakim's* head, if he does not disclose the fate of his 'brother'. Otis even manages to fall into a deep simulated coma which so frightens the *hakim* that that worthy at last relents and gives him the news he seeks:

> *John Geste was back in the hands of the French and all my work was to do again . . .*

The 'duel' between the Angel of Death and Otis begins again. While Otis' main concern is to rediscover the whereabouts of John Geste, the Angel refuses to tell him what he wishes to know and he refuses to respond to her overtures of love.

Otis is now 'Blue-Eyes' to her and when he refuses to respond to her kisses he receives a stinging blow in the face; of such stuff is the Angel made! She wants Otis and he wants to find John Geste.

To the observer it would seem that Otis adopts the wrong tactics. Had he humoured the Angel, had he made love to her, he may have got further down the line of his 'quest'. His fastidiousness, however, will not allow this line of attack.

So while the Angel of Death slaps him, bites him, strangles him, threatens to cut his lips off and put out his blue eyes, Otis remains steadfast to his resolution,

> I suffered most horribly in the next few minutes, but I can truthfully say that the idea of surrender . . . absolutely never entered my head . . . nor do I think that the reason for this lay in any Joseph-like virtue inherent in my character . . . But always I had to remember that a dead, maimed, or blinded Otis Vanbrugh would be of little service to John Geste . . . to Isobel . . .

The Angel, now desperate, plays her last card. She orders Otis be tied to a young palm tree and she proceeds to carve her name on his chest, ZAZA. Mercifully for him, though, she completes only the first 'Z' and decides to finalise matters by laying down an ultimatum: he either kisses her or she puts out his eyes.

Otis realises he must surrender – but he does not kiss her, he talks to her, calling her by her name, Zaza, and promising her that he will comply with any of her wishes on condition she helps him find John Geste.

Looking in from the outside this would seem to be a fair compromise.

John has been handed over to a *peloton méhariste* (French desert patrol) by Selim, for reward, and to sweeten his reputation with the French, a reputation that is in need of sweetening; and the Angel has kept Otis ostensibly to torture him.

Wren's plot is rather thin here as one feels that Selim would have served both *Roumi* prisoners equally and we know, too, that he has amorous feelings toward Zaza.

Be this as it may, the pact sworn is that Zaza will give Otis a year in which to find John Geste and get him out of the country and back to England; she will give him every assistance she possibly can. After one year (or sooner should Otis accomplish his task before the year was up) he will return and marry her.

An immediate manifestation is that no sooner has this pact been sworn to, than Zaza wishes to make love. Poor Otis! He insists that business is business and that love-making will come later – in fact in a year's time.

At this point Wren produces one of his master strokes of coincidence.

Two 'bad men'; now two eminent men make their appearance on the scene.

Having heard of the Touareg attack on the French road construction groups the Emir el Hamel el Kebir, his Vizier El Habibka and his famous and highly regarded camel corps travel north towards Zaguig to investigate the raid. The Emir will not tolerate Touareg activists in territory which he regards as his bailiwick.

Thus, before Otis can set out on the renewed search for John Geste, the magnificent entourage from the Great Oasis arrives in the village of Sheikh Selim ben Yussef and Zaza has an idea; she will visit the Emir and solicit his help as it is well known via the desert grapevine that he, the Emir, is interested in all *Roumis*, especially ones who have escaped or have deserted from the French authorities. One of the reasons for this benevolent interest, given by the Arabs, is that he is married to an English girl.

Otis has, independently, come to the conclusion that help for John Geste lies on the outside. He must operate from outside the ranks of the Zephyrs. Should he give himself up and regain the ranks of that notorious regiment it would be highly unlikely that he would be sent to the same *escouade* as John. Even if he were, the chances of the same sequence of events and coincidences that found them confined in a silo repeating themselves, are nil. And so Zaza's plan to visit the Emir el Hamel is fully endorsed by Otis.

Not much of Zaza's visit to the Emir is related. She returns to Otis full of praise for the Emir and with the additional news that the Vizier made love to her!

'Oh! la la! . . . he is one naughty little man . . . *mais c'est un grand amoureux* . . . he mak' love to me . . . oh, laike 'ell.'

This love-making does not trouble Otis as the main purpose of Zaza's visit has been achieved – the Emir will see Otis.

Seated on a rug-strewn carpet in front of the largest tent, were two richly dressed Arabs. They were alone, but within hail was a small group of sheikhs, *ekhwan*, and leaders of the soldiery.

Sentries, fine up-standing Soudanese, stood at their posts, or walked their beat in a smart and soldier-like manner.

I got the impression of discipline and efficiency not usually found about an Arab encampment.

The huge Emir, and his small companion, presumably the 'naughty Vizier', eyed me with a long and searching stare.

CHAPTER 9

Brothers

THE EMIR spoke first:
'Mawnin', Oats. How's things? . . . Meet my friend El Wazir el Habibka, known to the police and other friends, as Buddy . . .'

This speech, coming as it does on top of all Otis' other trials and tribulations affects him deeply.

Sun, fever, lunacy, hallucination? Buddy, though, is pleased to meet any friend of Hank's, and when told by the Emir that their guest is his brother, he remarks:

'That ain't his fault, is it, Hank Sheikh? Why wouldn't you say nothing and give the man a fair chance?'

Fever, sun, hallucination?

Only in dreams and in the delirium of fever do typical Arab potentates talk colloquial English. These men were most obviously Arabs; Arab to the last item of dress and accoutrement; Arab of Arabs in every detail of appearance and deportment . . .

Such is the metamorphosis of Hank and Buddy – ex French Foreign Legionnaires. Despite Hank's casual manner and laconic greeting, it must be remembered that he is better prepared for this type of encounter than his guest. He has been told by Mary that their brother was in Zaguig at the time of the massacre and meeting him like this, a few miles from Zaguig, can only mean that he survived the massacre; Mary has, however, slyly omitted to tell Otis that *their* brother is a desert potentate.

Things do, however, begin to fall into place. His brother, Noel, uses the boyhood name of 'Oats' for Otis. *Hank* Sheikh and *Buddy* strike a chord and when Hank mentions that Mary Vanbrugh (now Mary de Beaujolais) told him that their brother Otis had in all probability perished in the Zaguig massacre, Otis has to believe what his eyes will not confirm.

Otis asks if he may sit down and receives the reply:

'No, most certainly not. Common people like you don't sit down in the presence of royalty . . . don't you know *that* much?'

And so they go into the big pavilion tent, out of sight of the interested eyes of the *ekhwan*, and there greet one another in true brotherly fashion.

Gradually the story of de Beaujolais' visit to the Great Oasis, accompanied by Mary and Maudie, is told; the story of how, predating de Beaujolais' visit, they had slowly taken command of the Bedouin of the Great Oasis, and then came the realisation that 'Hank' and 'Buddy' were the men that John Geste had come back to look for.

Their amazement, when told, that John Geste had come back because he felt that they might still be alive, and perhaps in captivity, knows no bounds. These two hardened 'road kids' and now 'Sons of the Prophet' cannot believe that the gently nurtured John would even give them a second thought, let alone come looking for them.

That John, by the hand of Selim ben Yussef, is back in French hands, throws the usually sanguine Hank into a rage and he and Buddy mentally formulate plans for his rescue.

But before this they want to know whether John has married Isobel, why he left her and how he, Otis, knew the Geste brothers at all.

Otis tells them of his visits to Brandon Abbas and Brandon Regis in Devon. Hank (or Noel) did not know of this period of his brother's life and so missed the connection with the Gestes.

When the full impact of John's sacrifice for their sake is absorbed by these two hardened men they can heap no greater praise on him than to say,

'My God, he's like his brothers!'

Otis now demands to know how his brother knew of the wiping out of the road construction gangs and the confinement of French prisoners in the silo.

Noel puts the question: 'Who saved you, Son?'

Otis answers, 'Three aged scarecrows – united ages about three centuries . . .'

These three can only be, and are, Yacoub-who-goes-without-water and his two younger brothers – the back-bone of the Emir's Desert Intelligence Department.

> 'You were hardly above ground before I knew that there had been a raid on the road-gangs, and you were hardly in the power of Selim ben Yussef, before I knew that a couple of French prisoners had been found down in a silo . . . I rushed my Camel Corps straight here when Yacoub sent me word that the Touareg had got busy in my country . . . I surely will learn Mr Selim a lesson

he'll remember, and let him know who is Emir of this Confederation – when there are deals to be done with the French . . . It was his business to treat you properly and to notify me that he'd got you . . .'

It becomes obvious to all that the Angel of Death's timely visit to the Emir's encampment saved Otis from the same fate as John Geste and that Selim ben Yussuf was no friend of either the French or the Emir and his Confederation.

> Buddy: 'One thing, I kissed his gel for him, and that surely will get his goat *sur*-prising.'

There is no reply from Otis to this remark; revelation comes later!

Hank now tests his life-long friend and Vizier of the Tribe, by putting on the line what amounts to their life's work:

> 'We've built up a big business here . . . We've put the Injuns wise to a lot of things . . . taught 'em how to handle the Touareg, and got them in right with the French . . . It's a fine, sound, going concern, with me President, you Vice-President and the Board of Directors hand-picked, and a million francs invested under the old apple tree . . .'
> [Provided by de Beaujolais' Treaty.]
> 'Are we to lose everything to save John Geste? *Let's leave him where he is* . . .'
> 'Let's don't, Hank Sheikh.'

And so it goes on, Hank testing Buddy and Buddy testing Hank until Buddy cinches the matter,

> 'Ain't our friend in trouble . . . you stand by your pard through thick and thin . . . You remember what you said to me, Hank Sheikh? *It's all accordin' to what you call your "Bo Ideal".*'

It is thus decided that even if it means going back to 'riding the rails' the rescue and release of John Geste will be, along with Otis, their quest.

Soon Otis learns another fact about his remarkable brother – he is married and to an English girl. Buddy cannot refrain from telling Otis that it was he who should have married the English girl and that Hank had cut in and spoilt everything for him – but not to worry – he had found a new love – the Angel of Death.

'And she certainly is the Tough Baby . . .'

Buddy has to admit that it would be far harder for Hank to give up their power and wealth because:

> 'You got a wife, an' I ain't . . . Me! I got more sense . . .'

[And here Wren makes Otis sound a dreadful prig]

> 'Married, Noel? My congratulations. An Arab lady? Why now of course, I remember . . . the Angel of Death said you'd married an English girl like herself . . .'
> 'An English girl – very unlike herself.'
> 'I shall look forward to meeting her and paying my respects as a brother-in-law.'
> 'You have met her, Oats.'

And thus it is revealed to Otis that the wife of the great Emir is Maude Atkinson, his sister's personal maid!

The rescuing of John Geste from the Zephyrs, for the second time, develops into a tortuous exercise. The Emir has to keep up pretences with the French, and he does not want anyone hurt during the operation.

But before Hank can set the wheels turning he has to account for a missing French prisoner. Although, as far as the French are concerned, he may have perished in the massacre, more than one person in Selim's camp knows that the French prisoner is alive. One prisoner has been handed back to the French and there are strong rumours circulating that there was a second survivor from the silo.

Hank explains that once an escaped prisoner has been handed back that is the end of the matter.

> 'I myself couldn't do a thing, although I'm Emir of the Confederated tribes of the Great Oasis, and ally of France.'

If the French are to be duped it must be done in the nicest possible way. The prisoner must 'die' and must be known to have died and to this end the Emir, sitting on the judgement stool brought by Marbruk ben Hassan, addresses the elders of his tribe:

> 'And so there were two *Roumi* prisoners . . . and one of them was given up to the French, and the other died. Is it not so?'
> 'It is so, O Emir.'
> 'And his body was buried in the sand . . . you were all present, I think?'
> 'All, O Emir.'
> 'Was it a deep grave or a shallow grave, in which you buried this unfortunate prisoner?'
> 'Oh, a very shallow grave; O Emir . . . It might be found that jackals had removed the body . . . .should any search now be made for it . . .'

Such duplicity is necessary where it concerns the future life of his brother and the well-being of John Geste.

The second snapping of the bonds (of French authority) which hold John Geste would do justice to a Hollywood production. Or would it? Perhaps Hollywood would feel constrained to spoof it, as it did in 'Ten Tall Men', featuring Burt Lancaster, which dealt with the Foreign Legion at the time of the *Infada*. But no matter.

The Emir, Hank Sheikh, calls for ideas on how the snatching of John Geste from the grip of the French should be effected. His Arab followers all advise strong arm tactics. Sudden rushes – ambushes, suicide troops and stratagems suit their fiery martial temperament.

The Emir then makes it clear that there is to be no bloodshed – no loss of life on either side – French or Arab. His *ekwan* sit and stroke their beards. It is Buddy (Sheikh el Habibka) who introduces the yeast into the leaven, which through much kneading rises to produce 'the plan'.

The plan is one which involves hospitality, treachery and disguise, and culminates ultimately in honour for all, particularly for the French, whose good opinion the Tribe still needs.

The plan is to invite the French garrison to a great feast. During the festivities the French officers and men are to be drugged, their uniforms removed and donned by Otis, Buddy and several of the fighting men. Otis is to be in command as his French is less rusty than Buddy's. Arrayed in French uniform the group is to proceed to the road-gang camp and effect the release of John Geste.

A very straightforward plan – but beset by pitfalls.

Otis describes the feast thus:

> Surrounded by cushion-strewn rugs, on a large palm-leaf mat, slaves placed a shallow metal dish so vast as to suggest a bath. In this, on a deep bed of rice, lay a mass of lumps of meat, the flesh of kids, lambs, and I feared, of a sucking camel-calf. A sea of rich thick gravy lapped upon the shores of surrounding rice, with wavelets of molten butter and oily yellow fat.
>
> Around this dish we knelt, each upon one knee, his right arm bared to the elbow, and, with the aid of our good right hands, we filled our busy mouths . . .

Present at this feast, on the Arab side, are the Emirs el Hamel el Kebir, and el Habibka, Marbruk ben Hassan, Yussuf Latif ibn Fetata plus a dozen leading Sheikhs of the Tribe. On the French side are *l'Adjudant* Lebaudy, three corporals and two legionnaires.

Lebaudy we have met before. He was at Zinderneuf, serving under

Dufour and de Beaujolais and was reputed to have the loudest voice in the French Army.

Otis, who has not before encountered him and, as yet, does not know that Hank and Buddy have, has this to say of him:

> I put him down as very true to type, a soldier and nothing more, but a fine soldier, rugged as a rock, hard as iron, and true as steel . . .

Having all eaten from the common trough, liquid refreshment and soothing, settling tobacco, are served. But Lebaudy, to the horror and dismay of his host, does not drink coffee, nor does he take tea; both disagree with his digestion. Turkish cigarettes, too, do not agree with his digestion.

The party must go on. No sign of defeat must reflect on the Emir's visage.

The Angel of Death is next on the bill. She is to attempt a seduction of the adjutant, where coffee, tea and tobacco have failed. She throws her all into her dancing and Lebaudy, being a man of lesser moral fibre than Otis Vanbrugh, very nearly succumbs to her seduction. As Otis sees it:

> We sat and watched a wonderful exhibition of purposeful seduction . . . Before my eyes, this brave strong man weakened and deteriorated; ceased to be watchful, wary and alert; forgot his duty and his whereabouts – forgot everything but the woman before him, and succumbed.

Succumbed? Well, almost. When Lebaudy rises to follow her, as she withdraws, he becomes aware of the state of his fellow guests, his legionnaires – they are all asleep and sleeping soundly what is more.

'Get up you swine,' he growls in French.

A quick examination brings it home to him that his men have been drugged.

As a guest Lebaudy wore no visible weapon; his concealed one has been expertly removed by that jack of all trades, Buddy.

Lebaudy now shows his courage, (to the Emir):

'What's the game, you dog? You treacherous stinking jackal.'

The Emir, because he cannot do otherwise, shrugs off these insults hurled directly at his head, and calmly explains to Lebaudy the purpose of the invitation and his desire:

> The loan of the French uniforms and weapons in an endeavour to secure the

release of one single solitary convict. Not a throat to be cut, not a man to be stabbed, no one to be hurt.

He goes on to express his disappointment in Lebaudy not having played his part in falling involuntarily asleep, along with his men.

Lebaudy remains sceptical. He can only conclude that the convict the Emir wishes to liberate must have rich and powerful friends – all the more reason for the French to hold him.

The Emir then uses every subtlety at his command to induce Lebaudy to take part in liberating the convict. He would like Lebaudy to lead the liberation party, or give them the password so as to make things easier for the party and he finally resorts to bribery.

> 'Listen again, I beg – it is for the last time. One of your prisoners is going to be liberated, *now, by me*. It will be done more quickly and more easily with your help and presence, but done it *will* be. Give us that help and I give you my word, a word I have never broken, that you shall be set free, unhurt. And not only unhurt, my friend, but rewarded. As you remarked, the convict has wealthy friends – and I am one of them, What do you say to fifty thousand francs? Would you care to leave the desert, to retire to your home in France? Beautiful France. And sit beneath the shadow of your own vine, and your own figtree, a wealthy man. And no harm done, no betrayal, no treachery, no selling of the secrets of France. Just an act of mercy to an innocent man. What do you say *Sidi Adjudant*? What do you say to fifty thousand francs?'
>
> 'I say *nothing* to them. I spit on them. And on you. Now, you dog – lay a hand on me as I go to leave this tent, and you have assaulted a soldier of France – obstructed him in the execution of his duty. Already you have bribed and threatened him. *You*, calling yourself an ally of the Republic. *You*, who have taken French gold and would use it to bribe a servant of France – and if I live, I will command the firing-party that shall shoot you like the dog you are.'

Otis can only feel admiration for this soldier of France, and sorrow for his brother Noel, as he knows how much he loathes the part he has to play.

The Emir plays his last card:

'There is a lady in the case, a beautiful woman, a sweet and lovely woman whose heart is breaking!'

Lebaudy wavers for an instant, but then returns to his chosen path of duty and prepares to walk out of the tent.

He is immediately seized and held firm and then tied up and, being rendered immobile, can only use his lungs and his voice (reputed to be the loudest in the French army).

'*A moi! A moi! Garde!*'

The sound of his voice is enough to awaken the dead.

And the result of these cries is that a servant reports that 'One came running, a soldier. He heard the cry of this officer. We have bound him.'

The Emir has no option but to press on with his plan. Lebaudy is held captive. Otis, Buddy and others don the French uniforms taken from the drugged guests, their side-arms and *képis*.

Whilst the small band is busy arraying itself in the borrowed articles, the Emir speculates on the captive legionnaire who had come running (from the convict-camp):

> 'He may, for a few hundred francs, and his liberty, assist us, especially if Lebaudy is as popular as he used to be.'

Otis: 'Used to be?'

The Emir: 'Yes. Used to be, when Buddy and I were in his *peloton*. He surely was some slave driver.'

Otis is completely confused and demands further details.

The Emir: 'When we were in the Legion. You've heard the great tale of the Relief of Zinderneuf where Beau Geste was killed, and we started out with John Geste and his other brother, and tramped the desert for two years. Well, old Lebaudy was sergeant of our *peloton*, under our smart-Alec brother-in-law. Lebaudy is a great friend of ours.'

[De Beaujolais (the smart-Alex brother-in-law), Rastignac, and now Lebaudy, all failed to recognise Hank and Buddy. Even Hank's own brother Otis failed to penetrate the transformation!]

It is the turn of Otis to suggest a ploy which, he trusts, will refine the whole plan. His mounted unit is to ride away from the camp and re-enter it from the opposite side and ride straight to where the legionnaire is being held prisoner. He will see with his own eyes that a *peloton méhariste* has come on the scene. Otis, as commander of the *peloton*, will demand that the prisoner be released.

This plan is agreed on and put into effect, and Otis plays out his part with relish.

Wren, however, has another of his inevitable surprises in store.

On re-entering the camp the troop is challenged:

Marbruk ben Hassan: '*Franzawi!* Come in peace. By Allah, is it well?'

Otis: 'A *peloton méhariste français*. What camp is this?'

'The camp of His Highness the Emir, Sidi el Hamel el Kebir of the Great Oasis.'

And at this point the legionnaire is allowed to struggle free and present himself to the commander of the troop, with the complaint that he has been illegally arrested. The man is none other than Schnell who, quite understandably, on seeing Otis, cries out,

> 'Hankinson!'
> 'Sergeant Hankinson, please! Have you gone blind, Legionnaire Schnell?'
> It was the miserable Schnell, the butt and buffoon of my barrack-room in the Legion, and, in another second, I should learn whether he had heard that I had been court-martialled and sent to the Zephyrs.
> Schnell had not heard and could only stammer: *'Pardon, Monsieur le Sergent.'*

With the subservient Schnell's assistance the rescue plan becomes almost ridiculously easy. He discloses the password for the evening and is sent by 'Sergeant Hankinson' to warn the French camp that a troop is on its way to collect a convict wanted for interrogation by the authorities in Zaguig.

The camp, after exchange of the password, is entered without incident, and Otis and his troop are led by the corporal-in-charge to the tent where John Geste is held.

The story that he is to be returned to Zaguig for further questioning passes muster. John is tied to a spare camel in charge of 'Corporal' Buddy, and the troop rides away, ostensibly to Zaguig.

> Walk, march. The camels shuffled forward, the sentry saluted, and *John Geste was free.*

When came the meeting in the Emir's tent:

> Three Americans and one Englishman! Shall I attempt to describe that meeting? Tell how John cleared his throat with a slight cough and remarked, 'Thanks awfully, you fellows. Anybody got a drink on him?'

And, on the purely personal side, Otis tells us that:

> Words of fire capered through his aching brain, 'John Geste is free – John Geste is saved – Isobel – Isobel – Isobel . . .'

Wren leaves to the imagination John's thoughts on finding out exactly who the Emir and the Vizier and Hank and Buddy are. He does tell us, though, that both Hank and Buddy, those hard-bitten men, are deeply moved by their reunion with the last of the Gestes.

How does the Emir come to terms and reconcile his actions with *Adjudant* Lebaudy? This turns out to be fairly simple, but costly in lives, the bad men coming off worse.

CHAPTER 10

Exit Selim

SELIM BEN YUSSUF has been 'sulking in his tents'. He has lost his French prisoners; he has lost the Angel of Death; he knows that the French will continue to harass him, and so, what better than another lightning raid on the French convict camp, in the guise of Touareg?

But Selim has reckoned without Yacoub-who-goes-without-water! That worthy has returned to Selim's camp to do that which he does best, spying. Both Selim and the Angel of Death are objects of his scrutiny.

What better way of gaining Lebaudy's forgiveness and connivance at the freeing of a convict than to set him free and accompany him to his camp and help him defend it against the imminent attack?

And this is what the Emir does and when Selim's 'Touareg' descend on the French camp they are met by a hail of fire from both French and Arab rifles. Before being driven off Selim, accompanied by a small corps of fanatics, penetrates the French line and manages to seize Lebaudy, whom they carry off as they flee, no doubt supposing this officer a useful hostage.

Wren manages to present his readers with a duel which Hollywood would have been proud to screen. .

On being told that Lebaudy ('the French officer' in Marbruk ben Hassan's words) has been captured the Emir, mounted on the tribe's finest horse, gives chase. On seeing the Emir approaching at a gallop, Selim, never a coward, turns to meet the threat, at the same time urging his fighting men to ride on.

The two leaders, Selim armed with lance, and the Emir with sword and automatic pistol, gallop headlong towards one another.

The Emir wins a sharp encounter in which he with his sword knocks Selim's lance from his hand, and then, allowing his adversary to draw his sword, knocks that, too, to the ground. Finally he pulls Selim from his saddle and falls heavily on him, rendering him unconcscious. He does not kill him, but leaves him to be taken prisoner by the French.

With Selim out of the way the Emir's work is but half done. There is

Lebaudy to be rescued. Selim's last order was 'ride on', and this his men do, all except for the man leading the camel on which Lebaudy is bound. Haraun el Ghulam, the robber, shows fight, and as he prepares to use his rifle, the Emir has no hesitation in using his automatic, and Haram dies as he would have wished, facing his man.

By this time ben Hassan and his Camel Corps have come up at speed; Lebaudy is freed.

> *L'Ajudant* Lebaudy interested me greatly that night, when he returned the Emir's hospitality.
>
> He was not a man of breeding, culture and refinement, but he was a man of courage and tenacity.
>
> He somewhat pointedly assured the Emir that the latter could drink his coffee without fear, and he could please himself as to whether he slept where he dined. He was grimly jocular, and his jokes were not always in the best taste, but when we rose to depart, he shook hands with the Emir, stood to attention, honoured him with a military salute, and said:
>
> 'You are a brave man, Sidi Emir. You should have the Médaille Militaire for what you did this morning. Instead you have my complete forgetting of all that happened before dawn today. And if there should be a prisoner missing . . .!'
>
> Yes, an interesting man, our friend *l'Ajudant* Lebaudy . . .

CHAPTER 11

The Departure

WHEN HANK PUT BUDDY to the test regarding the possible loss of all they have achieved if their attempt to free John Geste misfires, he could already have been planning to forsake the Tribe and the Great Oasis and the desert.

Matters now move apace.

Otis tells of his meeting, on the return of the Emir and his retinue, with Maudie (Atkinson):

> ... I did what I had hardly ever expected to do – embraced and warmly kissed my sister's maid, Maude Atkinson, now my sister-in-law and something of a desert princess.

Apart from American democracy Otis, being a well-bred gentleman, had most likely overlooked Maudie's 'flirtatiousness', simply because she was his sister's maid!

It seems as if Maudie has grown tired of sheikhs and is not at all put out, when it is borne in on her, by slow degrees, that her lord and master, whom she worships, is in fact a westerner.

> Repeatedly she assured me that he was a 'one', and when at length she realised I was Noel's brother, and her own brother-in-law, she could only ejaculate a hundred times,
> 'Fancy that now! Whoever would have thought it! I can't hardly believe it!'

The Emir el Hamel el Kebir holds a solemn *mejliss* and takes leave of the assembled Sheikhs. The ostensible reason is that he, accompanied by his Vizier, is to make a long journey to visit their allies and protecting power the *Franzawi*. Otis describes the parting as 'heartrending' and 'pathetic'.

In due course a well-equipped and well-armed caravan leaves the Great Oasis and heads north. In the retinue are Marbruk ben Hassan and Yussuf Latif ibn Fetata, in command of the fighting men.

Wren does not tell us the port they reach but merely states that it is a great port on the southern shores of the Mediterranean – Algiers or Oran.

The caravan encamps near the town and Hank, Maudie, Buddy and John await a ship to bear them away. The ship will have to be of British or American register; a French ship will not do – all four men are wanted by the Legion and the arm of the Legion is long. It is decided that they would take the first of any American or British ship to enter harbour.

Otis will not be a fellow passenger.

Hank and Buddy are delighted that the first passenger ship turns out to be a cruise liner, flying the Stars and Stripes, and homeward bound. This seems rather hard on John Geste, but he is destined to cross the Atlantic, and a telegram to Isobel ensures that she will be on the harbour wall in New York City.

As this is almost the last we will hear of John Geste it is fitting that Otis has his say:

> I feel that I have not told all I should have done about John Geste –
>
> This dear wonderful John Geste – This true brother of Beau Geste and Digby Geste – This man who could not settle down in happiness even with Isobel, while his friends were stranded where he had 'deserted' them.
>
> Poor John Geste. I was almost amused – grimly, sadly amused, when he again tried to thank me and to say good-bye, on that last night:
>
> 'Vanbrugh, I want to say . . .
>
> 'What I want to try and tell you . . .'
>
> I would not help him. He was going back to Isobel; and I – to the Angel of Death.

In the end John comes out with it, and he says it while holding Otis' hand in a grip of steel:

'*Stout fella!*'

For the sake of his followers 'the Emir' decrees that they will remain 'Arabs' until the end. And so three Arab sheikhs and a heavily veiled Arab woman board the ship which will carry them to New York.

CHAPTER 12

Return to the West

OTIS NOW UNDERGOES a terrible mental struggle. Why is he not boarding the ship with his brother?

> I admit I was tempted and I thought it was fine of the other three to say nothing whatever to break my resolution. They knew I had given my word and would not ask me to break it, and when the Devil whispered in my ear, 'A dancing-girl, a half savage thing from the bazaars of Bouzen – she doesn't expect it of you,' I clung grimly to my poor honesty, and replied, 'I *do* expect it of me.'

The followers of the Emir, Shiekh El Hamil el Kebir, and his Vizier, Sheikh el Habibka, watch from a cliff-top, as the great vessel (something they have never seen before), puts to sea, carrying their lord and master with it. Otis, who is with them, tells us that 'they wept and literally rent their clothing'.

There are more serious repercussions than the rending of garments:

The Emir's body servant, El R'Orab, starves himself to death. His dying words to Yussuf Latif and Marburk ben Hassan are,

'We shall never look upon his face again.'

This statement, regarded as inspired as it comes from a dying man, causes Yussuf Latif ibn Fetata to go forth one night and stand beneath the stars and, looking towards the east, set up loud lamentations; and finally crying, '*Leila Nakhla! Leila Nakhla!*' he brings his unhappy life to an end.

As some time has elapsed since we last heard of Leila we should remember that she was the little girl, and Yussuf's promised bride, whom Suleiman the Strong had slain.

Otis' own parting from Marburk takes place near Bouzen, Marbruk leading his men south and Otis riding off to his destiny in the arms of the Angel of Death.

The Angel of Death arrives at their rendezvous with a small but nevertheless impressive caravan – a small village of tents springs up. Her plan is that they go to Bouzen where they will be married by one of the

'White Fathers' of the Catholic Church. It is implied that until such time as the 'knot is tied', the state of the game will be one of celibacy.

That night she gives a great feast in his honour and when they can eat no more and Otis is overwhelmed by wariness she sees him to bed.

> From her neck she took the curious book-like amulet, which was her most cherished possession and, putting its thin gold chain over my head, bade me wear it next to my heart, forever.
>
> 'My darling husband, I feel in my soul – yes, from the very depths of my soul – that this will save you . . .'

It does.

Lying in his bed of rugs and cushions sleep deserts Otis entirely; his hands stray to the amulet, and without meaning to, he opens it.

On one side of the inner flaps of the amulet, painted on ivory, is the beautiful face of Zaza Blanchfleur, the Ouled-Naïl dancing girl. On the opposite side is the face of a man, the man the Angel of Death had told Otis of, Omar, the Englishman.

Otis examines the face closely, closes the amulet, rises, writes four words on a piece of paper, dresses and flees.

Remarking to himself that the camp of the Angel of Death is, as far as security went, nowhere like that of the Emir el Hamel el Kebir, he is able to secure his camel and set off in the direction of Bouzen.

The four words, the number is exact, are never revealed.

Guessing at them, playing around with them, is an unrewarding exercise – but Otis knows that they conveyed to the Angel of Death a message of irrefutable finality.

Otis' journey from Bouzen to his father's ranch in Wyoming need not concern us. Journeys which in those days were long, six weeks, two months, would seem like years today – no Concorde to fly Otis across the Atlantic.

The ranch is a couple of hours' ride from the railway station and Otis arrives at the ranch-house in the midst of a family gathering.

His father dominates the conclave. Noel is there as is Buddy. Mary and Major de Beaujolais are there.

(Otis cannot refrain from noticing de Beaujolais' attire, 'the wide-cut, tight-kneed style, which our Western horsemen despise'. This cut has disappeared from Europe.)

The centre of the storm is Janey, the youngest of the Vanbrugh family. Buddy wants to marry her, she wants to marry Buddy, but her father says 'No'. Buddy wants to pull a gun on Vanbrugh Snr, but Janey says she will not marry him if he does, and adds that she will die if she doesn't marry him; her father says she would die if she does – with a father's curse on her head.

Into such an altercation Otis intrudes and it is an intrusion as he is ill-received by his father, getting in return for his warm and respectful greeting, 'a grunt and a contemptuous stare'.

Vanbrugh Snr is a tyrant that lives in a world long forgotten. In response to Buddy's request to be allowed to marry his daughter, he roars,

'. . . let me hear not another word about it, Janey.' And to Buddy, 'And as for *you*, my friend, you can get out of this just as quick as the quickest horse can take you – and don't you come on to this ranch again until you are quite tired of life. Get me?'

Strange how people call others 'my friend' when they mean exactly the opposite!

Noel intervenes – to no avail.

Mary urges Janey to go with Buddy.

De Beaujolais, mindful of his manners, refrains from taking sides. It is Otis who, so to speak, clears the decks. He holds a trump card which none of the others knows of.

'Will everybody please go away – for exactly ten minutes.'

'Come on,' I urged Buddy. 'Get out and take Janey with you – and come back in ten minutes. Off you go, Mary! Go on, Noel!'

And something in my voice and manner prevailed, and I was left alone with my father, to face him and out-face him for the first time in my life. He gave a bitter ugly laugh.

'Are you graciously pleased to allow me to remain? Or do I have to leave my house to oblige you? Why you insolent half-baked young hound!'

As he advances on his son, fists clenched and eyes blazing, Otis produces and opens the Angel of Death's locket. His father's eyes fall on the two portraits.

I thought, for one dreadful moment, that I had killed my father. He staggered back, smote his face with his clenched fist, and dropped into a chair, white, shaken and stricken:

'Oh, God! Where is she?'

'Dead.'

'How did you get it?'

'From your daughter. From my sister.'

'Where is she?'

'In Bouzen. Where you bought the Arab stallion – and other things.'

'To how many have you shown that?'

. . . and it seemed as though his whole life hung upon my answer:

'To no-one – yet,' I replied, and added, as I pocketed the locket:

'By the way, father, this chap Buddy is one of the very best. He'd make a wonderful overseer for this ranch, and a wonderful husband for Janey. And I might add that Major de Beaujolais is a most distinguished officer, whose visit to us is a great honour; and further, that Noel's wife, Maudie, is one of the best and bravest women that ever lived. You see, father.'

A long silence . . .

'I see, son. And you can give me that locket.'

'Why, no, I can't do that, father. When Janey's married, and Mary and de Beaujolais have gone, and Noel and Maudie have settled down here happily, and Buddy has an overseer's job, I must take it back to its owner.'

I shouted to the others to return. They found father wonderfully changed.

The trilogy, condensed and commented on, draws to its close. There are however several loose knots to be tied and one or two matters to cogitate over.

When de Beaujolais is a guest of Omar Vanbrugh, and Hank (Noel), Buddy, John Geste (yes, he was there too, but you'll only hear about him a little later on) and Otis were all there with him, does he realise that these men are deserters from the French Foreign Legion? Escapers from the Zephyrs? As they are not on French soil there is not much he can do in the matter. But with his high sense of 'duty' perhaps he feels a little uneasy. Above all, does he or does he not twig that Hank and Buddy are the western counterparts of the Emir el Hamel el Kebir and the Sheikh el Habibka? Maudie and the Sheikh? If he recognised neither the 'Emir' nor the 'Vizier', he could not have failed to recognise Maudie!

Wren does not tell us.

Neither does he care to elaborate on Otis' return to Algeria where he is to re-encounter the Angel of Death (his half-sister) and return the amulet to her! How does she receive him?

John Geste at the Vanbrugh ranch! Yes, he is, and Isobel is with him. You will recall that when her husband sailed from Algeria on the American ship he cabled Isobel to meet him in New York. It is thus natural for them to travel on with Noel and Buddy and Maudie to the ranch.

When Otis arrives at the ranch and is greeted by Noel's slow drawl,

'Hello, Oats,' he also manages to squeeze in the fact that John and Isobel are there as well but are out riding.

> John and Isobel returned by moonlight. John clasped my hand, held it, stared me in the eyes – his fine level steady gaze – gave his little cough of deepest feeling and embarrassment, and went into the house without a word. I sat down on the verandah steps, and Isobel, who had stopped to give sugar to her horse, came towards me. She did not know me until I removed my hat and the moonlight fell full upon my face. Like John, she said nothing, but, putting up her little hands, drew my head down and kissed me on the lips. She threw her arms tightly about my neck and kissed me again. Her little hands then stroked my hair, and again we kissed, and then, still without a word, Isobel turned and ran into the house.
>
> I took my horse and rode away. I rode further and harder than I had ever done in all my life, but I was not cruel to my horse. Who that had been kissed by Isobel should be cruel or even mean . . .
>
> Am I happy? Dear God! Who that has been kissed by Isobel is not happy?

BOOK THREE ENDS

An Ending

Omar Vanbrugh does not last the year. His puritanical spirit is so smitten at the discovery of his past sins that he succumbs and gives up the ghost.

Noel (Hank) inherits the ranch and makes Buddy the foreman. Hank and Maudie have four children and name them Marbruk, Leila, Digby, and John.

Buddy marries Janey; they have a little girl and call her Maude.

Otis remains a bachelor for the rest of his life. He joins the Diplomatic Corps and rises to the rank of Consul General in which capacity he serves his country both in Paris and at the Court of St James. His widowed sister, Mary de Beaujolais, becomes his companion and serves as hostess at all official functions.

Whilst in Paris he receives a letter from John reminding him of their pledge to Rien to visit Madame de Lannec. This he does and conveys to her John's apologies and best wishes for her continued good health.

Henri de Beaujolais rises steadily through the officer ranks. He falls at Verdun and is awarded the Grand Cross of the Legion of Honour, posthumously. He and Mary have no children.

John and Isobel live on at Brandon Abbas. They have four children whom they name Patricia, Michael, Digby and Otis. Except for a short period when John, owing to his knowledge of the desert and desert warfare, serves with General Allenby in the Middle East, he lives out his life as a country gentleman and squire. Isobel does not, this time, mind him going off to the war as she has her four children for companionship.

Before joining the Diplomatic Corps Otis, true to his word, returns to Bouzen and returns the locket, which has revealed past secrets of great importance, to the Angel of Death. She, realising that she could not marry her half-brother, decides to marry Sergeant Lebaudy. On completion of his term of service with the Legion, Lebaudy and Zaza settle on a small farm in Provence and live on her money. Lebaudy is good to her but it is on record that she goes off, from time to time, to take in the bright lights and the sights of Paris.

Marbruk ben Hassen serves the French, with distinction, throughout the Great War. On his return to the Confederation of the Great Oasis he finds much changed. The subsidy provided by the French is being frittered away on luxuries and trivia. Marbruk dies shortly before the *Front de Libération Nationale* insurrection was mounted in Algeria and so is spared the knowledge of the downfall of the Confederation which took place when the fundamentalists came to power.

Hank and Buddy think often of returning to the Great Oasis to pay a visit to their friends and check on their old stamping ground. Such is their fear, though, of the Legion, that they decide it is best to remain in the good ole' US of A.

THE END

Appendix 1

CONTRARY TO THE BELIEF of many the French Foreign Legion is open not only to foreigners but to Frenchmen as well. Another belief, propogated by some authors, is that the enlisted men are all Germans and the officers all French. This is incorrect.

As far back as 1881 enlistment was open to Frenchmen. (See Martin Woodrow – *Uniforms of the French Foreign Legion*.) This move, the acceptance of Frenchmen, proved beneficial for the Legion. The type of adventurous young man who would deliberately opt for the Legion instead of some 'Line' unit in a home garrison, proved to be of great value to the Corps.

Thus the men were of any nationality, including French, and the officers, whilst mainly French, could also be of any nationality. Several Britons attained high officer rank.

Although known as the 'foot cavalry' (*cavalarie à pied*) mounted companies were formed in the Legion before the turn of the century. De Beaujolais, when sent to Tanout to train the Mule Corps, was merely following a well established tradition. 'The mounted companies of the Legion would bring new fame to the corps.' (Martin Woodrow).

Appendix 2

JAMES WELLARD (noted Saharist) on the French Foreign Legion:

The *méheristes*, or *compagnies sahariennes*, which General Lapperine created and exploited so brilliantly, did not, for obvious reasons, ever catch the public imagination like another force of North African troops – namely the Foreign Legion, without which Hollywood would never have been able to make the films of the Sahara Desert at all. In point of fact, the desert was not the territory of the Legion, who were either confined to their barracks in Sidi-bel-Abbès just south of Oran, or sent anywhere in the world wherever there was some particularly tough and unpleasant fighting. In other words, the foreign legionnaire from the point of view of the French High Command was expendable, as commandos and parachutists are expendable in wartime. This 'expendability' – called in romances or film epics 'courage' – is the essential characteristic of the French Foreign Legion, making it a little different from most other military units.

The Foreign Legion as we know it today was officially formed in 1832 – *une légion composée d'étrangers*, stated the order of Louis Philippe, King of the French at the time. The idea, of course, was to attract to the French Army the mercenaries, revolutionaries and adventurers of the period in the belief that such men would be enthusiastic and experienced soldiers, grateful when their service was done for the reward of French citizenship . . . What the French Army got, however, and continued to get, was an assortment of thieves, cut-throats, deserters, criminals, vagabonds and unemployed, varied on rare occasions by some immature and misguided romantic who believed what he had seen in a motion picture or what he had read in a popular novel.

The French High Command turned over the organisation of the Legion to German and Swiss commanders; and the fact is that from its origin the force has been a quasi-Prussian outfit, in numbers, training, methods and outlook. It has always attracted Germans of the blond Nordic type so beloved of Hitler, who instinctively divined their 'killer' qualities; and, after the Germans, the dregs of the Mediterranean sea-ports. The few English and Americans who joined the Legion – and eventually wrote a book about it – were on the whole the 'romantics' who upheld the myth that a foreign legionnaire was a broken-hearted lover, an unsuccessful poet, or a religious mystic. As with all other books extolling military units, very few accounts of the Foreign Legion tell the truth about the organisation.

Wellard cites a man by name, Maurice Magnus, who joined the Legion in 1916. Magnus wrote a book, *Memoirs of the Foreign Legion*, in which he had this to say:

> I was but a few days in the Legion before I realised I had come to the wrong place . . . The typical legionnaire existed as he had existed ever since the foundation of the Legion: the murderer, thief, cut-throat, deserter, adventurer, embezzler, forger, gaol-bird, and fugitive from justice . . .
>
> [We now know where Wellard obtained his insight into the Legion.]
>
> Seventy per cent of the Legion were Germans; it was German food, German manners; German discipline, German militarism, German arrogance, German insolence . . . It was a German regiment of the lowest type transplanted to Africa. They retained all their German habits of excessive drinking, excessive smoking, swearing and blaspheming.
>
> There was not a man who could be trusted either as to his word or his honesty. Genuine feelings were unknown in the Legion. To rob openly, to steal secretly, to murder when lust prompted, were all one to the legionnaire. There was no friendship, no self-respect, no respect for others . . .

Harsh condemnation indeed.

But look at the date of Magnus' enlistment – 1916! At that time France was engaged in a war against Germany – a war which would cost her dearly in manpower, a war that, like Britain, drained her, by death in action, of the flower of her manhood. The Germans who had enlisted in the Legion before 1915 were not sent to France to fight against their Fatherland – they remained in North Africa, protecting French territories there. Thus the plethora of Germans.

This author disagrees with James Wellard. In 1960 he and his party met Foreign Legion troops – both foot and motorised – deep in the Sahara – in places such as In Salah, Arak, Tamanrassat and In Guessam. He can say too, without fear of contradiction, that most of the officers of the troops they met were Frenchmen; some of the enlisted men were undoubtedly of German origin. Two weeks before arriving in Sidi-bel-Abbès, two Captains – both British – had been killed in action.

As for Wellard's description of the troops being thieves, cut-throats *et al.*, neither P. C. Wren nor Bennet J. Doty, (educated at Vanderbilt University and the University of Virginia), write in this vein. Both found the men to be a fair mixture of what would be expected in a mercenary army.

Captain Liddell Hart's son joined the Legion after the Second World War. He deserted, but not because of the men – it was the French officers he could not get on with.

Nowhere can this author find substantiated that 'the French High Command turned over the organisation of the Legion to German and Swiss *commanders*'. The commanders, throughout the Legion's history, were, in the main, Frenchmen.

Wren, who served in the Legion prior to the First World War, has given a far different picture to that of Wellard. In Wren's day the food was French, the officers were French and the language was French – or at worst 'Legion French'. We do not know whether Wren found companionship in the Legion but we do know that life was better for those who did find companionship. Wren himself might have suffered as did Otis Vanbrugh, but even Otis managed to survive, thanks perhaps to an English *sous officier* in immediate command over him. But of course this was only Wren's version.

John Gunter, the noted American author (*Inside Africa, Inside Latin America* etc.), had this to say:

> . . . The most famous military body in the world, the French Foreign Legion . . .

Appendix 3

Senussi: The name of a North African sect which was founded by Mohammed Ben Ali El Senussi, an Algerian by birth . . . Before the Great War [the period of Wren's trilogy] it was estimated that the followers of Sheikh El Senussi numbered some three million, who were scattered widely over the whole of North Africa, and were especially numerous in Wadai [visited by de Beaujolais] . . . Gave indications of the probability that his son would be the Mahdi . . .

Everyman's Encyclopaedia (1931)